DETAINED

BOOK FOUR OF THE BENEATH THE MASK SERIES

LUNA MASON

Author's Note

Detained is a dark, stand-alone mafia romance. The MMC is a mafia boss and a complete walking red flag. Zara, the FMC, also comes with a host of red flags.

This is an enemies to lovers, mafia boss x detective romance. It does contain content and situations that could be triggering to some readers. This book is explicit and has explicit sexual content, intended for readers 18+.

This book does contain a first trimester pregnancy loss.

A full list of triggers can be found on my website. http://luna-mason-author-tr6ads.mailerpage.io/

Playlist

- abuse me – Ex Habit.

- THE DEATH OF PEACE OF MIND – Bad Omens

- *Too Late to Love you* – Ex habit

- Lethal Woman – Dove Cameron

- All that really matters – ILLENIUM, Teddy Swims

- Easy to Love – Bryce Savage

- PLEASE – Omido and Ex Habit

- Who Do You Want – Ex Habit

- Cravin, Stiletto – Kendyle Paige

- Outta my head – Omido, Rick Jansen, Ordell

- Tennessee Whiskey – Austin Giorgio

- Sleep Token – Jaws

- Chills- Dark Version – Mickey Valen, Joey Myron

- *Are You Really Okay?* – Sleep Token

- *Just Pretend* – Bad Omens

- *Atlantic* – Sleep Token

- *Final Judgement Day* – Five Finger Death Punch

- *Love me* – Ex Habit

- *You've Created a monster* – Bohnes

- *Rain* – Sleep token

- *Worship* – Ari Abdul

* To make the spice scenes even filthier, Ex Habit was kind enough to provide us with universal links for his songs (thank you so much for your service xoxo). So with the corresponding chapters I have picked, you can click, listen and enjoy however you please. Trust me, his songs paired with my spice is an experience.

To all my **filthy brats** who want to be fucked into submission
by the bloodied hands of the mafia boss.
Frankie is waiting to break you, choke you and leave his marks
all over you ...

Because that's what you get for being his good girl.

CONTENTS

Prologue   1

Chapter One   11

Chapter Two   19

Chapter Three   27

Chapter Four   31

Chapter Five   43

Chapter Six   53

Chapter Seven   59

Chapter Eight   65

Chapter Nine   71

Chapter Ten   79

Chapter Eleven   87

Chapter Twelve   97

Chapter Thirteen   103

Chapter Fourteen   111

Chapter Fifteen   119

Chapter Sixteen   127

Chapter Seventeen   135

Chapter Eighteen   143

Chapter Nineteen   153

Chapter Twenty   159

Chapter Twenty-One   161

Chapter Twenty-Two   173

Chapter Twenty-Three   179

Chapter Twenty-Four   183

Chapter Twenty-Five   189

Chapter Twenty-Six   195

Chapter Twenty-Seven   207

Chapter Twenty-Eight   219

Chapter Twenty-Nine   223

Chapter Thirty   231

Chapter Thirty-One   243

Chapter Thirty-Two   251

Chapter Thirty-Three   261

Chapter Thirty-Four   271

Chapter Thirty-Five   279

Chapter Thirty-Six   285

Chapter Thirty-Seven   291

Chapter Thirty-Eight	301
Chapter Thirty-Nine	305
Chapter Forty	309
Chapter Forty-One	323
Chapter Forty-Two	331
Chapter Forty-Three	339
Chapter Forty-Four	347
Chapter Forty-Five	357
Chapter Forty-Six	363
Chapter Forty-Seven	371
Chapter Forty-Eight	379
Chapter Forty-Nine	387
Chapter Fifty	391
Chapter Fifty-One	397
Chapter Fifty-Two	401
Chapter Fifty-Three	405
Chapter Fifty-Four	409
Chapter Fifty-Five	415
Chapter Fifty-Six	419
Chapter Fifty-Seven	425
Chapter Fifty-Eight	435
Chapter Fifty-Nine	441

Chapter Sixty   453

Chapter Sixty-One   459

Chapter Sixty-Two   465

Chapter Sixty-Three   473

Chapter Sixty-Four   487

Chapter Sixty-Five   491

Chapter Sixty-Six   497

Chapter Sixty-Seven   505

Chapter Sixty-Eight   509

Chapter Sixty-Nine   515

Chapter Seventy   525

Epilogue   533

Epilogue   537

THE MEN OF THE BENEATH THE MASK   541
SERIES BONUS EPILOGUE

Are you ready for CHAOS?   557

About The Author   559

Acknowledgments   560

PROLOGUE
Frankie

Ten years ago...

"You fucking did what?" I slam my fists down on the table as my asshole of a brother bows his head in shame. I told my father countless times Marco was not fit for the job. He isn't a leader.

Today has proven that.

"I had no choice. You said we needed to get the Capris under control."

I can't believe what I am hearing. My jaw ticks as I try to suppress some of this rage inside of me, so I don't shoot him in the head.

"So, you thought killing his wife would be the way to get him to back off our territory?" I spit out.

"He hasn't said a word since." He shrugs, and my hands ball into fists.

I lunge over the table, grab him by the throat, and squeeze. His eyes bulge as he claws at my forearm.

"You piece of shit," I seethe.

Blue begins to tinge the edges of his lips before I release him to fall back in his chair, gasping.

Pulling out my phone, I watch him closely and dial Leila.

The woman who's had me wrapped around her finger since we were kids. My blonde beauty who is carrying our daughter. I came here to tell my brother we were leaving. Our flight is booked to Cuba to start our new life away from the mess he keeps bringing to our door.

I don't want my family anywhere near him.

Holding the cell to my ear, I glower at him as it rings. "I swear to God, if anything happens to her, I will kill you. Blood or not, you will die."

His face pales.

Relief washes over me when I hear her sweet voice through the speaker.

"Baby, I need you to get home, lock the doors, and wait for me." I rush out my words.

"I'm at Marco's with Carla. We're safe here, right?"

I shake my head, my heart rate spiking. His protection is nowhere near the standard I would have over my family.

"Fine. Stay inside the house. I'm coming to get you."

As I sprint out of the door, I jump in the car and put her on speaker.

"Leila," I shout into the phone.

"I-I'm here. Do you want me to get Rosa and Eva inside?" Her voice shakes.

I press my fingers to my temple as I speed down the road. "Where are they? I need you and our baby safe, Leila."

There's a pause. "They're playing in the garden."

My hands clench the steering wheel. "Tell them to come in, baby. Please, just listen to me."

"Y-you're scaring me."

I bite my tongue before answering, 'good.' I know this life scares her. That's why I am taking her away. Why I never acted on my plans to take Marco out and assume his place as head of the family.

It's the reason I pretend to be a good man. For her. Anything for her. She doesn't need to see the cold monster I am beneath this.

"Sweetheart, it's going to be okay. I just need you to listen to me. Meet me outside the house. I'm just around the corner." I keep my tone calm, despite the fear running through my veins.

Her rapid breathing grows quieter. "Girls, I need you to come inside!" she yells.

"One second," I hear my niece, Rosa, call back. I wish I could take her with us.

"Now, Rosa. Inside. I am not asking again," Leila shouts like an angry mom. She is going to make the best mother for our children.

I turn onto Marco's road. "Leila, baby, I'm pulling down the driveway."

"Okay. I'm just coming to the front door. The girls are walking towards the back."

Marco's mansion, coming into view, lightens the load on my chest.

"I love you, Frankie."

I smile, entering the code to his gates. "I love you, too. Both of you."

The heavy iron barricades slowly open. I rub my hand over my short beard in frustration. Fuck waiting until tomorrow for a flight. We're going tonight. Marco can figure his own mess out. I am done babysitting his ass.

Racing down the long tree-lined lane, gravel flies as I skid to a stop before the wide marble steps as the front door swings inward.

A loud boom has me jolting back in my seat. I brace forward, covering my head with my hands on the steering wheel as the vibrations rock through the car, shattering my windows around me, piercing into my hands.

It falls silent, so I slowly look up towards the house.

"No. No. No."

Before I can register what is happening, another bang goes off, flames dancing in my vision.

This can't be fucking real.

Wiping my trembling hands over my face, I can barely see as the shock consumes me.

Leila.

I have to help her.

I race out of the vehicle, towards the rubble and smoke. My heart feels like it's been ripped from my chest.

Only half of the house is standing. The thick air makes my eyes sting. I only have one thing running through my mind: my girls.

Without thinking, I launch myself towards the rubble, pushing chunks of it out of the way frantically.

"Leila!" I scream at the top of my lungs.

Moving forwards, past the remains of the sofa and the sink, I can't find any trace of her. Fuck.

"Come on, baby. Where are you?"

I keep going on my hands and knees, tossing the debris out of my way. With every second that passes in silence, my hope fades.

There is no coming back from this. It isn't possible.

It's my fault. I told her to stay in the house.

My palm lands on something soft. Tugging on it, blood drips over my wrist. Looking down, my stomach rolls as I look at the severed hand in mine.

"No!" I can barely speak.

I choke on the knot that has my throat closing.

"Fuck!!" I roar, taking another look through my burning eyes.

Her engagement ring.

"Frankie, get the fuck out of there. The rest of it's gonna collapse!"

I swing around to see my brother, face streaming with tears as he looks at the devastation he's caused.

Reluctantly, I drag myself to my feet. The wall and ceiling groan and I hear wood break. A piece of plaster bounces off my shoulder, hurrying me to lunge out of the door before I'm crushed, dropping Leila's hand as I do.

Continuing past Marco, I can't look at him. Anger builds

within me so tightly, I might fucking kill him if I do. Each step crushes me as I walk away from her.

A hollow ache wraps around my heart.

She's gone.

Tears burn in my eyes, and my chest heaves as I sink onto the ground, wishing it would just swallow me up, too.

The pain is almost too much to bear.

"Frankie." I can hear the despair in his voice as he approaches me.

"Frankie, I know you're hurting," he repeats.

I suck in a breath, white rage taking over. It's a mistake to be vulnerable to him. To show him how badly this is ripping me apart. He'll never let me forget this if he sees it.

My gun points at him before I turn.

"Don't take another step towards me, or I will blow your motherfucking brains out."

He holds his hands up in surrender, tears rolling down his face. "My daughters. My wife."

My finger twitches over the trigger. But all I can see replaying in my mind are the visions of Rosa and Eva playing in the yard. That's the last place Leila said they were.

With a huff, I lower my arm. For them, I'll tolerate his presence. I need to find my nieces.

Let's hope Rosa and Eva didn't listen to Leila and stayed outside.

Without a word, I head off, and he follows behind me as we skirt the remains of the house. The girls always played by the swings. The glass crunches under my shoes as we step around the corner. Marco rushes past me towards the two small bodies lying motionless in the grass.

My knees sink into the soft earth as I pull a limp Rosa into my arms. Marco cradles Eva, and a low moan escapes his throat. I put two fingers to Rosa's neck, searching for a sign of life.

"She has a pulse," I call out to Marco, who nods.

I cuddle her into my chest, cupping her bloodstained head as I carry her to my car.

Carefully placing her on the backseat, a new wave of fury surges within me as Marco turns to face me.

I pull out my gun from my shoulder holster and press it against his forehead.

"Once I know the girls are okay, you won't be seeing me for a while."

Pressing the barrel harder against his skin, he gulps. I can't believe my brother would do this to us.

"I'm letting you live so you can care for my nieces. But, don't mistake that for anything more. They don't deserve to be orphans; they need you. Just know that I will be coming for you. I will make you pay for what you've done. You will die for this, Marco. And so will Romano."

I'd take them if I could, but they're safer without me. But when the time is right, I will be back for them. I'll make sure of it.

"I'm sorry, Frankie."

"No. We're done. Enjoy the time you have left with your

family, because I will end it."

My life has been ripped from under me. I have nothing.

I will hold on to this searing pain and use it for my revenge.

Today I watched my future go up in flames, and I left myself in the ashes.

CHAPTER ONE

Zara

Ten years later...

I duck under the yellow police tape and head over to my lieutenant, Alex. Forensics is busy sweeping the scene around us.

A female, late twenties, throat slit, ditched on the driveway of a house owned by Dante Capri. We watch in silence as they zip the pale body into a bag. I turn my nose up as I look at the dried blood covering her neck.

"Let me guess, mafia?" I ask Alex.

He looks at me warily and gives me a sharp nod.

These assholes think they own the streets. It's been escalating rapidly the last few weeks.

There was a shooting at a church. Warehouses burned to the ground. I've seen firsthand the destruction they cause.

My dad, the commissioner, works with Luca Russo, the head of the Russo family. Recently, I have been keeping tabs on the whole organization to report back to my dad. It's why I am here today. I can still see the piles of men outside the church. It seems now they've reduced themselves to killing women.

"Are we making an arrest?" I don't know where to start with

this mess.

Alex stands from where he was examining a bloody hand-print. "We have to now. It was called in by the public."

I hide my smile. I've wanted to bring one of these criminals in for months. My dad always dismisses the idea to keep the peace.

"Why would they just leave her here in broad daylight? Seems pretty dumb to me." I gesture at the row of suburban homes facing us. It is completely out of character for this tight-knit family.

He rubs a hand over his face, his tattooed forearm peeking out from his jacket.

"Probably to make a statement. If I'm correct, the stiff is Romano's daughter. This is her brother's home. They think they're above the law. With your dad on their side, they *are* the law."

Monsters. All of them. My fists clench as my heart picks up a gear. "So, this guy will actually get put away?"

He shakes his head, which deflates me.

In the six years I've been doing this job, no matter what their crime seems to be, they always get away with it.

Staring at the body bag as the guys lift it and carry it into the van, I wonder what she did to deserve such an end?

I wrack my brain, trying to think of who we can bring in for this. Years of cases, I almost feel like I'm on a first name basis with the big players. Luca, the big boss, is certainly a no. Keller and Grayson are his right-hand men, but their alibis are always flawless, covered by their lackeys from their gym. There is always one name that sticks out to me, an anomaly for the group. Frankie Falcone. He's a ghost. Long distance, grainy pictures are the best I've seen of him. Maybe he's my weak link.

As I look back at Alex, I see him wiping away the large handprint.

"What the hell are you doing, Alex?" I hiss.

"What I have to." His dark eyes peek over his sunglasses.

You have to be kidding me.

"A woman dies and the cops cover it up–fucking perfect." I nod over to the body being wheeled into the back of the van and glare at Alex.

He sighs. "They'll all end up killing each other, anyway. It's only a matter of time."

He rubs his hands together and heads off to his car, just as a bunch of cops walk onto the scene.

After what I've seen the last few weeks, one of these assholes needs to pay for this. Alex is clearly hiding something. It looks like I can take matters into my own hands.

I call over Chad as I make my decision.

"We need to make an arrest, okay?" I ask.

"Well, yeah." He rubs the back of his neck. I bite back my grin.

"Get all units out. This has Mr. Falcone's name written all over it."

He stares at me blankly, registering my words.

"Frankie Falcone. Call it in." I press. Alex won't, but Chad, as far as I'm aware, doesn't work alongside my father.

I was told we need to make someone pay, and Frankie Falcone seems like the perfect fit.

I cross my arms over my chest and sit back in my seat with a huff. "I'm not letting him free."

Just because my dad is the commissioner of the NYPD, doesn't mean I won't stare him down.

"Zara, how many times do you want me to explain this? *You* don't have a choice, sweetie."

I turn my nose up at his nickname for me. We both know that's far from the truth.

"Okay, so tell me, did he do it?"

He chuckles, running a hand through his gray hair. "Zara, you need to understand something: you do not mess with the mafia. This isn't a request, it's an order." He raises his eyebrows.

"He killed that woman and dumped her in a driveway. You saw the pictures on the crime report, right? Not only that, but the guy is rumored to have murdered his own brother, for Christ's sake! It's so easy to pin this on him!"

He shrugs, sliding the report I had slammed down away from him. "Mafia business is mafia business. We get paid well to turn a blind eye. I'm not prepared to risk myself for the sake of one body. You just arrested the new fucking mafia boss, Zara. Now you need to clean up your mess!"

"And where do we draw the line? When they start killing kids? Innocent people on the streets?" My arms fly out in exasperation.

His lips go thin. "This isn't up for discussion. I am your commissioner, and I'm giving you a damn order, Zara. Now suck it up, go in there, and release him." His coffee splashes as his arm jerks into a point.

I stand and rest my palms on his oak desk. "This is the last time."

It's becoming more and more. I thought to start with he just turned a blind eye, after seeing Alex at the scene, and now this outburst, I'm not so sure.

"With Frankie Falcone," he chuckles. "But this won't be the end of it."

"I thought Luca was the head?" I sneer.

"Luca handed the reins over to Frankie after the wedding fiasco. He asked me for this favor, and I don't have a choice. We have to stay on the winning side here." Pulling a napkin from his drawer, he dabs at the brown droplets on the cover of the report.

"Hmm. I suppose this is where the money is coming from for Mom's new fancy treatment?" I know Mom needs treatment for her heart. I've seen the way she's deteriorated over the last year and it breaks my heart. But at what cost is my dad paying to do this?

For a man who has berated me for the last six years for what I did, when he's no better than me. He made me become a cop to sort myself out and drag me off the path I was on. Or basically, to keep an eye on me, so he doesn't have to clean up anymore of my problems.

I watch as he balls his fists and his eyes narrow. Taking a step back, I straighten my jacket. "I am doing what I have to do to keep your mother alive, Zara. Now, roll down your sleeves. No one needs to see those god awful tattoos of yours, either." He drops his head back to focus on the paperwork in front of him, dismissing me.

Slamming the door shut, my middle finger sticks up as I leave. He has no clue about half of the ink that covers my body under these suits.

Storming towards the questioning room, I get there just as the door opens.

"You need to stay out of this," Alex warns, running a hand through his mop of dark hair.

"I got the message," I snap.

He leans against the wall, nearly blocking the narrow hall. "You sure you want to go in there on your own?"

"Why shouldn't I?" One of my hands lands on my hip.

"He's a dangerous man, and he's going to be pissed at you." His lips thin as he watches me.

"Is that so? Then why are we releasing him?" I straighten my spine. If one more man tries to tell me what to do today, I am going to scream. I hate this fucking place.

He stands in front of the handle as if to block me.

"Move, Alex. I have work to do. I am quite capable of dealing with Mr. Falcone *on my own*."

He throws up his arms and slides out of my way.

I hold back rolling my eyes as he slips away, and I stroll into the questioning room, shutting the door behind me.

My feet stop moving when Frankie swivels in his seat to face me. His icy gray eyes burn into mine.

Okay. This part of my investigation I appear to have brushed over. I've always kept my distance when keeping tabs on these men. I've missed one key detail.

The fact this man is drop dead gorgeous.

I don't know what I expected from the low-quality surveillance photos. All I've ever seen has been a partial profile or the back of his head.

Sitting at that table, handcuffed in a navy suit, is probably the sexiest guy I've laid eyes on. His dark chestnut hair is slicked back, and a tidy beard frames his chiseled jaw. With that moody, yet mysterious, look in his eye that tells me he could fuck me seven ways to Sunday.

I need to get a grip, not imagine the murdering asshole in front of me touching me in any way.

Dammit.

Chapter Two

Frankie

I tug on the chains connected to my handcuffs and lean back in my chair. There's just the meticulous ticking of the clock to keep me company. Whatever Luca's plan is to get me out of this questioning room needs to speed the fuck up.

The longer I'm in here, the more time Romano Capri has to retaliate. The police are right. I sliced his daughter Maria's throat and had her dumped at his son's place. You take one of mine, I take ten of yours. In fact, we've murdered all three of his kids. Although, I didn't bank on some of our new recruits missing some brain cells and leaving her body in plain sight.

I tap my handcuffs impatiently on the metal table in front of me. The cops were called out of the room thirteen minutes and twenty-three seconds ago. The fury in their eyes told me all I needed to know. They won't be keeping me here much longer.

The commissioner wants Romano out of New York. Well, that means he has no choice but to let me free to rid the world of that bastard.

The door creaks open and a grin twitches on my lips. I twist my head around as soon as I hear the clicking of heels on the tiled floor. A woman. Interesting.

Her dark green eyes meet mine and I'm faced with a scowl. "Are the cuffs really necessary?" I hold up my hands.

She ignores me and storms past the table, her dainty fingers grabbing hold of the seat in front of me. I cross my ankle over my knee and study her. Her silky black hair sits just on her shoulders and her plump lips are shining under the lights. The power suit that tugs her in so perfectly at the waist that I can see the outline of her breasts. Without even witnessing it, her curves tell me she has a perfectly round ass.

"You murdered Maria Capri." Her face remains stern. The woman has balls. She knows exactly who I am. The same as I know her. Miss Zara O'Reilly. Only daughter of commissioner George. Rose through the ranks of NYPD with an immaculate record, on her own accord. She's a force of nature here according to her stats.

I shrug. I did the world a favor, and it got me one step closer to my end goal.

"Why?" she presses. Any other cop would have just come in here, set me free without so much as a word. But not this pretty little thing.

My elbows rest on the table as I lean forward. "Do you really think I'm stupid, Detective?" I drawl out the last word.

Her eyes form into slits. "To kill a woman, the only daughter of the biggest crime boss in Europe. Yes. I think you must be pretty dumb, Mr. Falcone."

The way she says my last name has my cock twitching, imagining the way she would moan out "sir". I shake my head to try and free myself of the image.

"I didn't realize you were an expert on the mafia, Miss O'Reilly. Now, if you don't mind, I am a busy man, as you well know." I wink at her and hold up my wrists.

She pulls out a key from her pocket and leans over the table, just enough to give me a peek of the top of her full breasts hiding under her shirt. "Nice tattoos." I barely hold back a grin.

It's not often I get the opportunity to rile a woman up like this. I'm used to them doing exactly what I say. Zara is a new kind of game.

Her chin tilts down, and I let a smile play over my lips, watching her realize the button is undone. She doesn't rectify it; she just shakes her head and continues unlocking my handcuffs.

She steps back as they drop on the table. I rub my wrists and raise myself from the stiff confines of the chair. She stands her ground as I walk towards her. "Will it make you sleep better at night if you truly knew the monster you are releasing?"

When she takes a step back, I take one forward. I want to fuck with her. I like a challenge. Ideally, I want this detective on my side. But, it's not a necessity. I'm sure the commissioner can keep his daughter on track.

The blush spreading up her chest tells me what I need to know.

"You're free to go, Mr. Falcone. For now." She mutters the last part under her breath.

I lean down, my nose brushing against her cheek. I almost expect her to clock me in the jaw, but she doesn't. "I slit that bitch's throat and let her bleed out on the concrete. I laughed as I watched her take her last breath. And I will do the same to anyone who gets in my way."

She sucks in a breath and leans back, looking me dead in the eye. There isn't an ounce of fear there.

"Clock's ticking. You might have the commissioner on your side, but not everyone listens to him. Now get the fuck out of my personal space." She juts her chin defiantly.

I tilt my head and bite my bottom lip. Fuck, this woman. She struggles with control. She clearly isn't happy with her father's orders to release me.

"The clock's only just started, sweetheart. We're in a new reign."

I step back, despite my body not wanting to. I want to bend her over the table and spank her for speaking to me like this. I could fuck this defiance out of her in no time.

But I won't. I know my limits.

"You think you've got it all figured out, don't you?" Her sweet voice has my full attention, even if it is laced with venom.

"Hmm?" I respond, watching the color deepen on her neck. It's either from stress or my presence, or both.

Why is she still speaking?

"I'm sorry, I'm free to go right? I don't have to explain myself to you, detective. Now I suggest you run along back to your father to collect your next order."

I keep my expression stern and watch as her hands ball into fists, so tightly her black glitter nails dig into her skin.

"Fuck you," she spits back.

Instinctively, my hand shoots out and my fingers lace around her throat, pressing her into the wall behind. I feel her swallow against my palm.

"Silence. Much better." I can't believe I've listened to this woman for the last five minutes, no matter how beautiful and intriguing she may be. No one speaks to me like that.

The fact there's a speck of desire in her eyes behind the fury has me tightening my grip. She needs to learn her place. Clearly, she's more of a loose cannon than I first thought.

"Your kind are no better than mine. I don't hide who I truly am, while you all cower behind a badge. But you're different, aren't you, detective? Under this tight uniform, those tattoos, and that defiance against your controlling father. I can smell your desire from here. You want to fuck."

I loosen my hand to allow her to speak.

"I want to fuck." She rubs her neck, her gaze landing on my cock straining against my pants. The red marks around her throat are not helping the situation.

Her fingers pull my tie to tug me back towards her. Our noses nearly touch as she bites down on her lower lip with hooded eyes.

Those full lips brush the hairs on my jaw as the heat of her breath washes across my ear. "Anyone on this planet, other than you."

A smile teases the corner of my mouth. It's cut short when her knee slams into my balls.

"What the fuck," I mutter under my breath as I struggle not to bend over.

"I'm probably not your usual type. Let me guess, quiet and submissive. 'Yes sir, no sir. Oh, Frankie, please'." She fake moans the last part, and I have to stop my lips twitching into a grin.

This fucking woman.

She makes me murderous and turned on at the same time. My brain and dick are currently fighting a battle for blood.

"Now, get out. Touch me again, I will cut off your hands." She stomps over to the door and opens it, while flipping her dark hair over her shoulder. Gesturing me towards the hall, she wears a carefully polite expression.

I shake my head and follow her out. "You're crazy," I whisper.

She shrugs, keeping a fake smile in place. The lieutenant, Alex, from earlier watches our interaction from the corridor.

"I'll be seeing you soon, Mr. Falcone."

I lean towards her, watching her hand tighten around the doorknob.

"I hope for your sake, we don't meet again, detective," I say in a low tone and walk past her, ignoring her gawking friend as I do.

Pushing out the heavy door into the warm sun, I spot Grayson's white Audi in the parking lot next to a shiny black Porsche. The sign in front of it reads 'Detective'.

Interesting.

I loosen my tie and slide in the passenger seat.

"Morning, boss. Good night?" Grayson's blue eyes look over

his sunglasses, with one blonde brow raised.

"I've had worse. I miss anything?"

A few hours in this life, a lot can change. The last couple of weeks have been filled with bloodshed and death. The Capris have been fucking with my family right under my nose. Romano's long-lost son is my niece's rapist. The same guy who forced her into a marriage and fooled us all. I will live to regret missing that. I should have known.

But now she has Luca, which means we have to lose him as a leader. I have vowed to carry on our revenge. It's not just for me anymore, but for Luca's mom and Eva, my niece. We are in the middle of war, and this is what happens; people lose their lives. Grayson knows that. He's my new right-hand man, the ex-marine. We've come a long way from him wanting to murder me for kidnapping his wife. Luca's men have become mine. Their loyalty lies with me. Why? Because they know I can end this war.

My thirst for Romano's blood is unmatchable. The last ten years will come down to these next few months. Every part of my plot boils down to the end of the Capris. Only then can I breathe again, knowing I took my revenge.

"No, Luca and Rosa arrived in Greece safely. Enzo has started looking into Romano's whereabouts. Me and Keller have been rounding up the guys in the gym waiting for your arrival."

We built an army, now it's time to use it.

CHAPTER THREE

Zara

D ad calls us into his office as soon as Frankie leaves the building. Frankie has my whole body on high alert.

"What happened back there? What did he do?" Chad asks, stepping towards me.

The door flies open, and Chad creates distance between us. Clearly, he's scared about my father's reaction to him calling Frankie in on my orders.

"Ah, you're both here. Frankie left, I assume?" A grin spreads across my dad's face.

"You two have fucked up monumentally. So, you're both on paperwork for the next two weeks." He takes his seat at his desk.

"What–"

He holds up a finger to cut me off. "This is not up for debate."

Chad shifts uncomfortably on his feet next to me and I shoot him a glare.

"Sorry, it won't happen again." He looks down at his boots and I want to slap him. We all know it was Frankie who did this. He just admitted it to me.

Dad pins him with a hard stare. "No, it won't. Now, back to

your desk."

Chad opens the door, and I follow behind.

Father's voice freezes my movement. "Not you, Zara. Sit down."

My fists ball before turning back around to face him as Chad slams the door shut behind him.

My father leans back, his fingers folding into a point that he taps against his thin lips. "Zara, you need to stay away from Frankie."

A lump forms in my throat, making me swallow.

He takes a deep breath. "We can't trust him."

"Whatever gave you that impression?" I ask mockingly. Who trusts a mafia boss, especially one as ruthless and cold as Mr. Falcone?

"I know you, you won't let this go, but I am asking for all of our sakes–do not think about it."

This is not what I expected. "Why?"

I don't want to be anywhere near the man. A man who can wrap his fingers around my throat and spark something inside of me is someone I need to be far away from. But I can't help this nagging feeling there is so much more going on that I have to find out about.

"This is exactly what I am talking about, Zara. Just leave it. We have to focus on your mother. That's why I am going away."

I let out an exasperated sigh and slump back in my seat. He's right. With Mom's heart condition, it's a ticking time bomb.

"Is this where all the money is coming from?" I say, tapping my fingers against my jaw. She's recently started a clinical trial for a new drug, something that could add years to her life.

He starts to loosen his navy tie, a bead of sweat forming on his wrinkled forehead.

"If it works, it's worth every penny. You know that, Zara."

"Look, take me off desk duty and I'll leave him alone." I offer him a sweet smile.

His fingertips splay on the desk as he looks at me pensively. "I'll think about it."

I draw in a long breath. "Or, maybe, I could go to the feds and start asking questions about Frankie and the Capris? There is something big going on between those two, especially for you to have us cover his tracks on Maria. I wonder what else is hiding out there, on them both. I can imagine Romano must have done something pretty awful to get that kind of retaliation from Frankie."

His jaw starts to visibly shake, the vein on his forehead almost pops out.

Looks like I'm on the right track.

"Fine. Just leave it alone. Get on with your job, that is all I am asking."

I give him a curt nod, and we sit in a moment of silence.

This is what it's come down to between us. Since Mom started going downhill, it's put a strain on our relationship. Now, I know why that might be.

CHAPTER FOUR

Frankie

I slam my fists on the table, causing Carlos to jump back in his chair, so I lean over and grab him by the scruff of the neck.

"We are missing a whole crate. You have five seconds to tell me its location or I'll wedge a bullet straight between your eyes."

His whiskered upper lip trembles. "I-I don't know."

Why Luca didn't kill this useless prick years ago, I do not know.

I tug him closer to me. "Have you been stealing from me?"

He shakes his head. I can smell his fear. The worst part is that I can see in his eyes that he's lying to me.

He's the same weasel who used to steal Luca's shipments for my brother, who enabled Rosa's habit.

I pull him to his feet. His two men step towards me, so I aim my gun at the one on the left.

"Unless you both want to be floating in that fucking river with your friend here, I suggest you sit down."

I flick off the safety, and they step back.

I turn to Grayson and his new helpers, Jax and Kai, who are on either side of the door with their arms folded across their chests.

"Jax, Kai, go help the guys loading up the warehouse. We can't trust them."

"Got it, boss." Jax salutes me and waltzes out, tugging on his leather jacket. Kai, as always, follows behind his friend.

I drag Carlos across the desk, and he digs his feet in as I take him outside. His hands paw at my forearm the closer we get to the water.

"Please, sir, it won't happen again."

Weak, pathetic excuse for a man. Wrapping my fingers around his throat, I squeeze.

"Don't beg me for your life."

I let go, and he falls to the ground, holding his neck and gasping for air. As I go to retrieve my knife, I spot a shine coming off one of the windows at the entrance. I squint to get a better look.

A little black Porsche. I have only a single guess who it could be.

What are you doing here, detective?

I lift myself off him and pat down my suit.

"Grayson, take him back inside and finish the job there. Don't leave the warehouse until I say so."

He grunts in response and grabs Carlos, dragging the begging man behind him across the ground.

My arms cross over my chest. The screams ringing in my ears make a smirk twitch on my lips. I'm itching to get back in there and join the fun, but instead, I find myself in a silent battle with

Zara. Of course, I know it's her. I know everything about the woman that I need to.

That defiance in her eyes at the station, her threats. There was no doubt she wasn't going to leave this.

I've never been challenged by a woman before. It's exciting. I just wonder how far I can push her. So, I take my gun from the holster and aim it right at her windshield.

I bet she's biting that bottom lip, gripping her hands on the steering wheel, watching me.

She hasn't driven away. Impressive. Most people would have when a crazed man points a pistol at their car.

She really does need to leave, though. I can't have her or anyone getting in my way of ending Romano. Not the commissioner, the cops, and certainly not Zara.

I switch my aim slightly to the left, to the brick wall next to her car, and fire. The headlights come on and the engine roars to life. Running a hand through my hair, I watch as she erratically drives out of the lot. I don't know whether I'm pissed off or turned on by her bravery.

If she wants to play games with me, she better brace herself.

"Who was that?" Grayson asks, dropping Carlos's dead body on the floor. Jax and Kai are doing the same with one of the goons nearby. I look down and my nose wrinkles as my new loafers are spattered with blood.

"No one of concern, G. I'll deal with it."

He looks like he's about to say something, but his mouth clamps shut and his lips thin.

Pulling out my lapel, I slide my Glock back into the holster under my arm. "Once you've discarded the bodies, meet me at my place. Bring Keller."

"Got it, boss." He lifts Carlos and throws him over his shoulder.

"In the river?" I pull out a cigarette and light it. Anything to dampen the smell.

He grunts. "It'll have to be, unless you want me to blow up your warehouse?" He has a spark in his eye. In the year we've worked together, I never quite understood this man's obsession with setting everything on fire.

There's a lot cleaner ways to deal with a corpse.

I turn on my heel and head to my own silver Porsche parked outside and pull out my phone to dial Enzo.

We need a new plan.

If Zara is on my case, we need to know why.

Grayson, Jax, Kai, and Keller are in the kitchen raiding the drink cabinet. I recline on the couch and scroll through my phone.

For a detective, her social media is wide open.

Picture after picture, her off duty persona is revealed. The delicate ink that spans her right arm. Her green eyes that pierce into my soul, even through a screen.

I stop on the picture that holds my attention. She's unlike any other woman I've been with. She has a dark side, a rebellious side.

In this photo, she's at a concert, in a leather bra and high-waisted shorts, sticking her tongue out to the camera. Her raven hair frames her face, her lips are red and plump.

Clearly, she lives a different life outside of her day job.

A reckless one, which explains her behavior.

If she wants to be my enemy, I need to know *every single thing* about her.

I know she has an issue with control.

She hides behind that badge, which is probably why her body is scattered with ink.

My cock throbs as I remember her pulse increasing when my hand tightened around her throat.

She has a temper and will use violence.

But she doesn't like men ordering her around.

My fingers twitch as I imagine the ways I could control her.

The front door slams shut and I lock my cell.

Enzo appears from the entry hall. "You know you've got a car parked across the street? I ran the plates; it's her."

"Who?" Grayson looks at me with a frown.

"Zara," I reply flatly.

Grayson leans against the counter and tips back his glass. "The cop?"

"Yes, the detective." I clench my jaw.

"Why are you being followed by the cops?" Keller asks, taking a sip of beer.

"That's what we're all here to work out. I think I've got myself a little stalking problem."

"She's brave," Jax chuckles before jumping up to sit on the counter.

Sometimes his insolence is irritating. "Off. You can sit on a chair like a house-trained adult. This isn't a fucking frat house."

That earns me a snicker from Kai, who tugs on Jax's black t-shirt to get him back to his feet.

"You heard him," Kai says to Jax and gives me a nod.

These two are like a married couple. Jax, the wild one, the brute. And Kai is always there to calm him down and keep him out of trouble.

I stand and join them in the kitchen, taking a seat at the dining table. The rest of them all join me.

Enzo pulls out his laptop and puts on his glasses.

"I've never seen you with glasses. Very Clark Kent." Keller mocks and holds his beer up to Enzo.

"Fuck off," he retorts.

"What have you got for us?" I ask, looking at Enzo.

Enzo clicks a few keys before his eyes narrow at his screen. "Well, it looks like George took a private jet to Sicily."

"Of course he did."

He's always made clear of his hatred for my family. Despite the fact I am not my brother, the Falcone name sticks. Luca was the only reason George was on our side. Now that Luca is out, the responsibility falls with me.

And Romano can force anyone into doing what he wants

them to.

"So, how do we plan to keep power?" Grayson asks.

My chair rocks as I cross my foot over my knee. "We have to draw Romano here. I'm not fighting a war on anyone else's turf. We hold the upper hand here. We can't let the commissioner know that we're on to him. Let them think they have one over on us. I can feed him false information, easy enough. What about the lieutenant, Alex Pierce? Dig up any dirt on him?"

Enzo leans back with a frown. "Clean record. I'll keep digging."

"Alex is a lieutenant of the NYPD. There must be a way to get to him?"

He might have cleaned up the crime scene, I don't trust him nor George. If one switches, the other is bound to follow.

"We killing cops now?" Keller glances at Grayson with concern.

I shake my head.

"I was thinking we start with blackmail. We don't need that kind of heat on us. That is exactly what George will be waiting to pin on us. I've been playing these games with Romano for ten years now. I can be patient."

My hands clasp together on the table before I turn to Enzo.

"Don't forget we have a meeting at the club Friday," Enzo reminds me.

"Club?" Jax's eyes light up as he tips his chair back onto two legs, a grin on his face.

Barely containing an eye roll at his childishness, I simply give him a thumbs down. "I'll take you another night."

"Count me in," Kai interjects, shoving Jax's chair back on four legs. For a young guy, he certainly has his head screwed on.

"What about us?" A smirk creeps up on Grayson's lips that makes me laugh.

"You two are far too married for this kind of club. Sienna and Maddie would rip your balls off and shove them down your throat."

"Oh, that kind of club, yeah, I don't think so," Keller chuckles.

The two of them are so happily married it almost is revolting, popping out kids for fun. I'm concerned the organization is going to need its own fucking daycare soon.

"Speaking of, we better get back before we're in trouble." Grayson stands. "Let me know what you need from me. I'll get some recruits to take over the docks with Jax."

I nod. "I'll see you in the gym tomorrow."

Jax stands to leave with the other three. "You can stay." I point back to his chair.

He grins and sits his ass back down, shrugging off his leather jacket. His heavily tattooed arms prop on the table as he takes another drink. "Kai, I'll meet you at the gym tomorrow?"

"You got it, bud," Kai calls back, picking up his helmet from the table by the door.

"Are you two joined at the hip?" I ask Jax.

"Aww, you don't have a best friend?" Jax asks, sipping his beer.

"What do I need friends for?"

He shrugs. "He's basically my brother. I've had him by my side my whole life."

"Probably why your ass isn't in jail now."

Jax chuckles and nods. "For sure."

"What do you suggest I do about our little detective problem?" I turn and ask Enzo.

I have never come up against this kind of issue. I know what I'd do to resolve it. Although, with Zara's fiery personality, I doubt that would cause me anything but a further headache.

Enzo scratches the black scruff on his jaw. "Leave it alone for now. She could be useful. We could use her as an in to the commissioner. She would be easy to *take*." He raises his brows.

I bite the inside of my mouth. Having Zara tied up and gagged in my basement makes my dick come to life.

"Stop grinning, Frankie," Enzo smirks. He knows exactly where my brain went.

"Don't let her get to you. We don't know enough about her or her motives yet."

"A woman, get to me?" I scoff.

"You ready to get in deeper, Mr. Carter?" I turn to Jax, that fire in his eyes still there. I've watched him fight, the way he loses it. I've seen the joy he gets out on jobs. He's ready.

"Damn fucking right." Interlacing his hands, he turns his palms out and cracks his knuckles.

"Good. When is your next fight?"

Keller and Grayson have pitched him as the next light-heavy-weight champion. Kings Gym needs another hero and what an excellent disguise. Keller proved that point.

"Six weeks or so." He runs his fingers through his messy black curls.

"I want to bring you in, but you keep on top of your training with Grayson." He must be nearly fifteen years younger than me, yet is still learning the importance of discipline.

"Yes, *Dad,*" he mocks.

"I'll beat your ass like one. Remember who you're talking to." I watch as his jaw ticks at my comment. So, I clap my hand on his shoulder firmly. If I've learned anything in the last year, it's that I protect my family. No matter what.

The guilt that rips through me about Rosa and Eva eats me alive every day. Like everything else, I swallow it down and carry on.

Enzo shuts his laptop and stands.

"Need a lift?" he asks Jax, who shakes his head.

"I've got my bike out front." Jax lifts his heavy leather jacket back over his broad shoulders and follows Enzo out.

After they leave, I loosen my tie and pour a heavy measure of scotch, hitting dial on the commissioner's number.

"Frankie." He sounds less than happy.

"Call off your dogs, commissioner. She's your daughter, so I have allowed it this far. Enough is enough."

"Fuck," he mutters under his breath.

Hmm, so he didn't order this?

A smile creeps up on my lips and I can't help but lift the blind in the living room that looks out onto the road.

I wonder if she can see me.

"I'll take care of it, Frankie."

"Good." I cut the call with this new information. Knowing she is here for herself gives me a whole new outlook on our situation.

The way her body reacted to me, I bet she likes watching me.

"Night, detective," I say before I shut off the lights, knocking back the remainder of my drink. Each heavy step up the stairs is closer to another night of restless sleep, watching Leila go up in flames in my nightmares.

CHAPTER FIVE

Zara

I pull my jacket tighter as the cold air hits me. It's only eight am, so I drive to Frankie's house and park across the street. Reclining my seat, I blast the hot air and fight to keep my eyes open. With Dad being away, I've stepped in and helped Mom out. Every day is watching her fade away. She can barely walk five steps without getting out a breath. I swallow down the lump in my throat, as tears sting in my eyes.

Instead of dwelling on that, I focus on what I'm here to do. Despite my dad's angry call in the middle of the night, I'm still here. I might have promised I'd stop, I just can't. I know Frankie is hiding something. They all are.

His Porsche is parked in his driveway. The house is gigantic, a mansion even, with ivory covering the brickwork and black framed windows. An absolute dream. I tap my nails against the seat belt buckle and turn up the radio, slipping on my black Prada sunglasses. Even if they are oversized, I have no doubt Frankie would spot me a mile away. I don't think my father realizes just how clever this man is.

I sit up and lean against the steering wheel as his front door opens. My heart hammers as two stunning blonde women appear, stepping out onto the porch. They're followed by the man himself, his bare chest rippling in the morning sun. Oh my God. Even from here, I can see how perfectly built he is. Of course he is.

He grabs one of them by the back of the head and kisses her. I try to tear my eyes away, but I can't. The blush is evident on her face from here, almost matching the heat on my own cheeks. He forcefully slaps her ass in her tight red dress and turns his attention to hoe number two, who gets the same service.

When his dark gaze connects to me, my heart almost thuds out of my chest.

Shit.

I should be worried he's caught me. Again. Actually, what I'm more concerned about is I think that was a performance to get at me. The asshole knows he can get under my skin.

It only makes me despise him more.

He closes the door and I grab my phone, snapping pictures of the girls as they get in the car outside and note the plates to run when I'm back in the office.

It's half an hour before he finally makes his reappearance. I'm taken aback when I see him in a pair of gray sweatpants and a black hoodie. I've only ever seen him in his designer suits. He rolls up his sleeves, revealing his tattoos scaling up his right forearm.

Shit.

He breaks out into a jog, not even looking my way, and heads off down the road.

Shit. Shit. Shit. I wish I wore sensible shoes today.

I follow behind, keeping him far enough where I can just about have him in my vision as he jogs along the sidewalk. He takes a left; I quicken my steps to get him back in sight. The cold air creates a billow of fog with each breath.

"Fuck," I mutter as I round the corner. He's not there.

I do the best I can in my two-inch heels. Where the hell has he gone?

My pace slows, the bottoms of my feet are on fire. Reluctantly, I turn around and start to make my way back. A rustling sound comes from my left. As I spin, I meet a pair of piercing gray eyes that I'm starting to know too well. Before I open my mouth to scream, his hand clamps down over my lips and he yanks me down the alleyway, making my back crash against the brick wall.

A cool blade presses into the side of my neck.

"What did I say would happen if we crossed paths again, detective?" His tone drips with danger.

I can't speak, his palm restricts my air.

"If I remove my hand, do you promise to be a good girl and not scream?"

I nod weakly, letting him think he's won. It's a struggle to ignore the fact his words have me hot under his touch.

He peels back his hand and presses the knife harder against my skin. My breathing becomes heavy. Concentrate Zara.

It takes all of my willpower to make sure I speak even and calmly. "Screaming would mean I need help. I know you won't kill me. Not here, anyway."

Is that a flicker of a smile that is teasing up the corner of his mouth? "Hmmm, is that so?"

I close my eyes as he trails the edge to the center of my neck, then painfully slowly down the front of my chest.

He's consuming my space, his face just inches from mine.

"Zara, Zara, Zara. What am I going to do with you?" His eyes focus on my lips.

"Let me go, Frankie." My breath hitches as the knife brushes against my shirt over my stomach.

"Why would I let my stalker get away so lightly?" He grips my chin and turns my face left and right. I don't know what to say. Why is my heart racing? The thrill of his body wedged against mine feels better than I expected.

He can't ever know that.

"Get the fuck off me." I hate that I want the opposite. For him to push harder.

His nostrils flare as he looks me up and down before he chuckles. "Are you going to make me, dolcezza?"

What the hell is dolcezza, and why does it sound so damn hot coming from his deep voice? That line of thought has to stop. I need my brain to start working.

Sliding my hand down my side, I reach for the flip knife in my pocket and bring it up to his throat. I press a little too hard and droplets of blood start to drip down his neck. He doesn't flinch, but grabs my wrist and squeezes until the blade falls from my grip. Pushing my back against the bricks with a thud, one of his muscular legs wedges between my thighs.

"Don't fight me, detective. It will only make me harder for you. And that's the last thing either of us needs."

I gawp at him, fighting for air as his hand laces around my throat. He squeezes and leans in.

"Now, whatever this little mission of yours is, it needs to end. Maybe look a little closer to home for the real enemy, Zara. You never know what monsters are lurking in plain sight."

I swallow against his palm.

What the fuck does he mean?

"You're the only monster here," I croak out.

That earns me a full bellied laugh. "I didn't have you down as naïve. I thought you were smart, relentless with a disregard for personal safety. It seems I was wrong."

He releases his hold and my body sags. I rub my neck and he wipes the droplets from his. Staring at the crimson stain on his fingers, his eyes narrow, then lock with mine.

"Open your mouth," he demands.

I look up at him through my lashes. He cannot be serious.

He raises his eyebrow.

"No." My voice shakes as I speak. I can barely hear it through the pulse pounding in my ears.

"Have it your way." He shrugs and grips my chin and pries my lips open, slipping in his finger to the back of my mouth. The metallic twang of blood sours on my tongue, his eyes glint with hunger.

"I'll see you around, detective," he rasps. The way it rolls out of him with a deep Italian accent does something to me. He slips out his finger, still tightly holding my jaw. His mouth is just a breath away from mine. I'm fighting between the urge to headbutt him or kiss him, giving him back his blood from my mouth.

He gives me one last smug grin and backs away from me. Breaking into a jog, he veers out of the alleyway. Leaving me up against the wall, my body is tingling and the taste of him lingers on my tongue.

A new fire is set within me to take this asshole down.

"Hey, Alex. Can I talk to you for a second?" I ask as he pours himself a coffee in the break room.

His spoon clinks against the edge of his cup as he glances up. "Yeah, sure. Fire away."

"So, I'm working a case and the guy keeps going to this address." I lie. I spent the afternoon following Frankie around. First to King's Gym, then to Grayson's house and lastly, he met Jax on his bike outside this shady looking black building. I watched him swipe a key card to get in. I know there's something important behind that door.

So, I stayed for the rest of the afternoon and into the evening. It was either stunning women in hardly a shred of clothing or suited men.

I've got my bets it's a strip club, and what mafia organization doesn't have one of those?

I pull up the address on my phone and the picture of the entrance. Alex's brows bunch together and then his eyes go wide. Bingo.

"Oh, umm. I'm not sure that is the kind of place you want to be standing around, Zara."

I tilt my head, and he chuckles.

"Why? What is it?"

The look on Alex's face indicates something else is behind that boring black door.

"It's a sex club, Zara."

"Oh." My heart rate starts to pick up. The last place I want to bump into Frankie is in one of those, knowing the effect that man can have over me. It would be the place he least expects me and somewhere I have no doubts he would be too busy to even notice me.

It would be the perfect opportunity for me to plant a wire.

"It's run by the mafia. I would try to avoid that as much as possible. If you need to, I can send in a team, just send me the details of the case?" He eyes me suspiciously.

"No, no. It's fine. I'll keep digging. I'm not sure I'd find my answers there, anyway."

He gives me a curt nod, turning his attention back to his coffee, while I stand here trying to ignore the heat spreading on my cheeks. That isn't happening. I open my mouth to keep pressing, and quickly stop myself remembering how he hid evidence for Frankie. I can't trust him or my father at this stage.

It's perfect timing for Dad to be away.

"Thanks Alex." I shove my phone in my pocket and head straight to my desk.

If I'm going to do it, it has to be tonight. I just have to work out how the hell I'm going to get myself in to do some real detective work.

CHAPTER SIX

Zara

Song- abuse me, Ex Habit.

I park early and wait in the alleyway, so I have a view of the door. I'm going to have to think on my feet to get in here. It turns out the internet wasn't overly helpful in advising me on my latest predicament.

I pull my coat tighter around my waist and wait, hoping my opportunity hits soon.

"I wonder who you'll sub for tonight, Lex." A high-pitched voice has me backing into the hedge more as their heels click along the path.

"I hope Mr. F," the other one replies. I roll my eyes, knowing who they're talking about.

My heart races; this is my chance.

As they waltz past me in a fit of giggles, I step out of the shadows and slip in behind them as they approach the entrance. They swipe their keycard and it opens.

After they step through, I put out my hand to hold it open for myself. The blonde girl turns her head and looks straight at me.

"Thank you. It's my first night here." I smile as sweetly as I can.

She scrunches up her face, looking me up and down. I resist the urge to headbutt her for being such a judgmental bitch. Another reason I never had girlfriends growing up and found myself tied to a gang from the age of fifteen. I shake my head. I don't have time to dwell on that right now.

"Come on, I wanna get in there." Her friend nudges her and she lets go of the door, letting me step through.

The second I walk through, the aroma of vanilla mixed with sex fills my nostrils. The girls head off on their mission down the dark hallway, and I follow behind them.

"Come on, we can show you where to go," the other blonde girl says, pushing her hair from her bare shoulder.

"Can I take your coats?" The woman behind the desk asks as we approach.

I shuffle mine off and hand it to her, revealing my tight black dress that plunges between my breasts, showing off the tattoo between them that scales down across my ribs.

"Thank you." I give her a smile as I hand it over. The two girls push open the gold doors and saunter down the hall. I trail along behind, keeping my eyes down to not attract any attention.

If Frankie and his men are here, they would spot me. So, I try to hide behind these two bundles of joy in front of me.

"Girls, you're late. He's expecting you. Keep your head down, remember?"

I look up and quickly drop my gaze back down to the floor. It's one of the guys who works with Frankie. The one I can't put a name to.

A brunette hostess wearing only a set of stockings opens the red door up for us and I follow behind the girls, mimicking their position.

The first thing I'm greeted by is a woman's ass as she's bent over a dark-haired man. His navy suit pants are framing her, her hands gripped onto his muscular legs. Another dark-haired woman is positioned on her knees on the floor behind her, her face between her legs, pulling her ass cheeks apart and going to town.

Desire pools in my core. I scan my eyes up. I'm not one of these girls. Now that I'm in, I don't need to bow my head.

All the air is knocked out of my lungs as the man tips his head up, his cold gray eyes meeting mine. Him.

The shock on his face is there for a second before his cold resolve masks it.

He roughly laces his fingers through the blonde's hair and pushes her down so she gags. His eyes don't leave mine as he gives me a smirk.

The two girls I entered with discard every shred of clothing they have on and drop to their knees beside him, keeping their heads down.

I plant my feet firmly in place, tightening my grip on the door handle. My brain is screaming at me to leave. This is dangerous, not just for my safety but for my head. I can't let him get to me.

I shouldn't be turned on by him. Yet, I'm clenching my thighs together, a complete horny mess.

"Now you're here, why don't we play a game?" Frankie's voice just heats me even further.

I can't physically tear my eyes from his. I'm under his spell. His eyes dart to my hand on the handle and he raises an eyebrow.

He thinks I can't do this.

I straighten my spine, dropping my hand. "What do you suggest?"

A grin twitches on his lips. Frankie's grip tightens in the girl's hair, causing her to moan.

"You give me a show. If I come, I'll answer anything you ask me. If you can't get us both off with your performance, you stop this little mission of yours."

Desire flashes in his eyes. I lock my gaze with his as I step forward, slowly unzipping the side of my dress and letting it fall to the floor. He groans, raking my body all the way up. My red lace thongs and matching lace bra are a brilliant choice for tonight's activities.

"Show me what you've got, detective." He drawls out that last word in a way that has me soaking.

The two girls kneeling both look up directly at me. Frankie growls, making them turn their heads away.

"Lexie, here." Frankie's tone is commanding. For some reason, I open my legs, the pressure building in my pussy.

She saunters over, not before flashing me a malicious grin

and sits next to him, her legs spread wide as she leans into his shoulder. He slides a hand down her stomach and between her legs, starting to fuck her with them. His eyes still firmly on mine.

Fine. If he wants a show, I'll give him one. I can probably do that better myself, anyway.

I mimic his actions, brushing my hand along my bare stomach and slipping it under my panties.

I start to circle my clit lightly, and Frankie grunts in response. The thrill of it has me on the edge; my entire body is on fire. I start to picture him doing this to me and a moan escapes my lips.

Unclasping my bra with the other hand, it falls to the floor, letting my breasts bounce free. The cold air makes my nipples stand to peaks as I roll my nipple piercing between my fingers. Tipping my head back against the door as I slide in two fingers.

The pure fire in Frankie's eyes greets me when I look back at him. I can't focus on the other women. He is all I see.

I can hear the woman's moans. I can feel my temperature rising. I want the man who's staring at me like he's torn between strangling me and fucking me until I can't walk.

Gritting my teeth, my blood pounds in my ears. I shouldn't want him like this. I hate the man. I want to take him down.

I just can't stop.

CHAPTER SEVEN

Frankie

I can't concentrate on anything other than *her*. This blonde can suck on my dick for as long as she likes, the only woman I want wrapped around my cock is the one standing in front of me.

I groan as I imagine her sweet taste.

I'm riveted to her every movement.

She had a moment where she was debating leaving, it only made me want my stalker more when she slipped off that dress with a defiant glint in her eye and revealed her perfect frame, scattered with beautiful ink that spans a lot further than I first thought.

Her arms, her ribs, her thighs. I want to run my tongue along all of it.

The way she's eye fucking me and biting that plump bottom lip tells me she's not picturing anyone other than me doing that to her.

I lick my lips and fire flashes in her eyes. She needs more. She's desperate for it.

She needs to be claimed and controlled to truly be set free. I push the blonde's head forward so she chokes on my dick, my fingers still sliding in and out of Lexie, her legs shaking next to me. The girls might be moaning next to me, all I can focus on is the little breathy pants Zara keeps letting out.

I could have her screaming.

I bite down on the inside of my cheek. Fuck, I want her.

I push the blonde off me and slide my fingers out of Lexie, which earns me a displeased moan.

"You girls go and have some fun." I tap Lexie's ass as she stands and she giggles. I can't concentrate on them; my focus is entirely on Zara.

My hand grips my shaft, and I lean back, my other arm up on the back of the couch. I wonder how my little detective is going to play this one off. She's close, and I know she won't back down from a challenge.

What's your next move, detective?

I can almost feel the conflict happening inside her brain. She wants to finish. She hates herself for wanting me, but she's so turned on right now.

If she wants the answers, she has to get off.

I keep stroking myself. Her eyes zone in on my cock. I bite back a groan as she rolls that silver nipple piercing between her fingers. I can smell her sweetness from here.

It's taking every single ounce of restraint I have right now not to go over there and fuck her like she craves to be fucked.

Her back arches against the door, her head lowering, and her hooded eyes meet mine. The desire, the pure hunger in them, almost has my balls exploding. This woman is like none I've ever met. I have a nice slice on my neck to prove that.

"Fuck," she mutters as her body shakes.

I tip back my head and imagine her tied up on my bed; her spanked ass up in the air and me pounding into her from behind, over and over again until she passes out. Imagining her sweet voice screaming for me. My thighs tighten and with one last tug, I come all over my hand and I'm fucking breathless.

As I tip my head back up, I find her watching me, still rolling her lip between her perfect white teeth, brushing her hair out of her face and a beautiful blush spreading up her chest.

Without a word, I stand, tucking myself back into my pants and head to the bathroom to wash my hands. I catch a glance of my own reflection, the desire is hard to hide. Get a fucking grip.

She's still by the door as I re-enter, watching my every move. I walk towards her and her breath hitches. I bend down and pick up her dress and hand it out to her. She cautiously extends her hand out, and the second our fingers connect, a surge of electricity shoots down to my dick. I grab hold of her hand and pull her small frame towards me, leaning down so my lips brush against her jaw.

"You enjoy watching me, don't you, detective?" I huskily rasp in her ear.

She shivers against me. "No."

My lips twitch into a grin. "Liar."

"I-I'm not," she whispers, her warm breath hitting against my cheek.

"I'll warn you once. The next time we're in the same room

together, I will fuck you, Zara. I will ruin you for any other man. I've let you have your fun."

I rub my fingers along the cut she left me with on my throat.

I step back abruptly. I truly don't know what I want. Do I want her to stop following me? Do I want to fuck her? If I do, will I ever be able to stop?

"You owe me answers, Frankie." That fire in her eyes returns as she scowls at me, crossing her arms in front of her chest.

"You really think I'd make it that easy?" I whisper against her cheek and pull myself away before I take it any further.

Zara looks horrified as I open the door.

"See you around, angel." I wink and shut it.

CHAPTER EIGHT

Zara

I shimmy on my dress as fast as I can and zip it up, heading out of the room.

Jax is leaning on the bar with a beer, watching me with a knowing grin as I walk through. My cheeks are still on fire from my encounter with Frankie. I can't believe I just let him see me come, imagining it was him.

Fuck, it was hot.

Seeing him lose control for that split second, it was the hardest I've climaxed in a long time. That asshole owes me some answers.

I head towards the exit, the smell of cigarettes lingering in the hallway.

The door opens and two men walk in. That's when my eyes lock on Frankie's as he stands outside, hand in pocket, blowing a puff of smoke towards the door.

"Miss, your coat!"

I ignore the woman and slip out of the door into the darkness with Frankie.

"You didn't feel like joining the girls?" he asks, holding out a packet of cigarettes to me. I take one, place it between my lips, and he lights it for me.

"Not really my thing. Now, I want my answers."

"Go on, then," he pauses and smirks. "You get one and so do I."

I place my hand on my hip, the cool air causing me to shiver.

"That wasn't the deal, Frankie." I scowl at him.

He stretches one arm against the wall, framing me with his tall body.

"Tough. I'll go first. Do you have a boyfriend?"

I blink a few times at him, his face expressionless.

"No." I don't know why I felt the need to even reveal that to him. As stalkers go, I'm doing a pretty shit job at this. I just want to know the answer to one burning question.

"Good," he replies, blowing out smoke.

"Excuse me?"

He grins at me.

"I'd be pretty pissed if my girlfriend got herself off imagining another man fucking her."

My mouth gapes open.

"You have no idea what I was thinking about." I take a long drag. He leans towards me and I clench my thighs. Jesus, what is wrong with me?

I blow the smoke straight in his face, and he waves it nonchalantly out of the way.

"Now I know the most important thing there is to know about you, Zara." He licks his lower lip.

"Really? What's that?" I counter.

His head lowers, even with mine. "Just how absolutely breathtaking you look when you come thinking about me."

His hungry eyes scan my body as he scratches his beard.

"Fuck off." I glare at him.

He laughs. "You really don't learn, do you?" His eyes darken as his finger trails up my bare arm, making me suck in a breath.

"Stop," I whisper.

His chest rumbles as his voice deepens. "Admit you got off thinking about me."

I shake my head, dropping my cigarette to the ground. He stamps it out for me, stroking along my collarbone.

I won't ever let him know the truth. My heart races as his fingers loosely wrap around my throat.

"Say it." His lips hover over mine.

"Why? Will it make you feel better about coming all over your hand watching me?" I raise my eyebrow at him, biting the inside of my mouth.

"I didn't do that from watching you." The tease of his smile grows.

"Really?" I bite back.

"Yes. Really. I came thinking about you tied up on my bed, your red ass up in the air as I fuck that little tight hole of yours as you beg me to let you finish."

I gulp, snapping my lips together. That image forever engrained firmly in my mind.

"Quite the picture, isn't it?" He tips his head to the side, his warm breath hitting against my jaw.

We lock eyes, and he releases me.

"My question."

"Yes, detective. What have you got for me?"

"Maria. Why did you kill her?"

He rubs his beard. "Because that bitch deserved it."

He leans back in and I hold my breath.

"I'm sure I'll see you around, detective." He salutes me and turns his back to me and walks down the alley. It leaves me breathless and on fire.

The door slams shut behind me, the sound doesn't jostle me from the spell of watching him slip into the shadows.

CHAPTER NINE

Frankie

"What the fuck do you mean, there is a shipment coming in?" I shout into the phone to Enzo.

"It flagged up. Do you want me to send some guys down there?" Enzo asks, and I rub my finger on my temple.

"Yes. Get Keller, Jax, and Kai down there, too. Keep an eye on police reports. Keep your guys waiting on the sidelines until we work out what the hell is going on."

"Got it."

I cut the call, turning to Grayson, who abruptly turns the car around in the middle of the road.

"The docks, I take it?"

I nod. "Tell me we've got enough weapons in this car."

He laughs, putting his foot down on the accelerator.

"It's a fucking candy shop in the trunk. We're good. You think it's Romano?"

Most likely Romano's first power move. To remind me that he can try to take me down from Sicily. I could be wrong; it could be a coincidence.

The only downside is, we have no commissioner on board this time. We have no police units blocking the roads or the call ins. We do have Enzo, though, ready to intercept the response. The last thing I need is to get arrested again. I need Zara away from me, not even hotter on my tail.

If we are right and the Commissioner has switched sides, they'll be waiting for me to slip up. Like hell am I letting them take my docks. So, it's a risk we have to take tonight. It won't be the last one either. Until Romano is dead, we have to fight. I can't die until I end that motherfucker.

I spot Keller, Kai and Jax on the side of the road next to the entrance and G pulls up next to them.

"What the hell is going on?" Keller asks.

"We're about to find out." I grab the pack of cigarettes from my suit jacket and open them, offering Grayson one.

"Thanks, boss." He slides one out and sparks it up. Keller does the same.

"You're not wearing your famous mask anymore, Keller?" I ask.

"What do I need it for? I'm not hiding anymore. These fuckers can see my face just before they die."

Grayson raises an eyebrow at him. I can sense the tension from here. I won't be encouraging Keller to step back like Luca did. He's a grown ass man. If he wants in, he's in. I won't say no to a trained killer being on my side. It will be good for Jax and Kai to learn from him.

"What do we think is in there?" Jax asks from my right.

"Worst case, an army of Romano's men are sent here to slaughter us. Best case, more drugs and guns." I answer honestly.

We've never to this day had an unexpected shipment arrive.

Jax looks raring to go. Kai, behind him, shifts nervously from foot to foot .

"All good, Kai?"

He rubs his tattooed hand along the ink on his jaw and nods. It's his first time up here with me. Grayson assures me he's ready. Jax, I agree, he is ready for more. Kai may need more persuading.

"Likely, it's the first option," Grayson says, taking a drag of his cigarette and blowing the smoke up in the air.

I do the same; the nicotine calming the adrenaline pumping around my veins. It's been a while since I've had blood on my hands. I miss it.

As I step into the yard, I spot the commissioner watching the boat come in. There is movement next to the warehouse behind him. What the hell is he playing at?

I hold my hand up to stop the guys behind me.

The first boat starts to approach. I stand in front of my men and wait. Tossing my cigarette to the ground and stamping it into the gravel, I slip out the brass knuckles from my pocket and slide them on my fingers. My right hand rests on my gun, ready for whatever surprise they have planned for me.

Here we fucking go.

The second boat stops a few yards away from the dock.

"We need to move closer."

Glancing at Grayson, I catch his small nod.

I click my neck from side to side, unholstering my gun, leaving it at my side.

We crouch and scale the side of one of the containers, so we're close enough to see and hear what George is doing.

"Is that?" Grayson asks.

"Yes," I say through gritted teeth.

This confirms everything I need to know. That trip to Italy wasn't a vacation, it was an act of war.

The lackey on the boat uses a crowbar to tear open the front of the first wooden crate. Enzo's voice comes through the speaker in my ear.

"Armored vehicle approaching, ETA three minutes. Sending in your backup. They'll wait at the gates."

The last of the long nails screech as the face of the large box falls to the ground, the impact reverberating through my feet. As the choking dust clears, I can barely believe what I'm seeing.

"Oh fuck," Keller mutters behind me.

The gathering of George and his men startles the women cowering within the dark confines. Their hands raise, blocking the violent intrusion of light as they squint before cowering in a huddle in the back.

Rage burns through me.

Those dirty motherfuckers.

"What do we do, boss? He's the commissioner?"

My hands shake with rage as men jump off the boat and stand with George. I know we can take them out; that isn't a question.

"Kill every single one of them, leave George alive. Jax and Kai, you get the girls to safety." My blood boils, a stabbing feeling radiates through my chest as I think about Rosa, of everything that happened to her that I couldn't stop.

Over my dead body will any harm come to these women. Romano knows our stance on trafficking. A big fucking no.

"What if this is a setup?" Grayson asks.

"We can't leave these women." I take a step forward, my feet crunching on the gravel, and George's head turns to face me. Pure fucking horror on his features as I aim my gun at him.

"Kill him," George shouts at the man next to him, who pulls out his weapon at me, but he's too slow. I shift my aim and pull the trigger. The bullet hits through his cheek, and he drops without a sound. The screams get louder as our back up start to arrive, the men filtering out of the back of the armored truck just as the second boat pulls up.

We have enough safe houses while we work out where the hell the women came from. They could have information we need on Romano.

For now, we fight.

George takes his opportunity to run, but the old fucker can't keep up with me. I catch him easily, grabbing the back of his throat, turning him to face me as I slam my metal covered fist into the side of his jaw.

"You're going to fucking regret this, George," I grit out, throwing him to the ground.

He coughs, spitting blood into the dirt and laughs, looking past me as more black SUVs filter in.

"You touch me again, you'll spend the rest of your life behind bars, Frankie," he warns.

My finger twitches over the trigger. I could end him, here and now. I look back at the men coming out of the cars. My bet–dirty cops.

If I kill him, I'm done. We all are.

CHAPTER TEN

Zara

I've fucked up. Big time.

The heavy sound of the boat engines carries through the air as I slip between two containers. There is no way I can find a way out, not with this many of his men here.

I wrap my arms around my body and lean on the metal. Hopefully, it will be over soon. I'm far enough away to stay hidden, especially in the darkness. Still close enough, I can just about work out what's going on.

They all seem tense, which is making me on edge. I don't really know if I want to witness the monster in action again. Yet, I can't peel my eyes from him.

I lean forward, squinting, and my heart almost stops. My father.

He's standing with his hands in his pockets, watching the boats arrive. What the hell? He didn't even tell me or Mom he was home.

My eyes flick back to Frankie, who is next to the container closer to the docks. The way he commands his men, and the way they respect him, fascinates me.

I can hear shouting coming from the boat, I shuffle forwards to listen. That's when the unmistakable sounds of females screaming rips through the air.

"Shit," I hiss.

He's trafficking women. With my father.

I fumble back, the fear taking over. This is a whole other level of dangerous. Gunshots start to ring out and the cries get louder. Squatting against the cold steel, I wish I could melt through it. If anyone sees me here, I'm as good as dead.

Squeezing my weapon, I shuffle forward to get a better view. Frankie didn't strike me as the lowest of the low. A monster, yes. He seemed, I don't know, classier than that. A sliver of nausea boils through me. I let myself be turned on by him.

Fighting back the bile rising in my throat, I watch as men from the second boat swarm in from all angles. Behind me there is shouting, shots firing. Even with the chaos, I can't take my eyes off Frankie as he bolts towards my father.

I gasp as he shoots the guy next to my dad in the head and my heart is in my throat as my dad makes a run for it. I almost take a step forward and stop myself.

I shake my head. What the hell is going on? I thought my dad worked for Frankie. The next thing I know, my dad is thrown to the ground. Clamping my hand over my mouth, a guy runs at Frankie with a knife.

"No," I whisper.

I can barely breathe.

Jumping Frankie from the back, a hulking brute wraps his arms around Frankie's neck. Frankie grabs and slings him over his shoulder to land flat on the ground before pummeling the man in the head. The streetlamps reflect off the metal bands across Frankie's knuckles. He straddles him, and lets loose, his fists slamming into the prostrate man, blood splattering all over his shirt.

I watch as my dad takes his opportunity to make a run for it towards the black SUVs at the entrance.

Another man runs in my direction, and I press myself into the shadows. Keller darts after him and catches him easily, swiping a knife along his throat and stabbing it through his jaw before tossing him to the ground like trash.

My heart almost beats out of my chest. There are bodies and blood everywhere.. These men are feral beasts, and Frankie is the leader of the pack. His deep voice calls out orders over the screams and gunfire.

The fighting behind me gets closer, and I tighten my grip on my gun. Another van speeds through the gates. I am so far out of my depth here.

Frankie spots the van and runs towards it. They stop only a few containers down from me. I bite down on my cheek; I can't even risk them hearing me breathe.

"Jax, get these girls somewhere safe and hidden." Frankie's unmistakable voice sends my mind into a whirlwind.

This doesn't make any sense.

Grayson trots behind him. "What the fuck is happening?"

Frankie runs a hand through his hair, smearing the blood that was sprayed across his face.

"Romano is sending a message. We need to get out of here!" He shouts the last word and balls his fists.

My mouth falls open.

The ringing in my ears almost drowns out Frankie's voice. "G, get on the phone to Enzo. Send them to one of our safe houses." His jaw clenches. "They're all dead men."

I swear my heart almost stops and tears threaten to erupt. My dad did this?

Jax leads the sobbing girls past my container, speaking in Russian to them in a soft voice. I keep deadly still, praying no one spots me in the shadows.

Footsteps crunch on the gravel. With every step, they get louder. I feel like I'm about to pass out.

"Did they hurt you?" Frankie's husky voice asks. He's far too close to me.

My hands tremble on my face.

I can't make out her response.

"We will keep you safe, okay?"

The sickening realization dawns on me. He is saving them from my dad.

Chaos continues around them. Frankie, Grayson, and Jax lead the girls into an armored truck.

"Let's finish them off and get out of here."

A thump behind me makes me spin around, aiming my gun out in front. I have no clue who works for who. I keep my eyes set between the gap, where I saw a flash of movement.

Protect myself first. That's what my dad always taught me.

A heavy leather jacket is followed by a scarred face. My eyes focus only on the hefty knife he's waving. "Come here, whore," he shouts with a heavy accent.

"Stop, or I'll shoot," I say loud enough for him to hear me. Hopefully, it doesn't carry past the containers.

He hunches his shoulders and runs at me, blade extended.

So, I do just that, firing and hitting him in the chest. I back away as he charges forward. He lunges and I duck as he hits the side of the container.

Oh, shit.

I back out from the metal alley into plain sight. I fire again and hit him in the stomach. He doubles over, blood pours through his fingers clenching the wound as he grunts pain. My finger itches to pull the trigger again to finish him.

A gun goes off next to my ear. The back of my attacker's head splatters and he drops to the ground.

I spin around, running straight into a chest. Looking up, Frankie's familiar gray eyes lock onto mine.

He looks from the gun in my hand back to my face with a scowl. His jaw ticks and I swallow past the lump in my throat.

I'm in deep shit.

My heart races, knowing he's going to kill me.

His fingers wrap around the wrist that's holding my weapon.

"Are you hurt, dolcezza?"

I blink at him, registering his words.

He studies me as if looking for marks and blood. I shake my head. My hand starts to tremble, so he tightens his grip.

Weirdly, his piercing gaze makes me feel safe. His face is completely unreadable now. A shot fires and I jump. Frankie pushes us back between the containers. My back crashes against the metal and he cages me in with his grip still firmly on my wrist.

I should be petrified, yet for some reason, I'm not.

Chapter Eleven

Frankie

"I'm fine." She tips her chin up to me.

I study her as her chest rises and falls. My heart almost stopped when I saw her, before the rage returned.

"What the fuck do you think you're doing?" I hiss.

I can't trust her.

She tries to yank her arm away, but I tighten my grip, pulling her closer to me. Enough to feel her warm breath beat against my neck. I inhale her vanilla scent in an attempt to calm down, to settle my emotions.

The defiance in her jaw tells me she doesn't want to be here.

"Why are you here?" I press. I have to know.

"I-I don't know," she falters. I pull back and study her face. She's telling the truth. I doubt she even realizes I can read her like a damn book.

"Tell me what you're doing here, Zara." I drop her arm as she steps back, looking down to the ground.

What the hell do I do with this woman? She's a thorn in my side. I can't leave her here with Romano's men prowling around. It's irritating that I can't even seem to get her out of my mind.

"I followed you." That fire in her eyes returns, and I bite down on my tongue.

"You want me to believe you aren't here with your father?"

Her eyes flick to the dead guy on the ground beside us who has bullets from her gun lodged within him.

Pulling the magazine on my own weapon, I do a quick count before shoving it back into place.

"Frankie, move!"

I look up, and she shoves me out of the way into the side of the container, stepping in front of me. Before I have time to register what is happening, gun shots ring out and I grab hold of her.

"What the fuck are you doing?" I shout, looking over at the new body tumbling into the dirt. My nostrils flare as I spin her to me. Her hand trembles as she looks down at the smoking gun.

"He was going to shoot you," her voice shakes and I pull her against me.

"Don't fucking do that again." Keeping a tight grip on her biceps, I pull back and search those green eyes.

"I just saved your goddamn life. Why are you so angry?"

That, I don't want to admit the answer to. "I've never had a stalker before. I've become quite accustomed to it. I can't have you dying on me."

I can't help taking a moment to study her. Despite the burning rage at her putting herself in this much danger, I kind of admire her determination. She has guts and the potential to be a lot more than what she is.

I'm pretty sure she's just killed a cop. He doesn't resemble any of Romano's men. One thing this has cemented: she isn't working for her dad.

And she has a weakness.

Her feelings for me, whatever they may be. You don't jump in front of someone unless you don't want them to get hurt.

"I need to arrest you, Frankie." Her lips twitch into a smirk, shaking me from my thoughts.

Putting my theory to the test, I lean into the crook of her neck.

"Is that right, detective?" I slide my bloody hand down her side, reaching the hem of her jeans.

Letting my beard tickle against her neck, somehow I resist the urge to bite down on her flesh.

Her sharp inhale covers the moment I take the handcuffs from their holder.

This confirms exactly what I thought. I can definitely use this woman. She is so distracted by me, she doesn't realize I have her cuffs until they snap over her right wrist.

"What the fuck?" she hisses at me.

"I think you are the one under arrest, baby," I mutter against her throat.

Her body goes stiff against me. I clasp the other link over my own wrist. She yanks it, pinching my skin.

"I can get out of this, you know. I have the key," she says through her gritted teeth.

"I wouldn't dare, if I were you. You want to get out of here alive? I'll make sure you do. Seeing as you have a clear disregard for your own life, this—" I hold up our chained wrists, "—is non-negotiable."

She visibly shivers.

"Come on, I'm not that bad. Being cuffed can be fun." I wink.

Her nose wrinkles as she looks up at me.

I yank her towards me so her body slams into my side.

She relaxes against my touch.

My voice drops as my lips brush the lobe of her ear. "We are more alike than you think, detective."

She looks past me, deep in thought. "How is my dad involved in all of this?"

"That's something I still need to find the answer to," I answer honestly.

She holsters her weapon with her free hand. She could shoot me with the damn thing. Apparently, she seems to have me under her own kind of spell.

"Good shot earlier, much better the second time around," I chide her.

"I'm not supposed to shoot to kill," she snaps back.

"It's your life against theirs. You always put yourself first. There are no second chances. Remember that next time," I walk us out between the containers, spotting Grayson in front of me.

"There won't be a next time," she mutters to herself. Even looking slightly disheveled, with splatters of blood over her. To me, she is pure perfection.

I hope she's right and there won't be a next time. Yet, something is screaming at me that isn't true.

Grayson's head tilts to the side as we approach, his blue eyes focusing on the cuffs. One of his brows raises. "Boss?"

"I cuffed her, don't worry. Detective Zara O'Reilly, meet my right-hand man, Grayson Ward."

Grayson shifts on his feet, and his lips thin. He has a dead body next to his feet. Zara flicks her gaze from it to Grayson.

"Good to meet you, I guess," Grayson says, then turns his attention to me. "We really need to go. Jax and Keller are taking care of the last of the guys behind the warehouse."

"Excellent. I'll meet you later." I tug on her arm, breaking her stare at Grayson.

She takes a step closer to me, now flush against my side, which causes my mouth and brain to disconnect.

"Good girl," I rasp.

She stiffens beside me.

Shit.

Electricity fizzles around us.

Grayson clears his throat. "Enzo has the clean-up crew on the way. I'll do a quick count to see how many guys we lost."

His little dose of reality reminds me, Romano has to die.

"I'll take Zara with me. You head back with Keller? Text me the location. I'll have to take your Audi."

With a grumble, he tosses me his keys.

As I go to walk away, I turn back to face Grayson. "Good work today, G. We are one hell of a team."

He smiles back at me and slowly nods. "Yeah, we are."

I look back towards Zara, who's watching our interaction intently. Tugging on her wrist, I set a brisk pace.

She stumbles forward and walks beside me. Stepping over bodies, I'm surprised she's keeping her lips shut. I know her brain is working overtime as we approach Grayson's car.

Spotting the bobby pin in her hair, she sucks in a breath as I slide it out and open the metal up. She watches intently as I straighten it out and bend the top half over. Pulling our cuffed hands up in front of my face, I stick the makeshift key into the hole and jab around until it clicks, freeing my wrist.

She subtly nods her head, holding out her free hand.

"Let me try," she says.

I grin, placing it in her hand.

"Just wiggle it about until you feel it click."

It doesn't take her long to master it, releasing her wrist and rubbing over the skin.

Opening her door with a flourish, I step back and cup her elbow. "In you go."

She doesn't move.

"Zara, get in that fucking car before I drag your ass in there," I bark at her, losing my patience.

She blinks at me a few times, before huffing and finally obeying.

We drive back to her apartment in silence. My fingers tap on the steering wheel, weighing my options. She isn't safe to be around her dad, nor any of the cops at this point. Why do I care about her?

It's several minutes of blissful silence before she shatters it. "You okay over there?"

"Just plotting," I reply, keeping my eyes on the road. I can't look at her; she's far too distracting.

She turns in her seat, one knee shifting towards the center console. "Plotting what? My death? My kidnapping?"

I let out a groan. Jesus Christ, this woman. "Both are on the list."

Keeping Zara alive is my best bet. Keeping her close? Even better.

I pull up outside her apartment and spot the amused grin on her face.

She bites her lip. "Oh, you're letting me go?"

I give her a curt nod.

Her eyes thin to slits. "Why?"

"I don't need anything from you," I reply with my best neutral expression.

"Great." As she reaches to open the door, I hit the internal locks. She spins around to glare at me.

"That means no more following me, Zara. This is your final warning. If I see you skulking in the shadows again, I won't have a choice. Don't put me in that position."

She chews the inside of her mouth, looking deep in thought.

I swear she's fucking with me.

"Deal." A grin forms on her lips and she holds out her hand.

Reluctantly, I place my large palm in her little one, ignoring the protests from my dick as our fingers touch. I give a little pressure, and she doesn't flinch. I can't figure her out.

She's right, killing or kidnapping her would be the easiest option. I let out a breath. I can't do that. So I hit the button, and she slips out of the car, walking into her apartment without so much as a look back.

My fingers grip around the steering wheel before my head falls against it.

Fuck. What a mess.

I stay parked outside Zara's for an hour in silence, waiting for her lights to go off. Her dad had run off before he would have spotted her. I just hope none of the other cops saw what she did for me.

Fuck.

I pull out my phone and dial Enzo.

"I'm heading to the safe house, Frankie."

"Yeah, I'll meet you there. I need a favor."

I swear he mutters, fucker in Italian under his breath. I choose to let this one go.

"Keep a detail on Zara for the next few days, will you?"

I won't be able to rest, not if there is a chance they did see her there. In the meantime, I need to work out my next move.

I have to end Romano, yet nothing seems to get me closer to him.

CHAPTER TWELVE

Zara

Dread boils in my stomach as I knock on my dad's office door.

I spent all night tossing and turning, replaying the events in my head. I can't let this go. He might be my father, he isn't getting away with this.

Getting my mom new treatment is not an excuse for trafficking girls. He's actually putting both of us at risk. Mom doesn't need the stress. Not now.

Is he more dangerous to me than Frankie?

How deep is he in this?

I can't follow Frankie anymore. He gave me his warning and I believe him. I also know he doesn't want to kill me. Whatever this weird pull is between us, he feels it, too.

And we're both fighting it.

He might be dangerous, brutal, and the most powerful man in the city. I'm not frightened of him.

I am scared of the man behind this door. Frankie doesn't hide the monster he is, but my dad does. That's worse.

I'm stuck between two evils. One wants me to embrace the chaos within, while the other tries to force me to fight it.

"Come in."

A shiver runs down my spine, I won't let him see my turmoil. I tip my chin up and enter.

"Commissioner," I greet him, keeping my tone light.

"Sit down," he orders.

I smooth my skirt and take a seat in front of his desk. I made sure to dress 'appropriately', masking my tattoos so I don't anger him up any further.

He taps his pen, each time increasing the pounding in my head.

"What can I do for you, Zara?"

I shuffle in my seat, mustering the courage.

"You are a piece of shit, Dad."

I jerk back as his hands smash against the wood, sending our family picture crashing to the ground.

"Don't you dare speak to me like that," he grits out.

"It's the truth. I've seen enough. There is no excuse for what you're doing. I'm going to let everyone know exactly what kind of monster you are."

I don't owe either of them anything. Yet, only one of them stoops low enough to abuse and traffic women. The lines are blurring. Frankie's first concern last night was if I was okay.

"No. You won't."

He stands and steps around the desk, towering over me. I scoot my chair back and stand, looking up at him.

His fists ball at his sides. "Do you want to know why?"

I frown.

"You don't get to make the orders here, Zara. Otherwise, those bullets that were pulled from a cop's stomach, from your gun, might make their way into the right hands. Let's not forget, the murdered ex-boyfriend of yours. That's a lot of time in jail," he smirks.

My eyes sting.

"What kind of father are you?" I whisper.

He growls under his breath. "I told you to leave it alone. You just couldn't help yourself. Now look at the mess you've got yourself in. I can't protect you, not from this. So, you need to leave the NYPD and this family. We are done."

"W-what about Mom?" I hold back the tears. He can't stop me from seeing her. She hasn't done anything to deserve this.

His face reddens and his nostrils flare.

"If you can't understand that I'm doing this for my family, you are no longer part of it."

His hand starts to shake next to his leg.

"Fine. I don't want to be a part of any family who believes trafficking women solves their problems. You make me fucking sick." My chin juts defiantly. I'll find a way to take him down, and I'll do what I have to protect my mom, even if it is from her own husband. I'll make sure of it.

"You little bitch!" he shouts. His hand comes hurtling towards my face and connects to my cheek, sending me flying sideways. I scream out as my head smashes into the wooden arm of the chair.

I pull myself up on all fours, holding back the tears and rub my throbbing temple.

"You think you're any better than me? After what you did?"

My back presses against the wall as he looms over me.

"I did that to protect myself, you know that. There are no excuses for what you're doing. Those girls don't deserve this. You can still stop this; I can help you." My eyes burn, I won't let him see me cry. He's not the man I knew who had gentle words and treated the scrapes on my knees when I fell off my bike. It's like he's possessed, high on power and corruption.

I bring myself up to stand on unsteady legs.

He shakes his head violently enough that his hair ruffles. "Get out, Zara. I never want to see you here again."

I brush the stinging mark.

A life in jail would be better than this hell. I want to get out of here.

"If I go down, you're coming with me. Just remember that," I snarl.

His fingers twitch like he wants to hit me again. We enter a silent battle. This is the first time I've ever fought back, and it's electrifying. He lets out a grunt and leans against the desk.

The man looks defeated. I could feel sorry for him, but he got himself into this mess on his own.

I spin on my heel with the pain radiating on my face, my vision starting to blur. I force myself to walk out the door and slam it shut behind me.

Finding a cardboard box in the cupboard of the breakroom, I toss in the minimal items I own from my desk.

As I leave, I see the poster for tonight's Halloween ball, and stop.

I'm feeling particularly violent. He thinks he can blackmail me, hit me, and I'll just slink away with my tail between my legs? He's got me so wrong.

Especially now, I have something on him. Tonight is the perfect opportunity while he is distracted to dig a little deeper. I know all of his secrets will be in a drawer in his office. That old school asshole can barely use a computer.

If I can get the information about the girls, I can stop them. I can save them and my mom.

And I'm going to try and do what I can to make that happen.

Chapter Thirteen

Frankie

She seems to have stuck to her word and stayed away for a whole twenty-four hours. Yet, I can't seem to get her off my mind. I admire her strength, however reckless some of her decisions may be. There aren't many women who stand up against me like this.

She intrigues me because she isn't scared of me. Quite the opposite, actually.

I shift in my seat, pressing down on my semi-hard cock. It's the same every time I'm near her, or when she invades my thoughts. I can't fucking stop myself.

It's for the best that I sent her away. She's liable to get herself killed. I saved her ass last time, and I'd do it again in a heartbeat. That's what concerns me. I'm distracted and I can't afford to be. We are so close to taking down Romano, it's just a matter of time before he steps foot back in my territory.

Letting Zara too close to me opens up another weakness. Something he can exploit. Kicking up my feet onto the coffee table, I start scrolling through Zara's social media and try to delude myself that this will be the last time.

I groan as I open up the most recent post, from ten minutes

ago. Her in a tight red corset with a leather skirt, revealing all of those intricate tattoos on her porcelain skin. Fuck, she's beautiful.

The phone slips from my fingers as the front door crashes open. A red-faced Grayson, with a flustered Enzo following closely behind, push into my office.

I try to keep my expression neutral as they crowd into my space. "Well, hello. Come in, why don't you?"

Enzo sits down beside me and immediately opens up his laptop.

I shoot Grayson a questioning look. "Either of you care to tell me what's going on?"

"We have a big fucking problem, boss." Enzo ferociously jabs his fingers on his keyboard.

My patience is wearing thin.

"Spit it out," I say through gritted teeth.

"Here." Enzo turns the screen towards me, and I lean closer, looking at a page of numbers and some women's faces.

"What the hell am I looking at?" I rub my beard, shaking my head.

"It means this isn't the first nor the last shipment of women. It seems New York isn't their end goal. We need to dig deeper. The girls are coming from Russia, with George's involvement. It has to be Romano."

He leans back in the seat, looking pleased with himself.

"Well, continue," I say, bringing the computer onto my thighs.

Enzo shifts to face me. "We need to get to George. He must have some information on the end buyer."

I rub my hands over my eyes. "Why the hell would a commissioner be doing this? It makes no sense."

"What about that other detective, Zara?" Grayson asks. I straighten my spine at the mention of her name.

Her reaction to the shipment made it obvious she had no idea. No one can act like that, let alone put herself at risk like that, with no back up.

I shake my head.

"This isn't her, G."

She did everything I asked. She might be the only person in that force that isn't completely against us.

Shit, she could be deeper in this than even she realizes.

Enzo pushes his long black hair out of his face and lets out a long breath. "I agree."

Tapping my finger against the screen, I process all of this new information. The last thing I want is Romano having the complete upper hand with the police.

Looks like Zara may have some further use to me after all.

"I might have an idea." I bite back the grin.

Grayson raises his brows at me.

"You might not like it."

"Frankie," Enzo replies sternly.

I hold up one finger. "We need to stop them from trafficking women. It's non-negotiable. This shit does not happen in our territory. So, we need to get into the commissioner's office?"

Enzo nods. "Correct."

I decide to hold back my plans for Zara, just in case they go sour and she tries to stab me again. This game might take a little more work to get her where I need her.

"Where's Jax?" I ask Grayson.

"He's training with Kai, then we're going to the girl's safe house tonight."

"I'll take him with me." I can use his help in case things go south.

"Where?"

I clap my hands together and push myself up from the chair. "We're off to the annual police Halloween gala, boys."

"You think they're going to let you in?" Grayson chuckles.

"Not like this, obviously. They won't have a clue who I am in a mask." I wink, turning to Enzo. "Get your team ready. Looks like the key to Romano is the cops."

"You think this is a good idea?" Enzo asks.

Images of Zara in her little red outfit, and that lipstick that would look perfect wrapped around my cock, fill my mind.

"I don't see the problem. We can be in and out in no time."

Enzo leans back and rubs his face. "I can speak to Mikhail. Since he split the Volkovs to Vegas, I can see what he can find out about the Russian women. He should be able to confirm Romano's involvement."

"You do that. I'll go to the ball. Either way, we're getting closer to our goal."

"Let me go get changed. G, get Jax here; tell him to pick me up a mask that will hide my features."

I can't ignore the thrill I'm getting from turning the tables on Zara. Tonight, she won't have a clue I'll be the one watching her in the shadows. Let's see how much she likes it.

"You got it, boss."

He pulls out his phone and brings it to his ear. Enzo is already chatting away in Italian to his men.

By the time I shower and put on my tux, I hear Jax's engine revving up the driveway. At least it isn't that damn bike this time.

I open up the front door and roll my eyes. Jax is leaning against his new bright blue Lamborghini, still in his leather jacket and ripped jeans. The rings on his fingers catch the light as he holds up a mask with a long narrow white face and a gaping mouth.

"Looking suave, Mr. Falcone." He winks at me as I walk over to him and snatch the monstrosity from his tattooed hand.

"Nice wheels, very inconspicuous Jax."

He shrugs. "I come from a rich family remember, no one gives a shit about what I drive."

"We're breaking into a police event tonight. You think they might look twice at something that's worth more than what they'd earn in their life?"

He runs a hand through his curly black hair. "It was either this or the bike. Grayson said you'd prefer this one."

Out of the two, he was right.

I toss the mask on the floorboard and get in.

He speeds off and I'm pressed against the headrest.

"Jesus Christ, Jax," I hiss.

"You can't drive a beauty like this and not take her to the max."

He slows down as we pull up into the parking lot. He picks a spot far enough away to scope out the entrance.

"We're gonna have to go in the back," Jax says.

I agree.

Tugging at my collar, it suddenly feels tight around my neck. I hate to admit that I'm looking forward to my little reunion with Zara.

My vision fixates on the little red devil outfit walking towards the steps. Tattoos spanning up her left thigh, and a deep plunging neckline which has me licking my lips. Her hair is curly today, so it rests just above her shoulders.

"That one in red, fuck," Jax groans next to me.

The sight of her makes me dig my nails into my palms.

Mine.

Zara is mine.

Whether she likes it or not.

CHAPTER FOURTEEN

Zara

Song- THE DEATH OF PEACE OF MIND, Bad Omens

I sip on my champagne and plaster on a smile, just how Dad trained me to. With my black lace mask secured firmly on my face and my tattoos proudly on show. A final 'fuck you' to my father. He's lucky the mask covers the shiner he left me with. I've stayed firmly in the shadows, watching his every move, waiting for the opportunity to slip away to his office.

As soon as he's busy chatting to my superiors, including Alex in the corner, I down the last of the glass.

My breath hitches as an almost familiar figure enters the room. A designer black tux that hugs his frame perfectly. It's a shame he's wearing a scream mask, so I can't see his damn face.

I head to the back of the hall, keeping my distance from my father, brushing straight past that man in the mask. That's when that expensive aftershave hits my nose. The same one Frankie wears. My pulse picks up, and I quicken my pace, my heels clicking on the wooden floors as I head through the double doors into the dimly lit hallway.

I rush towards my dad's office, pulling out the spare key I have from my purse. Taking one last look around, I unlock it and push it open.

My heart is in my throat the entire time. Closing the door behind me, I toss my bag on the chair in front of the desk and start my search.

Pulling open the first drawer, I crouch down and start weeding out all the random paperwork. Old police reports, receipts, pictures of him and Mom from years ago. I toss it all back in and go for the next drawer.

Again, nothing.

"Come on, where are you?" I mutter under my breath.

If I know my father, he has always kept diaries. Every single day since the day I was born. My entire life is in one of his little black books.

A gust of cold air distracts me, I can't stop. I move on to the top drawer, rummaging through the vast array of pens.

"Fuck," I hiss. Every second that passes, someone could walk through that door and out me. I can't trust anyone who works here. Not my dad, not Alex. I'm on my own.

I go to stand, the sound of heavy breathing stops me. I am frozen in place as that familiar aftershave hits my nostrils.

I close my eyes, too scared to turn around. Goosebumps erupt on my skin as he trails his finger along my tattooed arm, all the way up to my collarbone, before lacing his hands around my throat.

He pushes me forward, so I'm bent over the desk, his body covering mine. I open my mouth to scream, his hand clamps over it, muffling the noise.

"What are you doing in here, detective?" he rasps. I'd recognize that sexy Italian voice anywhere.

I try to wiggle out of his hold, but I stop when I feel his erection press against my ass.

Oh, fuck.

Desire washes over me. He loosens his grip on my throat enough for me to turn my head, coming face to face with that white ghost face.

I'm fighting against being completely turned on. I should run. This is wrong. So wrong. The dampness in my panties is keeping me locked in his grip.

I want to know what it feels like. To see if this is really what I crave. Because I can't live my life thinking about him like this.

"If I move my hand, you won't scream?" he asks in a low, husky voice. I nod.

Sucking in a breath as he slowly removes his palm, he keeps me pressed against the desk with his hard dick.

"What are you doing here?" I croak out.

"The same as you, apparently. I thought I told you to leave it, Zara." There is a warning in his tone, yet all I can focus on is how his body is pressed against mine.

How I want him to do something more.

"I-I can't leave it."

He has no idea.

"Am I going to have to punish you, dolcezza?"

A smile spreads across my lips. I know just how to push him.

"I dare you," I bite back.

He growls in my ear, and my eyes go wide. His fingers trail along the back of my leg and I shiver as he stops and grabs my ass, his fingers digging into my flesh. And fuck, I want it.

"You mean you want to be spanked over your father's desk for disobeying me? Is that what you need?"

I bite back a moan. I should hate how much I want him. Right now, I don't care. His palm dips under my leather skirt, caressing me. Instinctively, my legs inch open as much as they can in this tight outfit and I press further into him.

"That's what I thought. You're a filthy slut, really."

I close my eyes, trying to calm down this burning desire within me that is only ignited by his dirty words.

His finger slips between my thighs and he follows the line of my thong all the way down towards my entrance. Pulling my panties across, I pant as he slowly slides his finger along my pussy.

"Fucking soaked, all for me."

My eyes almost roll back as he circles my clit before cracking his palm over my ass and clamping his hand over my mouth to muffle the scream that follows.

"Frankie," I moan.

"Fuck, the way you say my name, angel."

I can barely contain myself as I wait for his next move. I squeal as he lifts me by the hips, his fingers jabbing into my skin, and spins me to face him. He places me down on the edge of the desk and forcefully spreads my legs. Stepping between them, he lowers himself.

Anticipation sizzles as I look down at him. I bite back a moan as his fingers run along the inside of my thighs, hooking under my red lace panties, and lightly brushing against my needy pussy. The rip of the fabric fills the room before he pockets the remainder of my underwear into his tux jacket. I tighten my grip on the edge just as his mask connects with me, making my hips jolt. He slowly lifts it to the top of his head, but his face remains buried between my legs. When I look down, all I see is the damn plastic white face. His tongue connects with my clit and I arch my back, spreading my knees wider for him. He draws out slow licks from my entrance to my clit, which has my whole body vibrating against him.

"Oh, fuck!" I cry out as he slides a finger inside me.

He switches between licking, sucking, and finger fucking me.

"I need more." I let out a breathy pant.

He slides in a second finger, filling me up and biting down on my clit, which has me screaming out in pleasure. He finds a rhythm that has my thighs trembling next to his head.

"Fuck me, please," I all but scream.

If this is what he can do with his mouth, I have to know what he can do with his dick.

"Quiet, baby. Unless you want an audience."

I press my lips together, the realization washing over me.

His left hand shoots up and pulls down my dress, letting my breasts free, filling his hand and pinching the bar in my nipple.

"Jesus." I hear him grumble something against my pussy. The

next thing I know, he lifts me like I weigh nothing and my back crashes against the wall. My chest heaves, his mask is firmly back on, and his grip is tight around my throat. He adds pressure to the sides of my neck, not enough to restrict my air flow, I am desperate for more. I wrap my legs around his waist, pulling him closer so his dick rubs up against me. Rolling my hips, I beg him with my body to fuck me.

I've never wanted anything more in my life.

Chapter Fifteen

Frankie

H oly shit.

Her pulse hammers against my palm. Her sweet taste is fresh on my tongue.

I don't know what I expected to happen when I followed her into this room. It certainly wasn't the words, "fuck me". I groan just thinking about all the ways I could make her come, if she were mine. I'd have her chained to my bed, forcing her to climax over and over until her body finally gives up.

Her hands fumble around my boxers in desperation.

Just how I need her.

I'm in two minds about whether to stop before she comes to punish her for defying me at every turn. But, I think I'll save that for later. Now, I want to give her a taste of what I can give her.

I can use her and in return bring her to life. I squeeze her neck and she releases her hands, her eyes wide behind the black lace, filled with lust as she bites down on her bottom lip.

This is on my terms. It is always on my terms.

"Please." The desperation in her voice, begging for my cock, sets off a new wave of pure fire within me.

I yank down my zipper, freeing my throbbing length from

the tight confines of my pants. Dropping her ass down slightly, the tip presses against her soaking entrance. She's going to hate how she's dripping for me. Her nails dig into my shoulders through my jacket. I grunt, stopping myself from thrusting into her, instead tightening my grip on her throat. Enough to add that pressure she needs to add that euphoric feeling.

"Come on." She rolls her hips in frustration. If only she could see herself. That perfect flush on her pale skin, her nipples begging to be sucked, clamped even. Desperate for one thing... my cock.

I suck in a ragged breath and slide her down the wall so she's on her shaking legs.

She looks up at me, exasperated. "W-what are you doing?"

"Be a good girl and suck, dolcezza." When I fuck her, it won't be a quickie in an office. It will be so much more.

She doesn't move, her eyes focused on my raging hard dick, licking her lip I help her make her decision.

"On your knees, I won't ask next time."

I grab the bottom of the mask and go to pull it over my head, to show her I am not joking.

"N-no. Leave that on," she says.

If that's what it takes to get her plump red lips around my cock, then so be it.

She sinks to her knees in front of me and takes the tip in her mouth. My head tips back as she licks and takes me in like a goddamn angel.

Lacing my fingers through her soft hair, I take control. Pushing her to take as much of me as she can, looking down on her as she chokes on my cock. It's a perfect picture.

"Mmm, that's it, angel. Show me how much you want my dick."

She increases the pace and I can't contain myself. Her nails dig into my thigh. Those little gagging noises she's making as I thrust into the back of her mouth are too much.

Without giving her a warning, I coat her throat with my cum. Like the filthy girl I knew she would be, she swallows every last drop.

"Fuck, Zara," I pant out as she cleans my shaft with her tongue, looking up at me through her lashes. "A good girl dressed as the devil," I rasp, stroking her cheek.

She sits back on her heels with a satisfied grin.

I tuck myself back in my boxers and zip up my pants. She brings herself up to stand and tips her chin.

"You're joking," she mutters, shaking her head. I grab her jaw and force her to look at me. Those bright green eyes bore into mine and my heart races.

"There is only one way you get to come, and that is all over my cock, over and over again."

"What the hell?" she spits out. Moving my hand to her neck, I wrap my fingers around, feeling her heart rhythm match mine.

"Good work, detective." I drawl out every single word.

Her body shakes, probably with rage.

I take a step back, brushing the strand of hair out of her beautiful, shocked face. There she is. My demon.

"Fr–"

"It's only fair I get to see you now." I hook my index finger under her black lace mask and slide it up. I want to capture her expression forever. Furious at me. I freeze when I see the dark purple bruise under her right eye. The pure desire that flowed through me quickly morphs to rage.

"Who. The. Fuck. Did. This. To. You?" I grit out through clenched teeth. She closes her eyes as I brush my thumb along the angry blemish. She flinches and I am murderous. Someone marred her perfect skin. The only marks she should ever have are the ones I will give her on her ass.

"My dad," she whispers, trying to lower her face.

"I'll make him pay, angel. Don't you worry about that." My hand shakes as more guilt rushes through me. I should have stopped her games before the shipment. I need to clear my head, so I turn before I do anything stupid. I stop as she clears her throat behind me, my hand resting on the door handle.

"I'll never forget you couldn't manage to get me to come." There's teasing in her tone.

I bite down on my tongue to hold back the groan.

"Oh, you know where to find me, dolcezza," I say, leaving her cursing under her breath at me.

That nickname has an entirely new meaning now I have her sweetness on my tongue. She has to come to me. That is how this works.

As I open the door, I hear her pulling out another drawer.

"Wait," she calls out. "Fuck, Frankie, look at this."

I rush back over to her and rip off my mask so I can peer over her shoulder at the little leather black journal open in her hands.

Dates, Russian names, and addresses.

I quickly scan the page; every single one leads to Vegas. She has seen quite enough.

I pluck the book from her fingers and pocket it, despite her protests.

"Thank you, baby," I mutter against her cheek, placing a kiss. I can feel the heat radiating from her skin.

"Fuck you," she whispers sweetly. I can't hold my laughter.

"Maybe one day," I tease back.

There is no maybe. I will be coming back for my woman as soon as I deal with this shitshow.

I close the door behind me and head out the back.

Dammit, I left my disguise behind. I have what I need. I need to leave pronto.

I pass Alex as he comes in from the fire escape. I keep my face away from him and carry on walking until I reach Jax's car.

"Find anything, boss?" Jax tears his awful mask off his face, sucking in a lungful of crisp fresh air.

"Damn right," I reply, willing my cock to stop throbbing.

I hold on to the side of Jax's ridiculous car, as the consequences of what I've just done sink in. I know my fiery angel will come back with a vengeance. And I'll be waiting for her.

Jax pauses before opening his door. "You okay, boss?"

"Fine."

Zara is mine.

She was made for me, and there is nothing stopping me from going after what I want.

There are very few things I live with regret over.

Leila, Rosa, Eva, and not killing Romano sooner.

There is one more to add to that short list.

Not letting Zara come on my cock.

Chapter Sixteen

Zara

Song- PLEASE Omido and Ex Habit

I ran out of my dad's office, not even apologizing to Alex as I barreled into him. That book was filled with names and addresses. This clearly wasn't the first time Dad's been involved. I want to kill him myself.

Tossing Frankie's scream mask on my bed, heat burns my cheeks as I stare at it. I can still feel him on me, as I brush my fingers along my neck where he squeezed.

Even after I shower and get in my little pair of shorts and crop top, I can't stop thinking about him.

Lying down in the center of my bed, I stretch out and sink into the mattress. I slowly peel down my shorts and spread my legs, imagining he is here watching me. Sliding my hand down the front of my body, I start to circle my clit softly, letting out little puffs of air and my eyes flutter shut.

I replay his hands around my throat, how good it felt when he sucked my clit. Increasing the pace, I slide a finger inside, not holding back the moan that follows. His name slips from my lips and I arch off the bed, grabbing his mask.

I rub the fabric over my pussy, letting all my wetness smother it. He wants to play with me, I'm going to finish one way or another. And then I'll mail it back to him.

This will be his reminder of me. I roll my hips, grinding the plastic mouth against myself until I crash over the edge.

I lay here, waiting for my breathing to return to normal. It's not enough.

Holding up the damp façade, an idea springs to mind. One way I can dig deeper into Frankie. He might be the only person on my side, that doesn't mean I can trust him. Not yet. Jumping off the bed, I take the mask to my office, pulling out the drawer.

Perfect. I knew I had one in here.

Placing a listening device to the inside of the seam of his disguise, I set it down on the desk and grab my phone. The one thing that kept appearing in that notepad was Vegas shipping addresses. If I'm going to get the answers I need, it's going to be there.

So, I book a flight for tomorrow morning. After seeing that extensive list, I can't sit and do nothing. Despite Frankie's warnings, I know how to handle myself. Leaning back on the chair, my eyes are heavy. I check the time on my phone and it's one am. Grabbing the mask, I head back to my bedroom.

After tossing it on my dresser, a crash comes from the kitchen.

What the hell?

I creep down the hall, keeping my back against the wall. My breathing is shaky as I tiptoe towards the kitchen.

A hand clamps over my mouth and I'm pulled against a hard frame.

I claw at the powerful arms, thrashing against their hold. My arms fly out trying to elbow him in the ribs.

"Looking for this?" Frankie's deep voice sends shivers down my spine and I freeze. His erection presses against my ass.

Anger overtakes the fear, but I stop trying to fight back.

He takes his hand away from my mouth, still holding me tight against him.

"You here to finish the job?" I ask.

He brushes my hair away to expose my neck. I cry out as he bites down and sucks.

Picking me up, he props me on the counter and steps between my legs. I lean back on my hands and fumble them along the wall, flicking on the kitchen lights. I find his hooded eyes piercing into mine with a devious grin on his lips.

With my other hand, I push it back further to my knife collection. Pulling out the first one I touch, I lock my thighs around his waist, pushing him closer towards me so I can press the blade to his throat.

His gaze flicks down to my arm and back up to me, a spark of desire now muddled with anger. Just how I like him.

"Well played, detective." He licks his lips.

I stay frozen in place.

There is no fear on his face. He's looking at me like he wants to punish me, in all the best possible ways.

"What's your next move?" he rasps, his mouth dangerously

close to my own.

Blood hammers in my ears, and desire ignites in my core.

I open my mouth to speak, but no words follow. I can't even think coherently, let alone string a sentence together.

He rolls his bottom lip between his white teeth. I tighten my hold on the knife and gasp as he pushes himself forward against it.

"It will cut you, Frankie."

He stares into my damn soul. "You think a bit of blood bothers me, dolcezza? I have enough of it on my hands."

This is ridiculous. He shouldn't be here. I shouldn't be thinking about how hard he can fuck me. Yet no matter how much I want to stop, I can't. I keep the blade where it is, his eyes flicking between my lips and my eyes.

"I'm here to finish *you*. Now spread those legs wider for me and give me that pretty cunt to play with."

My heart rate picks up. "You think I'm that easy?" I raise my brow, looking down at the knife still on his throat.

"For me? I know so. I'm done playing games with you, detective."

"What if I'm n—"

He silences me by leaning forward and crashing his soft lips over mine. His fingers run through my hair and he pulls at it, arching my neck.

"Let go of the knife, dolcezza." His breath hits my burning cheeks and I do as he says. His hand covers mine and retrieves my last line of defense.

I hold my breath as he brings the bloodied knife up to my neck.

"It's only fair I get to mark you too, don't you think, dolcezza?"

I squeeze my eyes shut as the sharp tip presses against the skin of my collar. After a sharp sting, I open them and let out a ragged exhale. The pressure between my legs is almost unbearable.

Frankie leans in and runs his tongue along the wound, only intensifying the burning from the small cut.

"We need to stop this," I stutter.

"Not happening. I'm not letting you get away again. I've had one taste and I need more. Tell me, do you think you could go through the rest of your life not knowing?"

I nod weakly, but I know it's not true.

He's all I've dreamt about for weeks, no matter how hard I tried to stop it.

"Such a beautiful liar." He strokes my hair away from my face and crashes his lips over mine. His tongue pushes into my mouth and I can taste the metallic twang of my own blood.

Shivers run through me as he runs his thumb along the inside of my thigh, still ferociously kissing me.

"This time you'll see it's me fucking you, you'll feel it's me. You will forever remember this, the man who owns your orgasms. The man who owns your soul."

I roll my eyes and he forcefully grabs my chin between his fingers to face him.

"Do not roll your eyes at me, brat."

"I'm not one of your 'yes girls'." I glare at him.

He kisses along my jaw. "Trust me, I know."

I pull back. Weirdly, I don't like that comment.

"What do you mean?"

He chuckles. "If you were, you'd already be sucking my cock, and I wouldn't have had a knife pressed against my artery."

He has a point.

A darkness flashes across his eyes and he brushes his fingers along my arm.

"On your knees, Zara." His voice is deep and commanding.

I almost obey, but I stay strong, holding his stare.

"Submissives and I have a mutual agreement. You and I, however, do not have such luxuries." He taps the bloodied knife on the tip of my nose.

"You could be perfect for me." He tilts his head.

I gasp as he starts to slice through my crop top to expose my breasts.

I swallow past the lump in my throat as he watches with intent before his other hand shoots out and grips my neck.

"I'll get you to submit to me, angel. Just watch."

A smirk twitches on my lips. He's really messing with the wrong woman here.

I tear off the rest of the ruined shirt so I'm completely naked on the top and shuffle off the counter. I hold my hand out for him. "Knife, please," I say seductively.

He places it in my palm, amusement clear on his face.

I swipe up his blood from the blade, I don't break our stare as

I suck the coppery crimson off my index finger before dropping it. I push down my shorts and panties and step out of them, tossing the knife back on the counter.

"Fuck," he mutters. That turns me on more. I can get to him just as much as he does to me. He might want to control me, I want to break his resolve.

As I saunter to the couch, I hear him behind me unclasping his belt, his heavy steps following me. I choke on a breath as the leather loops round my throat and he tightens it, completely restricting my airflow.

I try to pull at it and he only yanks it up.

"Knees, now!"

Closing my eyes, I do as he says, my heart now beating erratically as he comes into view. I look up and the panic that was bubbling sates slightly when I see the way he eats me up with his eyes, like a man starved.

CHAPTER SEVENTEEN

Frankie

I don't think I've ever witnessed anything so erotic in my life. I have ultimate control over myself. I have always prided myself on that.

Until her.

Every muscle in my body is tense. There's a thin thread of restraint stopping me from saying 'fuck it' and both of us letting into our darkest urges. No dominance, no submission, just raw and intense fucking.

She's right, she isn't like any other woman I've met. That's probably why I'm so hell bent on claiming her. I see her potential. The fact she's on her knees, naked, with my belt squeezing her throat, tells me everything I need to know.

I'm just not sure I have the capacity to deal with a woman fierce enough to start her own fires. This distraction could be deadly for everyone around me. Yet, I can't stop myself around her.

My cock painfully aches in my pants, and I groan, tipping my head back. Never has my brain been so hectic. I grunt as she fumbles with my zipper. I should tell her to stop. I never ordered her to do that.

I will break her. It will be my mission to do so.

Just not today.

I need to punish her for getting to me like this. For putting herself in danger. I knot my fingers through her hair and pull tight, leaving her panting as she frees my cock.

Warm blood trickles down my neck. I swipe it up and look at it, coating my fingertips.

"Clean this mess up first," I grunt out. I bring my fingers to her lip and she opens for me.

As her fingers delicately gripping around my shaft, she sucks on my fingers.

"Good girl." That rewards me with a moan.

Knotting my hand back into her dark hair, I tug her closer so her mouth teases against the engorged head of my cock. "Spit on it." I look down at her and she licks her lips.

Her warm saliva coats me, remnants of the blood staining my dick. As she takes me in deeper, I loosen the pressure of the belt around her throat so she can choke on me properly. Squeezing my eyes shut as the sensation sets me on fire. The way she starts to gag, without even being told to and using her hands at the same time, it's perfect.

I pull on her hair, moving it out of her face and tipping it slightly to the right, so I can get a full view as I start to fuck her mouth violently. Tears run down her face, and she looks up at me through her lashes with mischief.

Biting down on my lip so hard I probably broke the skin, I'm fighting with myself to stay in control. Do not let this woman take it from you.

I yank her back and she pouts at me, before licking those luscious lips of hers.

She bats her lashes at me. "What next, *sir?*"

She mocks the last word, which only infuriates me further. She has no idea the power that word could hold for her.

"I'll ask you once, stop talking." Picking up her panties from the floor, I scrunch them into a ball.

She grins. "You're going to have to put your dick back in my mouth for that to happen."

It's getting harder to ignore the fact my cock is about to explode at her filthy words.

"Open." I hold them between us.

To my surprise, her chin drops and she tips her head back. I shove the silky thong in there, tapping her jaw lightly.

The shock on her face is evident. She starts to take them out of her mouth and I shake my head, giving her a firm stare.

I am about to give her a valuable lesson in not tempting the devil.

She asked for this.

Her whining is muffled as I pick her up by the waist and throw her over my shoulder. It would be so much easier at my home. I toss her down on the bed hard enough she bounces back.

A perfect mixture of fear and desire on her face.

"Lie on your back, arms above your head," I command, waiting for her disobedience.

She swallows, causing her neck to bob.

"What's the matter, dolcezza? Bitten off more than you can chew?" I taunt, striding to the edge of the mattress.

Her head shakes slightly, her hair cascading around her face, as she carefully lowers herself to lie flat. Running my eyes over her tattooed body, I pause to admire the intricate patterns that decorate the skin and encircle her ribcage.

As my finger glides along it, I feel the smoothness of her skin, following the tribal pattern until it ends between her breasts.

"Let's test it, shall we? How wet is my stalker for me?"

As I glide my index finger along her pussy, her body reacts instantly, arching in response.

"So responsive, detective," I growl, adding a second and third digit, admiring how well she stretches around me.

If I trusted her more, I'd remove her gag so I can hear her screams. Her time will come, I'm sure. I take my hand away, and she lets out a frustrated groan, her eyes locked onto mine.

"So fucking sweet, baby," I mutter, licking her flavor from my knuckle.

"In fact, I need a real taste."

As I position myself between her legs, I firmly push them apart until her knees are on the mattress. With my hands planted on her hips, I sensually suck on her throbbing clit, savoring the way her body shivers against my tongue.

As I retreat, she grabs a handful of my hair, guiding my face back towards her pussy. Yanking her hand from me, I sit up on my heels. She can't resist trying to take over.

Her eyes go wide and she reaches to remove her gag.

"I wouldn't," I warn.

Her eyes narrow, opposing the red blush running along her neck as she rests her arms above her head. My cell starts buzzing in my pants. I pull it out and rest it with my ear on my shoulder and trail my fingers along the inside of her thigh.

"Enzo," I greet him, keeping my voice neutral.

"Mikhail has an update on the girls and Romano. He's already on his way."

Shit.

Keller and Grayson have flown out to Greece for Rosa and Luca's wedding. There's no one I trust to take care of it. I have to take care of this shit myself.

"Okay. I'll see you soon." I cut the call and rest my body above hers, keeping the emotions away from my face.

She doesn't need to know. I'm still not sure how much I can trust her.

"Are you a patient woman?" I run my finger along her cheek.

She shakes her head erratically.

"Well, you are about to have your first important lesson. I need to deal with something. I will be back."

It's impossible to resist leaning down and taking her erect nipple in my mouth, then twirling the silver bar with my tongue. Her moans are completely muffled by the panties in her mouth.

Sinking two fingers inside her, I admire how her back arches off the bed. Her juices drip down my palm and my cock begs to explode at the sight of her.

With a sigh, I remove myself from her, bracing for her to slap me.

She doesn't. She just looks filled with disappointment. As I step back, my gaze fixates on my mask resting on her dresser. With a grin, I walk over, and the intoxicating scent of her fills my nostrils.

"I see you've had your own fun already," I growl, and her cheeks flush a deep red.

Pocketing the mask, I reach the door, but before leaving, I can't resist stealing one last look at her.

Perfectly naked and ready for me to use her how I need.

Another reason Romano needs to die has just been added to my list for tearing me away from this woman.

"Make no mistake. I will come for you, Zara."

There's a way, somehow, she manages to bend my control. The way she looks into my eyes, we are two of the same people.

A dangerous mix. Lethal even. I'm not sure if that's for everyone else or each other.

CHAPTER EIGHTEEN

Zara

My head drops against the pillow in frustration. Twice in one night. I am done with his shit. When I look over to the dresser, I want to squeal with excitement when I see he's taken the mask. I scramble across the bed and pick up my phone, logging into the app.

Whatever was more important than finishing me better be damn good.

After clicking it over to the speaker, I get off the bed and shove back on some clothes. It looks like it's going to be a long night.

Sitting on the sofa sipping some fresh coffee, I blink to keep my dry eyes open.

"Where is he?" Frankie's deep voice booms through the speaker.

Fumbling, I pick up the phone and bring it closer to my face. My heart pounds in my ears; any trace of sleepiness instantly disappears.

"In the dining room." The muffled voice that answers him sounds vaguely like the guy from the sex club.

A few moments pass before a thick Russian accent comes

through.

My fingers tighten around the phone, a bad feeling settling in my stomach. What if Frankie isn't who he said he was? What if he's framing my dad?

And I've let him do all of this to me.

I swallow, holding my breath; waiting for one of them to speak.

"Well, I'm here. What do you have for me?" Frankie says, and I want to throw up.

"Those addresses you sent me, they're run by the Reapers Motorcycle Club. Who apparently now have direct links to my father in Moscow."

"And this links to George and Romano?" Frankie asks.

I let out a whoosh of air.

"My father and Romano have formed an agreement. Romano is tight on cash. Since going off grid, this is easy money for them."

There's a pause before I hear Frankie's voice. "Can you stop them in Vegas?"

"I'm sure we can come to an agreement, Mr. Falcone."

The line is silent. My heart races. I want to believe him. He's saying all the right things. But can I really trust him?

A bang comes from the front door, and I scoot back on the couch. Muffled voices sound and I jump up from my seat. I know it isn't Frankie outside. Snatching up my phone, I sprint to the kitchen and pick up the knife that was left on the counter.

I make a dash to my office, closing the door enough that I can still peer through with a full view of the living room. Opening my gun safe, I pull out my backup pistol. I'd feel better with my service weapon, I had to leave that at the station along with my job.

I jump as the door is beaten off its hinges and my jaw nearly hits the floor when Chad waltzes into my apartment like he owns the place. A phone in one hand and a handgun in the other.

"Go and see if she's asleep." Alex orders Chad over the phone, who pushes my bedroom open slowly.

"She's not here."

"Well, go in and start looking for the book!" Alex's anger pours out of the tiny speakers.

Rage mixed with fear flows through me. I tighten my grip on my weapons.

Chad starts tearing through my room. Each drawer hits the floor with a thud.

These assholes.

"Anything?" Alex asks.

"Nope," Chad grunts.

"Go check the other rooms, then."

Shit.

I take a step back, pressing my back against the wall, aiming my gun in front of me. Heavy footsteps get louder and the door comes towards me as Chad steps in. I take a deep breath and hold it. If he doesn't find me, I won't have to kill him.

He moves across the room, closer to my desk. I keep my sights set on his head. Frankie's words replay in my mind. It's me against them.

Blood thumps in my ears, and everything is in slow motion as he turns to face me. The realization settles on his face and he reaches for his waistband.

Without thinking, I pull the trigger.

My feet are frozen to the ground as I slump against the wall.

"Oh fuck, fuck, fuck," I whisper.

"Chad, what the fuck was that?" Alex's voice yells out.

I look over to the phone on the floor and press the end button.

Chad's body lies in a heap.

I killed another cop.

Bile rises up my throat and my hands cover my mouth as I gag, scooting myself away from him until I'm at the door.

"What the hell have I done?" The tears start to freefall.

I can't fix this mess on my own.

I can't go to jail, either. These assholes were looking for that book. Alex saw me leaving Dad's office. That means I can't even rely on the justice system anymore.

I am truly fucked.

There is only one person on this earth that can help me. That has even just a small sliver of my trust.

I slide my cell out of my back pocket, blinking through the tears as my shaking finger hovers over Frankie's name. Sucking in a breath, I hit the call button.

He answers on the second ring.

"Couldn't wait for me?" His husky voice comes through the speaker and relief washes over me.

"F-Frankie?" I can barely get my words out.

"Zara, what's happened?" The concern in his voice is clear.

"I need you. I don't know what to do." Sobs consume me.

"Are you in danger, dolcezza?"

My gaze fixes on Chad's lifeless body. "Not anymore, but I don't know how long for."

"Don't move. I'll be there in a minute. Okay?"

"I've fucked up, Frankie. Big time."

"We will fix this, Zara. I've got you."

I pull my knees up to my chest and rest my head on them. I can't look at the spreading pool of blood for another second.

"Can you stay on the phone, Frankie?" I sniffle.

"Anything for you, angel." His soft words have my heart fluttering.

"Thank you," I whisper.

I look down at my hands, the gun still tightly in my right hand. I listen to Frankie driving, he keeps asking if I'm okay and reassuring me he's only around the corner.

"I'm coming up now, baby."

"Okay," I say weakly.

I tip my head back, looking up at the ceiling. Frankie's steps get closer, and the door swings open, letting the light in. I can't look at him, out of sheer embarrassment. He doesn't even flinch at the dead body, instead he steps in front of me and my heart pounds.

He tips his head to the side as I meet his dark eyes and he grins, holding out his hand to me.

"You good, dolcezza?"

He stares into my soul, waiting for me to respond.

I am now that he's here for me.

I give him a curt nod, placing my hand in his, and warmth spreads through my body as he pulls me to my feet. My body crashes against him and he hugs me tight. He pries the gun from my tight grip and shoves it into his waistband.

"You did what you had to do, baby. I'm proud of you."

I nuzzle my head against his chest and inhale his masculine scent, letting it soothe me.

"All that matters is you're okay," he whispers against the top of my head.

"W-what do you want from me?" I whisper.

"You. Simply you."

It isn't a question. It's a statement.

He tips my chin up so I face him, but I can't. Even if his eyes are filled with admiration. I killed another man.

I'm scared of myself.

I bow my head, looking at my feet and he forcefully grips my face, dragging my head back up again, his eyes piercing into mine.

"Never, and I mean ever, bow your head to anyone, Zara. Not even me. Not like this. You are a fucking queen, and you make them kneel before you." His face is stern, yet he's staring into the depths of me nobody has ever.

Tears sting in my eyes.

"Try it, baby. Embrace the power you hold." He presses a soft kiss to my temple.

When he is by my side, I do feel powerful.

"I killed him, Frankie."

"And?"

I blink a few times.

The corner of his lip turns up in an understanding smile. "He tried to hurt you. You reacted exactly as you should. Don't let anyone make you think differently."

My mouth opens, then closes. He's right. It was me or Chad. He went for his weapon.

"You truly are an angel," he mutters against my temple.

I push myself on my tiptoes and press my lips against his. His beard tickles my chin as electricity courses through me.

"Thank you," I whisper.

"What for?" His hands move up and down my back in a calming pattern.

"Seeing me." I give him a small smile.

He runs his fingers through my hair, pushing it out of my face before kissing the tip of my nose. "I told you before, you and I are the same. I see you for who you are."

He leans in closer, and my breath hitches as he licks the shell of my ear. "And who you will become after I break you."

Cupping my elbow, he begins to lead me out of the room. "Come on, let's go."

I look up at him and frown. "Go where? What about Chad?"

I can't just leave him here in my apartment.

"I have a clean-up crew coming to take care of that. You are coming home with me."

I step out of his hold, crossing my arms across my chest and shake my head. "No."

He steps forward, and I take one back.

"I don't need protecting. I'm capable of looking after myself." I gesture to the dead body on the floor.

He chuckles, towering over me.

I swallow as he leans down, running his mouth along my neck. Just from that touch, I'm on fire and I really shouldn't be. Not right now.

"Oh, Zara. We are far from finished. You just signed yourself over to me."

I close my eyes as his lips press against my jaw. "You made your choice when you called me, angel. No turning back now. You will be coming back with me, and you will be under my complete protection, capiche, dolcezza?"

He is my only way out of this, and that smug smirk on his annoyingly handsome face tells me he knows exactly just that.

I am his now.

Squeezing my thighs together doesn't quell the flurry of excitement. It won't be the worst thing in the world. I've had a taste of what he can give me and I want more. And, while under his roof, I can learn everything there is about him. Maybe I can still take my dad down.

"I want my own room." My bag is already out; time to pack.

A low rumble comes from his chest. "Let's see how long you last with that arrangement."

I swallow. I could live to regret this.

CHAPTER NINETEEN

Frankie

Closing the door to Zara's room, I let out a long, exhausted breath. She's sound asleep, so finally I get some peace. I need her under my roof and my protection, otherwise I can't think straight. That little demon is clawing her way under my skin, and I can't do a thing to stop it.

If I don't do something now, her kill count is probably going to go up and land her, and me, in a lot of shit.

Reckless doesn't even begin to cover her, but I'm damn proud of her. Once she gets in tune with who she really is, she will be a force to be reckoned with. She doesn't fully trust me, which I don't blame her for. Everyone is turning against her.

Soon she will realize I am not her enemy, far from it.

I pour out a generous measure of scotch, feeling the smooth glass in my hand as I slump back on the sofa and pull out my phone. I'm waiting for Mikhail's proposal for our alliance. If what I saw in that book is correct, there is another shipment of women somewhere in Vegas. Not only can I save them, it could lead me to Romano.

As I scroll through my phone, the soft glow illuminates the dimly lit room. The clinking of ice cubes echoes as I raise my glass of scotch to my lips, taking a long, smooth sip. With a sense of anticipation, I tap on the message from Enzo, feeling a slight buzz of excitement tingling through my fingertips.

> **Enzo: Miki's first offer- $500k cash plus a joint venture on the arms shipments. 25%.**

With a laugh, I shake my head while typing my reply. Mikhail is new to the States. Just because he's taken down the other mafia families in Vegas, doesn't mean he can come up against my army. He knows that.

> **F: I don't think so. Try again.**

The phone rings immediately after, and no surprise, it's Enzo.

"You know I'm not taking that deal, Enzo."

He sighs. "I know. We can at least counter it. We need that route into Vegas and Miki on our side."

I cut him off. "And what do the Volkovs have to offer me? If we come into Vegas, not only will we be dealing with his MC problem, he wants cash and fucking guns? Shall I draw some blood and send that to him, too?"

"He needs weapons. His supply comes from Russia. Since the split, he's had trouble getting them in."

Swirling my empty cup on the table, I take a moment before I answer. "You trust him enough to keep to his word and look after the girls? How do I know he isn't like his father?"

"I trust him. I'm working closely with him. Him and his brothers, they're different. Savages, yes, just like you. Your values align here. Think of the long game. Having the Bratva on your side isn't a bad thing." He sounds sincere.

As I run my hand over my face, I can feel the tension in my muscles and the weight of exhaustion settling in. This is just another distraction on top of hunting down Romano.

"This could be what we need to draw out Romano, Frankie. Mikhail is flying in tomorrow; I can arrange another meet."

Grayson's number flashes on the screen, and I frown. It's one am. He's normally tucked up in bed with Maddie and their daughter, Hope.

"One second, Enzo. G is calling."

I cut Enzo off and answer Grayson.

"Hey boss, we've got a couple of Romano's men snooping around the safe house where the Russian girls are. Kai and Jax are bringing them in now. Get your ass over here."

Jesus fucking Christ.

Rubbing my temples, I try to stop the throbbing now coming from my skull.

"Shit. Okay. I'll be there in a minute."

It's starting to look like Enzo is right. To end this, we may well need the Russians on our side.

As I make my way to the front door, my eyes are drawn to the grand staircase. There's no movement up there, so she still must be asleep. I'll be back by the time the sun rises and then I have big plans with her.

No more fucking around.

Chapter Twenty

Zara

As soon as the front door shuts, I sink down to the floor, my back pressed against the door. I can't let my feelings for Frankie skew my thoughts.

If there are more women that my dad has trafficked in Vegas, I need to do the right thing. Which is everything I can to save them from him.

I truly believe Frankie will protect me, that he's proven. Yet there is this nagging feeling in the back of my head that I can't fully trust him. He's cunning, ruthless. I could just be a pawn in this game to him.

Glancing at the suitcase I packed earlier, I remember my passport is inside.

There are a couple of the Vegas addresses I saw in the book that I memorized. I have to go and see this with my own eyes. Just sitting here, waiting for Frankie to make his next move, won't solve the problem. I need to stop my father.

I have to find out who I can really trust.

And there is only one way to do that.

It's about time I put my detective skills to use. I'm sure I can figure this out before Frankie hunts me down.

CHAPTER TWENTY-ONE

Frankie

I step over the body underneath my feet and turn my attention to the final asshole chained to a chair in my basement. His sobs echo in my ears, adding fuel to my fire.

As I stand before him, I let go of the hammer that had just caved in his friend's skull. Instinctively, I wipe my hands on the cloth, feeling the warmth of blood against my skin.

"Inspired you to talk yet?" I question, nodding over to his friend.

Spittle flies from his lips. "Please, sir."

I tut, shaking my head. "I don't do begging."

Well, unless it's coming from Zara's lips.

There is absolutely no doubt this guy is going to join his friend in a pool of his own blood.

"If you just tell me where I can find Mr. Capri, I will let you walk free."

The lie just falls from my mouth. I can't let him lose hope. If I want him to reveal anything, he has to believe he has a chance.

I take a step closer to him, and he squirms in his seat. His hands open and close, uselessly, in their restraints.

"I can be a very reasonable man." I lean over and pick up his wallet from the table, opening it to pull out his ID.

"Mr. Eduardo Fernandes. Age thirty-five. Oh, look an address."

"No." Snot bubbles from his nostril as he takes panicked breaths.

I wave the little plastic license beneath his bloodied nose. "Is that where I'd find the wife? The little kids running around? Huh?"

With a firm grip on the blade, I tap it against his card, feeling the vibrations travel through my fingertips.

"I'll tell you everything. Please don't hurt my family. They haven't done anything."

I toss his identification onto the floor and pull up a chair next to him, straddling it. I examine the silver blade, feeling its smoothness as my fingers glide along the metal.

"It's amazing what you can do with one of these, isn't it?" I say with a menacing tone.

"I could slice your throat. I quite enjoy watching someone's life slowly pour out of their neck. Or I could plunge it into your stomach as many times as I want. I could even-" I pause, tapping the knife against my lips. "Slice out your tongue."

He gulps.

"If you had a choice, how would you want to die, Eduardo? Personally, I'd have to choose a bullet in the head. Nice and quick."

He doesn't respond. I push myself up off the chair and kick

it out of the way.

"If you can't answer a simple question, how are you going to tell me what I need to know?" I press the blade just below his jawline, the sharp edge biting into his skin.

"The same. Shoot me," he croaks out.

I tap his cheek. "See? It's not that hard, is it? Answering simple questions."

He shakes his head with a rapid, short movement, and a tear rolls down his nose. "I don't know where Romano is."

The way his eye twitches as he speaks, the tremble in his voice indicates to me he's lying.

"Lies." Driving the tip of the blade through the back of his right hand, it lodges in the wooden arm of the chair.

When his screams subside, I jerk it loose. "Okay, tell me this. Where did the second shipment of girls go to?" Before I make any deal with Mikhail. I have to be certain it's Vegas.

He coughs hoarsely before answering. "To some motorcycle gang."

Well, there's a truth. "Where?"

"I think Vegas? I don't know. I was just told to see if the missing girls were here."

I nod. "Thank you."

Sweat drips down his forehead. A look of relief that washes over his face as I step closer.

"Now. Who gave you your orders?" I knock the blade against his cheek.

"I-I don't know," he sobs.

Bending over, I level with his bloodshot, dark eyes. "Do you know what one of the worst ways would be to die?"

He shakes his head. I untie his left hand and place the knife in his palm, closing his fingers around the handle. His jaw drops in surprise as he looks up at me.

"Forced suicide."

The sound of his gulp echoes in the room as he stares, transfixed, at the glinting weapon.

"Tell me what I need to know. If you can't, then slice your own throat."

As I take a step back, my attention shifts to Jax, who stands with arms folded across his chest.

"Make sure he doesn't do anything stupid," I say to Jax as my phone pings in my pocket.

He steps past me and stands next to Eduardo, who's now crying like a fucking baby.

My cell buzzes in my pocket again. As I open up the security alert, I watch as Zara drags her suitcase along my driveway and my heart thuds.

I feel my jaw ticking when she disappears from my view. My anger simmers and is ready to boil over.

Maybe I'll let her see how far she thinks she can get from me.

Because I'm coming for her, and I can't think of anything better than punishing her for every second she makes it on her own.

Once I'm finished, there will be no mistaking who she belongs to for the rest of her life.

You don't run from the devil and get away.

"I have to go. You good to carry on here?" I look to Jax and Kai. Between the two of them, they can get the job done.

"You got it." Jax grins and nudges Kai, whose green eyes flash with darkness as he turns his attention back to a shaking Eduardo.

"No problem, boss," Kai replies, blowing his dark fringe out of his eyes.

"Tell them where Romano is, you get to live," I call out, pacing up the stairs towards my car. Enzo answers on the first ring. Before he can even speak, I give him his order.

"Zara. Track her phone. I need to know where she is heading."

As I start up the car, I listen to Enzo tapping away.

"On her way to the airport, Frankie. Does this have anything to do with the dead cop you had me clean up at her apartment?"

"Yes."

It's more than that. So much more.

"Okay, hold on."

I enter the freeway, headed straight towards the airport.

"She's booked a flight to Vegas."

My fingers tightly grip the steering wheel as my eyes widen. Fuck.

There is only one reason my detective would be heading to Vegas. She saw those addresses in that book. She can't resist hunting the truth, even if it puts her life in danger.

"I need to speak to Mikhail, Enzo."

I grit my teeth, my palms itching to get my hands on her. She's forced my hand with Mikhail. I can't allow her to roam around Vegas unprotected. I'm about to prove to her how good I am at what I do.

I will have her craving me, hating me, and breaking under my hands.

She has no idea how far my obsession with her goes, but she's about to.

"He's on his way to the club. I'll let him know you'll meet him there." I hover my finger over her name on my contacts and stop myself. I don't want her to know I am coming for her. Perhaps I might even let her think she's won, just for a little bit.

Because she will soon realize neither of us wins apart.

It's together where we will rule.

Mikhail and Enzo sit across from me at the high table. Half-naked women surround us, I can't concentrate on anything other than the fact Zara has run from me.

I'm calculating and ruthless when it comes to getting what I want. And I want her all to myself. I haven't even broken the surface of what we could be together.

I haven't even seen her ass covered in welts, nor her tied up to my bed.

Mikhail has a gigantic frame, with a tight black top showing his bulging muscles. Even wearing a balaclava, there is evil in his black eyes. He picks up his glass, the dark skull tattoo spanning the front of his hand on show. His brothers stand stoically with their backs pressed against the wall behind him. Both with the same markings on the hands.

"What do you think, Frankie?" Enzo asks, shaking me from my thoughts.

"About?" I knock back my scotch, letting it scorch down me, a welcome distraction to the burning need I have inside me for her.

I've never felt something this powerful take over me.

"Mikhail will locate the women in Vegas. In return, we assist him with gun shipments while he is still solidifying his power."

Mikhail clears his throat, resting his large hands on the table. "I can also speak to my contacts in Moscow, see what they know about Romano."

"How is Vegas?" I need to know more about his empire before I decide anything.

"We've taken over the casinos, the clubs. There are no mafia families left." His deep Russian accent cuts through the air.

I sense some hesitation.

"But, the motorcycle club, that's where we are facing our biggest issues. We are recruiting more men. Our struggle is the gun imports. They run all of that across the country. I can't ship from Russia since I split. If they have the girls, which I think they do, we need help."

I run my hand along my jaw. Money means nothing to me,

not in the grand scheme of things.

"One month's worth is all I will be offering. Depending on how useful I find our alliance, we can renegotiate. You assist us find the girls in Vegas and find out what you can on Romano's whereabouts," I say.

"No problem there. If I have the guns, I can take them down."

I want Romano. That is my weakness here. It's been ten long years. I'm not keen on alliances, Enzo knows this. If it works in my favor, I'll trial it.

Mikhail's dark eyes don't leave mine as he lifts his scarf and takes his vodka shot before looking back to his men, hiding in the shadows of the room.

"Three," he counters.

I lean back in my seat, crossing my ankle over my knee. "I do have a further term to my agreement..."

Enzo gives me a questioning look and I shake my head. I'll be requiring his assistance for what I have planned.

I rest my hands on the table. "I believe Vegas will have something that belongs to me in a few hours. I'll extend my one month to three, with my guys overseeing the shipping to ensure it is delivered without any issues into Vegas."

He mimics my position as he leans back in his chair, fiddling with the rings on his fingers.

"What do you need us to do?"

Weighing the level of vulnerability I'm revealing, I opt to continue. "Make sure no one touches her until I decide to bring her home."

"Her? Just protection?"

I chew the inside of my mouth. "Well, I have more of a plan. Just make sure I can get in and out of the city with no issues."

Mikhail squints over his dark mask. "That we can do."

I lean my elbows on the table, fixing my gaze on him. "If I find a single mark on her body, the deal is off and I will tear down your empire myself. Do you understand me?"

He lets out a grunt. "Is she a danger to us?"

I chuckle. "She's unpredictable. She's also incredibly smart. Keep your distance until I arrive and keep her safe. Anyone touches her, they die."

The fabric over his cheek stretches. I'm sure he's grinning. "Sounds like more of a handful than you need."

"I like a challenge." I salute him with my scotch.

"The crazier the better, I understand," he says, and he is right.

"Do we have an agreement?" I ask.

"We do. Pleasure doing business with you." He takes out a card from his tailored jacket and slides it across the table. Picking it up, it's a casino business card.

"You need me. This is the only way you can contact me. Now, we have a flight to catch. We look forward to welcoming you to The Strip."

Zara will have no idea I have eyes on her from the second her foot touches the ground in Vegas. None of my men need to know why.

All I know is, she brings out a spark in me I thought had died.

And I want to watch it burn with her.

"You'll hear from me soon, Mr. Falcone." Mikhail raises his thick arm above his head before disappearing from the room. His entourage follows silently.

I'm sure I will. I, however, have more important things to attend to.

"That went well." Enzo grins, running a hand through his black hair.

"We'll see. They might come in useful." I shrug.

"I think they will. Mikhail is a strong leader."

I lean back in my chair, clasping my hands on the arms, feeling the cool leather against my skin.

"Don't you think we have other, more pressing issues to be working on here than some cop?" Enzo frowns at me and I ball my fists to stop from punching him.

"Clearly you don't see the bigger picture here, Enzo"

Enzo chews his bottom lip. He should know that pressing me won't get him anywhere.

"It depends on how much this woman means to you. Is she worth the risk?"

I tap my finger on my tumbler. I know my answer. I can feel it in my soul and my palm is twitching to connect to that ass of hers.

He closes his eyes and sighs as he stands. He knows. "Don't make me regret this, Frankie."

I can't have her running around that war zone, not with how reckless she is.

Lexie saunters in the room with a fresh glass of scotch, brushing her nose along my cheek as she places it in front of me. "Can I do anything else for you today, sir?" Her voice is sultry as she licks her bright pink lips.

I'm saving myself for one woman only. Even if she deserves to feel my wrath after her stunt.

"Not today," I dismiss her.

She pouts as she turns briskly on her high heels.

It won't be any day. I rub my palms on my thighs, trying to rid myself of the thoughts of Zara. I can still taste her sweetness on my tongue and feel her hot breath against my skin.

CHAPTER TWENTY-TWO

Zara

As soon as I'm through security, I pull down my aviators and keep my bag tight under my arm. I spent the entire flight knocking back whiskey, trying to numb the pain.

I was part of another murder, and I feel zero remorse over it.

I'm terrified of myself, but even more so, my feelings for Frankie. At every turn from leaving his home to arriving here, I expect him to turn up and drag me back kicking and screaming.

Yet, every time he didn't, I'm almost disappointed.

Stepping off the escalator, I unexpectedly bump into a guy, his chest solid and unyielding. I instinctively lift my arms and take a step away.

"I'm so sorry," I rush out.

With a swift motion, the guy's tattooed hand glides through his hair.

"It's okay, miss." His eyes travel down my body. His thick Russian accent has me taking a further step back.

I give him a sweet smile before swiftly ducking around him.

Just as I arrive at the taxi stand, a cab pulls up with a screech of brakes. I take another look behind me and see the guy I bumped into leaning against the railings, his eyes fixed on me. With a shiver down my spine, I quickly throw my bag into the back of the cab.

"Hotel?"

I nod again, another Russian accent. The guy's piercing blue eyes appear in the rear-view mirror. I tell him the address for the hotel I booked for two nights on the way here. It should be long enough for me to work out my plan.

I feel a surge of unease as the driver's phone punctuating the air before he responds in a flurry of Russian speech as he weaves in and out of traffic. The locks click on the door, making my heart rate spike. Vegas has recently been taken over by the Bratva. Is that what's going on here?

I grab some cash out of my bag. He smiles at me and holds out his palm.

He has the same skull tattoo spanning the front of his hand as the guy from the airport.

"Thank you. Enjoy your stay." One tooth in his wide grin reflects gold in the dim light.

"Thanks."

As he unlocks the cab, I quickly grab my bag and get out, exhaling with relief.

Maybe this wasn't a good idea.

I head in, not wanting to stay out in the crowds for too long. I hand over my passport to the blonde check-in lady.

"I have a two-night reservation. Under Zara O'Reilly."

She nods and chews on her pen. "Could you give me one

second?" she asks.

I frown. "Is everything okay?"

"Umm, yes. I just need to make arrangements for your room. If you'll excuse me."

I pull the sleeves of my leather jacket down. Something doesn't feel right.

She slips into the staff room, before the door closes, a large hand prevents it from latching. A hulking man dressed in a dark suit steps out and towers over me. His dark eyes meet mine, his face is completely masked with a black balaclava. He pulls his suit jacket and does up the button before breezing past me.

My stomach churns when I see he has the same tattoo on his hand as the last two guys.

Shit.

I pick my bag up off the floor. Just as I turn to leave, the receptionist re-appears, wearing a smile.

"All taken care of for you." She scans my passport and credit card, then hands them back to me.

"I'll show you to your room. You are room 554. We've upgraded you to one of our suites."

I let out a gush of air, maybe I am over thinking. "Thank you."

She leads the way to the elevator and presses the button as I step in. "Are you here for business or leisure?"

"Oh, I'm moving here. Start my new job next week." It's the first lie that rolls off my tongue.

Her bright red lips flatten into a practiced smile. "That's cool.

What do you do?"

"I'm a hairdresser." It seems safer to say than "cop".

Her eyes flick to my dark locks, and she raises one brow. "Awesome."

Entering the hallway, the sound of our footsteps echoes against the walls as she guides me towards the door. I slip the key card in and push into the room.

"Have a lovely stay." She pivots on one of her tall black heels and clicks away down the tiled hall.

I drop my bag to the ground and shut the door.

Wow.

She wasn't joking about the upgrade.

I walk over to the window, gripping the ledge, and take in the breathtaking views of the strip below. I watch the world go by. Even now, I can still feel him on me. It's as if he's here with me.

As the girl who has spent the last six years trying to be someone else entirely, I'm getting tired of it. Repressing my true self to please my father is getting harder, and I fear pointless, with what he's been doing.

That pivotal moment when Frankie accepted me, after seeing what I had done to Chad, is where I became who I was meant to be.

With Frankie by my side, I could hold on to that feeling forever.

How can I trust a man as cold and ruthless as him with my life?

Trusting only myself, I struggle to reach a conclusion that

doesn't leave a painful ache in my chest. There is more to him, far more beneath the surface than anyone else sees. Yet, he let me in, even if it was just for a glimpse of him.

You don't turn off your emotions to the level he has for no reason.

He wants me as much as I need him, yet why isn't he here?

He would have been alerted that I left. He let me catch this flight.

Opening my luggage on the enormous bed, I reach in and feel the smooth fabric of my black dress and matching heels. If I'm in Vegas for however long, I deserve a break. I'm not sure I'll ever be allowed to step foot in New York again, so this better be worth it for answers.

I'm not stupid enough to start strolling the streets of Vegas this late at night, so it looks like I'm heading to the bar.

Maybe there I might be able to clear my head and work out my next move.

CHAPTER TWENTY-THREE

Frankie

I pick up the call and stop in my tracks when I hear a Russian accent coming through the speaker.

"Frankie, how serious were you about killing anyone who touches her?"

My fingers squeeze the phone and I let out a breath.

"Deadly," I reply, anger now rippling through my veins. "Show me."

"Umm, okay."

A few moments later, a picture comes through and for the first time I can remember, jealousy hits me. I shake my head, looking at her in that tight black dress, the ink running down her arm. I can see the smile on her red lips. That should be for me.

As I zoom in, I see that asshole's hand on her lower back. Even from a picture, I can see she is doing this for one reason and one reason only.

To get at me.

I can see her side eying Nikolai. She knows. Of course she does. My girl isn't stupid; she knows how to watch.

"Let her have her fun, but he goes. I'll be there shortly."

I cut the call, dialing Enzo before the line even fully silences. "Get the jet ready now."

I sit in the driver's seat, with Grayson in the passenger seat, and Jax and Kai in the back.

"What did he want?" Grayson's eyebrows shoot up.

I chose to withhold the information about Zara for now.

"Change of plan. We are heading to Vegas," I say, turning on the ignition.

Grayson grunts, the sound punctuating the tense atmosphere.

"Let me reach out to Maddie," he says, pulling out his phone.

"You do that."

"She's going to be fuming at you, boss," Jax calls out from the back and I shoot him a look through the rearview mirror.

"Trust me, if anyone is furious, it's me."

CHAPTER TWENTY-FOUR

Zara

I signal the bartender for another Bloody Mary, adding to the collection of empty glasses in front of me. Somehow, I'm not even feeling tipsy yet. And I need it if I have to put up with any more of Paul's boring business chat.

I did plan to just have a quiet drink by myself in the booth.

That was until I spotted the same guy from the taxi watching me from the corner of the room. Call me paranoid, something about it is just screaming Frankie.

He's powerful enough to have allies all over the country. Whoever this Mikhail is that Frankie has been talking about with Enzo, I bet my life it's them.

Which is when Paul entered. I thought I'd test my theory. Just like that, one drink later, a few fake laughs, and my Russian friend is on the phone.

I'm pretty sure he even took a picture of me.

The bartender slides over my drink while carefully avoiding eye contact with me.

I swear, Paul has been gone for ages now.

My new stalker is also missing. I need to get back to my room and lock the door. I can't do anything tonight. Other than suck it up and call the one person who probably wants to strangle me right now.

I shouldn't have left. I'm way out of my depth here.

Holding my phone in my hand, my purse under my arm, I keep my head down and make my way as quick as I can to the elevators and jab the button. With my heart in my throat, I step in and let the doors close. As soon as I'm safe, I blow out a breath and rest against the mirrored back wall.

I have no doubt I am going to be in serious trouble for this.

It will be worth every second, I'm sure. He doesn't need to know I secretly enjoy it.

As soon as I get back in my room, I slam the door shut, pulling the chain across and locking the door. The deep Russian voices echo outside my door, and I step away and dial the only person in the world that can help me.

I start to shake as I listen to it ring.

"Shit," I whisper.

I pace the room, calling him over and over.

"Pick up, Frankie," I whisper-shout into the empty room.

The talking in the hall stops. I hold my breath and tiptoe over, placing my ear against the door, and wait. After a few minutes, I'm confident they're gone. Frankie still isn't answering. Disappointment fills me.

I unzip my dress and put on my nightgown before slipping under the covers and pulling them tight around my neck. It was probably all in my head, anyway. I'm safe in my room, I hope.

I wake up with numb arms, causing me to shake my head in confusion. I try to move them to rub my eyes, but they feel heavy and unresponsive.

What the hell?

As my eyes focus, I realize there are several men staring back at me. Those dark figures in the room come into sight.

"Morning, Zara."

The Russian accent slams into me, and I instantly recognize him as the guy from the airport.

I swallow hard, trying to suppress the bile that threatens to rise up my throat.

They all laugh. One steps to the foot of the bed. It's the huge guy from downstairs.

"You're in a lot of trouble, Zara."

"W-what? I'm a cop, you know that, right?" This is not a good place to be in. Might as well throw out all my cards.

Their eyes go wide, then they shrug it off.

Fuck.

My arms are pinned above my head. As I struggle, the ropes dig painfully into my wrists, causing me to quickly abandon my attempts.

"Don't do that," another familiar voice says from my right.

The taxi driver. My stalker from last night.

"We can't have any marks on you. Deal's off otherwise."

Deal?

I suck in a breath.

The room falls silent as the main guy at the foot of the bed pulls out his phone. "Sit tight, angel."

I stiffen at his use of the word. There's only one person who calls me that. I look down and I'm still under the covers, my body hidden from them.

The three guys all walk out, and the silence becomes deafening. I kick out on the bed, thrashing my body, trying to free my wrists. No matter how much it hurts, I have to get out.

The door clicks again, and my heart rate spikes as heavy footsteps draw closer.

Through teary eyes, *he* comes into view. In his navy suit and an expression I can only explain as pure fury on his face. Despite his anger, relief washes over me, followed closely by my own rage.

"Took you long enough?" I spit out, tugging my weak arms at the ropes.

He stops at the foot of the bed, his eyes fixed on me. "You don't get to run from me, dolcezza."

A lump forms in my throat.

I really am in trouble.

"Look, untie me and we can go back and talk about this." I give him a small smile to try to appease him.

"Do you honestly believe that's how this is going to go, Zara?"

He reaches the edge of the bed, his fingers closing tightly around my throat. Desperate for air, I strain my neck, trying to inhale.

As he eases his grip, I gasp for breath, my heart pounding in my ears.

"Frankie, please," I choke out.

He tips his head to the side, his thumb brushing against my lower lip.

"There isn't a single corner you could run to where I wouldn't scorch the earth to find you. I told you, you belong to me. Understand?" His dark eyes pierce into me.

I'm not scared of him.

The way he touches me has the opposite effect.

"Y-yes. Sir."

CHAPTER TWENTY-FIVE

Frankie

I slam my lips over hers the second she calls me "sir".

"I can't wait to punish you," I whisper against her lips.

With her eyes widening in disbelief, I gently run my fingers along her cheek. Even she can't hide the desire that appears at my mention of that, I doubt she's experienced anything quite like what I have planned for her.

When we get home, she won't ever doubt what she is to me.

That she is completely and utterly mine.

She isn't stupid. She knew I would come for her. As I go to possess her mouth again, she moves her head to the side. I growl, bringing her beautiful eyes back to me.

What she doesn't know is that I belong to her, too.

She juts out that perfect bottom lip. "You let the Bratva tie me up, Frankie!"

I shake my head, a smile tugging at my cheeks.

"You think I'd ever let anyone have their hands on you?" My finger glides down her jaw, gently brushing against her chin and down the graceful curve of her neck.

No matter how much she's pissed me off with her little stunt, the fact still stays the same—I won't let anyone else touch her.

"Y-you tied me up?" Her voice starts to shake.

"I did, and you had best get used to it, angel."

Her green eyes narrow. "What if I don't want to be yours?"

"Looks like I'll have to leave you here a little bit longer for you to think about it." I press a kiss to the tip of her nose, stand, straighten my jacket and turn to leave.

"Frankie! Don't leave me here!" she screams out in frustration.

I close the door behind me and knock on the room across the hall.

Nikolai greets me. "She's a feisty one."

"We are working on it." I step past him.

Mikhail is leaning back in his chair, his other tatted muscle man behind him, and my very own Grayson and Jax are sitting on the opposite side of the table from him.

"Take a seat," he says in a thick Russian accent, his words rolling off his tongue.

I join my men, resting my hands on the desk.

"Do we really need the mask here?" I ask Mikhail. I like to get a read of people's face. I assumed in his home city, he'd relax more. Clearly not the case.

"Yes," is all he says.

After giving him an unamused look, I pull out a cigarette and light it.

He pulls back the cuff of his black sleeve and checks an expensive-looking Rolex. "I don't have long. We are about to go after the MC's vice president."

I nod. "Sounds like a productive afternoon."

Leaning on his knees, he threads his fingers together. His brother, Nikolai, places a firm hand on his shoulder and leans down, whispering something in Russian to Mikhail.

Jax watches them intently before turning to me and translates quietly. "They've had a hit on one of their casinos."

I pull back, blinking at Jax, registering this new information.

"You speak fucking Russian?" It takes everything in me to keep my voice low after his surprising revelation.

He nods with a sneaky grin.

"My dad," he says with a shrug.

Mikhail clears his throat. "I've had confirmation this *zas-ranets* is holding some of the girls. After I threatened to release the information I hold over my father, I was given the first name. However, Romano's location, this could take me more time." He jots down the information on a small piece of paper fed to him by Nikolai. The chair creaks as he leans forward and hands it to me.

Not the answer I was hoping for, but this is the closest we have to Romano's location since he went off grid after Rosa's wedding.

After a quick glance, I tuck it into my chest pocket. "We have time. I've been waiting ten years to kill that piece of shit."

Mikhail laughs. "It's personal, then?"

"Very."

"Miki, we gotta go." His brother has piercing blue eyes that catch the light as he steps around the chair.

Grayson coughs behind me, we need the Volkov's on our side. Coming here and seeing their set up, they are responsive, quick and ruthless.

"Alexei, see our guests get home safely." Mikhail emphasizes the last word. He sticks his hand out across the table, the dark skull tattoo they are all marked with on display.

I give him a firm handshake.

The big guy to his left brings over six glasses and pours out a vodka. Mikhail slides mine over to me, followed by Grayson's and Jax's.

He holds up his shot. "To our alliance."

I hold up mine and knock it back, feeling the intense heat as the liquid scorches my throat.

His dark eyes watch me over his mask. "Are you sure you don't want the room for the night?"

I shake my head. "No. She's coming home."

Her home now for the rest of her life.

Chapter Twenty-Six

Zara

Song- Too Late to Love you, Ex Habit

Without uttering a single word, Frankie waltzes back in, his presence filling the air. The sight of him instantly raises my heart rate. And the anticipation of what he's going to do to me both excites and terrifies me.

"Have you had long enough to think about it?" he asks.

"Fuck you." I spit in his face.

Immediately regretting my decision, his nostrils flare as he wipes the saliva from his cheek.

He grabs my jaw, his grip firm and possessive.

"Say that again, I dare you," he grits out.

"I hate you, Frankie."

As he yanks the covers off, a blast of chilly air fills the room, causing a shiver to run down my spine. He unties my wrists, but keeps them bound in his grasp. Using his knee to spread my legs, he positions himself between them.

"Do you really? Hmm."

As I attempt to wriggle out of his strong hold, his grip only tightens.

"Yes," I say breathlessly.

His hand dips under my panties. I bite my tongue when his finger runs along my pussy.

He brings it up to my lip, gently tracing its outline.

"Taste how much you hate me, dolcezza." He forcefully pushes it into my mouth.

"Tastes like hate, doesn't it?"

I shoot him a glare, my eyes narrowing with anger.

"Tell me I'm wrong."

My body trembles under him. I squeeze my eyes shut. I don't want to look at him, to be put under his spell.

He's right though. Not that he deserves to know that.

"You're wrong. That isn't for you. Trust me."

My body is on fire as he hooks his fingers under my panties. I instinctively lift my hips to help him. He rewards me with a grin. And, hell, I've almost forgotten why I am so annoyed at him.

My mind definitely goes blank the second he slides a finger inside me.

"It's all for me and it will only ever be for me," he rasps, his hot breath against my cheek.

"No, it's not," I whisper.

My legs open wider as he presses himself against me, his hard cock straining in his pants. Tempting me.

"You don't want it? Fine," he murmurs against my lips.

He lets go of my wrists, but I don't move. Blood pounds in

my ears as his cock twitches against me. I inch my hips down so it connects with my clit and I let out a little moan.

As he pulls back, I realize how much I crave the sensation of his touch.

I want to scream out in pure frustration. How does he possess so much power over my body?

He sits back, a coldness on his face. Without hesitation, I sit up and snatch his tie, refusing to let go.

"Wait—"

With a wicked grin, he pushes me back down on the bed. The distinct sound of his belt being unbuckled fills the room.

"Do you think you deserve my cock, angel?" he groans, his hard tip teasing my entrance.

"Fuck, yes," I pant out.

He slams his fingers inside. A cry escapes my throat, arching my back off the bed. That isn't what I want.

"Mine," he growls in my ear.

Right now, I am. In every sense of the word.

"Frankie!"

He curls his fingers, lifting my hips to get a better angle so he can sink them as deep as he can go.

"You want more?"

I desperately nod my head against the pillow, whimpering as he hungrily kisses my neck before pressing his lips forcefully against me. Even like this, he's consuming me. I've never felt so alive.

"Fuck, Zara," he moans into my ear, which sparks me on

further.

He grabs onto my thigh and pushes it towards my chest.

"Holy shit, Frankie."

Pleasure courses through me.

"Don't you dare, come. Your punishment starts now. Prove you're mine."

Our eyes lock. He's dead serious.

Sitting back on his heels between my legs, he strokes his cock. Keeping his hungry gaze on me. It only increases the burning within me for him. With my name on his lips, he grunts and his warm come spills over my pussy. He doesn't even look at me as he shoves his dick back in his boxers and does up his pants. I throw my head back in frustration.

I try to catch my breath, my hands inching towards where I desperately need relief. He grabs my wrist and shakes his head.

"I own your pleasure, Zara. You'll come when I decide you can, not a second before."

"B-but, Frankie."

"You left me."

I swear I can see the hurt flash across his face as he looks at me. Even if it is just for a second, it's there.

"I didn't think you'd care that much."

He frowns and he settles back between my legs, which I clamp around his waist as he hovers over me, resting on his forearm. He strokes the hair out of my face. Just that alone has me burning with need for him.

"I care. More than I'd like to admit to even myself, dolcezza."

My heart sinks. When I ran, I didn't think this would be his reaction. Deep down, I hurt him. And I feel like an idiot. Despite our constant pushing, every single time I've needed him, he's there.

No questions, no consequences to my actions. He asked for one thing... and I went behind his back.

"I didn't run from you, Frankie. I only came here for answers. I was coming back to you."

"That isn't how we operate, you'll soon learn. We never go alone." He cups my cheek tenderly and I lean into his touch.

"What happens now?" I whisper, not being able to take his silence any longer.

"We go home, Zara." As if sensing my internal debate, he continues. "Nothing changes."

His lips hover just above mine, causing my heart to flutter wildly in my chest. "My property, my protection. End of discussion."

"So, you're kidnapping me?" I tease, blinking at him.

A mischievous smile spreads across his face as his finger glides sensually along my exposed thigh, his warm breath tickling my earlobe.

"The fact you have my cum dripping down you, tells me this isn't a kidnapping, dolcezza. You can't steal something that's already yours."

"Well, it feels like it if you're never going to let me get off."

"Oh, trust me. Once you've learned your lesson, I'll make you come as many times as you want. That's the beauty of it. The quicker you catch on, the better this will be for both of us."

"Are you really that pissed off with me?"

"Pissed off doesn't even begin to cover what I am feeling right now. Get dressed. We have a flight to catch."

After he lets go of my wrist, I shuffle into the bathroom, my legs trembling. By the time I've finished freshening up, I find Frankie waiting by the door with my luggage.

He roughly grabs my hand and we walk along the corridor. Grayson and Jax are waiting for us by the back exit.

"Zara." Jax nods at me.

I smile back and Frankie glares at me.

He tugs me into his side. "Be careful how you play this, angel. Remember who I am and what I can do. Unless you want more blood on my hands, like last night?"

My eyes widen in surprise as I look up at him, and he smugly lowers his aviators.

I figured something happened to Paul.

"And you say I don't care," he mutters, shaking his head.

I know I shouldn't want to jump him in a hallway, but right now, I really fucking do.

He doesn't speak a word to me the entire ride over to the airstrip. I keep my head down as we board the private jet. I guess this is where the next stage of my punishment begins and I already hate every second of it.

Guiding me to the seat by the small of my back, I sit down next to the window and he turns his back to me.

"Are you not sitting with me?"

"No," he grunts.

"Are you not speaking to me?"

He turns his head. "I just did."

I give him a curt nod to hide the overwhelming sadness that creeps over me.

He sighs, resting his hand on the headrest next to me. I can't stand how he's looking at me. Angry Frankie is one thing, but this scares me.

And I'm terrified of my uncontrollable feelings for him. I've been fighting against letting people control me, only to willingly be with a man who wants to break me.

I don't want him to look at me like he has today.

I want to feel empowered by him the same way he helped me with Chad. He sees the real me. I just seem to battle him.

He slides into the seat opposite me and gets out his phone with a frown. Every so often glancing in my direction, which makes me blush every single time.

"I need the bathroom." As I go to stand, his authoritative tone has me stopping.

"Sit. You can't be trusted."

And I do. Because I am desperate to be good for him to provide me with some relief when we get back. I've had a taste and I need so much more.

Once we pull up outside his mansion, I hesitate when he opens the passenger door. I look at his outstretched hand.

The instant our palms meet, a shock of electricity runs up my arm. I feel his strong pull as he lifts me to my feet, firmly clasping me, guiding me to his side.

Inside, he stops in his tracks and turns towards me, a chilling darkness flickering in his eyes. The touch of his hand around my throat is suffocating, his lips tantalizingly close to mine. It leaves me breathless. The scent of his masculinity engulfs me completely.

"Upstairs, you know where my bedroom is. I expect you to be naked and on your knees on the bed."

I shake my head.

"No?" His eyebrow shoots up. "You have three minutes before I take what's mine, dolcezza." He taps his watch and lets go of my neck. I stumble back as he turns away and walks towards the kitchen.

He leaves me in the middle of my choices, either up the stairs or out the door.

Right now, it's not my brain that's in control. The clock ticks. I don't belong to him, or anyone.

Resting my hand on the handle, my ears ring. It's all becoming too intense.

I'm on the verge of opening it when a scream bursts out of me, my hips forcefully pulled backward and I'm swiftly turned around to confront a furious Frankie. My back presses up against the wall.

"Wrong choice, angel."

My whole body comes to life as he lifts my hips and my legs wrap around his waist. His cock rubs against my center,

"One simple fucking instruction, Zara."

"I—"

He puts his index finger on my lip to stop me from speaking.

"That's fine with me. I'll just have to prove to you who that pussy belongs to for the rest of the night."

I take a deep breath, trying to calm the knot that has formed in my throat.

"Nothing to say now?" He raises a brow.

I'm torn between wanting to slap him and let him fuck me.

His beard tickles along the side of my neck and I tip my head to the side to give him better access as he starts to place rough kisses there.

"See, so responsive when you want to be," he mutters against my sensitive skin.

His arms tighten around my middle and I hold on to his neck. His lips slam over mine and it takes my breath away. I can't stop myself from deepening the kiss, moaning in his mouth as he carries us towards the stairs.

I bounce as he tosses me down on the bed.

"Clothes off." His tone is gruff.

Without breaking eye contact, he loosens his tie and unbuttons the top of his shirt.

He takes a step towards the bed, and I immediately get to work on my own clothes. I shrug off my hoodie and shimmy out of my leggings, leaving me in just my bra and panties.

He licks his lips, and that sparks something inside me to come to life.

There is no escaping him and right now, whatever he has to offer me, I want. In the middle of the bed, I lower myself onto my knees, my tongue darting out to moisten my lips, my eyes fixate on his cock straining against his pants.

With every second he doesn't touch me, the fire inside me builds further.

CHAPTER TWENTY-SEVEN

Frankie

Song- Who Do You Want, Ex Habit

I resist the urge to touch her. That isn't what she needs right now.

She wants discipline. She needs it as much as I do. For us, this is how we get what we need from each other.

With every step towards her, she takes a breath, watching me like a hawk. Even now, she defiantly lifts her chin up to me.

My cock throbs painfully at the sight of her on her knees for me.

To punish her, I have to punish myself. If that's what it takes for her to become the version of herself she so desperately deserves, then so be it.

I step towards her and caress her cheek. She presses her face into my touch.

"What am I going to do with you? Hmm?"

She peers up at me, giving me a naughty grin, which will soon be wiped off those plump lips when she learns what I have planned for her. She wants to come, that I can give her until she can't move. Until she's so ruined, she can only feel me inside her, claiming every single inch of her.

Cracking my knuckles, I step back, watching the steady rise and fall of her chest.

She lets out a shaky breath as my hands go to the buckle of my belt.

"Fuck me, preferably," she counters with a sexy smile.

I look down at her. "Enough talking."

My cock aches painfully in my boxers. She squirms beneath me, that fire still blazing in her eyes.

I've had enough of her trying to fight me for control.

Snatching her by the hips, I flip her over, tugging her by the legs to the edge of the bed, so she is bent over, her feet planted on the floor.

I drop to the ground, spreading her ass cheeks apart. I drive two fingers to her soaking entrance and I'm rewarded by a gasp.

"For the woman who just tried to run away from me, you're fucking dripping for me, baby."

A breathy moan escapes her so I slide in a third finger, curling them slightly to hit her G-spot. As her hips begin to rock against my hand, I lean forward and suck on her clit.

I pull back and she lets out a groan, so I adjust myself and withdraw my fingers, teasing her rear entrance. The way her body shivers as I barely touch it makes me almost come in my pants. Sucking the inside of my mouth, I spit my saliva on her asshole, using that to gradually push a finger in.

"Fuck, Frankie."

Her body jolts forward, and I instantly pull her back by her hip, sinking my finger deeper, holding her firmly in place.

"That's it, baby," I rasp.

With my hand on the base of her spine, I run it along her tattooed hip. I increase the tempo of my index finger in her ass and add another two into her pussy.

Her hands grip onto my sheets, squeezing her eyes shut.

"More," she says through gritted teeth.

I pull back my hand and smack her upper thigh. "I'll tell you when you can have more. If you're going to beg, it has to be better than that, dolcezza."

Sweat beads on her forehead and her walls clamp down on my fingers.

"You're so fucking close," I whisper, taunting her.

She wiggles her ass, bringing it up further in the air.

"Is my dirty whore going to come on my fingers?" I thrust into her down to the knuckle, over and over, causing her moans to turn to cries.

"Give yourself to me, Zara," I demand.

Her body convulses on the bed. I keep fucking her through her climax, her hips rocking violently against my hand.

"Take it, take what you want."

Just as she starts to fade from the wave of her first orgasm, I swiftly turn her over so her back is on the bed.

"Bring your knees up."

She does, opening her legs, and I step between them. I lean over and grip the sides of her throat. Her breath catches as I slide three fingers back into her.

"Another one."

Her cheeks flush as I keep pumping my hand. Her back arches off the bed and her juices smother my palm. It doesn't take long to have her balancing on the edge again.

"Look at me."

Her hooded green eyes meet mine.

"Look at the man who owns you as you come."

She opens her mouth, and I add the fourth finger to stop her speaking.

"Oh my god." She lets out a muffled cry.

Her pulse hammers against my grip, so I squeeze it tighter.

Before she can finish on my fingers, I drop down and hook her legs over my shoulders, tugging her body towards my face. I don't waste any time and start fucking her with my tongue, rubbing her clit with my fingers at the same time. Letting her completely soak my beard.

She erupts around me and I take everything from her, her hips bucking, her legs shaking next to my face.

"Frankie!" she cries out; it only spurs me on more. I hold her thighs down and keep thrusting with my tongue.

"I-I can't," she sobs.

Reluctantly, I inch my face back away from her.

"Yes, you can," I say and lightly slap her pussy, making her scream.

I feast on her like my life depends on it, sucking, licking and biting. Her legs start to close around my head and I push them apart again.

I'm desperate for my own release. I want to sink inside of her and fuck her until she can't see.

As soon as she is close again, I drive a finger back into her ass. She squeezes her eyes shut.

"Eyes on me, gorgeous."

I want to witness her fall apart. Over and over again.

She sits herself up on her forearms and does as I say, her green eyes glistening. With a suck on her clit, her gaze pinned on me, she lets loose. Her plump lips open and she screams my name. It is a fucking sight to behold.

She flops herself back onto the bed as I stand. We are far from done here. She watches me as I slide my belt from my pants, tossing it onto the bed.

"Pick a number."

"One," she replies, biting down on her lip.

I lean over her and tilt her chin up.

"Wrong answer." I shake my head.

I pull open the drawer, taking out a set of cuffs connected to metal chains and clip them onto the hoops on the headboard.

She doesn't move a muscle as I position her in the center of the bed and buckle her wrists into the leather.

Yes, I want to punish her for running from me. It's more than that. I want to show her how fucking freeing it can be, letting me take control. For once in her life, she can stop that brain from overthinking everything.

If she says stop, I will. This is a test. Can she trust me enough to hand over herself entirely to me? I want to prove to her she can give me every single part of her and I will protect her with my life.

I'm not her enemy here. I don't think I ever truly was.

I roll up my sleeves and she whimpers as I rest on the bed.

"What—"

I place a finger on her plump lips.

"No talking. You'll see you don't have to keep fighting me."

With a gentle touch, I run my finger down her chin, between her breasts, and trace the tattoos beneath them all the way to her bare pussy.

I flip her around by her hips then reposition myself between her legs, on my knees. As her hands meet above her head, the metal clashes.

Rubbing my hands over her perfect body, I ache to be in her.

"Such a gorgeous fucking ass, Zara. It will look even better covered in my marks."

Her soft moans are replaced by screams as I smack my palm against it.

"Count for me, dolcezza."

"O-one."

"Good girl. See, you can listen." My hand cracks down again. I run a finger along her soaking cunt and she jolts forward.

"Two," she stutters, and my cock is begging to explode.

"So fucking wet."

With her ass spread open, I lean forward and lick from her entrance to her asshole, then quickly withdraw. That was for me—I needed another taste.

I pick up my belt and climb off the bed, admiring the view.

"Look at me. I want to see you."

She turns her flushed and sweaty face to me.

I slap the belt down over her pale skin on the perfect swell of her thighs. Her face squashes into the pillow and she cries out. I suck in a breath as the welts start to appear. It's perfect.

"Beautiful." I stroke along her back.

Her fists clench as I slide two fingers inside her, letting her balance on the edge of pleasure and pain.

Now, let's see if I'm getting anywhere with her.

"Who does this pretty pussy belong to?"

"M-me," she moans.

I withdraw my fingers and follow it with another lash of my belt on her other cheek, causing her to cry out.

"Try again."

She sucks in a shaky breath.

I push three back inside her. With each thrust, I grunt out a word.

"Who. Do. You. Belong. To?"

"You," she screams out at the top of her lungs. "You, only fucking you," she cries.

Tears roll down her face and a fire spreads through my chest. I free my fingers and proceed to lick them clean, one by one.

"You are so sweet," I groan.

"Please, Frankie." She pulls her knees closer to her chest. Her soaking cunt has me salivating.

I keep my touch light as I slide my index finger from her entrance to her clit.

"La mia ragazza perfetta." *My perfect girl.*

I keep my gaze locked on hers as I undo each button of my shirt.

I'll give it to her. She is the first person to almost make me break my resolve. It took everything not to tear off my clothes and sink into her the second I walked in here. She is addicting in every way, both in and outside of the bedroom.

"Please, Frankie?" The desperation in her voice has me groaning.

"What do you want, baby?" The cool air is welcome over my fevered shoulders as I toss my sweaty shirt aside.

"You."

Her response has me pause, kicking my shoes off. "Me? Really? I didn't get that impression earlier."

"I'm sorry."

"Stop apologizing." My pants hit the floor, freeing my eager cock.

I clamber behind her, staring at her beautifully red ass and curl my hands on the underside of her thighs, bringing her up to me.

"What do you want, dolcezza? My fingers?" I say, pushing them inside her.

I quickly pull them out and her body sags forward, so I tug her back, holding her hip tightly.

I hover my mouth over her pussy. "Or my mouth?" I say and

take a slow and sensual lick before sitting back on my heels.

"Fuck, Frankie. Please fuck me."

"Oh, is it my cock you want sinking deep inside you? Do you want to be fucked like you're my dirty little slut?"

"Yes!" She writhes against the silken sheets, her flushed body begging for me.

Turning her over onto her back, I remove the restraints on her wrists and place her hands on the pillow above her head. I stroke myself, not breaking eye contact with her.

"You want me? Is that right?" I bite down on my lip and tug on my dick. The sight of her by itself is almost enough to get me off.

"Yes, Frankie, I want you."

She can't take her eyes from my hand, moving up and down my shaft.

"Are you mine?"

"I'm yours. I promise." She squirms around me, her legs hitting against mine.

"I don't believe you."

She sits up and I clench my thigh muscles as she runs her nails along my skin. She squeals as I pick her up, my mouth hovering over hers and my cock nudging against her entrance. Her legs wrapped around me so tight.

I don't sink into her. I hold her tight as she tries to wriggle her hips.

"I haven't heard you beg yet, baby."

I bite down on her neck and suck, using my other hand to

grab one of her breasts and roll her nipple bar between my thumb and index finger.

I slide the tip in just a little more and pull back, she cries out in frustration.

I bite down on the skin between her neck and shoulder and lick all the way up the column of her throat to her ear.

She sucks in a breath. My defiant little thing is fighting herself.

I pull back her bottom lip and a little moan comes out.

"Now, beg like a good girl."

"I need you to fuck me more than I need air to breathe. Please, sir," she purrs the last word. It sends blood rushing straight to my cock.

I waste no time slamming into her. I can't take it anymore. I need to know how it feels to claim her.

"Fuck," I hiss out as her pussy clamps down so tight on my cock.

"Oh my god, Frankie!" she cries out and nuzzles her face into my neck to muffle her screams as I sink as deep as I can go.

I pull nearly all the way out and thrust inside her, over and over again.

She bites down on my shoulder, I grit my teeth as the pain shoots through me.

I slap her thigh hard. "I am earning every one of those screams. Let me fucking hear them."

Her fingers claw at the air. "Frankie, fuck, shit."

"Now, Zara," I hiss out.

Together, we both tip over the edge. Coming with such force that my entire body is ablaze. Her name escapes my lips as I reach my peak.

Leaning over, I let my cock twitch inside of her and rest against her exhausted body on the mattress. The room is filled with nothing but the sound of our heavy breathing.

Brushing her dark hair off her sweaty forehead, her eyes open with a flutter as I smile.

Freshly fucked and perfect.

"That was pretty good." She bites back a grin.

I tilt her chin up so she can see me. "You think we're finished?"

CHAPTER TWENTY-EIGHT

Zara

Song- Cravin, Stiletto, Kendyle Paige

As he pulls me close, his heart races against my cheek. He lifts me as if I weigh nothing. My body feels heavy, making me question my ability to give him anything else.

"On your knees, dolcezza."

He spins me round so I'm sat up on my knees, my back pressed against his hard chest.

"Spread them nice and wide."

I shuffle them out, too exhausted to argue.

His arms wrap around me, pulling me tightly against him, and his lips graze my shoulder with soft, lingering kisses.

"So fucking perfect," he whispers.

He strokes down my side. Just that simple touch alone forces me back to life.

His other hand tightly wraps around my lower stomach, causing me to gasp in surprise as he gently slides his fingers between my legs.

He kisses up my neck, sending shivers down my spine.

"Can you hear how wet you are for me?" he groans.

Yes. Embarrassingly so.

He increases the pressure on my stomach and fucks me harder with his fingers, lightly nipping at my jaw. His cock presses against my ass.

"Come on, baby. Let me have it all."

He circles my clit with his thumb. I start to pant. My head tips back and I rock against his hand.

"I'm so close," I whisper.

As he twists his finger inside me, the sensation intensifies, and a mind-blowing orgasm ripples through me, sending waves of pleasure coursing through my entire body. I give in to the feeling, losing myself against him, and the wetness spreads from his fingers down my legs.

"Oh, holy fuck, Zara."

I can barely see, let alone do much else. I wriggle in his grasp. His thigh between my legs is absolutely drenched.

"Did I just—"

"Squirt? Yes, you did, all over me."

His husky voice sends flutters in my stomach. I lower my head, not sure what else to do.

"Zara?"

"Hmm?"

"Look at me."

I don't know what comes over me. It's all too much. All I know is, I don't want to look at him. I'm suddenly completely vulnerable to him.

He guides my face up with his thumb.

"Don't you dare be embarrassed, dolcezza. Do I look anything other than completely turned on right now?"

The way he is looking at me, he slides his finger along my pussy bringing it up to his lips and licking it clean with a glint in his eye. "Well?"

"N-no, you don't," I stutter.

"That's because it's true. That was so goddamn hot," he rumbles and steals a kiss.

CHAPTER
TWENTY-NINE

Frankie

I pull her spent body into my side and listen to her steady breathing. This isn't something I've done in the last ten years.

And now that she's here, she isn't going anywhere. Even if she wants to fight me on it, it's something I've come to love. She might be a brat, but she is my brat. She lets out a soft snore, her warm breath hitting against my chest, and my dick is instantly hard for her.

As my phone starts ringing on the nightstand, I hiss in frustration. Jax's name flashes up on the screen.

"Jax." I keep my voice quiet to not to disturb her.

What the hell is he doing up at this time of the morning?

"Have you seen your messages from Enzo?"

I rub my eyes. I've been far too occupied with Zara to check anything. I swipe up and see the onslaught of texts from Enzo.

I open up the attachment and I stare back at a Lieutenant of the NYPD, with a hollowness in his eyes. As Zara stirs beside me, the warmth of her hand glides down my chiseled abs.

"What does that picture mean?" I ask.

"That guy and one of his cop buddies have requested a membership at Enzo's club. Using fake papers, obviously."

"Oh." Interesting.

As I pull up my text chain with Enzo. I can hear the faint sound of my fingers tapping on the screen as I type out a simple instruction.

> F: Approve their memberships and invite them this evening. I'll be bringing Zara.

"Okay, Jax. I've sent instructions to Enzo. Round up a team, we will be meeting there at 6pm."

"Nice." I can hear the excitement in his voice.

"This is work, Jax," I remind him.

"Work hard, play harder."

"We'll see." I cut the call just as Enzo's prompt reply comes in.

> Enzo: All arranged. There won't be any trouble inside the club and I expect Zara will still be on a guest pass?

A smile creeps up on my lips as I recall our last encounter in Enzo's club. He's right. She has absolutely no need to participate in any activities.

F: Yes. I'll see you there.

I place my cell back on the table. I don't want Zara knowing anything about the cops. I want to see if I can really trust her. I'll be able to sense her alliance from a simple interaction with them. It will prove if we're really on the same team.

Her leg brushes up along my thigh, resting over my morning hard on. When I look down, I am captivated by her big green eyes, sparkling with mischief.

"Morning, gorgeous."

"Are you always this busy?" she asks in a husky tone.

"It would seem that way."

"How could you possibly have time to fit me in that busy schedule?" she teases, biting down on her bottom lip.

I brush my nose against hers. I don't think she quite understands what I expect out of our arrangement, especially if she passes my test tonight.

"Don't worry, I'll have plenty of time to make sure all your needs are met, baby."

"Is that so?" She pouts, and I bite down on her protruding pout.

"I'll always make time for people who deserve it from me."

Rolling on top of her, I firmly grasp her hands, restraining them above her head with one hand.

"Can I trust you to behave today if I leave you for a few hours?

I need you to do something for me."

Her eyes light up.

"You can trust me."

She sounds sincere enough, but words mean nothing to me. Actions are the only thing I take note of. What she doesn't realize is, I'll have my men tailing her wherever she goes, until she fully earns my trust.

"What do you need?" she asks as I plant wet kisses on her neck.

"For you to buy yourself a new sexy dress, something you want me to rip off of you. I'll give you my card, buy whatever the hell you need for tonight and, well, for the rest of your life."

As she wiggles her hips, her laughter fills the air.

"Frankie," she says with warning in her tone.

"What, dolcezza?"

"I'm not just going to sit around here and look pretty for you, waiting for you to take me out and shower me with gifts. If that's what you think is happening here, I won't be here when you get home." That fire in her eyes is back.

I tighten my hold around her wrists. "You'll do exactly as I say."

I hide my smile against her neck. Fucking with her is still one of my favorite past times. This woman is wound so tight it's almost too easy.

"Like hell—"

I silence her by sinking my teeth into the column of her neck. A soft moan escapes her lips beside my face.

"You think that is what I want from you? I've told you I want a woman to stand alongside me. It's up to you if you become that."

"Oh," she says in a breath.

"Oh, indeed."

"Money doesn't mean power with me, Zara. Take my card, max it out if you want. Buy something from a thrift store, I don't care. I won't ever have you going without. You're unemployed, remember?"

I smirk at her. She shoots me a look that tells me to fuck off.

"Just make sure whatever you buy, I have access to your pussy whenever the hell I want it," I murmur against her skin and she shivers.

"Where are we going?" she asks as I roll my hips, pressing my dick against her heat.

"We have a meeting to attend at the club."

"The End Zone?"

Of course, she knows about Keller's club. I doubt there isn't much she doesn't know.

"Nope, the club we're going to, I'll actually be able to touch you this time. And I won't just know what you look like when you come thinking about me. I know what you look like when my cock sinks so deep inside you that you can barely contain yourself."

"So something short, tight, and revealing?" I can sense the tease in her tone, I can't help but growl at her words.

"If you want anyone who looks at you to die, then go ahead,

angel." I pull back, my eyes searching hers.

She isn't remotely worried about my threats. In fact, that desire written across her face tells me the opposite.

"You think that bothers me?" she says with a menacing grin. I swear my heart almost pounds out of my chest.

"Jesus, fuck." I rub a hand over my face, letting out a breath. This woman.

I need to marry her and never let her out of my sight again.

As she giggles, I seize the moment and press my lips firmly against hers.

I really hope she proves me right tonight because now I have her, I don't think I'd ever be able to let her go. The more she lets me see, the deeper she digs her claws into me.

"You're crazy, you know that, right?" she says between kisses.

I raise an eyebrow. She's right. I'm crazy about one thing.

Her.

"I may have been told that one or two times before."

CHAPTER THIRTY

Zara

Song- Tennessee Whiskey, Austin Giorgio

I start applying my makeup in the mirror of his en-suite. His predatory stare meets mine in the reflection as he slowly approaches. No, Zara. Today is a new day. But damn, him in that navy suit, his brown hair perfectly styled and a hunger in his gray eyes is certainly what I need in the morning.

His fingers brush against the back of my neck, lingering on the raised, angry red marks.

"How am I supposed to go out like this?" With a playful smirk on his lips, he pulls down his collar, revealing a glimpse of the red scratches that trail along his throat and shoulder.

"Oh, shit." I cover my mouth with my hands.

I mean, it's really hot knowing this powerful man is walking around with marks I gave him.

"I think you got away lightly, Zara. I have to walk around looking like I've had a fight with a damn tiger," he says with amusement.

My stomach erupts into butterflies.

The touch of his lips on my neck ignites a fire within me, and

I struggle to suppress a moan.

"Come on, I've made us breakfast and we have things to discuss." He slaps my ass before he turns and leaves.

I'm not far behind him, breathless and needy for him, admiring his ass in those tight suit pants. As the scent of freshly cooked pancakes wafts through the air, my stomach grumbles and my mouth waters.

"Sit." He gestures to the large dining table, set up for two people. There's coffee and orange juice for each of us.

My eyes are glued to him as he places the food in front of me. As he sits down, the subtle contact of his knee against mine sets my heart racing. I have no idea what is happening to me.

Picking up my fork, I shove in a bite of the most delicious fluffy pancake I think I've ever tasted.

"So, what do you want to discuss, Mr. Falcone?" I ask between mouthfuls.

With a swift motion, he pulls out a key and slides it across the table towards me, the sound of metal against wood filling the room, causing me to catch my breath.

"Our living arrangements," he says, before popping a piece of pancake between his lips. "I assumed I was going back to my place now it's been cleaned up?" I tease, taking another bite and fighting my grin.

His eyes blaze as I push the key back towards him.

"You think I was joking?" His fingers tighten around my wrist.

With a chuckle, he shakes his head, unable to contain his

amusement.

"You think once was enough? You think that was you truly being mine?" I hold my breath as he leans in, feeling a surge of nervousness.

"We barely even scraped the surface, angel."

I open my mouth to speak and snap it shut.

As we lock eyes, neither of us is willing to back down.

"I still want my own bedroom." I bite down on my lip.

His eyes go wide, as if he was expecting more of a debate with me. "No deal."

His touch on my thigh sends a jolt of electricity through me, making me squirm in my seat.

"This is all mine, dolcezza. I can do as I please with you wherever and whenever I decide to. You are mine, therefore you belong in my bed."

I pout at him, crossing my leg over the other, squeezing his hand tightly.

"I don't want to be controlled by any man." I narrow my eyes.

"It's different with me. I take some of your control, in return you gain the freedom you need." He grabs my chin, forcing me to look back at him.

"And what if I say no?"

His perfect white teeth appear as he smiles. "Try it," he breathes out.

I can feel his warm breath on my lips, distracting me from whatever I was thinking about. There is one burning question

I can't stop thinking about.

"Why me?" I ask.

"You want a challenge? Is it because I'm different from all those other girls?"

I know I don't fit in his mold, of most people's, actually. The ink that spans my body often gets me dirty looks. The fact I've never had girlfriends, I've always been more comfortable with the men. It's why I got myself involved in a gang in my teens.

I chase that excitement. That's why I thought being a cop wouldn't be so bad. It was still dangerous.

He shakes his head. I can sense the conflict running through his mind right now.

"You're different from them, yes. That isn't why."

He pauses, causing me to frown in response.

"It's because deep down, you and I are similar. That fire in you—I want to tame it for me, never for anyone else. You, Zara, were meant for more in life. I can give you that. You have shown me that time and time again."

I stiffen at the reminder of what I've done.

His lips purse as he watches me. "Please don't insult me by thinking I care that you killed that cop. One thing you need to quickly understand is that it was by far the sexiest thing you could have ever done in front of me."

I can't help but notice the fire in his eyes, mirroring the desire in mine. He isn't lying. He genuinely likes the dark streak that I try so hard to hide.

He picks up a pancake, holding it in front of my mouth.

"Open."

Leaning forward, I open wide enough to suck the offered morsel from his fingers , biting down on them as I do. I slowly lick them and then chew my food.

"Well, looks like I better go get a dress sexy enough to have you and every other man in there distracted tonight," I say, pressing my hands on the table and standing.

His jaw clenches, a subtle twitch in his facial expression, and he shifts restlessly in his seat.

"You like me being different. Remember that, Mr. Falcone. You wanted this."

I flip him off and rush up the stairs two steps at a time, expecting him to chase after me and bend me over his knee. Slamming the door, I lean against it for support.

Why do visions of him doing exactly that make me so hot for him?

It's late by the time I get back from my shopping spree, courtesy of Frankie's black AmEx.

The house is cold and empty without him here.

I didn't miss the fact Jax and Kai were tailing me the whole time. I'll be having words with him about this.

I know I fucked up; I ran from him. I will have to earn his trust, but he has to earn mine, too.

There's a feeling that I can't shake that tonight's events are a test for him. All I know is, I want to pass it with flying colors.

He's promised me power, and to work alongside him if I prove myself.

I can't help but smile as I pull my new dress up, mesmerized by the way the small diamante's glimmer in the light. It's the most stunning thing I've ever laid eyes on, like it was made for me. With a black leather skirt, the top half is a sparkly meshed material, with a halter neck, plunged neckline and open back.

There is a jacket to put over the top. I'm not sure how he's going to feel about introducing me to his friends and people at the club with all my tattoos out. Especially having one arm fully covered in ink.

I don't want to embarrass him. Men don't always take well to seeing my skin.

I love them. I started getting them after what happened with my ex, Ash. Dad controlled every part of my life, so every time I felt overwhelmed or pissed off, I'd go and add to the collection.

It's freeing. The pain and the reward. Perfectly imperfect.

For years, I've had to hide them. That's why I always avoided putting them on my neck and hands. These are for me more than anyone else, something I could have control over.

I spend the next hour applying my make-up and straightening my silky black hair, finishing off the look with a swipe of deep red lipstick. Running my black nails through my hair to give it some volume, I take a look at myself in the mirror. My dark smokey eyes bring out the green, the lipstick a pop of color against the black.

Finally, I shuffle into my dress, making sure my tits look perfect for him.

I want his jaw to hit the floor when he sees me. I finish off the look with a pair of heeled biker boots, fully embracing my style.

As the door crashes open, I look up and see Frankie freeze in his tracks, his eyes slowly traveling up my body. I feel my cheeks heat up as he bites down on his fist.

"Holy fuck," he hisses out, and it sets my whole body on fire.

"I-I'm speechless, dolcezza." His tone is husky as he stalks toward me.

My breath catches as he traces his finger along my throat and down the neckline of my dress. I've never felt more beautiful in my entire life. The way this man is looking like he wants to bend me over and fuck me like an animal has my heart racing.

"The most beautiful woman I have ever laid eyes on." There is a sincerity in his tone that has me speechless.

His touch ventures down my dress, reaching the hemline that stops at the center of my thigh.

"How am I going to concentrate on anything other than this perfect body?" he groans, his hot breath beating against my sensitive skin.

His other hand tightens around my ass, causing me to snug against him, my body pressing into his solid chest.

"It's a sex club. You don't need to think about work." I smile.

"This is work, baby." His lips graze against the shell of my ear. "We might be able to fit in some fun," he whispers.

I shiver in anticipation at his words.

"You might like this, then," I whisper. Placing my hand over his at the hem of my dress and guiding him underneath, his fingers brush along the lace at the top of my crotchless panties and he trails it down towards my bare pussy, sucking in a breath as his finger circles my clit.

"Just for you, sir."

"Such a good little slut for me."

I can't deny the way his words get to me. He withdraws his hand and taps my ass.

"I've got a bottle of champagne chilling downstairs. Let me go and have a shower and I'll meet you downstairs."

My hand trails over his hard cock, straining against his zipper.

"You don't want me to fix this for you before?"

With a wicked grin on his lips, he shakes his head in amusement.

"You'll be getting plenty of it tonight. Don't worry about that." He places a fierce kiss on my lips, almost leaving me breathless as he waltzes off into his en-suite.

Bringing the glass to my lips, I savor the sensation of the fizzy bubbles dancing on my tongue before the silky liquid goes down my throat. Sitting on the barstool, I keep looking over to the hallway, waiting for Frankie to come down. Even from just a little bit of the alcohol, I have that buzz of excitement running through me.

For the first time, I think I belong somewhere. I'm accepted for exactly who I want to be. Even with my recklessness, my defiance.

My mouth gapes as Frankie walks through the door, tugging his black suit jacket tighter, giving me a boyish grin, letting me get another peek of the tattoos on his forearm. His crisp white shirt with the top button undone. That smart yet rugged look about him, a perfect match to me.

"Look at you, handsome." I wink at him and hold out his flute of champagne. His hand wraps around my waist, and the familiar aroma of his masculine aftershave fills my senses.

With a swift motion, he tilts his head back, emptying his glass in one gulp. After he places it on the counter, I feel a rush of warmth as his nose brushes against my neck.

"We have to go, baby."

I run my hand along his coarse beard, feeling the roughness against my fingertips, before bringing his lips to mine to steal a passionate kiss.

I grab my jacket from the counter and put it on.

"What are you doing?" He pulls back with a frown, looking at the black leather covering my arms.

"Take it off."

His harsh tone catches me off guard, causing me to blink at him in surprise.

"Don't you think this dress would look better with all my tattoos covered?"

My dad always told me that my skin looks a mess and they make me look unprofessional and reckless.

He pushes it off my shoulders and tosses it across the room

onto the dining table.

I look away, staring down at the snake tattoo I have wrapping around my forearm. This one was always my favorite, so I put it in a prominent place. Why do I want to hide that?

As he grips my chin, he turns me to him, his touch gentle, yet firm. His face softens and I feel a warmth in his gaze as our eyes meet. "No, dolcezza. That ink is a reflection of you. If they don't accept you for who you are, they don't deserve a single fucking second of your time."

I don't know what to say.

His finger trails down my arm, tracing past the flowers, the butterflies and on the delicately detailed snake. "I never want you to hide, not from me, not from anyone. You need to realize just how special you are, angel."

I blink rapidly, trying to keep the tears from welling up in my eyes. Never in my life have I been accepted, not like this. "Thank you, Frankie."

As he leans in, his tongue glides across my shoulder, leaving a trail of tingling sensations down my arm. His eyes never leave mine as he explores every inch of my skin, finally ending with a tender kiss on the top of my hand. I squeeze my thighs together as his face is just a breath away from mine.

"Plus, every time I look at them, I get hard as hell thinking about tasting every single one." With a panty dropping grin, he takes a step back, his hand outstretched towards me.

Without hesitation, I place my hand in his.

CHAPTER THIRTY-ONE

Frankie

Song- Lethal Woman, Dove Cameron.

As we head to the bar, I keep a protective arm around Zara. She took my breath away with her beauty tonight. The fact that every man in here has spotted her makes me murderous, but I know she is only mine.

"Your usual, sir?" Candy asks, fluttering her eyelashes at me. She completely ignores Zara standing beside me.

"Only if you'd like to take my girl's order." I raise my eyebrows at her.

She quickly shifts her attention to Zara, a forced smile on her face.

"Oh, of course, sorry." Her cheeks flush.

My hand finds its way to rest on Zara's ass, her obvious irritation becomes apparent.

"Champagne, please." Zara turns her attention back to me with a tight smile.

"I'll bring them over."

Nodding, I guide Zara to our table in the center of the room, my hand lightly resting on the small of her back.

It's easy for me to spot the two cops we have here tonight, propped up in the corner of the room. Their eyes have been on me from the second we walked in. Tonight is a statement. Firstly, that Zara is mine. Secondly, no matter how close they think they can get to me, I'll always be the one in control.

Candy returns with our drinks and I feel Zara tense against me as the woman's fingers lightly graze the front of my hand. Zara seems to be far too concerned with her presence to have even noticed her colleagues.

Her reaction will tell me everything I need to know about her.

"Can I get you anything else?" Candy purrs at me.

"No, thank you," I reply flatly and take a sip of my drink, not taking my eyes off my beautiful girl. Which gives Candy the hint she has been dismissed.

"So, do you come here often?" Zara asks, keeping her tone cool and looking anywhere but at me.

"Less so recently," I respond, fighting back a smile.

I have absolutely zero interest in anyone else. In fact, even these half-naked women strolling around haven't caught my attention.

Only the woman next to me does that.

As Lexie and Rae approach our table, she takes a step closer to me.

"Good evening, girls," I greet them with a smile.

"Sir," they say in unison, bowing their heads to me.

I lace my fingers through Zara's and her nails dig into my

flesh.

"Would you like us tonight?" Lexi asks, fluttering her lashes at me.

"No. I'm here for a meeting."

Zara drops her hand from mine and I snatch it back. Rae props herself up on the barstool and purposely pushes her breasts out further and pouts at me.

"You might need us after?" she whispers.

I chuckle in response. Zara's throat clears audibly next to me, and the girls' eyes dart in her direction.

"I—"

"I'm Zara. Nice to meet you." She cuts me off and smiles at them.

Anticipation fills the air as they await my reaction to Zara's interruption.

I tug her into my side and squeeze her ass. She picks up her glass and knocks back the contents before looking up and glaring at me.

Startled by my actions, the girls gasp and begin whispering to each other while I dig my fingers into her buttocks.

Sensing her flinch, I lean down and softly whisper in her ear. "Something the matter, angel?"

Suppressing my laughter, I clench my teeth and bite down on my tongue, watching her face turn red with fury.

"Are you going to let her talk to you like that?" Lexie asks. I hold a finger up to silence her noise.

"What do you think?" Zara angrily whispers back.

"Are you worried?" Using my thumb, I tilt her chin upward. "Eyes on me, dolcezza."

"You're mine, remember," she says, loud enough for the girls to hear.

The intensity of her anger is evident in the way her eyes flash, prompting me to lean forward and kiss her. She tries to deny me, so I thrust my fingers in her hair and pull her flush against me so she can feel my raging hard on pressing against her.

She melts against my touch, and I keep kissing her, showing her she's right. And fuck, if that isn't the hottest thing I've ever experienced, Zara claiming me as hers.

"Does that show you?" I grab her hand and run it along my dick, and her face flushes.

I bury my face in the crook of her neck, inhaling her sweet scent, before softly nipping at her.

"You girls can go now. You won't be required. Ever." Her voice carries loud enough to be heard over the pulsing of the music.

I nibble on the lobe of her ear. "You're going to enjoy the reward you've just earned yourself, baby."

As she pulls my hair, her intense gaze locks onto mine, the fire in her eyes searing into my soul. "Touch another woman, I will cut your dick off and make you eat it. Do I make myself clear, *sir?*"

Having done that to a man, very recently, I can confirm, I want to keep my manhood very much connected to my body. "You wouldn't. You enjoy it far too much."

Her head tilts and a mischievous grin spreads across her beautiful face. "You have plenty of other uses besides that. I'll survive." The tip of her pink tongue wiggles between her deep red lips, teasingly.

Just as she is about to speak again, I seize her by the back of her neck. "Mine will be the only dick that you will have for the rest of your life." I growl, sliding my hand underneath her dress, letting her juices coat my fingers. "You think anyone else could make you feel like this?"

With a shake of her head, she releases a gentle, breathy moan.

"Do you want to come?"

A tinge of panic clouds her features. I firmly push her face back towards me.

"Y-yes." Her heaving chest tinges red with a blush.

"In front of all these people? Will you give in to me?" I want to test her, see how far she is truly willing to go for me, how much she trusts me.

"Anywhere," she pants.

"Hmm." I slide a finger in and she nudges open her legs, giving me better access. "Such a temptress," I mutter against her neck.

"Oh, Frankie," she moans, resting her head against my shoulder.

"Soak my fingers, angel. Show me how wet you are for me."

Everyone is probably watching us right now. This is not something I'd usually entertain, preferring private rooms only. I have nothing to prove to anyone. Well, that is, until Zara.

Enzo clears his throat behind me. I tug her flush against my front and turn my back to him.

"Come for me," I whisper into her ear.

She trembles against me with her jaw clenched.

"Bite my neck, I'll let you save those screams for when it's just us, dolcezza." I bend down so her teeth can sink into me as I twist my fingers inside her. She shudders against me. I brush her silky hair away from her cheek and place a kiss there.

"Good girl." I slide my hand out and when she looks up at me with her blush, wild eyes and a gorgeous smile, my heart almost stops.

"I think someone wants to speak to you," she whispers, without a hint of embarrassment.

"Us. Baby. They'll be speaking to 'us'," I correct her.

With my hand resting on her lower back, I swallow my drink in one gulp, but it fails to quench the fire inside me. I want her so fucking much.

I turn to Enzo, who has his usual unamused look on his face.

"Enzo, meet Zara."

His eyes narrow. "Miss O'Reilly," he greets her, purposely using her last name.

"Mr. Testa. Pleasure. Nice place you have here." She gives a broad smile as she holds her hand out to him.

Enzo keeps his face expressionless, but his body goes rigid. I can tell he's impressed. I can't keep the amused grin off my lips.

There are only a few of us who know his real last name. How the hell she found that out, I don't know. I've never doubted her intelligence. This should prove to him that she deserves her place here.

He brushes his dark hair back and loosens his shoulders. "Our guests have arrived. I have business to attend to. I'll leave it in your capable hands. Jax and Kai are in one of the rooms to keep an eye on things."

The cops wouldn't be stupid enough to pull anything in here. Not unless they have a death wish. I cast a glance over to them, both of them are looking at us, sipping their liquor.

"Have a good night," Enzo says, turning his back and leaving.

Zara places her warm palm lightly on my arm. "I need the ladies' room. Where is it?"

"Just the other side of the bar. Don't be long," I whisper in her ear. It's hard not to fixate on her ass as she walks away.

When she's nearly to the door, she stops and looks at Alex, then continues into the restroom.

Fuck.

CHAPTER THIRTY-TWO

Zara

What the hell are Alex and Lee even doing here? I slam the bathroom door shut and lock it. There is absolutely no way this is a coincidence. This has my dad written all over it.

Alex is damn good at his job. We have a serious problem.

Shit. I should have never asked him about the club.

What if they're here to mess up whatever meeting Frankie has tonight? He would have seen Frankie get me off at the table.

My dad will find out, and that makes me a target for them to get to Frankie. The cold water from the sink doesn't stop my blood from boiling. At every turn, my father is there to get to me.

I hate him. I hate what he is, what he stands for.

He can't control me anymore. I have something more powerful than any of them.

Frankie.

Running my hands through my hair, I take a deep breath and make my decision. I need to get back to him. I couldn't stand seeing him with another woman earlier; it made me murderous.

I've been through this before, and I don't want the same ending this time.

I don't want more blood on my hands.

Heading back into the bar area, I keep my eyes fixed on Frankie, who watches my every move. Holding my chin high, I walk past my old colleagues, deliberately positioning myself next to Frankie while turning away from Alex and Lee.

I lean in close to Frankie and whisper, "You have a problem."

"Tell me more, baby." He grips my waist, hugging me closer.

"You've got two high-ranking cops over in the corner. They know me. Alex is working for my dad. I'm sure of it. He was the one telling Chad to raid my apartment."

"Hmm." Scratching his beard, he leans his face closer to mine. "What are their names?"

"Alex Pierce and Lee Mitchell," I say without a pause.

Frankie leans back, his hands firmly planted on the smooth surface of the table. Completely unbothered by this news.

"Why do you not care? They could be here to find out who you're meeting? They know we are together? This is bad, Frankie!" I whisper shout, annoyed by his lack of interest.

His fingers tap against his glass. I can't get a read on him at all, and then a smile creeps up on his lips as he faces me.

"Thank fuck for that," he says, almost to himself. I shake my head in confusion at his reaction. He almost seems happy.

I don't get a chance to question him as his lips crash over mine and his fingers lace around my throat.

He pulls back with a glint in his eye. "How do you suggest we deal with them, dolcezza? Should I kill them?" he asks.

My eyes slide over to where they are sitting, watching our interaction. Of course, that's Frankie's answer. My first instinct is that we need more information as to how and why they're working for my father.

I chew on the inside of my mouth, with all these ideas spinning around. I want to impress him, show him I can be useful.

As bad as it is, I understand his need to eliminate the problem.

"I guess you could? Or use them to blackmail my way back into the force? That way I can dig for information there?"

A smirk creeps up on his lips as he leans forward.

"Perfect answer, baby. But, no. I don't want you near them. Not without me."

I roll my eyes. "You haven't heard the rest. My dad will give me my job back, thinking I'm an easy target to get to you. I don't know what Romano has on him or why he's so involved, I want to know. I can find out."

He slowly traces the rim of his empty glass. "Your dad will just let you in?"

I shake my head. "What if I tell him I'm pretending to be yours to get closer to you? It would be the ultimate in."

Darkness flashes across his eyes. "Are you?"

"Are you fucking serious?" I say, too loudly.

"You said it yourself. Is that why you gave in to me?"

"How do I know you're not using me to get to Romano?" I cross my arms over my chest, taking a step back.

We stare at each other, neither one of us giving up. It is quite plausible we were both using one another. I thought this was more than that, though. What I feel towards him is something I can't fight.

"I didn't expect to fall for you, dolcezza. I don't play games. I certainly don't open my heart to anyone. Yet, here you are."

As I step towards him, I can't help but notice the intensity in his eyes as I tilt my chin up to match his height.

"You think I'd let a guy do the things you do to me, if it wasn't real?" I feel his imposing presence as he stands, towering over me. Forcefully pushing against his chest, I fail miserably trying to move him away.

"I don't play games either, Frankie. Either trust me and let me help you or leave me. I ask for two things: trust and respect. If you can't give me both of those, we are done." My heel clicks against the floor as I stomp my foot for emphasis.

His jaw tightens, and I hold his stare. I'm not giving in. He came after me; he made me his. If he wants to keep me, I'm not settling for anything less.

He wraps his arms around me, his solid frame pressing against me. Softly, he moves my hair away from my neck.

"You aren't going anywhere, Zara. Not now, not ever."

I blow out a breath. It's terrifying how deep we are. He nudges my legs open with his thigh, planting wet kisses below my ear.

I want to know everything there is about this man. "I meant what I said, Frankie."

"I know. I expect the same back. Don't ever disrespect me like that in public. I don't care how pissed off you are, save it for when we are home. Do you understand me?"

I can feel my body trembling as his fingers tighten around my throat, the weight of his threat sinking in.

"I understand, sir." I bite down on my lip. "Am I going to be punished?"

"Absolutely. Right now, I just need to be inside that tight pussy. You have no idea how hard that made me."

With a firm grip, he pulls me away from the bustling bar, revealing a gleaming gold door to our left, which he locks behind us. It's just like the room I was in before, except this one is adorned with black accents. A velvet couch is in the corner and a pole is in the middle of the room.

"We have a meeting in ten minutes, so we have to be quick," he groans, tugging my back against his chest as his hand slides under my dress.

I can hear my wetness as his fingers start to fuck me, this burning need for him taking over and consuming me.

"That all depends on how well you can take me, sir," I tease. A moan escapes me as a third finger slides in.

"Now stop talking and bend over and take it like a good fucking girl," he rumbles into my ear.

He owns my body and my pleasure completely.

As Frankie guides me into a private conference room, his hand sits possessively around my lower back. I can't help but feel a growing sense of panic. Enzo and Jax are sitting opposite the three Russian thugs from Vegas.

The one in the mask is built like a wall of pure muscle. The black balaclava doesn't hide his black eyes staring at me. He looks so much more intimidating here in the dim lights than he did at the hotel.

There are two seats at the head of the table. I hesitate as we reach them.

Frankie leans in, his lips brushing my ear. "This is where you should be, dolcezza."

I can't help but shiver at the sound of his husky whisper as he pulls out my chair. Ignoring the empty spot beside him, I make myself comfortable on his lap. His chest vibrates with a low chuckle against my body, and his arms tighten securely around my stomach.

"I don't have long, so tell me, do we have updates on the status of the girls in Vegas?" Frankie's fingers trace my knee as he speaks.

The masked man leans back languidly. "Yes. We have located eight of the ten, each to premises owned by a Reaper. We will begin our operations to save them tomorrow."

Frankie nods. I shift uneasily on his lap, the pressure of his throbbing dick against my ass intensifying as he holds me closer.

"Don't Zara," he warns under his breath, making my body heat at his commanding tone. "And where will you be housing them?"

"Enzo will source them new identities. We will question them for information surrounding my father and Romano. They can have new lives in new states, under our protection, with some of our alliances elsewhere. They can't stay in Vegas, not with the MC issues." Mikhail's face turns to watch Candy saunter by.

Frankie doesn't look, just focuses on his tech guy. "Enzo, can we organize the same for the girls we have in our safe house?"

Enzo types on his phone. "I've already started on the paperwork. Give me a couple of days. It will all be done."

"Jax, are you good to question the girls tomorrow?" Frankie turns to his right-hand man.

"You know it, boss," he says enthusiastically.

"Good. So, Mikhail, if we get these girls to you, can you keep them safe until they can be moved somewhere permanent?"

"Another hundred thousand on top of our deal, yes," the masked man answers in his deep Russian accent.

"What is the original deal?" I ask, my voice quiet as every man in the room stares at me.

"Half a million and three month's worth of weapon supply," Frankie responds. I can hear the amusement in his tone.

"If we're taking care of the paperwork and getting the girls to you, plus providing weapons, why would we pay you anymore?" I idly trace one of Frankie's tattoos that thread across the back of his thumb, I keep my focus on Mikhail.

Mikhail cracks his knuckles with his harsh gaze locked on me.

"Why are you speaking to me?"

"Why not?" I counter, lifting my chin.

"You don't run Frankie's business. You are just a hot piece of ass. I don't answer to you," he says gruffly.

I can sense Frankie's anger radiating off him as he stiffens beneath me. Oh shit.

"If you don't apologize to Zara in the next thirty seconds, the whole deal is off and I will take my entire army into Vegas and we will tear your empire to the ground. She is my woman and she will be treated with respect from all of you. Do I make myself clear?" The chill in his voice brings goosebumps to my arms and makes my heart pound faster.

Fuck, he's sexy.

Mikhail's eyes widen in surprise. "I didn't realize. I apologize." He holds up his open hands, stopping his two bodyguards from stepping forward.

"That is your first and only warning, Mikhail. Now answer her questions. I could do without another war."

I can feel the heat radiating from my cheeks, as if my entire body is being consumed by fire.

"We need the funds to relocate the girls safely."

"Would fifty thousand cover it?" I ask.

His jaw grinds beneath the fabric covering. "We can make that work."

I fake a smile at him, pressing my ass harder against Frankie's lap. "Good."

"Looks like we have a deal, then." Frankie taps my thigh.

Standing up, I feel his hand on my waist as he joins me, his touch reassuring as he addresses the table. "Feel free to stay here and enjoy yourselves. We have a busy few days ahead."

He leads me out of the secluded room, back to the bar area where Alex and Lee are still sitting.

"Now, about that punishment," he whispers in my ear.

CHAPTER THIRTY-THREE

Frankie

My phone buzzes, and Grayson's message appears.

> **G: Raid by NYPD on the safe house. Eight girls are gone.**

"Fuck!" I angrily toss my phone across the room, the sound of it hitting the wall echoes in the silence.

"Frankie, what the hell?" Zara emerges from the hallway, her footsteps echoing softly on the tiled floor.

"Fucking cops," I mutter, making her frown.

"What now?" She rushes over, sitting on my lap.

"They raided our safe house with the girls. They've taken eight of them."

"Assholes," she mutters, fury in her eyes.

She pulls her phone out of her pocket. "Was this in the middle of the night?"

I nod.

She starts scrolling with a look of concentration on her pretty face as she chews on her lower lip. "It didn't even make the news. This wasn't a real raid, Frankie."

Now that they've taken the girls back means not only are they all in danger, Romano has his line of funding back open.

Her green eyes meet mine. "What about your guy in Vegas?"

"They've got two of the girls back there. Enzo is going to start digging. We need to find them."

With a quick movement, she turns and straddles me, her legs wrapping around my waist.

"I can help him. If he lets me into his systems, I'm a good detective. I've worked on trafficking cases before."

I pause, considering her proposal. It does make sense.

"Plus, I feel obligated. My father helped put them in this situation. I want to fix it." Her eyes briefly drop.

I gently lift her chin back up, acknowledging the guilt behind her unspoken request.

"Okay, baby. I'll have Enzo come over and set you all up in my office. You sure you're ready to start tracking down corrupt cops?"

Her face lights up and I'm rewarded with a smile, which makes my heart race.

"I worked with them long enough. I know how my dad works. I'm the best person there is to do this. They all deserve to be brought to justice." That fire in her eyes leaves a heavy feeling in my chest. I love it when she's like this. Her passion, her grit. It gets me every damn time.

"What about the two girls?" she asks.

"We're going over there now. Jax is going to ask them some questions and then escort them to Vegas."

She makes a perfect 'o'. "We?"

"Yes, 'we'. I need you there."

If those girls can identify the cops, Zara can pinpoint who they are.

"Well, let me get ready, I can't see everyone looking like this." She looks down at her sexy lace nightgown.

I lean forward and suck on her nipple through the translucent material, rolling her piercing with my tongue.

"Frankie." She bats at my arm, and I hold her firmly in place.

I can't help myself. Whenever she's around, I have this all-consuming need to have her. "Are you telling me no, angel?"

I kiss my way up to her throat and she tips her head back, giving me the access I need.

"I didn't think so."

Lighting my cigarette, Jax slides the door open and joins me and Grayson.

"They don't know anything, boss. They don't want to go back to Russia, though." He shakes his head, making his dark curls bounce.

"When in the hell did you learn to speak Russian?" Grayson asks.

"My dad was Russian."

"I've never heard of a Russian with the last name of Carter," I say, exhaling smoke.

"Carter isn't my real last name," he replies, sparking up a joint he pulled from his pocket. "After dad died, my step-dad tried to get me to change it to be the same as his. Over my fucking dead body was that happening, so I changed it to my mom's last name instead."

"How did he die?" I ask, remembering the way Jax tenses up at any mention of his father.

He takes a long inhale. His scruffy jaw clicks as he puffs out a series of concentric smoke rings before he answers. "That's a story for another day."

I don't want to press him. I need his head in the zone. He is doing well in his new role with me. He'll tell me when he needs to.

Hearing the sweet sound of Zara laughing drags my attention away from Jax. I look inside and spot her chatting to Maddie and Sienna with a bright smile. Maddie's blonde pony tail bobs as she talks animatedly and I dread to think what she's saying about me. I shouldn't worry, she's one of the few people who sees the good in everyone, including what little there is in me.

"Has he got any updates on Romano?" Grayson asks beside me.

My patience is wearing thin, waiting for answers. "No. For now, we wait. We take care of the girls first, then we may have to work on a plan to draw him out before this escalates any further."

"Where is Kai?" I ask. I rarely see one without the other.

Jax drops his butt on the ground and grinds it out with the toe of his heavy boot. "He has some family shit going on. He's still on for our first run to Vegas tonight, don't worry."

I nod, taking another drag. We are sending over the two girls we still have, so Mikhail can protect them.

"Jax, go in there and help the girls figure out the paperwork. Then you can head home."

He grins and turns to his reflection in the window, where he adjusts his curly hair, giving it a tousled look.

"Don't forget we have training in two hours, Jax!" Grayson calls out.

"I know, I know!" He waves him off, sliding the door shut behind him.

"You think he's going to win?" I turn to Grayson.

"It's not so much the winning, it will be stopping him from killing his opponent we have to watch out for." Grayson rubs the back of his neck.

"That temper needs fixing."

"I'd say so. Kai is the only one who can get through to him. I'm working on it. I think him working with the Russians will help keep him busy and out of trouble."

"We shall see." I stub out my cigarette. I can sense Grayson wants to say something else but is hesitating.

"Spit it out, G."

He crosses his arms and leans against the wall, tilting his nose down to look at me over his sunglasses. "So, Zara?"

"What about her?"

"She's sticking around? The girls seem to get along well with her." He nods towards the glass door where I spot them sitting in there laughing together.

Another icy layer of my heart melts.

I want her to be part of this dysfunctional family we have. "She is."

Grayson grunts. "Did you kidnap her, too? She's not anything like I expected you'd go for."

A smile dances over my lips. "I didn't. She's here of her own choice. What did you think would be more fitting?" I can't wait to hear his reply.

"I don't know, not a cop? One that would cause less of a headache?"

I let out a laugh. "I can't say I saw this coming."

Now she's here, I need to make sure she doesn't go anywhere. She was made for me, that I am sure of.

Zara looks up, and waves at me and I shove my hands in my pockets giving her a grin, my heart racing.

I approach her with a determined stride, and she instinctively stands up as soon as I arrive at the table.

"You ready to go, gorgeous?" I whisper in her ear, wrapping my arms around her.

"Awww, look at you two, all in love," Maddie says.

We both stiffen.

"Maddie," Grayson says in a warning tone, before lifting her out of her seat.

"What?" she squeals, already distracted by her husband.

"Yep, home sounds good." Zara rushes out her words.

I can't seem to respond, so instead I lace my fingers through hers and lead her out of the safe house. I know I loved Leila, but it didn't feel anything like this. There wasn't this fire. We grew up together; we fell in love over time.

This is the opposite. Zara threw herself into my life and consumed me entirely.

It's as if without her, I can't fucking breathe.

I've never felt this. I never want to with anybody else.

This need to own her, for her to be mine. For her to stand by my side and be my queen.

Fuck.

It's quite plausible this is even more than love. She is my life.

We drive home in complete silence, both of us having the same dilemma in our heads. When she isn't talking, I know it isn't good.

I'm not going to deny my feelings for this woman. I'll do whatever it takes to keep her by my side.

It isn't until we're home and I'm pouring us a drink that she breaks her fretting silence. "Why did you kill your brother?"

Her new line of question brings a knowing smirk to my lips. "Because he deserved it."

Her red lips pucker as she mulls over my answer. "He's your blood, your family?"

"Blood and family are not the same thing, angel."

My family is this dysfunctional one we've created. Men who would lay down their lives for me, that I trust. This woman is also part of that.

"I'm starting to realize that," she whispers and bows her head.

I admire her strength, but sometimes seeing this other side of her means she is letting me in.

Stepping around the counter, my hand slips around her waist. "We make our own family of the ones we choose."

I gently tilt her chin upwards, pressing my lips against hers.

"And those are the ones you never let go of," I whisper against her mouth, hoping she understands my meaning behind them.

"The ones you fight for," she says, and kisses me.

"Exactly that, dolcezza."

"Now, what do you say I make us dinner and then have you for dessert?" My hands grip her perfect ass tightly before lifting her onto her stool.

She purses her lips together, as if she has to even think about that. It has become our routine since she moved in. We cook together, we clean and then we fuck. Pushing each other's boundaries. Every day that passes, she is starting to understand. Yet, she still won't let up on that last little shred of control she has in the bedroom.

That urge to fight me. To talk back.

"Can we have steak? I've been dreaming about that all week."

"Whatever you want, baby. Now let's go. The quicker we eat, the quicker we get to the good stuff," I say, biting on her bottom lip.

CHAPTER THIRTY-FOUR

Zara

Song- Outta my head, Omido, Rick Jansen, Ordell

"Wakey, wakey, baby," I hear Frankie whisper in my ear.

I keep blinking through my blurry vision. I can feel his lips ferociously kissing my neck. I dig my nails into his back and he grunts.

"Frankie?" I croak out.

He pulls his face away and his lust filled eyes meet mine. His fingers are turning me on before I can wade out of the haziness of sleep.

"You can't escape me. Even in your dreams, dolcezza." His voice is husky.

He laces his fingers with my left hand and places it on his chest with a mischievous grin.

"What's so funny?"

His eyes flick down to our hands.

I'm staring at what could be the biggest pear-shaped diamond ring I've ever seen in my entire life, on a thin gold band with red diamonds clustered on either side.

It's absolutely gorgeous.

But, wait. I know what this is. "You are joking, right?"

I try to pull my hand back and he holds it in place over his heart.

"Mine, dolcezza. See what happens if you take it off. Try it. I dare you."

His face is stern. I swallow past the lump in my throat, my cheeks on fire.

"I-We, Frankie."

He chuckles. "Lost for words?"

"Well, yes." My palm flattens against his skin as I watch the gems glitter in the morning sun.

His smile broadens. "That's the correct answer."

A moment of silence passes with my mind going into overdrive. "What? No. Why?" My thoughts jumble into a mess of words.

He traces my snake tattoo with one finger, raising goosebumps with each feathery touch.

"You're mine. I want you in every sense of the word. My wife."

"It only counts if you get down on your knees, sir."

Holding back a grin, I roll back onto my back.

Frankie remains silent behind me, I can feel the anger rolling off him.

I pad to the ensuite. As I go to shut the door, his voice echoes through the bedroom.

"'No' isn't an answer, Zara."

"Well, maybe try the proposal again," I shout back and slam the door.

Every day I give him more and more of my heart, willingly.

If he wants to marry me, he can damn well ask me properly. I'm certain my heart belongs to him. No matter how much I tried to fight him, it was always meant to be his.

Turning on the shower, I let the steam fill the room and start brushing my teeth. I frown, looking at my pink bag on the counter.

Shit.

I forgot to take my pill.

I fumble with the zipper and pull out the packet. When I find it, my hands start to shake making dropping the toothbrush into the sink. I storm to the door and it opens before I reach it. Leaning against the frame, Frankie crosses his foot and wears an amused expression on his face.

"What the fuck is this?" I shout, holding my empty pill packet.

He takes a step towards me, I hold my ground, trembling with rage.

"It's exactly what it looks like." He stops in front of me, and I grit my teeth as he tips my chin up to him.

I shriek as he lifts me and drops me on the sink, settling between my legs. I press the empty packet against his chest.

"Why did you do this? It's a pain in the ass to get more."

"You don't need them." He snatches it from me and tosses it behind his shoulder.

He's lost his damn mind.

"You are un-fucking-believable." My finger pokes against his solid abs.

"Watch your mouth," he warns.

I glare at him.

"You really want me to pop you out a goddamn heir?" I laugh, because this is a joke.

A serious expression settles on his face, his jaw visibly clenches.

I stop laughing. Shit. "You're for real, aren't you?"

He leans in, his lips grazing my ear. "Deadly. I want you by my side, where you belong." He grips my arms almost hard enough to bruise in his intensity.

I suck in a breath.

In this second, I'd give this man whatever the hell he wants. He was right. You chose your family, and I chose this one.

"Give me one good reason."

"Just imagine, coming home from work and mini versions of us running around the house causing chaos. With two parents who will burn down the earth to protect them. Family, dolcezza. We can build a legacy, a home. We can have everything we fucking deserve in life. I want that with you."

One where I am accepted for who I am. That doesn't stop me from wanting to mess with him. I won't let him think I'm that easy.

"You think it's a good idea to have kids with our genes running around? I don't think the world will know how to cope with that." I flash him a teasing smile.

He drops his head so his eyes are level with mine. "No one else matters. They will have an empire to run."

"You really want this?" My voice is a squeak, heavy with doubt.

In one swift motion, he yanks me flush against him, my hands pressed against his chest, feeling the frenzied pounding of his heart. "I have never been more sure of anything in my life."

"I'm not marrying you until you get down on your knees and do it properly."

"We'll see about that."

I slip away from his grasp, brushing past him with a subtle hip sway.

"The baby–all you had to do was ask," I say, looking back over my shoulder at him.

I hear him growl behind me.

"Don't fuck with me." His tone is gruff, setting pulses straight to my core.

"Me? Never." I hold my breath. If he wants to play games, then so will I.

As soon as I take a step into the bedroom, he grabs ahold of me by the back of the neck, spins me around, and forcefully presses me against the wall. Our eyes lock and I slide the ring from my finger, pressing it into his chest as his fingers tighten around my throat.

A darkness flashes across his features as he retrieves the ring from my fingers.

"That was a mistake." His teeth sink into my shoulder and I stifle a moan.

With my legs wrapped around him, his dick presses against my entrance.

"You will wear my ring. You will be my wife. You'll see."

I want both of those things, his last name and his baby.

I gasp as the cold metal of the ring presses against my throbbing clit. My body starts to shake as he circles the diamond against me.

"Maybe you can't have it all," I reply, my breath caught in my throat.

His jaw ticks. "Wrong answer." Pinning my arm between our chests, he pushes the band back onto my finger.

"What the f—"

He cuts me off, clamping his hand over my lips, which has my senses dulling to anything outside of him. His grip tightening around my throat, my lungs burning as he plunges into me, fucking me into oblivion, taking what he wants.

My nails dig into his muscular back as he removes his hand, replacing it with a ferocious kiss that steals the last of my breath. He consumes me in every way possible.

My body shakes in his hold, sparks ignited in my veins.

He plunges his cock deeper inside me.

"Come for me, dolcezza," he pants out, upping the pace and squeezing my throat. "Now!"

When he moans into my ear, I scream out his name, and he joins me with a few final thrusts.

He drops his forehead to mine and I try to regain my breath. That was hot.

Dragging my nails along his shoulders, resting on his front. A smirk dances on his lips as he removes my ring from his little finger and slides it back onto mine.

Licking my lips, I shake my head.

"Is that really how you're going to put a baby in me? A quickie against a wall?"

"Oh, Zara. You have no fucking idea what I'm going to do to you."

CHAPTER THIRTY-FIVE

Frankie

I glance over to the fight going on in the ring. The sound of the crowd erupting around us drowns out all other noise as the home fighter delivers a powerful blow, knocking his opponent to the ground.

"I'm so fucking proud of you." I pull Zara's slim body into mine and kiss the top of her head.

Between her and Enzo, they have managed to track down three of the missing girls in just a matter of days. She was so focused, I had to drag her out to make sure she was eating. Once she gets something in her head, there is no stopping her.

"Grayson and Kai still have to save them," she replies, nuzzling her head against my chest.

"They will, baby."

"Hey, look, Jax is the next fight!" She spins in my arms, wrapping hers around my neck.

Turns out, one of the undercard fighters at Jax's fight is a Reaper, and he has three of the girls hiding in his mom's house. Which, of course, has protection of the motorcycle club. But, a lot of them are here tonight for his fight.

So, with the help of Mikhail, we got the cards switched. Jax is his new opponent. If this asshole comes out of the ring alive is now another story. I've given Jax strict instructions to go out there and fight, not kill. If he wants a future in boxing and if we want the Reapers off our backs, he has to keep his cool.

It will be an excellent test for him.

While that is going on, it's a perfect opportunity for Grayson, Kai and Mikhail's men to swoop in and take the girls back to the Volkov's safe house.

"I need another drink." She looks up and grins at me.

"Won't be long before you can't have any more of those," I whisper against her lips and she blushes instantly.

"Let's hope." She presses a kiss to my lips as the lights dim, replaced by red strobes.

As Jax 'The King of Chaos' walks into the ring with his hood up and his red and gold shorts, we take our seats and watch him put on an absolute masterclass of boxing.

With Keller shouting orders at him, he does us all proud. Knocking that fucker out in the sixth round. That split moment when his opponent was on the floor, darkness crept over his eyes and I thought he was gone. Yet, much to my surprise, he stopped himself, took a step back and claimed his victory after the ref counted down.

The crowd goes wild. With blood dripping down his forehead, Jax's wild eyes find mine and I give him a nod. I'm damn proud of him. He kisses his glove and shoves it in the air before Keller jumps over the ropes to lift him up in victory.

I look back over. The Reapers are filtering out of the arena. I discreetly slide out my cell and shoot a text to Grayson, warning him.

He replies instantly.

> **G: All good, boss, Mikhail has taken the girls to his safe house. Tell me Jax beat the shit out of that asshole?**

I chuckle, showing the Zara text and she laughs.

> **F: Easy win. He did you proud, G. I'll see you back at the jet.**

> **G: Fuck yeah!**

"You ready to get outta here, baby?" My arm winds around her waist, tugging her closer.

Her hopeful green eyes look up to me. "Did they get them?"

"Damn right. We won both battles tonight, thanks to you." I place a kiss on her temple and her eyes flutter closed. She pulls on my tie, dragging me to her, and crashes her lips over mine, leaving the taste of sweet champagne on my tongue.

"What was that for?" I tease.

"I'm just happy."

I steal another kiss. "Me too, bella. Me too," I mutter.

For the first time in ten years, I truly mean those words. With her by my side, I am happy. I can see a future, one that exists outside of hunting my enemies.

"One day, we need to come back here and do Vegas properly," she says.

I snug her against me tighter.

"Anything you want in the world, it's yours, dolcezza. You want me to shut down the entire city for you, I will."

She bites her lip and my cock twitches.

"Even if I'm a complete brat?"

I brush my fingers along her jaw, not giving a fuck to who is around.

"*Because* you are my brat. I know you're a good girl deep down somewhere,"

She turns her face towards me, her glossy lips pressing against my cheek. "I don't want to be your good girl, Frankie."

"Is that right?" I rasp.

My hands slide down her back and rest on her perfect ass.

"I want to be your dirty little slut."

I choke on a cough, and she giggles in my ear, causing me to squeeze her ass. My dick is aggressively throbbing as she runs her long nail along the back of my neck.

"You're going to pay for that one."

"Good," she whispers.

CHAPTER THIRTY-SIX

Zara

After finding and successfully getting the first three girls to safety, I have a new determination to find the remaining five. I don't care what I have to do. I know I have Frankie and a whole army behind me on this mission.

It's more rewarding than any police work I've done to date.

Once I know they're all safe, I'll happily make my father pay for this.

My fists tighten, fueled by the burning fire of my hatred for him.

My eyes are fixed on the screen, where the slimy mug shot of my latest target stares back at me. He fits the bill, late fifties, multi-millionaire property tycoon. Wife, two kids, perfect family.

I flick through the next pictures. This has him standing next to the Mayor of New York. The one that really nails it for me is him standing in our precinct shaking hands with my father two years ago.

Enzo sent me over the suspicious transactions to dig into. He makes a lot of payments, all low value to shell companies in

Moscow, Albania and Mexico. He has no registered businesses I can find in any of these countries. But, what he has done recently that really caught my attention, opened a new hotel in Vegas.

"Here you go, baby."

I jump back, not even hearing Frankie sneak through the door and place a steaming mug of coffee next to my computer.

"Thank you. I think I'm onto something, Frankie," I say, tapping my pen against my chin.

He steps behind my chair and wraps his muscular arms around my shoulders. "I'm all ears."

I turn, bring the screen closer and pull up the report I've collated on Mr. James Thompson.

"This guy. He's from New York. High up in the chain with the Mayor and my father, property developer. Links to Russia and Vegas. Recent transactions are telling me he's involved."

"I know of him. He wanted to buy the End Zone from Keller last year."

I spin the chair around. He's just given me the perfect idea.

"What's got you grinning like that? Is your wicked brain working?" He smirks.

I tap my finger against my chin. "What if we got Keller to invite him to the End Zone? Tell him he's looking to sell?"

He scratches his beard. "He's not going to just give us the location of the girls."

I can tell he's impressed.

"That's nothing a little bit of interrogation won't fix. I can be quite resourceful at getting people to talk." His eyes light up as he speaks.

"You can't kill him, Frankie."

Not yet anyway. James is far too high profile for that to get brushed over. We need to find the girls before we do anything.

Frankie crosses his heart with a mischievous grin.

"I'm coming with you. I can easily slip something into his drink. Keller and Jax can tie him up in the office and then you can work your magic."

He nods, grabbing my legs and wrapping them around his thighs. "I like that plan."

"Well, get it in motion. We have women to save." I tap on his cheeks.

"We have babies to make." He lifts me into his arms and sits me up on the desk, being careful to move my paperwork and the array of colored pens out of the way.

"Text Keller, then you can do what the hell you want with me." My body is on fire just saying those words.

"You drive a hard bargain, future Mrs. Falcone." He winks and I roll my eyes, bringing my left hand up and resting it on his chest.

And there it is, that stunning diamond ring, slipped back on my finger. Like he does every damn day.

"I told you, I'm not keeping it on until you get on your knees, *sir.*" I try to keep my face stern.

"And I told you, there is only one of us on our knees here, dolcezza."

I run my fingers through his hair, hovering my lips over his.

"Well, looks like dolcezza will always be my name, Mr. Falcone." I slide the ring off my finger and place it inside his suit jacket pocket, and tap over his heart. "You know the rules. Now get texting. I'm so fucking ready for you."

Reluctantly, he pulls out his phone and starts texting with concentration on his face. I reach for his belt and he slaps my hand away.

"You know my rules," he says in a low tone.

I put my hand back on the desk, anticipation sizzling in the room.

He finishes and tosses his cell on the desk before turning to me with a darkness in his eyes. "Now, where were we?"

My fingers tug again at his waist. "You were about to drop to your knees and show me how good that tongue is."

His hands slam down on either side of me, his nose touching mine.

"Oh, angel. You don't realize how long you're going to have to wait to come now."

CHAPTER THIRTY-SEVEN

Frankie

Settling into Keller's luxurious leather office chair, I gaze at the monitor, the soft glow reflecting off the smoke swirling from my lit cigarette, while Jax and Kai set up our latest torture area.

A decent selection of knives, nail pullers, and tooth extractors are laid out on the desk and a chair with rope in the middle of the room.

Jax leans over my shoulder, looking at the monitor I'm watching, waiting for Zara to do her thing with James.

"Wow, Zara is looking smokin' tonight, boss."

I look up at him, grinning ear to ear and blink a few times at his stupidity.

"Jax, one day he is going to knock you the fuck out," Kai says to Jax. He's a smart boy.

"I'd listen to him, Jax," I warn.

"I was just winding you up, boss." He taps my shoulder and I take another inhale.

"Try it again. You don't need your tongue to work for me." It's a struggle to keep from smiling.

His eyes go wide and he steps back. I don't miss Kai laughing in the background.

They start bickering behind me.

Tuning them out, I sit forward with my elbows on the desk and zoom in on Zara as she walks into the VIP area with the tray of drinks for Keller and James.

Stubbing out my cigarette in the ashtray, I watch as his eyes roam her body and anger boils through me. I might not be able to kill him, but I'll certainly make this hurt.

She leans over the table, purposely brushing her hand on his arm as she straightens up, placing two shot glasses next to their beers.

He says something to her, and she fakes a laugh dramatically. I watch as her tits bounce in her revealing dress. Much like our friend James, I can't take my eyes off them.

She shakes her head as Keller knocks back his scotch.

Giving James a wave, she turns and looks up at the monitor and winks. She knows I'm watching.

It doesn't take long for me to hear her heels clicking in the hallway as she approaches. She steps inside the secluded room and waltzes towards me, sitting on my lap.

"How did I do, handsome?"

She picks up the packet of cigarettes and lights one, leaning back on me as she exhales a plume of smoke into the air above us.

"Jax, Kai, out!" I order, and they silently slink to the exit, closing the door behind them.

"You're lucky I'm about to torture the guy." My jaw clenches thinking about his slimy hands itching to touch her.

She purses her lips and looks at me through her lashes. "I've heard you used to be quite good at sharing at the club."

"That was different."

She raises one of her elegant eyebrows. "Oh, really?"

"Yes really. Those girls were never mine to be possessive over. You, however, are all mine. And I don't share. At all." It's hard not to squeeze her tighter than I should.

She bursts out laughing.

"You're too easy to wind up sometimes, Frankie." She blows out her last drag and stubs it out.

Her hands frame my face. My nostrils flare as I fight the heat of anger burning within me. I've never been a jealous person, but, for Zara, I'd kill someone for looking at her the wrong way.

"I'm only yours, sir. Always."

I let out a breath. Hearing her say the words out loud calms the rage burning inside me.

The door opens and Jax and Kai drag in a drugged and unconscious James.

"Well, that worked quickly." The green of her eyes grow as they widen.

"It's good stuff," I reply. "Do you want to go out there and have a drink with Keller? I'll deal with this asshole and then I'll join you."

She nods, pressing a kiss to my cheek. I grab her face and claim her lips, reminding her who she belongs to.

"Have fun." She winks at me breathlessly before lifting herself off my lap.

Pouring myself a glass of scotch, I sit back and sip as Jax finishes tying James to the chair, leaving his head slumped over. Glancing over to the array of supplies, I know many of them I won't be using. I know his type. He will talk at the first chance to save himself.

Picking up the taser, I shoot it at him and watch him vibrate on the chair. He breaks out into a coughing fit, gasping for air. I step in front of him, smiling down at him when his pale, wrinkly face looks up.

"Mr. Thompson, how are you feeling?"

He looks around the room and starts tugging at the ropes around his wrist. "Who are you?"

I step forward, forcefully grabbing his face, noticing the tension in his jaw as I tip his head back.

"I could be your worst fucking nightmare," I say through gritted teeth. I release my grip and tap his cheek. "Or I could be your savior."

He looks at me blankly. I clearly need to step it up. Heading back to the tools, I pick up a thin knife, bringing the blade up in front of my face.

"We can make this really easy, James. Am I okay to call you James?" I ask.

He frantically nods, his legs starting to tremble.

"This knife, I can either cut your ties and let you go, or I could gouge your eyes out and remove your fingers."

His pupils dilate as I let the reflection of the bright light flicker across his face.

"Ooh, it's sharp," I say, swiping the blade across the tip of my finger, watching the blood drip down.

His chest rapidly rises and falls as a tide of sweat breaks across his forehead. "What do you need to know?"

"Where are the girls, James?" I step towards him, towering over this pathetic man.

"W-what girls?"

I raise my eyebrow, lowering the sharp edge to his throat. "Don't play dumb. I know you're an intelligent man. Tell me where you sent them. Once I have them back safely in my care, I'll let you go."

He swallows against the cold metal. "I-I haven't touched them."

I tilt my head. "What did you do with them, then?"

I take a breath to calm myself before I really stab him through the neck.

"I'm using them for cheap labor in my hotel."

"How many? Where are they?" My jaw ticks.

"Just three. I've got them in a house just outside Vegas. I was told it wasn't safe for them to start yet."

"By who?" I press hard enough to break the skin. As blood trickles down his throat, it stains his pristine white collar.

His head quivers and he squeezes his eyes shut.

"James. Come on. It's your life or theirs. Think about your wife, your kids." It's the one threat that will break any man.

His eyes fly open, full of fear. "George O'Reilly."

Fucker.

"Anyone else?"

"Some Italian guy he works for. I only dealt with George. He wanted them out of the city. He knew I had properties. I normally deal with Ivan."

"Volkov?"

He nods, and the smell of sweat and urine starts to seep from him. That explains the ties to Moscow that Zara found. I bet he's been buying women from Mikhail's father for a long time. I might not be able to kill James now, I will be coming back for this piece of shit at a later date.

"Address."

He reels it off and I pull out my phone, texting it to Enzo, so he can orchestrate the operation with Mikhail and his men, who are on standby waiting.

"Once we have them, I'll let you go." I back away, tossing my weapon into the pile. I take a seat, leaving my phone face up on the table. I light a cigarette and wait, listening to the clock on the wall tick.

Forty minutes later, I have confirmation that Mikhail has all three girls.

"Looks like it's your lucky day, Mr. Thompson." I cut his ties, letting him stand. Before he can pass by me, I grab hold of his throat and forcefully slam him against the wall.

"Breathe a word, I'll kill you. Buy more girls, I'll kill you. I'll have men watching your every move, tracking every fucking call you make. You can't escape us. No matter where you are. Remember that."

I drop him, and he lands on the floor in a heap, clutching onto his neck.

"I won't," he croaks out.

Just in time, Jax and Kai reappear with a grin, looking at James on the floor.

"Take him home," I purposefully say as a reminder to James we know everything about him.

As I stride into the VIP area, I find Zara giggling away with Maddie sipping on champagne, while Keller and Grayson nurse their scotch.

When our gaze connects, she abruptly halts her laughter, her tongue darting out to wet her lips.

"Well, how did it go?" she asks, sliding out of the booth and wrapping her arms around me.

"We saved three more girls."

Her brows furrow as she tosses back the rest of her drink.

"What's the matter, baby? This is good, right?"

"There are still two missing, Frankie."

I tighten my embrace, stroking her bare back. "I know. We will find them."

Zara has taken this on like a personal vendetta. She feels responsible because of her father's involvement. I get it. The woman has determination like no one I've ever met. That's what makes her special.

Sienna waddles over with a fresh bottle of champagne and a

glass of water for herself, taking a seat on her husband's lap.

"Hey, Zara! Do you want another one?"

She looks up at me holding an empty flute on the verge of pouring.

"You deserve to let go. Enjoy yourself, baby." I place a kiss on her temple.

"Yes please," she says.

"Frankie?" Maddie asks.

"Is it your best stuff?" I ask Keller.

He chuckles. "You know I don't serve shit in here."

I slide into the booth next to Zara, resting my arm around her shoulder.

"Well, tonight was a success. Enzo is working with Mikhail to track down a location on Romano using his father's links. The end to this is near." I hold up my drink and the rest of the group joins.

"Do you think Luca and Rosa will come home when this is over?" Maddie asks.

"I'm sure they'll be back, baby," Grayson replies before kissing the side of her head.

Keller clenches his jaw and traces his hand up and down Sienna's arm.

Having spoken to Luca and Rosa a few times, they are happy traveling through Europe. I won't be forcing them to come back. They deserve a break. Looking at Keller's face, he needs his brother. We all miss Luca's sarcastic persona. Even me. We are their family. I'm sure they'll return when the time is right for them.

"If not, then we will just have to go and visit them. I'd like to meet them," Zara says with a smile.

"We will, dolcezza," I reply, rubbing small circles lightly on her shoulder.

CHAPTER
THIRTY-EIGHT

Zara

As another wave of nausea washes over me and I tightly grip the toilet bowl with my hands. My stomach physically aches as I heave relentlessly.

I only had a few glasses of champagne last night. I don't remember having a hangover like this since I was eighteen.

"Zara!" Frankie's voice echoes into the bathroom.

"In here," I call out. Just that alone has my mouth watering again.

The door opens and I pull myself away and sit down on my butt, finding Frankie leaning on the door with his arms crossed in front of his six-pack.

"Someone had too much to drink?" he says with a smirk.

"I'm not a lightweight, Frankie. On a good day, I could drink you under the table. I clearly have a stomach bug," I say. The words have barely left before I throw myself back over the toilet and empty the contents of my stomach.

The soft touch of Frankie rubbing my back provides me with some comfort as I sag back onto the floor and he joins me, spreading his muscular thighs on either side of me and holding me against his naked body.

He strokes my hair behind my ear.

"Are you okay, angel? Can I get you anything?" he whispers.

I shake my head, sinking into his embrace. "Go back to bed, Frankie. We can't have both of us getting sick. We have too much to do."

His chest vibrates against my back as he chuckles. "I don't think this is a bug, baby."

I scoot forward, turning to face him, pulling my brows together. Shock ripples through me as the meaning behind his words sink in. "Y-you think?"

His hands band around my waist, pulling me closer to him. "I do."

I've been using one of those cycle tracking apps. I was due yesterday, I assumed stopping the pill might mess things up.

My heart starts to race. Could this really be it? "Well, what are you waiting for? I need tests, about twenty of them, to make sure."

His hands frame my face as his eyes search mine. "You have no idea how much this means to me, angel."

I smile back at him. I do. Because I want this as much as he does. I want to be next to this man and the power he has for the rest of my life. I want our kids to see their dad rule the world.

"I have a good idea, handsome," I whisper, stroking his cheek.

"You're mine, Zara. Mine forever." His words make butterflies erupt in my stomach.

"That's all I want."

His lips feather over mine for a soft kiss. One that shows me exactly what I need to know. That this right here is everything. Even if we don't say the words, we show it every day.

"I probably should take a shower and brush my teeth." I forgot I was just puking.

"I couldn't give a fuck. While you do that, I'll go to the pharmacy. I won't be long. Call me if you need anything else. Okay?"

I roll my eyes and he grips my chin.

"Don't do that. You aren't in any fit state for me to punish you," he whispers against my lips.

Despite the heat spreading across my chest, I know he's right.

As he leaves, I stand up, looking at myself in the mirror. A tear slips down my cheek. I want this. I want those two lines to show up more than anything. I know with Frankie by my side, I can do anything.

CHAPTER THIRTY-NINE

Frankie

Song- All that really matters, ILLENIUM, Teddy Swims

As I enter the house, I discover Zara fast asleep in our bed. I leave the bag on the nightstand and crawl into bed, wrapping my arms around her.

This changes everything but also nothing at the same time.

I never had any intentions of having kids again. I wasn't looking for it.

She is the only reason I wanted a baby, because it's her.

She rests her hand on my neck and lets out a little snore.

I look down at her ringless finger and stiffen. I know she's teasing me, pushing me to get down on one knee.

She always keeps it in the box in her drawer. I carefully reach over to take it out of the box and slip it back where it belongs.

"You're here," she says in a sleepy haze.

"You need to pee yet?"

She laughs, rolling on her back.

"I could, yes."

She yawns and stretches out. Even like this, with mussed hair and tired eyes, I've never seen a woman more beautiful than my Zara.

I pat her on the ass, and she rolls out of bed dramatically. I follow her in and give her the test.

She stands in front of the toilet and gives me a flat stare. "You don't need to watch me pee."

I ignore her and kick the door shut with my foot.

When she takes the test out of the packet, the room suddenly feels suffocating. My hands are all sticky. I rest my back on the cool tiles, hoping it tempers this new fever in me.

"I'm scared." She looks up at me with her big eyes brimming with tears.

I won't tell her, but so am I. I imagine for completely different reasons.

"Why?"

"Is this even a safe time to have a baby with what's going on?" She sniffles as I stroke her face with my thumb.

"Baby, no one will ever get close enough to our child to harm them. They will be the safest person in the city. I promise you that, dolcezza." I mean every single word. I won't be repeating the mistakes of my past. Even if it means sacrificing myself. Zara and our baby will always be my priority.

"I can look after them, too, you know."

I nod and smile at her. I have no doubt. With that kind of fire behind her eyes, she will make a wonderful and fierce mother.

"Has it been two minutes yet?"

With the sound of my heartbeat filling my ears, I pick up the test. My fingers tremble slightly as I hand it to her.

She lets out a shaky breath before she looks.

Her hands cover her mouth, tears well in her eyes. I know what it says before she utters the words.

When she flips it around, two pink lines stare back at me. Without thinking, I lift her into my arms, hiding my face in her neck as she sobs against me.

I never got the chance to be a father, to be a husband. I've spent the last ten years running from these thoughts. I buried those dreams the same day I lost them.

And now, they're creeping back and it hurts as much as the day they died. Like a fucking spear through the heart.

The only thing that stops me from spiraling is Zara. Yet, I've never felt so out of control in my life.

"We're having a baby, Frankie. We are really fucking do this. Are we crazy?"

"Yes, we are crazy, in the best possible way."

Now she really can never leave me. I can't shake this feeling, this voice screaming at me that we can't have this. I don't deserve it.

And maybe I don't. That won't stop me from taking it, anyway. It only gives me the determination to finally end this war, and with Zara by my side, we can take over the world.

Chapter Forty

Zara

"Hey Enzo, I think we're onto something here. Let me send it across." I look up at Enzo sitting at the other side of the dining table, typing away.

"Send it," he says without looking up.

I don't think there is a single place on earth Enzo wouldn't be able to hunt down someone. I thought some of our systems in the NYPD were advanced, but shit, what Enzo has created is a whole new level.

That does make me think, how dangerous is Romano? For someone to go off grid and have Enzo not being able to find them, that doesn't sit right with me.

"Sent. Enzo, can I ask you something?"

When he looks up, his fingers thread through his dark hair, and his striking blue eyes find mine as he stretches away from his keyboard.

"What happened with Frankie and Romano? I know a little bit about Rosa's wedding. I err, saw the aftermath of that. I don't understand the determination. This is more than just a territory war, isn't it?"

I was thinking about this last night, why Frankie killed his brother and Romano's kids. There has to be more. Frankie doesn't look for trouble, even if it seems to find him. He acts like he is out for revenge.

Enzo's gaze shifts momentarily, his attention elsewhere as he anxiously chews on the inside of his mouth. "Zara, look, it's not my place to say. Yes, there is a lot more to it. It isn't my story to tell."

"Right," I say, while tapping my finger against the table.

His palms flatten on the table. "Ask him. In all the time I've known Frankie, he's never let anyone in. You're different. If you need the truth, demand it. We both know that's who you are."

I take a sip of water, the nausea starting to make my head woozy.

He's right. I'm not scared of Frankie. But, maybe deep down, I'm afraid of what he might tell me.

I look at the time on the screen. Frankie was training with Grayson and Jax at the gym today and then coming back for a call with Mikhail any minute now.

"I can see you scheming," Enzo laughs.

"Me? Never." I like working with him. We make a good team.

"This guy, you know him?" Enzo asks as he flips his laptop around.

"I've heard of him. He's SWAT. He was part of the raid on the safe house. I think he's holding the women for my dad until they find buyers. We should scope it out before we do anything. I'm not 100% on this one."

"Sure. I can send out a team."

I shake my head. "He's NYPD. If he is hiding the girls, he's going to be on high alert. I'll go."

He frowns. "Take Jax and Kai with you, otherwise Frankie will kill me."

I roll my eyes dramatically. He's right. Frankie would flip if I went on my own.

"Will I ever not need a babysitter?"

"It's not babysitting, Zara. It's protecting. We never go out on our own, none of us." His finger stabs the table emphatically.

"Oh, okay."

He pulls up his phone and leans back in his chair as he texts. "Let me get Jax and Kai here. We need to act fast."

I stand. "You got it, boss! Let me get changed."

I hear the front door slam shut and Frankie double steps up the stairs, heading straight into his office. I put my hoodie on and finish the look off with some sneakers, just in case I end up needing to run today. Not that my body is ready for that.

As I enter the hallway, I can hear Frankie's raised voice. "It's not fucking good enough. We can't keep waiting around for answers. We are going to have to draw this fucker out from hiding. This has to end, Mikhail."

I stop outside the door, listening to Mikhail's aggressive Russian tone coming back through speakers, but I can't understand the words.

Frankie's voice mellows. "It has to be money. That's why he's doing this. See what you can find out from your sources in Moscow."

I quietly open the door and peer through, desire flowing through me as I watch him toss his sweater across the room, revealing his toned physique in a tight black tee. His skin glistens from his workout. I look at his computer and see Mikhail's masked face on the screen.

Dropping to my knees, I silently start to crawl towards him so I'm not seen on the video call. I stop as I reach halfway and Frankie's eyes flick to mine and back to the monitor. He spreads his legs apart and leans back, gesturing me closer with two fingers. I make my way over and sit between his knees, careful not to hit my head on the desk.

Mikhail's voice has a tinny sound. "The girls, I'm keeping them here for now? Correct? I have the paperwork ready for your say so."

"Yes," Frankie almost grunts out as I run my nails up his thighs.

In one swift motion, he frees his cock from his shorts and grabs the back of my head, pushing me towards him so I can take him in my mouth.

I hear the mouse click.

"Not a single sound from you, capiche?"

I look up at him through my lashes and nod, getting to work without making a noise. Taking him as far back as I can without choking.

The mouse clicks again.

"I'll speak to my contacts tonight and get back to you, Frankie."

"You'll have the next shipment on Monday."

I lick up his shaft and watch as his jaw clenches, his thighs tightening under my hands.

As soon as I suck on the tip, he pulls my hair so tight at my scalp that my eyes start to water. I squeeze my legs together, the need for him taking over.

"I have to go. I'll speak to you later." He cuts the call and turns his attention to me. The desire in his eyes is mixed with that darkness that hides there. He stands, towering over me, not taking his gaze off me.

"Now, let me hear you gag," he says with a smirk, pushing my head down so he hits the back of my throat and starts fucking my mouth. I grab his ass and dig my nails in, taking everything he gives me.

He lets out a deep moan, which sparks me to start caressing his balls. He tenses against me. Just when I close my eyes, thinking he's going to come down my throat, he pulls me off him. Wasting no time, his hand strokes his cock as he yanks down my top.

I look up at him as he tips his head back, stroking himself with his hand, squeezing my shoulder.

"Fuck. Zara." The way my name rolls off his tongue as he loses control catches my breath.

I bite down on my lip as his hot cum smothers my chest.

Lifting me to my feet, he holds the back of my neck and crashes his lips over mine.

"Your turn, baby," he whispers against my lips.

I pull back and give him a playful smile. "I can't. I'm going out for work."

His thumb delicately strokes my bottom lip.

"Let me clean you up."

He releases me, and I lean back on the desk. It doesn't take long for him to return with a wet cloth. He starts to delicately move the fabric over my skin.

"Where are you going?" His tone has dropped, the sincerity in it moving over me as tenderly as the soft material as he cleans me.

"Checking out a location for the girls."

"Get Enzo to send his men," he says gruffly.

"I'm perfectly capable. Don't keep me locked up, because I'll only want to escape. Remember that." I keep the warning in my words.

"Fine."

I let out a long sigh. "I'm taking Kai and Jax."

I can see the worry on his face.

"Don't do that to me, Frankie. Trust me?" I tilt my head to the side and offer him a sweet smile.

"All I ask is don't take unnecessary risks. Okay?" His hand dips under my top and splays on my stomach. "I can't lose either of you, baby."

These damn hormones have my eyes stinging. I wrap my arms around him and squeeze him tight. "You know I'll do everything I can to keep us safe, Frankie. I promise you."

"I know, angel," he whispers into the top of my head.

I push my chin up and press a kiss to his neck. "When I'm home, can you tell me what happened with Romano? Why do you hate him so much? I feel like I'm missing a huge piece of the puzzle here."

As his body goes stiff, his jaw ticks, and he averts his eyes from me.

"There are things that are best left in the past." The conflict flickers across his features as he looks into my eyes.

"Have a good day at work." He kisses me softly, pulling away and running a hand through his hair as he walks out of the office, slamming the door behind him.

It leaves me standing in the middle of the room, staring at a closed door, wondering what the hell just happened.

I look in the rearview mirror as I pull up next to the curb. There was a silver Chevrolet tailing me for most of the journey over. I sit and wait, watching as Jax and Kai park their bikes behind me. Running my fingers through my hair, I shake my head.

I'm probably overthinking it.

I just can't help thinking I've seen that damn car before. I jump as Jax taps on the window with a grin.

"You good?" He gestures for me to get out.

Blowing out a long breath, I nod to him and get out.

I look past them both and down the road; there are no signs

of that car.

"What's up?" Jax asks, concern etched across his face.

"Did you notice a silver Chevy tailing us on the way here?"

Jax turns to Kai, who shrugs and shakes his head.

"Want me to go check it out?" Kai asks.

"Yeah, just have a look down nearby roads. It's probably nothing. Jax, you can stay with me. We can go scope out the road, see if our SWAT guy is home."

"You got it, boss," Jax says playfully.

I take off, wrapping my long black coat tighter around me. I can't stop thinking about Frankie shutting down on me. Now, more than ever, I need to find out what happened. If he wants it all with me, he needs to tell me the damn truth.

As I approach the little picket fence around our target's house, there isn't a car in the driveway. I keep walking past, checking to see how many of the neighbors are in. I know I can't break in, not in broad daylight.

Pushing down my sunglasses over my eyes, I circle back around, crossing over the road and walking to Jax and Kai on their bikes next to Frankie's Porsche.

"He's not in, seems pretty dead down there. What do you say? Do some snooping?"

Kai warily looks at Jax. This wasn't part of the mission.

A grin spreads on Jax's lips. "Fuck it, let's go. Kai, you wait here and keep watch."

"You got a gun?" Jax asks, taking his out and offering it to me.

"You think Frankie would let me leave the house without

one? Put it away." I push his weapon back to him.

I follow Jax's lead. He scales the side gate, dropping down the other side and opening it up for me.

With my pistol firmly in my grip, we creep around the alley into his small yard. I open up the shed and am disappointed to find only a mower.

Jax checks the back door. "It's locked."

Something tells me the girls aren't here. The neighborhood is far too quiet. There would be someone here. The SWAT guy might know where they are, but he isn't hiding them. That's what my gut is telling me.

"Want me to fix that?" Jax asks, his eyes bright.

"No. They aren't here. Let's just go."

Jax jogs in front of me, checking it is clear before we walk out. He tugs my arm and we break into a fast walk until we round the corner.

Kai tosses Jax his helmet as we approach.

"Anything?"

"No," We both reply in unison.

Kai raises a brow, looking between us.

I unlock the car. "You two can head home. I'm just going to call Enzo. I'll be right behind you."

Holstering my gun, I lean against the smooth hood as the boys ride off. I'm sure this cop knows something, I need to dig deeper to find out where he's hiding them.

I dial Enzo's number, pulling my sleeves over my hands to warm them up.

"Zara, everything okay?"

"Yeah, I'm just leaving now. The girls aren't here. No way would they be stupid enough for that. Can you start digging deeper, maybe see what properties he owns?"

"Yes, of course. I'll see what I can do, and we can have a look when you're back."

As I reach to open the driver's door, I cast my eyes across the road, and squint.

I swear that's the same silver car from earlier.

"The boys are on their way back, and I'll be back in twenty. Can you look up a license plate for me?"

"What is it?"

Grabbing a hold of the handle, I open my mouth to reply and a hand wraps around my arm, making my phone drop to the ground.

"Get the fuck off me." I pull my elbow back and slam it as hard as I can into my attacker's stomach.

As I stumble forward, my lungs strain for breath and my ears are filled with a deafening ring. The masked guy lunges towards me. I duck out of the way, kicking him in the shin.

"Fucking bitch," he grunts.

Seizing the opportunity, I sprint towards the car.

Before I can get there, he grabs my shoulders and pushes me up against a retaining wall. As my cheek grazes against the rough brickwork, a sharp hiss escapes my lips.

"I'm not here to hurt you, Zara. I'm just the messenger."

"For who?" I spit out.

"Your father. You think he doesn't have eyes and ears? Especially when you go parading yourself in front of his friends?"

He slams me further against the wall, and I squeeze my eyes shut.

James. It has to be him telling my father.

"Get the fuck off me."

"Keep out of your dad's business. Do you understand? If you don't, he won't have a choice."

With that, he releases me. I turn and watch as he sprints off, with his hood over his head. Bringing my fingers over my stinging cheek, I swipe the blood from my skin.

"Shit," I whisper.

Frankie won't let this go easily.

I rush over to the phone, picking it up from the ground. Frankie's furious voice bellows through the speakers.

The rumbling of Kai and Jax's engines makes me look up and see them driving towards me. Relief washes over me. With trembling fingers, I put the phone to my ear.

"Zara, what happened? Are you okay?"

"I-I'm fine. My dad sent me a warning. I think James told him I'm involved with you."

"Is that Jax there?" he growls.

"Yes."

"Hand him the phone." The anger is clear in his voice. I swallow the bile down in my throat. Jax kicks out his stand, taking off his helmet.

"Here." I give him an apologetic look.

Even from here, I can hear the wrath of Frankie as he shouts at Jax through the tiny speaker.

"I'm sorry," I mouth to him.

Jax shakes his head, giving me a smile. I'll make sure Frankie doesn't continue on his war path with these two. They're good guys. He's just upset.

A red faced Jax hands the cell back to me.

Frankie's voice sounds slightly calmer. "Stay on the phone, dolcezza. I can't think straight until you're here."

CHAPTER FORTY-ONE

Frankie

I jog out of the house as soon as I hear them pull up in the driveway. Before she can open the door, I do it for her and pull her into my arms, taking a deep inhale of her sweet vanilla scent in an attempt to calm myself.

She's okay.

"I'm sorry, Frankie."

"Shhh. It's fine."

I flash a warning glare at Jax. I know it isn't completely their fault. It's mine. I should have gone with her. Even if it was just scoping out a neighborhood. From now on, she doesn't leave my fucking side.

I place her back down on her feet. She flinches as I cup her face and that's when I see the cuts on her cheek. Murderous doesn't even begin to explain how I feel.

There is a fear in her eyes. She's scared I'm going to blow up.

I press my lips over hers, reminding her what's most important. Reminding myself that she's okay. Whoever hurt her will die.

As will her father.

I swear to God, my heart stopped when Enzo came to me with the phone.

"Come on, let's go inside," I whisper, taking in a deep breath. I need to be calm, for her, for the baby.

Jax and Kai stay on their bikes. Now that she's home, I want to murder them both a little less. I still don't want to see them for the next few hours, though.

"Go back to the gym, fill Grayson in, and work with Enzo to bring me this guy's head."

They both nod and head out, knowing better than to even utter a single word to me. I lead Zara back inside and she sits herself down on the couch. I take my place next to her, pulling her up onto my lap.

I can honestly say for the first time in forty years, I felt pure terror.

Lacing my arms protectively around her middle, I soak her in, stroking light circles around her toned stomach. Her presence calms the fire that was burning in me.

"I should have gone with you today," I say, resting my chin on her shoulder.

"I told you before, Frankie. I don't need babysitting. Not by you. I handled myself, didn't I?" Her lower lip sticks out in a delicious pout.

Sighing, I push a tendril of hair from her cheek. "That isn't the point, Zara. That's not how we work here, baby."

"Give me some credit." She turns in my arms to straddle me.

I brush a hand down her thigh and slip under her tights. Her legs twitch open instantly.

"Always so ready for me, even if I should be punishing you," I whisper in her ear.

I slide out my hand and settle it back on her stomach.

Her breath hitches. "I don't deserve to be punished. I deserve a reward."

I tap her jutting lower lip. "Putting yourself in danger does not deserve to be rewarded, Zara. Not a fucking chance."

I just want to keep her safe. To keep her happy.

"I can't stand you sometimes, Frankie." She glares at me in annoyance.

I bite back a laugh. Moments ago I was so mad I could have broken even Jax in half bare-handed. Now she's here, on my lap, pushing my buttons.

And I wouldn't have it any other way.

"Well, you better sit then. I might be able to change your mind."

Her green eyes narrow. "I am sitting. What are you talking ab—"

"Sit. On. My. Face."

Her mouth makes a perfect 'o' as a blush works its way up her neck.

I peel her tight leggings over her ass and she lifts her hips to help me while tugging off her sweater and bra. I slide down between her legs as she holds onto the arm of the couch, giving me a perfect view of those pierced nipples.

She lowers herself against my nose and I lick gently to get her started. I hold on to her as she rolls her hips, her little moans spurring me on.

"That's it baby, ride my mouth. Show me how much you need this."

She lifts herself up and I slap her ass, inching my tongue out further.

"I told you to sit on my face. So why the fuck can I still breathe?" I slap her hip again, this time harder.

She screams out and drops, grinding against me.

I feast on her, ignoring my dick painfully straining in my pants. I'm too distracted by this beauty acting like she's never been eaten out before. I squeeze around her thighs, switching between licking and sucking until her legs quiver.

I pull her downwards, so she's covering me completely and thrust three fingers inside her soaking pussy.

"Fuck, Frankie!" she cries.

I let her ride her climax out on my face. She slows down and eventually lifts herself up, looking down at me with perfectly flushed cheeks and a wild hunger in her eyes.

"Only one?" She grins mischievously.

I slide out from between her legs and pick her up, tossing her over my shoulder. Then, I slap her ass for every step I take up to our bedroom.

Rolling over, I run my hands along the cold side of Zara's bed. Panic tries to take me as I sit up.

I pause, my heart sinking at the sound of Zara's heart-wrenching sobs echoing from the bathroom. Even over the shower, I can hear her muffled sobs.

I don't care what it is, I will find a way to stop her from hurting.

I walk in and frown as I don't immediately see her, but then I spot her on the floor, nestled against the cold tiles, her head tucked against her knees.

Without hesitation, I hastily enter the shower, collapsing onto the floor as I draw her soaked body close to mine, surrendering to the cascade of water.

"Speak to me." I hold her face in my hands, swiping away her tears with my thumb.

"It's mom," she sniffles.

"What's happened?"

"I've been trying to get through to her hospital room, she's not answering. She has a heart condition and is in a place to help her. It's not good. They won't tell me anything, except she's been transferred. What if something bad has happened? I need my mom, Frankie. After today, I need to tell her the truth, and about the baby, too. It's not safe for her to be around dad. I need to do something."

I hold her tighter, feeling the tremors in her body as she sobs. I stroke her back, resting my head on hers.

"I never told her I was leaving. She doesn't know what's going on. She could be thinking anything about me if it's up to dad. I need to see her, Frankie. I need to make sure she's okay."

"She's fine, angel."

With a shake of her head, she pulls back.

"How do you know that?!" she shouts. I raise my eyebrows at her to remind her who she is talking to.

"Because I've taken care of it. I'm having her moved to a secure hospital in Vegas. No one can get to her and she's being looked after. She knows you didn't abandon her, Zara."

Her eyes narrow. "What? How?"

"With Enzo's help. We explained the situation to her."

She blinks rapidly at me with her mouth wide open. According to Enzo, Jane has the same attitude as her daughter. She's strong. She knew something was happening with George. That still didn't stop her from making Enzo promise to video call me. He said she wants to grill me about Zara to make sure that I am taking care of her.

"All of it?"

I nod.

"We gave her a choice. To get her out of there and move her to a facility that is safe away from your father. One under the protection of Mikhail. Or she stays with George and loses her daughter."

She blinks, wide eyed. "She believed you?"

"She knows more than you think, baby. When you speak to her, she will explain."

"She can't afford all those fancy new treatments."

"I have that covered, Zara. I told you before, money means nothing to me. She will have the best care, with new specialists and whatever treatment plan will help her."

She slams into my chest and clings to me tightly.

"Thank you, Frankie. I don't know what to say."

"We take care of our family. I don't need thanking." I run my fingers through her soft hair.

She looks up, her puffy red eyes staring back at me.

I stroke her cheek. "You know I'll do anything for you," I say and mean every single word.

"Can I see her soon?"

"Once it's settled down more, I'll take you. In the meantime, we're setting up a phone system you can speak to her on that will be secure. When we have the girls safe and finish this, we can look at our options. Whether she moves in with us, or we find somewhere nearby. Whatever you want, baby."

She wraps her hands around my neck, pulling me down to her and capturing my lips with her soft ones. With a firm grip, I bring her closer, feeling her trembling body gradually subside, enabling me to lift her out of the shower.

CHAPTER FORTY-TWO

Zara

I chose a flowing black dress with intricate lace details and paired it with a cozy white cardigan.

As Frankie drives, his hand tightly grips my exposed thigh. "You look absolutely fucking divine, angel."

I blush at his words and place my hand over his. My leg starts to bounce, and he tightens his grip.

"It's all going to be fine, Zara."

"You don't know that. This is one thing you don't have control over, Frankie."

His lips form a thin line.

"I know if you could, you'd do anything to make sure they're okay." My heart is full. I don't need anything else. My stomach tightens as he parks outside of the doctor's office. I don't know what strings he pulled to get this on Christmas Day, but I'm not arguing with him.

"You know, we could have just waited for the twelve weeks?" I say as Frankie rings the bell while squeezing my hand.

"After yesterday, we need to make sure."

"It's a damn scratch on my face!"

He tugs me into his side. "Shh."

The door creaks open, and an older lady with a warm smile greets us, guiding us to the waiting room.

"Dr. Edwards will be ready for you both in a minute. Is this your first pregnancy?"

Frankie keeps quiet next to me. I nod slowly.

A bright smile spreads across her face as she claps her hands together.

"How wonderful, first-time parents. The first scan is always the scariest, you'll be fine."

I direct my attention to Frankie. I swear he's stopped breathing; his face is incredibly pale.

"Are you okay?"

He sucks in a deep breath. "Yes."

Perfect. Looks like both of us are on the edge today. I take a seat and Frankie stands in front of me, tapping his foot on the floor repeatedly. It makes me grit my teeth.

"Can you just sit down?" I hiss.

He turns his head to me and raises a brow. I snap my lips shut.

"Ah, Mr. and Mrs. Falcone."

"Umm—" I reply, Frankie cuts me off by pulling me up out of the chair and smiling at the handsome doctor. He holds out his hand to Frankie, who firmly grips it to shake.

"Follow me."

I pause, fear slowing my movements.

"Come on, it won't hurt." He presses a hand to the small of my back and guides me into the room.

"How do you know? Have you done this before?" I ask sarcastically.

His lips thin, but he doesn't answer.

The doctor is putting on the latex gloves as I stare at a stretcher with stirrups in the middle of the room. I want to run away.

My mouth goes dry and I'm stuck in my place.

"You've got this, dolcezza," Frankie whispers on the top of my head and places a kiss.

"If you could get yourself undressed from the waist down, prop yourself up with a leg in either stirrup, that would be great. Just give me a shout when you're ready."

Dr. Edwards pulls a curtain around the bed after handing me a paper towel material.

I nod.

Frankie takes the paper from my hand. "Breathe, Zara."

I look up at him. He looks no better than me right now.

I shimmy off my panties and hold them out to Frankie. He gives me a weak smile and shoves them in his suit pocket.

"I want those back." I squint my eyes.

I shuffle my dress up and position myself, exposed, with my legs open. Frankie places the paper over the top of my thighs and pulls up a seat right next to me. I expect him to sit, but he walks around, taking a step back.

"What a view," he rasps, looking straight at my naked pussy and licking his lips.

"Stop it." I do *not* feel sexy like this.

"We're ready!" I call out, and Frankie glares at me.

As the doctor enters, he steps around the monitor and sits next to me. I pull down the sleeves of my cardigan over my hands and stare up at the ceiling.

He starts the machine, and a low hum fills the room. He picks up a stick looking thing. I bite back a laugh as he squirts some lube on it and Frankie clears his throat.

"Okay, Zara. If you can take a deep breath in for me and then slowly let it out, I will insert the transvaginal probe inside. It will be cold, but hopefully not too uncomfortable," the doctor says matter-of-factly.

I respond by nodding and taking a deep breath.

"Good girl," the doctor says.

A growl rumbles through Frankie's chest and his jaw tightens as he glares at the doctor. I grab his hand in mine and dig my nails into the skin.

I release my breath through my nose and wince as the cold object slides into me.

"Okay, nearly there, Zara. Relax for me," the doctor says in a soothing tone.

I take in another breath, keeping my eyes locked on Frankie's.

His face softens as I smile at him.

The monitor starts making rumbling noises, so I look over at all the gray and black on the screen and try to make out what the hell it all is. The doctor wiggles the probe around and I bite down on my lip, completely on edge, waiting to see something, anything appear.

"Well?" Frankie asks.

The doctor doesn't reply. He's fixated on the screen.

Frankie's grip on my hand tightens, providing a reassuring squeeze as my fear intensifies.

"Ah-ha. Gotcha." The doctor beams and turns the screen to face us.

"There you have it." He points to the little blob on the screen, and my eyes start to sting.

Our baby.

My attention is completely captivated by it.

Dr. Edwards clicks a few buttons, and a white line appears over the picture. "From this, I'd say you are around eleven weeks."

Frankie's bloodshot eyes meet mine, filled with sadness.

"Would you like to keep some images?" the doctor asks, I can't stop looking at Frankie. Why the hell is he so pale? Neither of us reply.

"Please," I whisper.

My heart is in my throat. Something is wrong.

"Would you mind giving us a minute when you're finished?" I ask the doctor.

"Of course."

He continues taking a few more measurements. We all sit in silence until he finishes and quietly leaves.

I pull my dress back down and toss the paper in the trash, sitting in front of an unmoving Frankie, who looks as though he is about to throw up.

"Hey." I cup his cheek.

Nothing. I place a kiss on his cheek.

"I'm going to need you to talk to me, Frankie Falcone." I keep my voice stern, forcing him to look at me.

My own eyes brim with tears, and I let out a shaky breath.

"Please. What's going on? Our baby is fine. Don't make me do this on my own, Frankie. I need you here with me."

He tips his head down, so I stroke his hair lightly.

I want to know what has caused this reaction, but equally, I know he isn't ready to tell me. If this is ever going to work between us, he has to open up to me, to trust me.

Maybe I have to show him I trust him, too. Completely and utterly.

Chapter Forty-Three

Frankie

"Are you coming to bed?" Zara stands by my desk with her hand on her hip. Even in her tone, she's had enough of me today.

After spending the rest of the day at Grayson's for Christmas, I couldn't shake that grief that crept over me. It's something I've worked so hard to keep away.

I shake my head, not looking away from the screen. My heart races as the office door slams shut. Leaning back in the chair, I release a tired exhale.

I have everything I want in my grasp. Pouring myself another glass of scotch, I pull out the ultrasound picture from my pocket and fixate on that little dot.

Our baby. Our future.

All fucking day, all I can replay in my mind is that house going up in flames.

The way Zara looked at me with pity in her eyes earlier.

I don't know how long I sit here, not letting go of the pictures. Fearing that If I do, I might lose them again.

Staring until my eyes physically hurt, I drag myself out of the office and creep towards our bedroom, not wanting to disturb Zara. I just want to crawl in next to her and remind myself that she is mine. She isn't going anywhere, despite what my brain might be telling me.

I feel my heart pounding in my chest as I see our bed is empty.

"Fuck," I whisper.

Making my way down the hall, I open doors until I stumble upon her, nestled on her side with her tattooed arm wrapped around the blanket.

I swiftly undress and slip into bed beside her, wrapping my arms around her as tightly as I can. My arm encircles her stomach protectively, and I rub small circles around her belly button.

"I'm sorry," I whisper, closing my eyes and inhaling her sweet scent. The only thing that provides me calm right now.

"It's okay," she whispers back.

A smile creeps up on my face.

She wiggles her ass against me, which has my cock springing to life.

"I don't think so, Frankie. Not until we talk," she says in a sleepy voice.

"I don't think you get to make orders around here, angel," I reply, but she's right.

"Trust me, right now, I do. Now, goodnight." She sighs against me and I can't help the guilt swirling around in my chest.

I hug her tighter as her breathing settles. This woman is my life.

"Ti amo, dolcezza," I whisper against her hair.

I thought I knew what love was ten years ago. Leila never loved me for who I was, simply who she wanted me to be, for her. Zara, she knows my flaws. She sees every single part of me and craves more.

Every moment in my life happened for a reason. To bring her to me.

And there is not a single soul on this earth who can take that away from me.

I peer out of one eye and find Zara straddling me with a naughty grin on her lips.

"Morning, gorgeous." She bites down on her lip and rolls her hips against my cock.

She peels off her tank top, and her perky breasts have me salivating. I tug my hands forward, only to have metal digging into my wrists.

"Zara." I look up and find both of my arms cuffed to the bed.

"You really don't want to do this," I say, trying to remain calm. She rubs her pussy against me again, sending bolts of desire through me.

"I don't?" she pouts at me.

When her wet heat connects again, I can't hold in the groan that escapes.

"I think I could get myself off just by doing this, you know. Your dick is so perfect, Frankie."

"Uncuff me, now," I growl.

Leaning forward, she shakes her head and runs her nails down my abs.

"See, I was thinking, after what happened yesterday. I need to know what the hell went on. I need you to trust me, Frankie. In return, I will show you how much I trust you. I will give my body over to you, completely."

She pauses to grind her hips again.

"Exactly how you want me to." She cups her breasts and lets out a moan.

I yank at the restraints. My body is on fucking fire.

"Don't fuck with me, Zara."

She rolls her eyes, making me want to bend her over my knee and slap her ass raw.

"It's up to you." She shrugs and slides her hand down the front of her body and between her legs. "I'll get off either way."

Her mouth parts as she starts to play with herself.

I grit my teeth together, trying to calm this raging inferno inside of me.

Her eyes fall closed as she gyrates her hand faster between her thighs.

"Well?" She pinches the silver bar in her nipple and cries out.

My balls tighten and I thrust my hips up. "Uncuff me, then we talk."

She shakes her head.

"Oh god, I'm so close." She tips her head back, exposing her slender neck, which I want to wrap my fingers around and squeeze.

"Fine!" I snap.

She stops everything, and her eyes widen in shock. "You'll tell me?"

I nod. I planned on telling her, anyway, except this time, I get something in return.

"It isn't pretty, Zara."

"I gathered." She offers me a sad smile and crawls up my body, brushing her lips along mine.

"You think my past is all sunshine and teddy bears?"

"I was waiting for you to tell me the truth, angel. If I'd have known this was the method, I would have cuffed you to the bed and edged you until you told me."

"We're having a baby, Frankie. That changes everything. If we can't open up, at least to each other, we have nothing."

"You want me to change?"

She shakes her head. "Not even a little, I don't mean that. I quite like you, all cold and ruthless. What I mean is you need to let go of the demons in your past, accept them and focus on what we have here. I'm not going anywhere."

I may not like being at her mercy, but she's right. We are so close to having it all, ruling our empire and building a family. My past and a quest for revenge have fueled me for ten years. Now, I have an end to this and a fucking perfect future almost in my gasp.

She goes to free me, and I bite down on her nipple.

"I suggest you sit that pretty pussy on my face first."

Her green eyes light up and she blows a strand of her black hair out of her face. "I'm not going to argue with that."

CHAPTER FORTY-FOUR

Zara

Song- Sleep Token, Jaws

With his shirt draped loosely over my shoulders, I find myself absentmindedly tapping my fingers against the rich oak dining table, the sound blending with the aroma of freshly brewed coffee he's making.

He's dragging this out.

Whatever happened, he really doesn't want to speak about it.

He places the steaming cup in front of me, and I lick my lips, needing the caffeine. I tossed and turned all night against him in anticipation of this morning.

"Thank you."

"Decaf, sorry." He winks.

It's going to be a long seven months without real coffee.

He pulls out the chair next to me and sits, tapping his thigh.

I slip over and sit on his lap, sliding my cup along the counter as I move.

I'll wait for him to start. I'm already on the edge of his patience today after my stunt upstairs.

"Ten years ago, I was going to be a dad to a little girl. Her name was going to be Valentina. Her mother was my childhood sweetheart."

Was.

As his arm wraps around my middle, I run my fingers along his forearm to provide reassurance.

"The day before we were meant to leave, my older brother, Marco, told me he had murdered Romano's wife."

"Wow, it's been going on since then?" I ask, turning to look at him.

"Yes. My idiot of a brother didn't think the retaliation would happen so soon." He swallows, tightening his grip on his drink.

He takes in a sharp breath and shakes his head. "I watched the house burst into flames. With Leila inside."

"Oh my god," I whisper, bile rising up my throat. He watched his whole future explode in front of his eyes. It's understandable why he is now so cold and emotionless.

I don't know how anyone could recover from that.

"Marco lost his wife, his mother-in-law, and almost both of his daughters."

"Rosa and Eva?"

"Yes. Eva was murdered by Maria. That is why you found that bitch's throat slit." His fist tightens, making the veins bulge beneath my fingers.

"I don't blame you. She deserved a way worse death."

Frankie chuckles. "That isn't what you said when you released me from jail, angel."

I shrug. "Things change."

"That they do." He strokes my stomach.

Biting my lip, I jump in. "I know you don't want to hear this, but I'm going to say it, anyway."

"Of course you are."

I turn around on his lap and straddle him, my legs dangling on either side with his strong hands cupping my ass.

"I'm sorry that happened to you. I'm sorry for your loss." A tear slips down my cheek and I rest my forehead against his. "I never want to replace them, Frankie. You are allowed to grieve, to feel. Don't shut it out."

His jaw clenches. "I'm fine."

"Are you? Because yesterday didn't seem like you were." I watch him look away, his darkened eyes unfocused as he stares at some place long ago.

His hands run up and down my thighs before he speaks again. "I-I never expected this, you to happen."

"I'm happy I can be here to see you get your revenge."

As he tilts his head back, I sink my teeth into his neck.

"You're perfect, Zara," he groans.

I flash him a wide grin. "I know."

His lips claim mine and I let his tongue explore as I run my fingers through his soft hair.

I pull back, cupping his cheeks. "Thank you for trusting me, Frankie."

"I look forward to earning yours in a minute," he winks.

"I'm serious."

"So am I, angel."

I roll my eyes.

He grips my chin. "This doesn't change anything."

I place his hand on my stomach. "This might, though."

"I'll protect them with my life. That would always be the case, don't ever doubt that."

"Well, I hope you don't have to. I wouldn't mind some help with the night feedings. I'd rather not do it on my own."

"It will all work out, baby. Now, what's your dirty secret?"

I suck in a breath. I've never said the words out loud. What if he really thinks I am crazy?

"I killed my ex-boyfriend."

"Was he hurting you?" He frowns as he studies my face.

"No. He was part of a gang, a drug dealer. I was eighteen. I thought it was cool. Well, it was until one night he left me to do his deals for him. It was freezing cold, and I got robbed. When I got home, he wasn't there. One of his junkie friends let slip that he was at Anna's."

His eyebrows raise as he listens to me.

"How did you do it?"

"I waited outside her house. He got on his bike and I ran into him with my car."

"That killed him?"

I shake my head.

"Me then reversing back over him is what killed him."

His eyes go wide, followed by a burst of full bellied laughter.

"Well, this means I can't be your boyfriend, dolcezza."

My heart races. "What do you mean?"

He smiles. "I will have to be a husband, so I don't meet the same fate."

I blow out a breath. "Fuck, you scared me."

He strokes my face tenderly. "You did what you thought was right. You're feisty. The guy was clearly a loser to cheat on you in the first place. I take it your father knew? That's why you never fought back against him?"

"He helped me cover it up, then got me into the force to keep an eye on his 'crazy daughter.'"

He shrugs. "There wasn't anything you could have possibly done in your past that would have kept me away from you."

"So, you don't think I'm crazy?"

"Oh, you are, baby." He leans in, brushing his nose along my neck. "But so am I."

His hands gently touch my belly.

"How many of these things did you see yourself having?" I ask, out of curiosity. I've never put much thought into this. I never imagined this would be my life.

He looks deep in thought. "Three?"

"Let's see how we do with one first."

With a soft touch, he presses his lips against my neck, his fingers venturing beneath the fabric of my top.

My eyes close and I lose myself to the bliss of his touch. "You were in love with Leila?"

"I was." His words feather against my skin.

"Is that why you wanted us to have a baby so badly? You want another chance at being a dad?"

"No. That wasn't why." He pulls back, his face now expressionless.

I push one of his dark locks away from his temple. "I'm not mad, Frankie. I get it. You lost everything, now you can have something back."

"You think I don't love you?" His eyes squint.

It's hard processing all of this new information. Finding out this was the life he had ripped away from him hurts because I know it must have ruined him.

I've known that I was in love with him for a long time. I tried to fight it, but it was a losing battle. My heart belonged to him from the moment we met.

"I love you, Frankie. You brought me to life and I want to give you this, the family you deserve. I'll always be by your side, no matter what. Even if you never love me completely, I know I'm enough for you. I know, in your own way, you love me, too."

I press a gentle kiss to his cheek, closing my eyes and resting my forehead against his.

"Look at me, Zara."

I feel the tender touch of his hands as they rest on my cheeks. I couldn't tear my eyes from his, even if I wanted to. That is the effect he has on me. It will only ever be him for me.

"In every single lifetime, it will always be you, Zara. I would go through the torture I've dealt with a thousand times over if it meant that you were my reward. You make everything worth it. Every ounce of pain I've ever felt was to bring me to you.

My undying love for you is unquestionable. No matter what life throws at us. You, Zara. You are my inevitable, my love and my purpose."

My cheeks are stained with tears. My heart feels like it's about to burst.

"I love you, Zara. With every part of me. Our future is not my past. It was never about that. It was purely out of my love for you."

"Frankie," I whisper. I can hardly get my words out. "I shouldn't have said that. I'm so sorry."

I'm ashamed I even accused him, my own insecurities getting in the way. If this man never said the words, he shows me every day he loves me. He proves it in his actions.

"I'm glad you did. You needed to know everything. Now we've laid it all out, we don't look back, only forward."

"I never realized you could feel a love this strong. It's kind of scary, isn't it?"

"I'm not scared of it. It's our power. It's what will set us apart from the rest."

"Any change in your stance on the proper proposal?" I pout at him. Not that I need that now. I will be Mrs. Falcone, regardless.

"Yes," he mutters between kisses. "If you pass the last test."
"Which is?"

"Giving yourself over to me, let me take away all of your control. Let me set you free."

He slides a finger along my pussy,

With a swift motion, he scoops me up by the waist and delicately sets me down on the smooth surface of the table.

"I need to go and get us set up upstairs. Give me ten minutes. I want you naked with your head down as you enter the room. Upstairs, I own you. This is the ultimate statement of trust. I won't take that lightly, I promise. Do you want this, Zara?"

I swallow, looking into his eyes.

I trust him to protect me, to protect our child. It's an easy answer.

"Yes, sir."

He drops a hot kiss on my lips.

"Good girl. Ten minutes, okay?"

"Okay."

He runs his hands through my hair, looking into the depths of my soul that he owns.

"I love you."

I can't even hide my smile.

"Ti amo," I whisper back. "Sei la mia anima gemelli." *You are my soulmate.*

CHAPTER FORTY-FIVE

Frankie

Song- Easy to Love, Bryce Savage

I swear to God I stop breathing the second she appears, head bowed, hands clasped, and completely naked.

I take a second to admire my view.

It's like a weight has been lifted from my shoulders. Telling her the truth, both of us laying our cards on the table.

There is nothing either of us could have said that would have changed how we feel.

Pure fucking love.

"W-where do you want me?" she whispers. I can smell her desire from here.

"Shh, no talking." I walk towards her and she stays completely still. "Take my belt off."

She sucks in a quick breath, and her hands reach for my waist.

She slides it from my pants and holds it out to me. I take it and wrap both of her wrists behind her back. Then, I pick up the black blindfold from the bed and slip it over her head.

"Perfect," I groan, tipping her chin up to see her. I taste her lips and she moans into my mouth instantly.

"I bet you're already soaked for me. Aren't you?"

She nods silently. I trail my hand down her trembling chest and smooth belly. She opens her legs as I reach her pussy. Lightly, I stroke along her slick slit.

"So wet," I whisper against her ear and watch the goosebumps form. I bring my finger to her lips and pry them apart, sliding the tip in.

"Isn't it delicious?"

"Hmm hmmm," she swirls her tongue around my finger and my dick wants to explode.

"Let's get you prepped, shall we?" I lead her to the edge of the bed and bend her over, so her ass is in the air. Stepping behind her, a whimper escapes her as I drag my index finger down her spine and between her cheeks.

"Wider."

She shuffles her legs apart, her dripping pussy now on display for me.

I drop to my knees and part her ass and start feasting on her. She lets out a strangled cry, as if she's holding back.

"Be as loud as you want, dolcezza. Let me hear you."

I lick all the way from her clit to her entrance and up to her tight, puckered hole. I circle it lightly and she jolts forward.

I pull her back and keep going.

"Frankie," she pants and I reward her by thrusting three fingers in her pussy all the way to the knuckle.

I tease her ass with my wet finger, and she sucks in a breath.

"Yes," she cries and I bite back my smile.

Complete and utter perfection.

"You like being filled in both holes?"

"Y-yes," she whimpers.

My cock painfully throbs at her words. I slap down on her hip with my free hand and she screams.

"Come for me."

She's so close, her walls tighten around my fingers. She's resisting, holding back.

"Surrender to me. Fucking. Come. Now."

With a final smack, she explodes around me and I keep fucking her through it, as she squirms on the bed.

I let her catch her breath for a moment as I free her wrists.

"Now you're ready."

As I lift her body, she clings to me, her arms tightly wrapped around my neck, and we make our way towards the sling hanging from the chains to the ceiling.

She lets out a small gasp as I lay her chest on the cool leather. It pushes her breasts up, teasing me with her piercings.

Brushing her hair away from her neck, I tighten the collar around her throat and spread her arms so they can be snugged into the wrist restraints.

Seeing her like this, hanging and fastened at my mercy, she is magnificent. Her dark tendrils splay against the pale skin of her back. Suspended and waiting, she has me aching in need.

A shaky breath escapes her lips as she nervously bites down on her bottom lip.

"Such a good fucking girl."

"Frankie, please, I need you." Her voice is barely a whisper, laced with pure desperation.

"We had one rule, Zara. You let me make every choice. You don't get to beg, not now. So, it looks like I'm going to have to punish you."

My cock throbs painfully at the thought of my belt welting her delectable ass.

Chapter Forty-Six

Zara

Song- Chills- Dark Version, Mickey Valen, Joey Myron

My body vibrates against the leather as he picks up my ankle and clasps it to the chains. All my weight is held in the swing. Between that and the blindfold, every single sense is heightened.

I can feel his breath beat against my skin.

The anticipation in itself has me teetering on the edge.

"How badly do you want my cock?" His husky voice sends ripples through me.

"I need it, sir." I barely recognize my own needy words.

His firm hand caresses my ass. I bite down on my tongue as his belt cracks down. Stars fill my vision and I scream, shaking in my restraints.

I try to lift my head, but it tightens the collar around my neck, leaving me gasping for air as he places a soft kiss on my tender flesh.

I open my mouth to beg him to fuck me and quickly stop myself.

"Just one more, baby," he groans.

My pussy pulses. I can't concentrate on anything else other

than the sting on my ass. I clench my fists. The belt connects with my flesh on the other side and I lose it.

Tears slip from my eyes, and I tug on my restraints,

"Fuck!" I cry out.

Before I can register the pain from the spanking, he thrusts inside me and it is pure ecstasy.

"Ride out the pain, angel."

I stretch around him, focusing only on the sensation of him hitting against that sweet spot.

"Fuck, yes," he grunts.

I gasp as he slaps my pussy, ferociously pounding into me from behind.

"Let me come," I beg, "please."

I can't hold it off. My whole body is tingling. I'm ready to combust.

I shiver as he pulls out, then I hear the familiar buzzing of my vibrator. I try to push myself back as I feel the tip of his cock press against my asshole.

Frankie growls out my name as he starts to fuck my ass, and the vibrator enters my pussy. He ups the momentum, both thrusting inside me at the exact same time. I've never felt so full, so completely consumed.

"I can't take anymore."

"You can and you will. You will take everything I give you."

"Frankie!"

"Jesus, Zara." His voice is strained. "Break for me, baby," he orders.

I shatter around him until I can't physically give him anymore.

I drop my head, focusing on my breath as Frankie pulls out of me. He lets my ankles free first and they fall to either side of the sling.

I squeeze my eyes shut as he removes the blindfold.

"Look at me." His face softens as I do as he says.

He releases my wrist, pulls my spent body up and cuddles me against his chest before laying us down on the bed.

My head hits the pillow and my body sinks into the soft mattress.

Without a word, he presses his lips to mine.

"How was that?"

Overwhelming, intense, perfect.

"Everything I never knew I needed."

He nods.

"For you?" I ask, curiosity getting the better of me. Is this what he does with every woman? Is this what he expects all the time?

"Complete and utter perfection."

I roll onto my back and wince as my ass hits the covers.

Frankie rolls off the bed and disappears into the bathroom, reappearing with a bottle of lotion.

"Lay on your front for me, baby."

I do and rest my head on my hands.

"God, just looking at this is making me hard again."

In response, I let out a soft hum as he begins to gently massage my delicate skin, causing my eyes to flutter shut.

"That feels so nice," I whisper.

His hand slides between my thighs, and I open my legs. Despite my body being completely exhausted, I can't resist him.

"Let me take care of you?"

"Please do."

After massaging the lotion, he turns me over and positions himself between my knees, settling his face beneath my belly.

He keeps his eyes pinned on me as he starts to softly lick me. I bring my knees up and run my fingers through his hair.

"Mmm, yes."

He slowly circles my clit with the tip of his tongue and I roll my hips, letting the waves of pleasure roll through me.

He reaches over to the bedside table and picks up what looks like a small white ball.

Sitting on his heels, he places it in his mouth and I cry out as the icy cold connects with my pussy.

He runs the smooth ice along my hot center.

I spread my legs wider, desperate for more. I've never experienced anything quite like this in my life. His frozen touch isn't melting away any of this burning heat inside of me.

His eyes pin on mine. "Take a deep breath, baby."

I do as he says, watching him intently, my body shaking from built up desire.

"All the way out now."

I blow out the air slowly. He licks his lips and pushes the ice inside of me. My eyes go wide as I adjust to it.

What the fuck.

He crawls up my body, laying on top of me, his hand between my legs still circling my clit lightly.

"How does it feel?"

"Good, cold, burning."

His fingers tease my entrance and I'm a quivering mess.

"You are soaking my fingers, baby. So Goddamn perfect."

I can feel the cold liquid spilling out of me as it melts. I wiggle my hips, trying anything to release this pressure.

"Focus on how good it feels, dolcezza. Just relax for me," he says in a low and commanding tone.

I grit my teeth together, trying to hold off for him.

"I need to come, Frankie, sir."

"And you will, the only way you get to do that is with my cock buried deep inside of you."

That's exactly what I want. I want him to consume every single part of me. Anything is his.

He presses his lips against mine.

I open my mouth to let his tongue explore and his hands fist in my hair.

"Oh, my god." I arch my back off the bed. I can't take much more. All I want is him.

I gasp as he thrusts his fingers inside me, his name rolling off my tongue. Lining his cock up to my entrance, he cups my face with one hand, while the other grips onto the headboard.

"So beautiful." He thrusts into me. "So perfect." He kisses me.

"Mine," I reply.

With every thrust bringing me closer to the edge, the way he commands my mouth, stroking my face, it sets me on fire.

"Always mine, angel. I love you."

"I love you, sir."

CHAPTER FORTY-SEVEN

Zara

By the time we arrive at the End Zone, Maddie and Sienna are busy decorating the VIP area with gold and black balloons, ordering Keller around to reach all the high spots. They're throwing one hell of a party for New Year's Eve and we've been summoned in to help.

Just after me, Jax walks in, letting out a tired yawn.

"Long night?" I ask him.

"You could say that again." He throws down his helmet on one of the tables as Kai passes him a beer.

"You look like you need one of these," Kai says.

Jax shakes his head, almost going green. "I can't."

"Pussy!" Keller shouts out, just as a balloon pops above his head.

It makes me jump back into Frankie's arms.

"Keller, concentrate!" Sienna admonishes him.

"Where do you need me?" I ask.

Maddie bundles a few boxes of red confetti at me. "Can you start throwing this over the tables, please?" She blows her bright blonde hair out of her face and gives me a smile.

"Jax, get your ass up. I need you checking the bar stock," Keller calls over his shoulder.

Jax groans, nudging Kai next to him.

"Give me a hand?" he says, his voice croaky.

"Fine." Kai rolls his eyes at his friend.

"Where do you want me?" Frankie asks and Maddie turns, beaming at him.

"You can go and help Grayson move the DJ equipment into the other side of the room."

"Fine," he responds, unamused.

With a smile, I turn to Frankie and place a gentle kiss on his cheek, feeling the warmth of his skin against my lips.

"Have fun with that."

Before I can retreat, he holds me tighter, pressing his tongue into my mouth.

"Enough of that, we don't have time!" Maddie claps her hands next to us and we both pull back and laugh.

"You heard the boss," Frankie whispers.

I watch Frankie stride out of the VIP area, and I get to work throwing confetti over the tables. As I look up at Maddie, the room begins to whirl around me, and a wave of nausea washes over me.

"Zara, are you okay?"

My mouth starts watering to the point all I can do is nod.

"I'll be right back." I hastily exit the room and sprint down the hallway, the nauseating sensation building until I finally reach the toilet to empty my stomach.

When I finally finish, I sit back on the floor, rubbing my lower belly with a smile on my face. "You're already just like your daddy, always testing me."

Even feeling like complete crap, I know it will all be worth it in a few months to hold this little one in my arms.

Dragging myself up to my feet, I go and splash some cold water over my face. As I leave, a breeze brushes along my shirt and I take in a deep breath. The chill instantly makes me feel better.

I head towards the fire escape, slipping out and feeling the cold air embrace my body as I lean against the rough brick wall. Closing my eyes, I take deep breaths in and out to mellow the queasy feeling.

Footsteps crunch on the leaves on the floor. I look up and Alex's imposing figure walking towards me. My eyes quickly dart down, and I catch sight of the pistol in his hands, causing a rush of adrenaline through my veins.

Shit.

"Alex, what are you doing?" I try to keep my voice calm.

"If you want to save yourself, I wouldn't move."

"Don't do this, Alex." I warn as he takes a step closer.

He lets out an exasperated sigh. "I'm not here to hurt you, Zara. I just need to talk to you somewhere, not here."

"You say, with a gun pointed at me?"

As I reach for my own weapon, he raises his other arm.

"Zara, I have the location of the last two girls. Please, just come with me."

I hesitate, searching his face. He's pleading with me, his eyes filled with desperation. A slight tremor runs through his hand as he holds it out.

"Give me that."

"No," I reply.

He lunges forward, wrenching it from my grasp, and it clatters loudly to the pavement.

As he grabs my wrist, I feel the cold metal of his barrel pressing into my back, urging me to move.

"I don't want it to be like this, Zara. You have to believe me."

I suck in a breath. It's not just me anymore. I have to think about our baby. I can't be reckless or scare Alex into doing something stupid.

He leads me down the alleyway to his black mustang.

"I'm sorry, Zara," he says with sincerity. I frown as he cuffs my wrists and forcefully pats me down before taking my phone.

"Get in." He opens the passenger door and waits, his tone leaving no room for argument.

"Don't fucking touch me," I hiss as he reaches to help me.

The engine roars to life, its thunderous sound echoing through the air as he pulls out. His jaw clenches and his knuckles turn white from gripping the steering wheel.

"Well? Start talking, Alex."

"I will. I just need to get us somewhere safe."

My heart rate picks up.

"What do you mean 'safe'?"

He shakes his head. "Look, I'm under instructions to keep

you away. I can't risk my family."

"Well, I can't risk mine either, Alex."

Tears sting in my eyes. I have to warn Frankie. I have to do anything to get out of this.

He continues the drive, the only sound being the loud hum of the engine. We must have been on the road for half an hour. My hands rise, brushing against my face as I pretend to scratch it. In my balled fist, I securely hold on to one of my bobby pins.

"Why do you care about protecting me?" I ask, trying to get him talking to me again.

"I was told to keep you away from Frankie, okay? I just think something else is going down and I can't have you getting caught up in this."

My body stiffens.

"What do you mean?"

"I can't do this anymore, Zara. I fucking hate what I've become. I don't know how to escape; they are holding my father's life over my head. I couldn't let them hurt you. You don't deserve it. I've seen you working your ass off to save those women. You're a good person."

"I don't care about me. What do you mean, you 'think something big is happening'?"

"I heard them talking, something about making a play for power."

"Where?"

"I don't know. All I know is, I was told to be on duty and keep you away from Frankie. That was my order."

I pound my fists against my knees in frustration. "Turn the fucking car around and take me back to him, Alex."

His jaw tightens.

"I can't, Zara, I'm sorry."

As we pull up into an abandoned warehouse, I notice the broken windows and graffiti-covered walls in front of me. As soon as he pulls to a stop and the locks click, he jumps out.

I keep the bobby pin tight in my grip as he opens the passenger door and helps me out.

Before we reach the front of the building, I dig my feet into the ground, forcing him to face me.

"You're pathetic, you know that, right?" I spit out, full of venom.

"I've only done what I had to do. Same as you, right?"

"Trafficking women? Really, Alex? How the fuck is that the same?"

"Chad, did he deserve to die?"

I take a step forward, straightening the bobby pin discretely as Frankie showed me to do at the docks.

"He did, yes. He went for his gun. He was in my goddamn apartment under your orders. You killed your own friend, Alex. Not me. You put him there, because your spineless ass couldn't do it."

"I don't have a fucking choice," he shouts, throwing his arms up in the air.

"There is always a choice, Alex. You just picked the wrong side of this. Let me guess, you're getting paid a good sum for this, too?"

His face drops, telling me everything I need to know.

"You better hope to god nothing happened to those girls, or my Frankie, Alex. Or, I'll end you myself."

With each step I take, his piercing stare intensifies.

Keeping him distracted with my onslaught of aggression, I start wiggling the metal in the cuffs, waiting to hit resistance.

"I want out, Zara. I need your help."

I let out a laugh. "You have to be kidding me. You'll be lucky to get out of this without a bullet through your skull."

"I'm doing this for you! I don't want to be doing this anymore, Zara!" His face reddens.

"Do the right thing, then. Let me speak to Frankie and let's save the girls. That's the only way you get out alive, Alex."

He shakes his head. "I can't do that."

The lock clicks. In a swift movement, I shake them off and make a lunge for the gun in his holster.

CHAPTER FORTY-EIGHT

Frankie

"**F**rankie!" Maddie's piercing shriek sends me scrambling back into the VIP area.

Tears stain her cheeks. "I can't find Zara. She ran out to the bathroom a few minutes ago. She was so pale. I just went and checked. She isn't there."

With each step I take, my heart races faster, each beat reverberating through my entire body.

"Start looking!" I order the rest of them and storm out down the hall.

"ZARA!" I shout, barging open the doors along my path. Nothing.

"ZARA!" I repeat, heading out to the back. Maybe she needed some air. She's been struggling the last couple of days with dizziness.

My gaze falls to the ground, and a jolt of agony pierces my chest as I spot her gun lying there.

Fuck.

Dialing Enzo's cell, he picks up on the first ring.

"Track Zara's phone. Send me the location."

"Shit. Okay."

Keller, Jax, Kai and Grayson appear by my side.

Enzo's voice cuts in over the clicking of keys in the background. "She's on the move. I'll send you live updates."

Grayson tosses me his keys to his Audi.

"Let's go. Keller, you stay here with the girls," I order.

"Got it, boss," he says, his hands clenched into fists at his sides.

I look at the moving dot on my screen.

"Can you find her on the traffic cams? Who's fucking car is it, Enzo?"

He pauses before he answers. "It belongs to an Alex Pierce."

I don't have time to spare; I have to get to her.

As we jump in Grayson's car, the engine roars to life, and I put my foot down as soon as we hit the road. My heart is in my throat the entire time.

A million different visions running through my mind of losing her.

"Boss, we've got her. Keep your head," Jax says from the backseat.

"I can't. Not until I've got her back."

"We will, Frankie." Grayson chimes in.

I really fucking hope we do.

We follow the live tracker for twenty minutes, heading further into the outskirts of New York. Where the fuck is he going?

"They've stopped," G says beside me.

"Where?"

About three minutes away, I glance over and he's zooming in on the screen.

"I don't know, maybe a warehouse? Regardless, we're ready." He pops open the glove box and starts handing out weapons like candy.

"Oh, fuck." I mutter, slamming on the brakes as we enter the parking lot. All I see is Zara pointing a gun at Alex, who has his arms up, his back against the wall.

I throw open the door and run towards her.

"Zara!"

She doesn't take her aim from Alex when she turns her head to me. I quickly scan her body, looking for marks and relief washes over me when I don't see any.

The guys follow behind me as I unholster my pistol.

"On your fucking knees, Alex," I command.

G steps to his side as Alex drops to the ground, a quivering mess, and presses his barrel against his head.

"Jesus fucking Christ, Zara." I let out a breath and wrap my arms around her.

My eyes flick to the abandoned building behind us.

"Take him in there, tie him up. I'll be there shortly," I say to Grayson.

Kai waits with me as Grayson and Jax drag Alex into the warehouse.

As I cup Zara's face in my hands, I can feel her pulse quickening beneath my fingertips.

"Are you okay, dolcezza?"

I glance down, spotting the handcuffs on the ground. She follows my gaze and grins.

"I used the trick you taught me."

"Good girl." I press a kiss to her forehead.

"Alex knows something, Frankie. He's on the verge of breaking. He's going on about something going down tonight and how he wants out. He said he knows where the last two girls are."

Interesting.

"Fine work, detective." I smirk at her.

"What do we do now?" she asks.

"You and Kai go back to the End Zone with Keller and the girls. I can't concentrate unless I know you're safe. We are sitting ducks here, Zara. I don't know who owns this place, or what the bigger plan was here. I can't risk it, not now."

I place my hands on her stomach, reminding her of the importance of not just her safety, but for our baby as well.

Handing her the keys, she shakes her head, refusing to take them.

"I don't want to leave you, Frankie." She blinks back the tears and I stroke her cheek with my thumb.

"I'll be perfectly fine. I'll get what I need from Alex and I'll have Enzo come and get us. I won't be long, baby. I promise."

Pressing a kiss on her lips, I pull her tightly to my chest. I need her protected and away from this.

"You made me proud today, baby," I whisper.

"You found me pretty quick."

"I told you, I'll always find you. Now, get your ass back to the club." My hand pats her hip as I let her free from my embrace.

"I will." She takes her hand back with the keys, looking behind me to Kai. "I'm driving!" she calls out, looking at the RS7 Grayson owns.

"Be careful," I warn her.

"Always." She winks.

I stand back, watching as she pulls out of the lot, and I can breathe again. She's safe with Kai and Keller; the End Zone is on lockdown for now. My phone buzzes in my pocket.

> **Enzo: I'm on my way to you. Will be 15 minutes. Your army is at the End Zone.**

With the knowledge that Zara will be safe, I head into the dark warehouse.

"I suggest you start fucking talking, Alex," I spit out as Jax is putting the rope around his neck. I look up and find Grayson tossing the end over one of the metal beams in the ceiling.

"Get him up on the crate, Jax," G calls.

Sweat drips down Alex's forehead. "Please, Frankie."

I nudge my head, instructing him to listen to them. With a sigh, he steps up on the wooden pallet and G sets the length.

"Why did you take my girl from me, Alex? Of all the things you could have possibly done. Why?"

"I-I was trying to help."

"Help?" I laugh and step towards the edge of the crate. "Help me how?"

"I was trying to keep her safe, okay?" His voice cracks as he speaks.

"Safe from who?"

He stares hard at me, following me with his eyes as I walk behind him. "You, Frankie."

I pull back my fist and slam it into his left kidney. He screams out in agony.

CHAPTER FORTY-NINE

Zara

Keller's eyes remain fixed on the phone, his grip growing tighter with each passing second.

"Can't we just go back?" I ask, sipping on my water to try to calm my nerves.

I don't want to be here. I want to be with Frankie.

Keller's piercing gaze darts around the room, his tense jawline making me feel uneasy.

He shakes his head.

"We have our orders, Zara. We sit tight. We've shut the place down and put armed guards outside. We have to keep you and the girls safe. End of discussion."

He looks over at his pregnant wife, who is busy with Maddie taking down some decorations, seeing as the party is officially over. "He's just protecting you, Zara. We would all do the same."

"I don't need protecting, Keller."

He hums and takes a swallow of his scotch. "Sometimes we need protecting from ourselves."

I sigh, watching how Keller softens the second Sienna slips

on his lap. His huge hand strokes her belly bump.

I wonder what I'm having. Maybe it's a little boy with Frankie's gray eyes and my black hair. I hope he has Frankie's tanned skin rather than my pasty white Irish skin.

I shuffle in my seat as tears brim in my eyes.

"Are you okay, Zara?" Kai whispers beside me. I can't speak. I just want Frankie back here. This waiting around is killing me.

"Not really," I whisper back, wiping away a stray tear.

Placing my hands on my belly, I have to focus on them. I have to be strong.

I look up to see Sienna and Keller are both watching me with confusion on their faces. If anyone can understand, it will be them.

"I'm pregnant," I blurt out.

Keller's eyes widen. "Well, congratulations." The shock is clear in his voice.

"Oh, Zara." Sienna jumps off her husband's lap and rounds the table, wrapping her arms around my shoulders. "It's all going to be okay, I promise," she says in her soft British accent.

I nod, but her words don't bring me any comfort.

"I can't just sit here and do nothing, Keller. It's not who I am."

Something isn't sitting right with me about Alex. Why did he need me away from Frankie? What did he mean about tonight?

"I've sworn to protect you with my goddamn life, Zara. That is what being part of this family is about. Stop fighting me on it."

I know exactly what he means. It's the same way I feel about Frankie and our baby. It's the kind of love you would take a bullet for.

"I get it, Keller, I do. I just don't expect you to put yourself in harm's way. Like you said, you've got a family, they need you."

He nods, a solemn look passing across his face.

"I need a pee. I'll be back in a minute," Sienna says, looking at her husband.

Keller points to the guards by the door who open it for Sienna, and Maddie runs after her.

"We are all a family here, Zara. You included," Keller says, still deep in thought.

I smile up at him.

"I appreciate that. Thank you."

For the first time in my life, I belong somewhere, just by being myself. My past doesn't matter to any of these guys.

CHAPTER FIFTY

Frankie

With anticipation building inside me, I place my foot on the crate, fully prepared to bring an end to his existence. I wipe the sweat beading on my forehead. I just want to be back with Zara.

"W-where did Zara go?" Alex asks, looking around the room, making me hesitate.

"Someplace safe."

"No, no. She's not." The panic in his blue eyes has me taking a step back.

"You don't get to mention her name," I say through gritted teeth. "Where is Romano, and where are the girls, Alex?"

"I-I don't know where Romano is. All I know is he's planning something big. George just instructed me to keep Zara away from you."

My pulse picks up as the realization settles over me. Jax shoots me a worried look. I bet he's thinking the same as me.

"What specifically did they say about Zara?"

"I was just told to keep her busy tonight, keep her away from you. I just wanted to keep her safe, Frankie. I'd never harm her."

I swear my heart fucking stops.

"No." I close my eyes. This cannot be happening.

"We need to go," I say to Grayson and Jax, already making my way to the exit. I'm not about to let history repeat itself.

"You can't just leave me here!" Alex whines as I reach the door.

"You better hope to fucking god nothing happens to her, Alex," I seethe at him.

We jump in Enzo's Aston Martin. "We gotta get back to the End Zone, as quick as you fucking can, Enzo." I can barely get my words out.

"What's going on, boss?" Grayson asks.

I hope I'm wrong.

I need to get her away from here–far, far away.

Keller picks up on the first ring.

"Tell me Zara is still with you."

"Yes. She's sitting here with me. Sienna and Maddie are in the ladies' room. We have our men surrounding the club. We're all fine here."

"No one is to come in or out. Do you understand me, Keller?"

"I got it, boss. They won't."

I won't be able to breathe until I have her in my arms. I turn to Enzo, who concentrates on the road.

"I'll have some of our guys pick up Alex and bring him back to the safe house. We can finish him off there and get the girls location," Grayson says from the back seat.

"That's fine."

The tension is so thick, I could cut it with a knife. I need that asshole alive. I'll get the answers I need and I will fucking end this.

Romano may be out here somewhere. I have lived, breathed and survived with one aim; to kill him.

Now, my life has a new purpose. I will still end that motherfucker and I will make it hurt. But it is not anywhere as important to me as Zara.

There isn't a price on my devotion to her.

I rush out of the car as Enzo pulls up, not waiting for him to stop.

The information Alex shared does not sit right with me at all. I need her as much as I need air to breathe.

With every step closer to the entrance, the more I can relax. She's inside. Nothing has happened. I can protect her and our baby with my life from this second on.

Grayson, Jax and Enzo are right on my tail as we approach the neon signs of the club. That big red door to the VIP area is in my sights.

The echoing boom, a sound that is deeply ingrained in my memory, resonates along the street. The crowd outside erupts into a frenzy of screams that engulf me, causing my heart to fucking stop.

The force of the impact knocks me down to the ground. My hands instinctively shield my head, the explosion rips the air from my lungs.

My vision is completely consumed by the sight of angry

flames pouring out of the club's shattered glass windows.

I can't let this happen again. Not a chance in hell.

As I claw to my feet and stumble forwards, a deep roar erupts from deep within me. I feel a searing pain slicing through my chest, causing my vision to blur.

Time goes still, and I am completely numb to the pain.

"Zara!" I scream.

The smell of smoke fills the air as I drag myself towards the burning building, the sound of glass crunches beneath my feet. I don't even allow myself time to think as I run as fast as I can towards the VIP entrance.

Not a single thing matters in my life. Her life comes above my own.

If I have to follow her into the next life, I fucking will.

Chapter Fifty-One

Zara

I just manage to open my eyes.

Orange embers float around the room, and as I look up, the red confetti breezes past me. The room is filled with the suffocating thick smoke as it boils from the flames around me.

Fire engulfs the main area of the club. With each attempt to roll onto my side, the glass embedded in the ground cuts deeper into my arms.

"Keller," I cough as soon as I speak.

The air is heavy, making it hard to breathe.

I try to move my numb limbs, it's like I'm in water.

He has to be here somewhere. The last thing I remember was him sitting opposite me.

With each movement, I can feel the strain in my arms as I drag my body across the floor.

"Here," he croaks out, sitting up. A gasp escapes my lips as I take in the sight of the gaping wound on his head.

"Fuck, Zara. Don't move." His eyes go wide and he scrambles across the rubble, holding onto my face and shrugging off his jacket, placing it over my stomach. "It's going to be fine. Just don't look down. I'll get you out of here."

"How bad is it?" I rasp out as I struggle to keep my eyes open. The pain is there, but the adrenaline flowing through my veins is blocking everything else.

He lifts my top half of my body, as I look up I see Kai. He's so pale. A steady flow of blood is pouring out from his head and forming a pool beside him.

"Keller, you have to get Kai out of here." I nod over to him.

He glances over, then drops his chin. "Shit."

The thumping in my head gets louder. I rub my temple and hiss out in pain.

"Kai," I say weakly. Why isn't he answering?

A warm liquid smothers my hands, and I bring my fingers in front of my eyes. All I see is blood.

A loud creak comes from above us and the chandelier starts to shake.

"Keller, what the fuck is happening?"

Before he can reply, he looks up. The crack that splits across the concrete above us is getting bigger. Before I can speak, he drops his body over me, covering me completely.

The ceiling collapses. The impact on Keller's body crushes me further into the rubble.

It's hard to breathe. He's too heavy. Weakly, I try to push his arm as stars begin to fill my vision. I feel like I'm floating as everything blurs together into one haze.

"Zara!" I faintly hear my name.

I'm not sure if I'm hallucinating. It sounds familiar; it takes away some of the fear.

CHAPTER FIFTY-TWO

Frankie

"Boss, come on." Jax calls out as we head into the smoke and towards the big double doors that lead to the VIP area.

I hold my breath, knowing this could very well be the moment that shatters me into a million pieces.

I almost stumble over an unconscious body on the floor. One of Keller's men is laid out but breathing. My guys rush in to evacuate as many people as possible as ambulance sirens blare in the background.

"ZARA!" I call out.

Glass cracks under my boot.

"Over here, Frankie!" Jax calls out, and I follow his voice.

"Fuck!" he shouts, and it makes my heart drop.

That's when I see her arm, blood dripping from the shards splintering her skin.

I fight the urge to throw up as I see Keller resting on top of her. Rubble from the ceiling covers them.

Crimson drips from the back of Keller's head onto the broken concrete.

I dive across, feeling the sharp edges of debris scrape against my skin, while Jax positions himself on the other side of an unresponsive Keller. Together, we carefully push away the chunks and roll him onto his back. "Don't move his head. Keep him as still as you can. We need a stretcher in here!" I hope my voice can carry over the cries of so many injured.

Jax's hands are covered in Keller's blood as we maneuver him.

I carefully pick up Zara. I can barely see through my blurry vision.

"No," I whisper as I spot the glass sticking out from her abdomen.

"He has a pulse. It's fucking weak," Jax says. I can't even comprehend his words.

"Go and get a fucking stretcher!" I call out to our guys coming in through the door.

"I gotta find, Kai. Where the fuck is he?" I can hear the panic rising in Jax's voice as the stretcher gets placed next to Keller.

"You can't move, not until they take Keller, Jax."

"Kai!" he shouts out.

Nothing.

"Come on, baby." I pick Zara up in my arms, cradling her to my chest.

As I reach the door, I stop as Jax lets out what can only be described as a scream of utter heartbreak. Enough to tell me that Kai didn't make it.

I know his pain, I've felt it.

I close my eyes, resting against Zara's cold face. Her little shallow breaths are enough to keep me sane.

Grayson strides in, fury on his face. "Maddie and Sienna are safe. Keller?"

Jax's cries rip through the building and Grayson looks at me.

"Kai," I whisper.

"Go and help him, G. You know what to do." I nod to him.

I head straight to the nearest ambulance, and they help me lay her down on a stretcher inside. I take a seat next to her as the paramedics get to work, placing an oxygen mask over her mouth.

My entire life is on that bed and now, there isn't a single thing I can do to make this right.

"She's pregnant."

The paramedics look at each other. I know what they're thinking.

The same thing as me.

"Are you the father?"

"Yes."

"How far along is she?"

"Eleven weeks."

Resting my head in my hands, I pull at my hair. Romano is going to fucking pay, him and anyone involved will die for this.

I keep my eyes on Zara, the woman who owns my damn heart, and remember this moment. I will use it to fuel me to end this war. For her and for our baby.

CHAPTER FIFTY-THREE

Frankie

With one hand holding hers, the other stroking her stomach, I am completely fucking numb.

"Come on, angel. Come back to me."

I can't do this without her. The thought of having to rip her heart out when she wakes up makes me want to vomit.

She went straight into surgery and it was the worst two hours of my life. They managed to remove the glass and fix any internal damage. The scans showed there is no major head trauma. A few broken ribs, she's going to be fine.

That's the only thing keeping me together.

I squeeze her hand tighter. We have lost our future. Our baby is gone.

I stroke my thumb along the front of her hand. I'm so distracted in my own head, I don't hear Grayson come through the door.

"Any improvements?" Grayson asks, and I shake my head.

"Keller?" I ask.

The pain flashes across his face.

"The surgery went as well as they could hope. They stopped

the bleeding on his brain. It's all on him waking up now. He's in an induced coma."

Fuck. I will forever be grateful to Keller. He saved Zara's life.

"Did you call Luca?"

"He's on his way home, boss. We need all of our family together to get through this."

I let out a shaky breath.

My family is lying next to me on a hospital bed.

I rub my eyes. I'm almost too tired to think. "Have Enzo pick them up. Rosa can stay with Maddie and the kids at the safe house. Luca needs to be here with his brother."

"You got it."

"Where's Jax?"

Kai's death is going to hit him hard. We have to do what we can to stop him going off the rails.

"With us, boss. He's not in a good way. He hasn't said a fucking word." Grayson runs his hand through his hair. The bags under his eyes tell me he feels just as exhausted as I am.

"As soon as Zara wakes up, I'll speak to him. We'll get him through this, G." I am not leaving this woman's side. Not now, not ever. "Until Zara is awake, I'm not moving."

"You really love her, don't you?"

"More than life. I'd take her fucking place in a heartbeat." I bow my head, not being able to say anymore.

Grayson's eyes go wide, fixating on my hand over the bandages on her stomach.

"Fuck. I'm so sorry."

"I don't need sorry, Grayson. I do need something else."

"Anything."

"Make sure Alex has been delivered back to our safe house and get the location of the girls. Tell Enzo we need Mikhail. I'm done fucking around. We're ending this."

"How much will the Russians want this time?"

"Like I said, I'd give my life. It doesn't matter."

"Got it." As he turns to leave, he stops. "Let us know about Zara, Frankie. We are all here for whatever you both need."

"Thank you, G. Keep me updated on Keller, and don't leave Jax on his own."

He gives me a curt nod and quietly shuts the door, leaving me with just my thoughts.

I squeeze my eyes shut. All I can see are the flames. The way her lifeless body felt in my arms. I trace circles around the engagement ring I slipped back on a little while ago.

Gently, I lift her hand to my lips and plant a soft kiss on her skin.

"I will make up for this. I will prove to you every day for the rest of our lives how much I love you. Let me worship you. Wake up, dolcezza. Please? I fucking need you, baby." I rest my head against her hand as my heart rapidly thumps in my chest.

I've fucked this up again.

But she's still alive. I know my girl is strong.

We can get through this, and we will burn the fucking world down, together.

CHAPTER FIFTY-FOUR

Zara

The intense brightness of the white lights makes my eyes ache as I struggle to keep them open. With a groan, I tilt my head from side to side, trying to alleviate the stiffness in my neck.

"Zara?" Frankie's voice floats around the room.

I can make out a shadow. I can feel him around me.

"Frankie?" I cough and pain rips through me.

"Don't move."

Alarms start ringing, causing my head to pound against my skull. "Turn it off."

He squeezes my hand, which calms the rising panic. Jesus, my mouth is so dry.

"You're okay, angel." Frankie reassures me and strokes my cheek. I can hear the pain in his voice, and it makes my heart start racing.

My eyes go heavy as I try to focus on him. But with the agony deep in my bones and throughout my entire body, it's too much.

All I can see is the flames, the blood on my hands. Keller's face as the ceiling collapsed.

Kai's lifeless body.

Fear takes over.

"Hey, stay with me, baby."

"Hmm," is all I manage to say before I fail to keep my eyes open any longer.

"We need to keep monitoring her, Mr. Falcone. Your fiancé has had surgery and inhaled a lot of smoke." The woman sounds like she's on her last leg of patience.

His voice is rough. "You said the scans showed no lasting damage. So why the fuck isn't she waking up?"

"Because she isn't ready, sir."

My eyes flutter open at the commotion. I squeeze Frankie's hand and he turns to me, his red eyes meeting mine.

"Zara."

"Frankie." My throat is so dry, it hurts to talk.

"How are you feeling? Does anything hurt?" His hand cups my cheek and I lean into his touch.

"Everything." I try to laugh, but it sends pain shooting through my ribs.

"Do you remember what happened, Zara?" the woman doctor asks, stepping forward next to Frankie.

"There was an explosion. Keller, he dived on top of me.

Maddie and Sienna–" I start to tremble, tears sliding down my face. "Please tell me they're okay, Frankie."

"Shhh, yes. They're both fine." His thumb wipes the droplet from my skin.

"What about Keller?"

He took the brunt of the force. I don't remember much else.

"He's had surgery. We're waiting for him to wake up." Frankie hesitates, as if he's holding back.

A sliver of fear shivers through me. "How bad is it?"

"His prognosis could be better." He leans closer. "Kai never made it though, Zara."

A sob catches in my throat. Frankie joins me on the bed, holding my hands. "It's going to be alright."

"The baby?" I all but whisper.

I hold my breath, waiting for the next blow. I don't know how much more I can handle before I break.

Frankie's face pales, grief written all over it.

"No," I cry out. "Don't say it."

I let out a whoosh of air, and the tears flow freely.

Frankie carefully wraps his arms around me, and I nuzzle my face into his chest.

"I'm sorry, Frankie. I'm so fucking sorry."

He sucks in a breath and hugs my head against his chest, my sorrow seeping through his white shirt. How can he be so calm?

How can he go through this again?

"No, angel. I'm fucking sorry."

I grip onto his suit and squeeze, wanting to rid myself of this agony.

"It hurts, so bad," I sob.

"I know, baby. I know."

I don't just mean the physical pain, it's the pain in my heart. The way it's crumbling is enough to make me numb.

He rests his head on mine, holding me so tight I can barely breathe.

"I love you," he whispers. His voice breaks, which shatters my world.

We've had our future, our baby, painfully ripped from us.

Nothing has felt quite like this in my life.

Chapter Fifty-Five

Frankie

Everything is a blur, as I fight to keep myself together for her. How much can one person lose before they finally snap?

I'm not sure, I must be seriously close now.

The second the door closes, she rips her hand from mine and balls her fists, bashing them against the bed, letting out a scream that is laced with raw agony.

"Why! Frankie! WHY?" she asks in defeat. She holds her face in her hands and her chest heaves.

Without thinking, I pull her tight against me.

"Shhh, it's going to be okay, baby." I don't know what else to say. I failed her. I failed our baby. I should never have let her leave my side.

This is my mistake to live with.

"It's not. It's not ever going to be okay." She shakes her head, her body trembling against me.

I ignore the pain in my chest. She needs me to be the one to pull her through this, no matter how hard that might be.

"Maybe we're just bad people who don't deserve to be parents,"

I stiffen at her words and pull back.

"You fucking deserve every damn thing in this world, Zara."

She sniffles, and I wipe away her tears from her puffy face.

"Then why would this happen to us?" Her bottom lip trembles and makes my heart splinter. I can't take much more.

"Because life is so fucking cruel, Zara. That doesn't mean we give up."

It's not her fault. It's mine, for letting Romano live. For not getting to the club quick enough.

I will never forgive myself for letting her down like this.

She tries to press her face into the pillow to muffle her sobs. I stroke her hair away from her face and gently pull her up. I need to look at her.

"Ti amo, Zara," I whisper, pressing my forehead against hers and closing my eyes.

"I love you, Frankie." It's barely a whisper. "I just want to sleep. Everything fucking hurts. I can't deal with it right now."

I pull back, searching her eyes. There is nothing there. It really fucking hurts watching the life drain out of the strongest woman I've ever met, and there isn't a single thing I can do to make this right.

I cuddle her against me, stroking her hair. Eventually, her sobs subside, I still don't let her go. I never will.

I will bring her back to me.

And we will seek our revenge against the entire fucking world for taking this away from us.

Chapter Fifty-Six

Zara

Song- Are You Really Okay? Sleep Token.

I lie still, my eyes fixed on the ceiling while Frankie peacefully slumbers beside me. We were supposed to go back to the safe house with everyone after I was discharged from the hospital. I couldn't face it.

Not with Sienna being pregnant and babies around.

It's too much.

I didn't want to be at the hospital either. Frankie called in a private doctor for the next few days.

I've barely spoken a word today. I thought when I woke up, it would hurt less. It doesn't.

Except now, my sadness is joined by hatred for the people who did this to us.

They took Kai's life and left Keller fighting for his.

It's hard seeing a man, as big and powerful as him, attached to monitors to keep him alive. It broke my heart that little bit more, I had to see him. To say thank you. He saved my life.

Now, I just want to be locked away from the world with Frankie.

I've cried so much, I've run out of tears.

The wound on my stomach might hurt, the cuts on my arms, the pounding headache I have. None of that compares to my broken heart. Painkillers can't fix that.

Frankie has barely left my side, trying to get me to eat something and take my pain meds. He's hurting, too. But, he puts on a brave face for me.

I sit up and lightly stroke his cheek. How he's been through this twice and is still standing, I don't know.

He never falters. He stays strong when I need him to. He has the strength for both of us. I'm spiraling down a path I don't see a way out of.

My every thought is, what could I have done differently?

"You okay, baby?" he whispers in his husky, sleepy voice.

"No. Not really." I fight the next onslaught of tears away.

"Come here." He opens his arms and I fall onto his chest, tracing my finger over the bullet wound on his shoulder.

"Who shot you?" I ask, needing a distraction from my own head.

"Maria. Well, the bullet was meant for Grayson."

"You're crazy, you know that? Not many people take a bullet for someone, let alone if that person hates them," I say.

"I'd do the same for you. It might make me crazy, but we're all a little mad."

"Hey! I'm not!" I laugh and immediately feel guilty for being anything other than sad.

He rumbles with laughter, sending vibrations through my

body.

"You stalked a mafia boss, kicked him in the balls, stuck a knife into his throat, and killed two men."

When I press my palm over his mouth, his eyes pierce into mine.

"Okay, okay, no need to continue–"

He licks his lips as I remove my hand,

"I love your crazy. I'm damn proud of every single one of those things. It's what makes you so perfect. Mine."

Sitting up, I press my lips against his, and the sensation of his fingers tangling in my hair heightens the intensity. It isn't our usual hungry and ferocious kiss. This is us, showing each other how much we truly love one another.

I squeeze my legs together. The urge to go to use the toilet is starting to make my lower belly ache. I've held off for as long as I can.

In the hospital, the nurse changed the pads for me. I don't know why, it made everything more real.

Seeing the blood as the loss we've had.

"I need to pee." My voice trails off in a silent plea for his help.

After a few seconds, he rolls out of bed and pulls on his boxers before making his way to my side.

He scoops me up with ease, his strong arms effortlessly carrying me into the bathroom.

"Sit. Keep your eyes on me. Don't look anywhere else."

The weight of his actions brings tears to my eyes, their meaning overwhelming. He knew my fear without me even saying a word.

As he pulls down my shorts and panties, his gaze remains fixed on me. I take in a trembling breath and settle onto the cold seat.

I close my eyes and try to relax, ignoring the pain in my stomach as I do.

"You're okay, angel."

As he opens the packet of pads, the crinkle of plastic echoes in the room.

My tears free fall down my cheeks. Wiping them with the back of my hand, I sneak a glimpse of him.

This moment is completely raw.

Bending to his knees, I stare into his loving eyes as he swiftly changes me. He hands me one of my cooling wipes, holding onto my fingers before I can take it.

"You are incredible, Zara. Truly."

I can't control my sobs, bowing my head to bury my face in my hands.

I don't feel incredible. I feel useless. I'm a failure.

"Come on, baby." He rubs small circles on my bare knees.

"I failed, Frankie. I couldn't do the one job I have as a mother: protect our baby."

Frankie helps me to my feet and pulls up my shorts for me. I wrap my arms around his waist and press my face into his naked chest, letting his steady heartbeat soothe me.

"Don't ever say that again. You are perfect. This was not your fault; you didn't fail them. Please don't think you did. No one except Romano and your father are to blame."

"Thank you, Frankie."

He gently rubs my back, soothing the tension in my muscles. "Anything, I mean every word. Now, just tell me what you need."

I pull back. His face is stoic, his jaw tight. I cup his face in my hands, and he leans into my touch, closing his eyes.

"Are you okay, Frankie?"

He simply nods. He's so good at burying his emotions, he could believe he truly is fine.

"You aren't sad?"

A darkness swiftly flashes over his eyes as they open. "Sad? No."

"Oh." I didn't expect that.

"Completely and utterly fucking devastated? Yes." With a gentle gesture, he covers my hand with his own.

"How do you stay so strong? I want to be like that." I'd give anything to not hurt like this.

He half laughs and shakes his head. "Trust me, you don't."

"You are just as strong as me, Zara. If not fucking stronger. Remember that," he whispers, nuzzling his head into my neck and kissing me softly there.

This is the first time I've felt anything other than numb in twenty-four hours. He brings me strength, and he brings me to life.

With him by my side, I can conquer anything.

CHAPTER FIFTY-SEVEN

Frankie

Song- Just Pretend, Bad Omens.

I wake up in the middle of the night to find Zara downstairs in the kitchen, sipping coffee at the dining table, staring at her engagement ring placed in front of her.

Just seeing it off her finger again has my heart racing.

"Zara, baby. What are you doing?" I ask, edging closer to her.

"Just thinking," she mutters, not looking up at me.

"About?" I ask softly, stepping behind her chair and holding onto the back.

"Us."

I blow out a breath. Fuck.

"I need more than that, Zara."

She slides the diamond ring further away from her.

I can feel my jaw ticking with frustration. So, I lean over and retrieve it, my fingers brushing against her left hand as I carefully place it back where it belongs.

She flattens her palm onto the smooth wood, and she sighs.

"Was any of it real?" she asks.

"Excuse me?"

She bows her head and sniffles.

I can't move. I don't know if I can breathe.

"I'm useless to you now."

I swiftly spin her chair around to face me, then fall to my knees, clutching onto her thighs. "Zara, tell me what's going on in your head. I need you to let me in."

She chews on her trembling lower lip as she focuses on some distant place over my head. "You wanted me for a baby. I can't even give you that."

"Is that honestly what you believe, Zara?" I try to keep the bubbling anger out of my voice. She's grieving. She's been through more than I can imagine. I can't lose my temper with her, but I also can't lose her.

I gently intertwine my fingers with hers.

"You don't think I love you? You think my fucking chest doesn't burn every time I'm near you? That I'm not completely and utterly obsessed with you? That I don't have an overwhelming need to protect you, where not a single thing else matters to me more than you?"

"I-I don't know anymore, Frankie. I just feel lost and so fucking useless. I'm not what you need. Maybe I'm not the woman you should have by your side."

My hand runs through my hair as I shake my head in disbelief, unable to comprehend what I'm hearing. I need to get it through to her before it's too late.

How I live purely for this woman.

"Zara, you are the strongest woman I've ever met. You're far stronger than me."

"You said love is a weakness," she whispers. I tip her chin up, forcing her to look at me. The sound of my pounding blood is drowning out everything else.

"I was wrong. Not ours. Ours is my fucking strength, baby. I love you."

She fights back welling tears.

"Tell me you don't love me, Zara. I dare you." I pin her with a glare.

It's the only way I can snap her out of this. She needs me to help get her emotions under control the only way I know how.

"Nothing? You still have nothing to say?"

I've never known this woman to be stuck for words.

"What, you want me to prove it? Show you how completely and utterly committed I am to you and us for the rest of our lives? Is that what it will take for you to wear my damn ring?"

Filled with frustration, I storm around the breakfast bar, grab a knife, and place it over the gas fire to heat it up.

"Frankie! What the hell are you doing?"

Frantically, she rushes towards me, her sole focus being on taking it out of my hand. I swiftly snatch it away from her grasp.

"You want my commitment, you want me to prove my love, well here it fucking is."

I take a slow, deliberate step towards her.

"And you have the nerve to tell me I don't fucking love you."

"I didn't say that."

She grabs my wrist, but I pull away. Taking off my top over my head and tossing it on the floor.

"What the fuck are you doing?" Her voice raises an octave.

I look down at my bare chest and push the tip of the hot blade on my pec. Blood drips as I start carving the letter 'Z' into my skin.

She grabs at my arm. "Stop it! Look, I get it. You love me, I believe you."

I reach the last line of the letter, ignoring the stinging of my flesh. "Now. Tell me I don't love you. I dare you."

She looks down at the blood dripping off my knife and back up to me.

This is the man she needs right now.

I swipe the fresh drop up with the tip of my finger.

"I just carved your initial into my skin. If that isn't love, I don't know what is."

I stalk towards her and open up her legs. Sliding between them, I trace an 'F' across her chest with my blood.

Her mouth gapes open, but now she's looking at me how she should.

With love in her eyes.

I drop down onto one knee, grabbing her left hand. "Marry me, Zara. I'm down on my knees for you. I love you. Marry me."

She taps her chin, pretending to be deep in thought, before she bursts out into laughter and my heart nearly explodes.

"I can't even hold it in. Yes, a million times, yes."

I jump to my feet and swoop her up into my arms and kiss her like my whole life depends on it.

"Don't ever doubt my utter devotion to you, Zara. It's real, it always has been, and it is never going anywhere. No matter what, we are in this together."

"I'm sorry, Frankie."

"No. I don't want that. Whatever grief you have, whatever emotions they may be, let me have them. I can handle it. Just never, ever doubt me. That's all I ask, angel."

"You do deserve better than me, Frankie. I won't do that again."

Maybe we both needed this to realize what is important beyond anything else.

Us.

"I love you, Frankie. More than life, I'm just so angry and hurt, I took it out on you. I want to blame myself, to punish myself for losing-"

"I know, baby. I know. We don't punish ourselves, we destroy the ones who did this to us. When we're ready."

I press my lips over hers. For one night, I think this is enough.

"Now let's get some sleep and we can talk tomorrow. I just want you in my arms, with that ring on your finger for tonight."

"I'd like that, Frankie."

"Good girl," I whisper, kissing her again.

Squeezing Zara's hand as we walk into our new home for the foreseeable. When I say home, I mean mansion, complete with two separate wings. Everyone is here in the safe house, and I still have my space.

We need to all be together. We are stronger this way. That is the only way we can all get through this. We have all lost someone.

And we all are seeking our revenge.

As we enter into the hallway, I can hear the chattering coming from the dining room, so I lead us in.

In reality, all I want to do is look after Zara. She is a shell of herself, both physically and mentally.

She sees herself as a failure and I can't make her understand how, if anything, she is the opposite. To me, she embodies strength where it truly matters.

She hasn't let me down. This isn't her fault. I won't stop until she believes me. My girl is still in there somewhere, I know it.

I saw a glimpse of it last night. It's just going to take some time. Time we don't have.

"Uncle Frankie!" Rosa squeals and runs into my arms.

I hold her tight. I have a lot of making up to do with this girl.

As I raise my eyes, I notice Luca standing to the side, intently watching his wife. I give him a nod.

"Hello, little thorn." I rustle her hair, and she whines, pulling away with a big grin on her face. It's the Rosa I remember.

Luca walks over and wraps an arm around her shoulder, holding his other hand out to me.

"Well, look at you two all tanned and in love," I say to Luca. His laughter fills the room as he shakes his head.

When I link my fingers through Zara's, their eyes widen in surprise.

"I think it's about time you two met my fiancé, Zara."

"What!! Frankie! Why didn't you say anything?" Rosa hugs Zara, who winces but smiles through the pain.

"Frankie fucking Falcone. In love. I can't believe it." Luca assesses Zara, before holding out his hand to her with a genuine smile. "I'm Luca Russo."

She shakes his hand firmly.

"Oh, I know. I'm Zara, O'Reilly." She emphasizes her last name.

It's quite entertaining watching the recognition wash over Luca's face.

"Oh fuck," he coughs out.

He turns to me. "Please tell me you didn't kidnap her."

Zara laughs. "No, I'm here out of my own free will."

I shoot a glare to Grayson, who is sitting next to Enzo at the dining table.

"See? Did you hear that?"

He shakes his head and chuckles. "You might have paid her to say that!"

The room erupts into laughter. I pull Zara into my side and press a kiss to the top of her head. "We're going to head upstairs. Let me know when our meeting with Mikhail is arranged."

"We need to speak to you, Uncle Frankie." Rosa looks up at

Luca with a smile on her face. She's glowing.

I swallow past the lump in my throat. I have a feeling I know what she's going to say, and I can't let them say this in front of Zara.

Hell, I don't know if I can hear it right now.

I look over to Grayson and tilt my head to Zara, who cuddles into my side. Silently, Grayson gets up and steps around the table.

"We can all catch up over dinner later," he says, casting a meaningful glance at Luca.

Luca's eyes bounce from me to Zara and he catches on, silently offering his apologies to me.

Cupping her elbow, I encourage her to follow. "Come on, baby, let's get settled."

"Okay," she whispers, her voice hoarse.

"What do you want us to do with Alex? Enzo's team have secured the girls, they're safe." Jax says as he leans back in his chair with a beer in his hand.

Zara looks up at me, her eyes alight. "He's here?"

"For now, yes."

She needs time to heal before she learns the truth. Yet, even now, I can hear her mind ticking.

Chapter Fifty-Eight

Zara

I lie awake, tossing and turning, my mind refusing to shut off. A burning rage that is inside me is taking over my every thought.

The people that killed my baby are still breathing.

Sitting up, I peel the covers away and tiptoe over to the wardrobe, trying not to disturb Frankie. He's finally getting some rest. Pulling on my sneakers, Frankie's phone keeps lighting up on the nightstand. Shit. I need to make sure it isn't anything important.

I quietly pick it up. Messages from Enzo flash up one after another. I should be happy we saved all the girls, I just can't focus on anything other than my grief.

The last one catches my attention. It isn't from Enzo, it's an email invoice from the hospital my mom used to be at with her name on it.

I tap the screen and open it up. Outstanding fees. My eyes widen as I take in the staggering amount. Hundreds of thousands of dollars' worth of treatment dating back to the start of the year.

"What the fuck?" I whisper.

My hands start to shake. My fucking father was never using Romano's money to pay for Mom's treatment. That was the only explanation I had for his part in all of his involvement with the shady organizations.

Anger clouds my vision, making it difficult to see. I feel my chest tightening as I grip the phone tightly.

That asshole.

He was the man who was supposed to protect me and Mom. Now he's the man who is partly responsible for me losing the baby.

I can't take it anymore knowing he's out there making money trafficking innocent girls.

I hate him and everything he's become.

"Fuck!" I scream, letting some of the pain go with it. Frankie's phone launches across the room.

All I see is red. I look up at all of our clothes hanging perfectly in the wardrobe and start yanking them off and throwing them across the room.

"Zara!" Frankie calls out, I can hardly hear him over the ringing in my ears.

His hands grip onto my shoulders, and he spins me to face him.

"Zara, I need you to calm down."

"No. Frankie. I'm not doing that. I fucking hate him!" My chest heaves.

"Who?" He blinks at me in confusion.

"My dad. Romano. Fucking Alex downstairs. All of them. They need to go. They've done this to us!"

My cheeks are wet with tears, and my fists are clenched as my body trembles uncontrollably.

"They will, baby. I promise you, not one of them responsible will make it out alive. I need you to be okay first." His warm palms run up and down my arms.

I grit my teeth. "I won't be. Not until they die for this. Starting with my father."

He tilts his head and his eyebrows knit.

"I saw your phone, Frankie. I know Dad hasn't paid a single cent towards her treatment. You're covering it. Where the hell is his money going?"

He sighs softly, pulling me into an embrace.

"He was never the man you thought he was, Zara. I'm so fucking sorry," he whispers.

"What do you mean?" I ask, looking up at him.

"He's been having an affair. He used the money to buy properties from what we can see so far. One of which his mistress lives in."

"Who the hell is she?" I try to free myself from Frankie's hold, but he only tightens it.

"We are looking into it. She isn't our priority."

My whole body trembles. "I want him gone, Frankie. I need him to pay for this."

I feel his hand under my chin, guiding my gaze to meet his intense eyes.

"And I will deliver him to you, Zara. I will stop at nothing to end this, if that is what you want right now?"

"I do," I say, without hesitation.

Sitting around here won't fix anything. I can never get our baby back, but I can send the assholes down to hell that did this.

"I fucking love you, Zara. So much." He tucks my hair behind my ears, stroking my cheek.

"Together, we can take these fuckers down." A fire dances behind his eyes, fueling me further. If I only get to do one more thing in life, I will be happy knowing it is finishing them.

For the girls they trafficked, for my baby, for Keller, Kai and everyone else they've hurt.

It ends now.

"How do you suggest we get to my dad? I want to be there. I want to make him feel my pain, Frankie."

"You will, angel. I'll make sure of it. We do this, together." He pauses. "I think it's about time we went and spoke to our friend Alex, don't you?" he says with a smirk.

"I do."

CHAPTER FIFTY-NINE

Frankie

The guys have all come down for our meeting. If we end this, we do it together. Killing Romano has been on the forefront of my mind for ten years. Yet, I can't concentrate on anything else except this gaping hole in my chest, which only fuels my hatred further.

"You okay, boss?" Jax asks, handing me a coffee.

"Fine. You?"

The dark circles under his eyes, the messy hair and outright misery that seeps off of him tells me he's not.

"I'm fucking lost."

I wrap an arm around his shoulders, pulling him against my side.

"I can't take away your pain. All I can tell you to do is use it. Every ounce of it for Kai, we will destroy them all. Do you hear me? I fucking promise you. Don't let this kill you; we need you, Jax."

He sucks in a breath. "I can do that."

"Make that your focus. We've got your back. You are our family now." I pat his back.

The rest of the crew walks over, taking their seats at the dining table.

"Frankie, you ready?" Luca asks, pulling out a chair at the end for me.

"The meeting starts when Zara arrives."

My heart stops as I see her pad down the stairs in a pair of ripped black jeans and a tight cami top that hugs her curves perfectly. Her eyes meet mine and she gives me a devious smile.

"I'm here!" she says, taking my seat at the head of the table.

With each tap of her nail, her intense gaze never wavers from me.

Grayson wears a wide grin, clearly entertained by Zara.

I rest my hands on the back of her chair, the scent of her perfume lingering in the air, and lean down, brushing my lips against the delicate contour of her ear.

"You're sitting in my seat, baby," I whisper.

She turns her head to face me, the first time I've seen any light in her eyes since we lost the baby.

"Fine, I'll sit on your lap."

I bite on the inside of my mouth. As distracting as that may be, I need her with me. She slips out of the way and I take her place, sitting back so she can perch on my thighs. Wrapping my arm around her stomach, I pull her against me so her ass is rubbing on my dick.

"Well, who has a plan? Because I've spent ten years hunting this fucker."

Zara clears her throat. "I do."

Pride fills my chest. Of course my girl has a plan.

"Let's hear it." I nod to her.

"Well, I was thinking, what if we use Mikhail to proposition Romano using the girls we saved? Obviously, we would never give them back."

I scratch my beard, taking in her suggestion.

"We can do that," Grayson says.

"He has an inside track with George. He will still be getting money. We have to stop all other routes for him..."

I trail off.

"My dad is the answer," Zara says calmly. All the guys at the table look at her.

Romano always thinks he can outsmart anyone. I need to get ahead of him and cover all bases to end this.

"And I know just the man who can give us that information." I look to Jax and Grayson.

"Alex. Once we get to George, we use him to cut Romano off completely. That way, he will jump at Mikhail's offer. He's in this life for one thing only; money. Are we all in agreement?" I look at each of them around the table.

"Yes," Grayson replies.

"I'm fucking in," Jax says, slamming back a scotch.

I narrow my eyes to Grayson. He has to get a handle on Jax.

"Luca?" I ask.

"I'm in. For Keller, Mom and Rosa." He deserves his revenge just as much as I do. I want him by my side for this.

"Good. Any improvements with Keller?" I know Luca has

spent nearly every free moment at the hospital.

"They're going to try to wake him up from his induced coma tomorrow. We won't know more until that." He stretches back and runs his fingers through his hair.

"So, after we finish this, your break is over?" He looks like the time away was good for him.

"It's looking that way." He bites back a grin.

Zara turns in my lap, and her warm hands frame my face, demanding my attention. "You deserve your revenge."

I suck in a breath.

"We," I answer. This is no longer just about me. "We will never be able to get back what we've lost. But we will burn the fucking world down to get ours, dolcezza. That, I promise you."

Fire starts to emerge in her eyes, and a smile creeps up on her lips; the first one I've seen in days.

I've missed it.

"Well, what are we waiting for? Let's make them pay. I want to watch them begging for their lives. I want them to feel even just an ounce of our pain."

My chest fills with pride. This woman is truly everything.

"Fuck, I love you," I mumble against her mouth.

The sound of Luca's cough to my right forces me to reluctantly break away from Zara.

"Won't taking out the commissioner of the NYPD raise questions?" he asks.

"Not if we clean it up good enough. Me and Enzo can work on that. They'll replace him in no time, especially if information was to be leaked on my dad. They'll cover up that he ever existed," Zara replies as she wriggles in my lap.

"Now this I'd like to see," I say, tightening my hold around her.

I tap her ass, and she stands.

"Well, are you guys coming?" she asks.

"Come on, she might be able to teach you a thing or two." I step behind her, wrapping my arms around her.

"You've got this baby," I whisper in her ear.

"With you by my side, Frankie. I've got everything."

"Rise and shine." Grayson bangs against the door, and Alex sits up on his single mattress in the corner.

His eyes fill with fear as we approach.

"Z-Zara?" he croaks out.

"Get up, Alex. Take a seat." She gestures to the metal chair and Luca pulls another one across the room.

Alex scrambles out of bed, his face swollen and purple. Jax obviously took some of his anger out on Alex's face.

He sits down, and Zara rests her hands on the back of her chair as Luca ties up Alex.

"You don't look too good, Alex."

"No thanks to your *family.*" He spits out the last word.

I keep my feet rooted in the ground, with Luca, Jax, and

Grayson by my side. This is her time to shine.

Alex's eyes flick to me.

I return his glance with a furious stare.

"Don't look at me, Alex. Zara is talking to you," I say, crossing my arms over my chest. I'm too busy watching my woman pick up a knife from the tray Jax bought in.

"I need you to do something for me, Alex." She holds the blade up to the light. "Wow, this is clean."

Alex pales, and Grayson shoots me an impressed look. I keep my eyes zeroed in on Zara. Fuck, I'm proud of her.

"I suppose this would feel similar to the glass that sliced into my flesh, don't you think?"

Shivers run down my spine at her words, leaving a cold ache in my chest.

"Zara, what the fuck has gotten into you?" Alex splutters.

"Nothing. This is who I am. Do you want to know what happened to the last guy who hurt me?"

"What?"

"I ran him over, killed him." She pauses, tapping the knife on her palm as she smiles sweetly at him.

"You're all fucking crazy," Alex hisses.

"No, we aren't. We are just sick to death of being betrayed, and of people taking things from us. Things no one can ever replace."

She steps towards him and his fists clench. As I go to move forward, she presses the knife against his throat.

"You have a choice though, Alex. Make the right one, you can live a happy life. The wrong one and we will send you and your family to your graves. I know how much you love your dad. It would be a shame if he paid the price."

Sweat beads on Alex's forehead as he looks up at my girl.

"What do you want from me?" His eyes plead with her.

"I need you to tell me where I can find my father."

"How the hell would I know? I've been in here for days. He could be anywhere!" He wipes his hands on his thighs, leaving a damp trail.

"Use your fucking brain. You're telling me you don't know about his other properties, his meeting spots? Hmm?" She pushes the knife in further, this time enough to release blood down the blade.

"Zara! Okay, okay. Give me a second!"

She releases the pressure, wiping the blade on her jeans.

"He had an apartment not far from our office. I met him there once to drop off some keys?"

Zara looks over her shoulder to me.

"What do we think about that one?"

"I can have Enzo check it out." I shrug.

She turns back to Alex, who's now the same complexion as the gray flooring.

"Actually, I have a better idea. What if you just called him? Maybe you can tell him how he needs to hide from me, because I am after blood for him killing my baby. We will give you the location to tell him," she says, with no emotion in her voice.

I know deep down that hurt her worse than any wound ever

could.

"W-what?" Alex says.

Zara's gaze unfocuses to some place on the wall in front of her.

"Dolcezza, concentrate."

She takes a deep breath and returns her attention to the bruised and beaten man in front of her. "Yes, Alex, that's what happened, and that's exactly what you'll tell him. He knows what I am. He will believe you and he will run there."

"I'm sorry, Zara. Truly. You don't deserve this. I can do it."

"Maybe you should have thought about that before you decided to help the men who did this to me." A flush of red works its way up her throat as the pitch in her voice raises.

He leans away from the knife point she brandishes inches from his nose. "I didn't have a choice."

I step forward, place a hand on Zara's shoulder and squeeze.

Her body is tense beneath my touch. "That's bullshit, and we both know it."

Grayson hands me Alex's phone.

"What's his number stored under?" I scroll through his contacts list.

"Dad New."

Zara laughs. "Of course it is."

George's croaky voice fills the air, causing my fist to tighten.

"It's about fucking time, Alex. Tell me you're okay?"

Alex coughs, looking up at Zara, who presses the knife against his skin to remind him.

"Yep, look. You need to get somewhere safe, George. Zara's on a rampage. She was in the explosion, and she lost her baby. She's out for blood, yours specifically. Do you have somewhere to go?"

"H-how do you know that?" George stutters.

"She came to me looking for you. I'm lucky I only ended up with a black eye. She's crazy." Alex swallows hard and looks up at Zara.

"I know. Shit. Okay. Where?" The stress oozes out of the speakers of the cell.

"I'll send you the location. It's not safe over the phone."

Clever. Maybe he isn't as useless as I first thought.

"Well, hurry the fuck up. I've got Romano breathing down my neck, asking questions. Do you know if Frankie survived?" George sounds almost frantic.

"I-I don't have a clue, sir. She seemed really upset, so I don't know."

"Text it over now. I need to leave." George cuts the call.

Alex's eyes widen as he leans back, and she follows his throat with her blade. "I did what you asked!"

Her hand quivers and she chews on her lower lip.

I cup her elbow and bend to whisper in her ear. "Take a few steps back, baby."

With a slow nod, her knife slips from her grasp, making a loud clatter as it hits the floor. She then steps back in line with my guys.

We can't move on until every single one of them involved is

dead. Alex is no exception.

His part in our devastation weighs just as heavily as the rest. He had his chances for redemption. Now it's too late.

Alex's eyes plead with me, but it's pointless.

I feel nothing.

I unholster my gun and pull the trigger.

Zara's eyes dart back and forth between me and Alex's lifeless form.

"You did a good job there," Grayson says to Zara, squeezing her on the shoulder.

"Thank you." She returns with a smile.

I toss Grayson the phone.

"Send the location to George. Get Mikhail on the line and be ready to move as soon as we tell him."

"Will do, boss."

"Jax, Luca, go with G. I'll be up in a minute."

Once Grayson is out of sight, I grab her and hold her close.

"I'm so fucking proud of you, angel."

I can feel her tears soaking through my shirt. I withdraw and brush them away with my thumb. "They're going to pay for this, Zara. We are going to win this."

"It still doesn't bring our baby back, though, does it?" She sniffles.

I sigh. "No, Zara. I'm sorry."

"Maybe when I watch them all die, I'll feel better." She hiccups as she laughs.

I can't help but chuckle with her.

"Yeah, I agree." I press a kiss to the tip of her nose. "Together, we can get through this."

"I hope so." She sniffles.

"I know so."

We have a lot to do to pull this off.

CHAPTER SIXTY

Zara

All the color drains from Dad's face when the elevator door opens into the penthouse apartment Enzo owns.

Stepping into the living room, his gaze quickly shifts from me to Frankie.

"Nothing to say, commissioner?" Frankie asks, raising his gun.

He looks past Frankie, straight at me.

"Zara, sweetheart. This is all a misunderstanding. I can explain."

I let out a malicious laugh. I can't wait to unleash hell on him for everything he's done. This is the least he deserves.

"A misunderstanding, Dad?" I step closer and Frankie falls behind me. He has my back, he always has. Unlike this asshole I call my father.

"You put me in a burning building. You killed your own fucking grandchild."

My fist shakes by my side, and my grip tightens around the gun in my right hand.

He takes a step forward, and Frankie clears his throat behind me. "Go any closer to her and I'll shoot you, George."

Dad shakes his head, running a trembling hand through his greasy gray hair. He's a damn mess.

"It wasn't me! I tried to get Alex to keep you away. I didn't have a clue." His voice shakes. "Don't do this Zara. It isn't you. You didn't mean to kill Ash. You aren't anything like *him.*"

I follow his line of vision straight back to Frankie and my blood boils.

How fucking dare he.

My arm raises on its own, aiming my weapon at his forehead.

"You can't even apologize for what you've done to me? Can you?" It hurts to say out loud.

His palms show in a sign of surrender. "You're alive, aren't you?"

I hear Frankie tutting behind me. The sound amplifies the pounding in my ears.

"I am, but my baby isn't. Your grandchild," I spit with venom, and he starts to back away from me.

He can't escape us this time.

"Zara, be real here. It isn't the worst thing in the world to happen. You don't want to have a kid with him. You should be thanking me for giving you your freedom again."

All I can see is a blinding, white rage as my blood boils with anger.

"How fucking dare you!" I scream and lunge at him. The butt of my pistol connects to his cheek and sends his head flying back. I keep hitting him. Every blow that connects just fuels me further.

"I hate you!" I cry out.

"That's enough, baby." Frankie pulls me back to him by the waist.

"Fuck you." George looks up with blood dripping down his cheek and spits at Frankie's leg.

I look down in disgust and shake my head.

Without a word, Frankie bends and removes the knife from my boot and places it in my hand. I watch in awe as Frankie grabs Dad by the throat to pin him in place against the wall.

"How about you show him some of the pain you felt?" Frankie says, looking only at me.

I look at the blade in my palm, then back up to Frankie.

"You can do this, baby." A fire burns in his eyes as he watches me.

We both deserve this. We need this.

"Zara." Dad addresses me in a stern tone as I approach him.

"I meant what I said before, you're dead to me, *Dad,*" I grit out, and drive the steel into his stomach. He grunts, looking down at the black handle sticking out with shock on his face.

Frankie edges behind me and covers my hands over the hilt and twists it. The guttural sounds of my father's cries fill the room.

"Anyone who hurts my family dies, George. Don't worry, I'll do the one thing you failed to do as a father. I will protect your daughter with my life."

Dad trembles as Frankie shoves the knife in deeper.

I look at my father, the tears streaming down his face, and bile rises up my throat. How has it come to this?

He went against us. He took away my future. That is what I'm grieving. Not him.

"Please, Frankie. We can fix this," he begs.

"You're pleading with the wrong person here, Commissioner. It's your daughter that holds your life in her hands, not me."

"You're pathetic, Dad. You really think you can beg for your life now? You're not only a useless father, you're also a useless husband. Mom is better off without you."

"I-I love your mother. It was all for her, Zara," he sobs. His words provide a stark reminder of why we're doing this.

I tug the knife out of his stomach and press it under his jaw, above Frankie's grasp.

"You think I don't know you haven't paid a single one of her medical bills? That you've been off fucking some whore while you sit back and watch my mom die? You two might have thought you would have it all, I'll make sure you both burn," I whisper against his cheek. My hand holding the blade starts to tremble.

The weight of what I'm about to do is taking over.

He's my dad.

"He's lying." He glares at me as his hands cling to his stomach, trying to stem the flow of blood spilling onto the floor. "You know what he's like. You've seen he's a monster. He's brainwashed you, Zara. It's all a lie. I was protecting you this whole time."

"Your call, baby," Frankie says next to me.

My eyes narrow in disgust as I take my father.

Letting out a shaky breath, I lower the knife and step back. Tipping my head to the ground, I can't look at him. Tears sting my eyes. With everything that's happened. I'm a mess.

"End this, Frankie. I can't listen to it anymore," I say quietly.

Without a word, Frankie reaches out and strokes my cheek, tracing along my skin. "Go back down with the guys. I'll meet you there."

It isn't a question, it's an order.

I nod, taking one last look at my piece-of-shit dad. We are better off without him. So is Mom.

"You did this to yourself. I hope you fucking rot." I keep my head held high as I reach the elevator. Once safely inside, I slump back against the wall and cover my face in my hands.

CHAPTER SIXTY-ONE

Frankie

I wait for the elevator doors to close, then throw him onto the floor, pressing my boot onto his neck.

"It didn't have to be this way, George." I shake my head.

It really didn't.

"Romano will kill you, Frankie. It's only a matter of time," he gurgles through his swelling lips.

"Wrong. See, I'm about to offer you a lifeline, Commissioner."

I release my foot. He scrambles to sit up, clutching at his stomach.

"What lifeline?" he coughs out with blood dripping over his eyes.

"See, I don't give a fuck about you. In fact, having you alive in the NYPD is useful. It's Romano I'm after. I need you to make the call. Tell him he can't have any more shipments in New York, that it's too risky with the heat from the feds. You're going to need at least a month to be able to facilitate any more women coming in."

"Why?"

"That is none of your business. Just make the call and you can live." I need to cut all of Romano's funding off, so he snaps Mikhail's offer up. As it stands, he still has George as a backup. Once that is gone, Mikhail's deal will sound a lot more appealing to someone in hiding.

"You've got ten seconds to decide." I point my gun at his head. "Nine, eight."

"Fine, fine." He holds his arms up in surrender. "I need my phone out of my pocket."

Training my gun between his eyes, I watch him make slow movements to pull it out of his chest pocket. As soon as it's free, I snatch it from his fingers.

"I'll dial and put it on speaker. Passcode."

He calls out the numbers and I jab it in.

"Contact for Romano?"

He looks down.

My anger bubbles just beneath the surface, practically begging for him to fuck this up. "Spit it out."

"Helen."

I laugh. Fucking idiots.

I dial *Helen*, and someone picks up after a couple of rings. I hold my breath, feeling a rush of adrenaline as Romano's voice fills the room.

"George. Tell me you have good news."

George clears his throat, and I raise my brows, gesturing with my gun.

"No. Not really. New York is out for shipments. There's way

too much pressure on me after Alex's disappearance. You're going to have to find another dock."

"Motherfuckers," Romano spits out in his deep Italian accent. "You better help me fix this, George."

"You don't know anyone who can help?" George asks.

"I have one option. I'll speak to him. How long are we talking? I need to fix this before Frankie catches on."

George's eyes widen and his mouth falls open, he quickly shuts it when I give him a stern glare.

"I'll see what I can do. It will be at least a month, Romano. I'm sorry."

He cuts the call and I place the cell on the counter next to me for Enzo to collect later.

"Can I go now?" he asks, glancing over at the elevator.

"Not a fucking chance. You think I'd ever let you near Zara again? You lost the right to live when you hurt her the first time."

I can still see the bruises he left her; I've wanted to do this for a long time.

"No–"

I pull the trigger and the bullet hits in the middle of his forehead. The metallic scent of gunpowder fills the air as he falls to the floor, staining the wood with crimson.

One down. One to go.

I let Enzo know it's done so he can clean things up and make my way back to Zara.

I slip into the backseat of Grayson's Audi. Zara looks up at me, her eyes glassy. With no need for words, I gently bring her onto my lap, feeling the weight of her settle against me.

Grayson looks at me through the rearview mirror and I simply nod. That's enough for him to know. She lays her head on my shoulder, and I stroke her silky hair.

"You okay, baby?" I whisper softly.

"Yeah, I am."

I press a kiss on the side of her temple and her eyes flutter closed. Her tears drop against my shirt.

"Even though he's dead. We still don't win, do we?"

I swallow the lump in my throat. She's right. It's the reality I've faced for over ten years. You can't change the past. You can't stop the pain.

You can't get back what you've lost.

"No, dolcezza. But it does mean we can close the door behind us and move on knowing they can never hurt us again."

Her face brushes against my throat as she nods.

"I can't believe he did this to me. He's my dad."

"He never deserved to have a daughter as brilliant as you." I grin as a smile twitches on her lips.

She huffs as she pushes herself back far enough to face me. "At least I know, if we have kids in the future, their dad will be incredible. You'd never let them down." Her warm palm strokes my face.

"Never, Zara. You have my word."

I can smell the subtle hint of her perfume as I hover my lips over hers.

"It's not *if*, it's *when*."

Her perfect white teeth bite down on her lip.

"Soon." I whisper against her, before pressing my lips over hers, losing myself in her. I vow to be everything she needs. She's right, I'd do anything for my family.

CHAPTER SIXTY-TWO

Frankie

"I'm with Mikhail now. We're waiting for Romano to bite. I don't expect it will be long after George's message. There was nothing useful on his phone, according to my team," Enzo says over the phone.

"Keep me updated. I'll have everything taken care of here so we can leave on the jet within the hour once we have the confirmation."

"You got it. The time has nearly come, Frankie. Are you ready for this to be over?"

I run a hand over my face. Am I ready for my new future? I glance over to Zara and Rosa chatting by the door. Her smile makes my chest swell. To have my past dead and buried with Romano? Absolutely.

"Damn right, Enzo. Now, make it happen."

I cut the call, heading towards the yard where we have gathered all of our men. It's the safest place right now. While we go on our hunt for Romano, we have to be prepared for just about anything here in New York.

I have to protect our family.

I need to make sure our army is strong, that we have enough to out gun Romano. He's had plenty of time to regroup and we are missing Keller, Kai, and a lot of other casualties along the way.

Although, looking at the way the grounds are overflowing with men, each one ready to kill for me, I'd say we have a pretty good chance if it comes to it.

We just have to wait for Mikhail and Enzo to come through.

"Can I speak to you?" Rosa asks and I stop, looking down into her shining blue eyes.

Zara and Luca stop by the doors.

"I'll be out in a second," I nod to Zara and she smiles back.

Both of them retreat, leaving me and Rosa.

"Everything okay, little thorn?"

She twiddles her thumbs nervously, which concerns me.

"Rosa?"

"We want to move back to New York, to be with our family again."

I blow out a breath. "Of course. It's where you both belong, Rosa."

She looks down, holding back the tears, and I frown.

"But?"

"What if something happens to Luca? I can't go through that again, Uncle Frankie."

I won't let it. I refuse to bring this girl any more pain.

"Have you spoken to Luca about this?"

"He's been through so much, Frankie. He needs his brother

to get better. I'm worried he's going to lose it if he doesn't."

I can imagine he's struggling. Especially after they lost their mother so brutally. "He needs your strength. We will look out for him, Rosa. Never doubt that he is family."

"Is he coming back into the business?" She twists her hands nervously.

I shrug. "We haven't discussed it. He won't be taking control back, if that's what you're asking. We all know that isn't what he wants."

For the first time in my life, I truly do understand Luca's utter devotion to my niece. The way he was willing to give up everything in a heartbeat for her.

I know now, Zara is my person. There isn't a single thing on this earth I wouldn't do for her.

"If you kill Romano, does that mean it's safe for us to be home?"

"Yes, Rosa. I'll make sure it's safe for you both to return."

She wraps her arms around me and squeezes. I freeze for a second before relaxing and returning the hug and softly stroking her back.

"You know I don't blame you, right?" She mutters against my shoulder.

I sigh. She might not, but I do.

"I shouldn't have let that asshole return, Rosa. I should have known something was wrong. I should have been someone you could trust to confide in. I fucked up; I am responsible for a great deal of your pain. I'll never forgive myself."

Fuck, I should have taken her with me ten years ago. I should have been the uncle she needed.

I can't change the past. If I did, the glowing woman before me wouldn't be the Rosa she is right now.

She shakes her head against my chest and releases me, wiping her tears with her sleeve.

"No, you're not. You helped save me. You kept me strong. You kept me from drinking when Luca was hurt. You're making up for everything now by being who you are meant to be, their leader. Romano is the cause of my pain and Luca's. I forgive you, Frankie. If that's what you need to hear, but I didn't blame you in the first place. My dad fucked up and Romano did, too. You hurt as much as I did."

The knot of anger I hold for them tightens, knowing she needs this as much as I do. "I'll make sure it fucking hurts him, don't you worry."

She laughs with a little hiccup.

"Come on." I wrap my arm around her shoulder. "I am sorry, Rosa. For what it's worth. If I could turn back time and change what happened, know that I would. All I can offer you is revenge."

"Luca deserves his revenge too, Rosa. For you both. I'll see you soon, okay?"

He might have handed control over to me. He made me their leader, but I understand his need for blood. Revenge for his brother, the only family he has left.

"I get it. You better come back this time. That, and I want

my uncle Frankie back, my friend." She looks up at me with a mischievous smile, just like she used to when she wanted ice cream after school.

"Easy."

"Hey, don't I get an apology yet?" Grayson calls out behind me, throwing on a black t-shirt.

"You'll be waiting a long time for that, G. The bullet hole I've got in my shoulder is good enough."

He rolls his eyes at me and slams his hand over the wound with a tap. "You're still dwelling on that?"

"Yes, and I will for as long as I see fit. Or you take a bullet for me."

It's completely plausible in our line of work.

Grayson gives me a lopsided grin and turns to Rosa. "Maddie's got the kids settled while Sienna is at the hospital. She said she's put on some film called Bridesmaids for you guys to watch?"

A smile erupts on Rosa's face. Despite everything, she is happy.

The hundreds of men fall silent as me and Grayson step out onto the patio. I find Zara and pull her into my side. "You good, baby?"

"Now I am." She snugs herself against me.

We form a line in front of the crowd, with Jax to my left and Luca and Grayson to my right.

"As you all know, everything we've worked for is falling into place. This is our opportunity to end this war and come home victorious. If we don't, we're fucked. I won't lose any more of my family. We can't. So I need you to fight for your lives, fight for your families, for our future. Because we will rule New York. I can't do that without each and every single one of you."

I can feel the nervous energy from them. Hell, I feel it in my core. I know as well as they do, it's possible that we will come under attack after wiping out the commissioner. Romano will be desperate. I don't know if I'll be walking away from this.

I've come to terms with that.

One thing I am sure of is, if I go, I'm dragging that fucker down to hell with me.

"Now, I understand, this is the biggest ask I've had to make of you yet. I'm giving you all one chance to walk away. No questions asked. If you can't fight for me, now is your only chance to leave with no repercussions."

I feel Grayson's glare on me, but I can't have men who aren't prepared to die for me on this task. It's either all in or nothing. I'm trusting Grayson and Keller have only bought in the best, most bloodthirsty killers there are.

I cross my arms across my chest, the icy breeze blowing in my face as I look at the men before me.

I need their trust and loyalty.

Not a single person moves.

"You did a good fucking job here, G." I turn to him.

He chuckles. "Never doubt me, you want an army? That's what I'll give you."

I turn back to the sea of faces.

"Well, it looks like we have a fucking war to end. You'll all be given your stations by Grayson, Jax, and Luca. Once this is over, the drinks are on me. Now let's finish this, for Keller and Kai."

They all cheer, the energy shifting from nerves to excitement.

CHAPTER SIXTY-THREE

Zara

Song- Worship, Ari Abdul

I sit back and gaze at my reflection, the mascara enhancing the darkness of my lashes. Frankie hasn't touched me since the miscarriage. He's cared for me, he's helping me heal. We're taking our revenge.

It's not enough. That isn't the Frankie I need anymore. Running my finger across my lip, I just want to feel alive again, even just for a moment. I now understand why Frankie spent all these years fixating on his revenge.

Because when you stop and truly give yourself the time to think, the time to grieve what you've lost, that's when the pain starts. And right now, I feel useless, now even to Frankie. I'm so caught up in watching the people who did this to me die, I've forgotten how much I need Frankie. All I want is for him to take control and remind me of who I am.

I need him to stop this cycle of pain the only way I know how. So, I slip on my red satin robe, its smooth fabric sliding over my lace lingerie, and stand outside his office door.

Mikhail's heavy accent echoes through the heavy wood. "He's taken the bait, Frankie. I have a call with him in an hour. Enzo will intercept and get the location."

I hesitate, waiting for Frankie's response. I quietly open his office and step in. His wild eyes meet mine and his face softens before he turns back to the screen. "I will only be taking a small team with me. I need the rest here to protect my family."

"Your funeral." Michail's words sound final.

Frankie laughs and I feel sick to my stomach. "It just means you and your brothers will have to come on the adventure with me." His eyes flick to me again and I blush as he bites down on his lip. "I have to go. When you have the updates, let me know immediately."

He spins in his seat to face me, his muscular legs spread, and he runs a hand through his messy hair. "Everything okay, baby?"

I shake my head, biting down on my nail. "I need you, Frankie."

He raises an eyebrow. "I'm here; I haven't gone anywhere."

"Not like that." I bow my head. I hear his heavy footsteps as he reaches me and tips my chin up.

"Use your words, angel. Tell me what you need from me."

His lips hover over mine.

"I need you to help me feel normal again—sexy. Make me forget who I am, even for a little while. Break me to make me whole again."

"Fuck," he whispers.

He leans back, his eyes searching mine.

"Please, Frankie." I bat my lashes at him.

"I'll give you what I think you need," he growls.

I nod, not taking my eyes off his lips that I so desperately want on mine. He tucks a stray strand of hair behind my ear.

"I need you, too, dolcezza," he mutters against my cheek, feathering his lips down my skin towards my jaw.

His fingers trail up my arms and he pushes the robe from my shoulders, letting it drop to the floor. He sucks in a breath, with a hunger in his eyes as he takes in my little red outfit.

"My beautiful girl," he whispers. He traces his tongue along my throat and down my chest. As I tilt my head back, I intertwine my fingers in his hair.

His hands continue down my stomach and he cups my throbbing pussy through my silky thongs.

"You really are desperate for me, aren't you? My filthy little slut," he growls.

"So bad, sir."

"Turn around, arms up against the door."

I don't hesitate. I do exactly as he says, pressing the side of my face against the cool wood.

He groans in appreciation as he grabs my ass cheeks and runs a finger down the center, hooking it under the thongs and pulling them down to my ankles.

"As perfect as you look in these, you naked will always be my favorite."

My arms start to ache, so I let them sag down to the frame.

His hand connects with the top of my thigh in a sharp snap.

"Oh my god." I squeeze my eyes shut as the sting takes over.

"Stay still. You aren't going to move a muscle until I tell you to."

I hold my breath as he presses his hard cock against my ass and his fingers lace around my throat.

I try to steady myself, but as he circles my clit, my legs feel like they're giving out beneath me.

"My girl lost her voice, hmm?"

I let out a whimper as he slides his fingers deep inside me and increases the pressure on the sides of my neck.

"Is this what you need, Zara?"

"M-more," I beg him.

"Is that right?"

When he removes himself from me, I nearly collapse against the door, feeling weak and shaky. His fingers dig into my hip as he spreads my cheeks, his warm breath sending ripples of pleasure through me.

"Fuck, dolcezza truly is the right name for you," he whispers against my pussy and takes a slow lick from my slit all the way back to my asshole. "So fucking sweet."

He continues to alternate between licking, sucking and fucking me with his tongue, all while his finger circles my tight hole.

"I'm so close, sir."

I can feel the strain in my muscles as I fight to keep my arms elevated. The more my legs tremble, the harder it gets. He stands and whips me around to face him, lifting me in the air so my legs wrap around his waist, his rock-hard dick rubbing against my pussy.

His lips crash over mine for a hungry kiss as he presses my body against the wall. I grind my hips to try to relieve some of the pressure, but his firm hand on my hip holds me in place.

"Keep doing that and you won't get to come," he warns.

With his kisses stealing my breath, he walks us over to the couch and lays me down, settling himself between my thighs. I watch as he unzips with his pants, releasing his cock and wipes the pre-come from the tip.

"Open," he commands.

I do as he says and suck the salty liquid from his thumb. He removes his shirt and sits back on his heels, taking long slow strokes on his dick.

His eyes are piercing as he watches me squirm. He must be waiting for me to start pleading with him to fuck me into oblivion. He needs me desperate for him, and I am.

"P-please, Frankie. I need your cock inside me."

With him positioned above me, his arm supporting his weight, I let out a sigh as he guides himself closer, the tip tantalizingly rubbing against my sensitive clit.

Holy fuck.

The longer it goes on, the harder it is to resist pushing my hips down to force him to fuck me.

"That feels so fucking good, sir," I pant, tipping my head back. My whole body is ablaze.

"You don't want my dick sinking deep inside of you?"

My eyes open. "That's what I thought," he bends down for a kiss and flips me over onto all fours, his fingers digging hard into my hips as he sinks inside me, letting out a moan of his own.

"Do that again," I whisper.

"What?" he asks breathlessly.

"Moan, that was so fucking hot."

He pushes back inside me, pressing a firm hand down on my lower back. Another rumbling sound rips from him and I nearly lose control.

He fucks me with no holding back, slamming inside me over and over again. I'm screaming out his name, all while fighting for breath. I can't take much more.

I grip the overstuffed arms of the loveseat tightly, my knuckles turning white, as I lean forward. I feel his strong grip tighten as he pulls me back, securing me in place.

"Did I say you could move?"

The second his finger starts to circle my clit, I crash over the edge. I come harder than I ever have before. He takes every single ounce of pleasure from me, without letting up. I feel as if I've died and gone to heaven. He slows the pace and slides out of me, my body sagging into the cushions.

I don't even have a moment to catch my breath before he yanks me up by my hair, pressing my back tightly against his chest, our bodies slick with sweat, sticking together.

I lean my head to the side and he nibbles softly on my cheek.

He releases me, and as I turn around to face him, I find myself mirroring his position on his knees. As we stare into each other's eyes, his hand comes out and cups the side of my face and he pulls me into him, claiming my tender lips for a passionate kiss.

"I love you, sir."

"I love you, angel. You have no idea how much."

Oh, I do.

"I want to come with you to get Romano, Frankie. I'm not staying here without you. We do this together."

We haven't spoken about this. It's all happened so fast.

He won't stop me.

When Romano dies, he will look us both in the eyes as he takes his last breath. I deserve this, too.

"I wouldn't have it any other way, baby. It's us against the world, remember? It's your revenge as well. I'd never take that from you."

Pressing my face against him and I hug him tight, listening to his fast heartbeat.

"I want to try again for a baby when this is over. I want everything."

I can feel the warmth of his fingers as they trail up my spine, before lacing around my throat and pulling me back in front of him.

"I'll give you the world. We will have it all and it will be beautiful."

A wave of emotion washes over me, causing tears to well in my eyes.

"I wish I could take this pain away, dolcezza." He lowers his forehead to mine.

"You do. Every day, you make it better."

"I'm so fucking lucky I get to call you mine," he says, pressing a kiss to my lips that has me craving more.

"You're quite the catch yourself, Mr. Falcone."

"Is that right?"

I squeal as he lifts me over his shoulder, slapping my ass as he carries me to the door.

"We have time to kill before Enzo calls, and I'm making use of every single second with your perfect body."

It's been a whirlwind twenty-four hours since Enzo called. Between the rapidly scheduled flights to Italy and the coordination of getting the army brought over and tracking down lodging and supplies, we're all living on nerves and caffeine.

I lean back on the kitchen counter as the men line up their weapons on the dining table. Frankie is in his element, dishing out armament to his men. When he looks up and catches me eyeing up, he blows me a kiss and I can't help but blush.

Frankie held me so tightly in his sleep, like it could be the last time we do this. No matter how confident we may be, there is that doubt in all of our minds. We've all lost so much, realistically, this could go very badly.

Just because we've narrowed down Romano's location, we're in a villa in Sicily with the Russians. I should feel safe, but it doesn't mean the unexpected can't happen. A bit like the End Zone blowing up with me inside.

I just have to pray to God it doesn't.

Jax waltzes over with a teasing grin on his face to hand me a vest.

"For you, queen Zara."

"Knock it off." Frankie slaps him on the back of the head.

I've been waiting for Frankie to change his mind and make me stay behind. He knows I'm capable of looking after myself, he's my protector.

We're just waiting on Enzo to scope out the exact coordinates. We want to catch Romano when he least expects it.

"Go and put it on for me." Frankie leans over and drops a kiss to my lips.

"Get a fucking room," Jax calls out.

"I swear to God, Jax," Frankie growls.

I can't help but laugh. Jax knows how to get under Frankie's skin as much as I do.

I head over to the coffee machine and jab the button, placing a black mug underneath. Frankie's arms wrap around my stomach, his lips brushing along my neck.

"How long before we need to leave?" I ask just as the coffee machine beeps.

"Twenty minutes."

"Okay, I'll get my vest on. Grab me a couple of guns."

"Only the best for you." He kisses my jaw and releases me, not before slapping my ass.

I stop by the door as I hear Luca and Rosa coming down the stairs.

His deep voice precedes them. "I'm coming home, tesoro. To both of you. Don't doubt me on that. Once this is over, we can finally be free."

My heart sinks in the most selfish way possible. Despite the stinging sensation of tears in my eyes, I manage to suppress them as they come closer to me, replacing any trace of sadness with a forced smile.

Luca pulls her into an embrace, and I look away, not wanting to invade on their moment.

I need space. I clasp tightly to my vest and bolt out up the stairs, slamming our bedroom door shut behind me. I pull my black cami over my head and toss it next to the vest on the bed.

I'm still fucking broken. All the years of my dad chipping away at me, everything Frankie rebuilt within me, has been shattered again. If I lose him, I lose everything. I'm so consumed by my guilt and anger, I can barely see.

A squeak escapes my lips as Frankie spins me around. His lips crash onto mine, leaving me gasping for air.

"What was that for?" I say when he pulls back.

"I just wanted some time with you before we go."

"You mean in case you don't come home, don't you?"

He shakes his head, stroking my face.

"Baby, you know if it comes down to it, I'm taking a bullet for you, for my family. Will I try my fucking hardest to make it home to you? Yes. You know that is my driving force now. I can't lie to you, though. This isn't going to be pretty. There is a chance. This could be the last time I get to steal a kiss from my dolcezza."

My eyes sting. I can't bring myself to look at him. "Don't say that, Frankie."

"Zara, this is our life. This is how I have lived for years, except this time, I truly have something to live for, to fight to come back to. So, I will."

He kisses me again, but I don't return it. I refuse for it to be our last.

"Don't deny me," he growls.

He grabs my hand, my engagement ring sparkling between us.

"You think I won't do everything I can to make sure I make you my wife? That I won't come home to give us that family we want, our legacy? Give me some credit."

I suck in a breath, looking into his eyes.

"Now, kiss me like you mean it," he demands.

I jump into his arms, causing him to stumble back against the wall. Slamming my lips over his, I kiss him with everything I have, pulling at his hair as he moans into my mouth.

His hand slides down into my panties, his index finger circles my clit until my entire body begins to quiver.

Just as I'm about to start begging, he pulls away with a grin. "I'll be finishing what I started when we're home."

I stare at him, open-mouthed and breathless. "You asshole."

"Yeah, I'll fuck your ass too, if you want." He winks, and

removes his hand. "I love you, Zara. You know that, right?"

I nod. "Oh, I know. I love you too, my crazy man. Let's get this done, so I can have you all to myself."

He turns away and swipes up the vest from the bed.

"Arms up," he commands.

He slips it over my head and starts to adjust the sides first, followed by my shoulders, without saying a word.

"I'm going to be fine, Frankie. You've seen me in action."

He swallows, still staying silent as he hands me my black sweater. "You are all that matters, dolcezza."

I gently cup his face in my hands, tracing the short dark beard with my fingertips.

"I mean, I think I look pretty hot like this. Badass, right?" I wink at him, trying to shake him out of any dark place he might be sending himself to.

"Badass, now that is the perfect way to describe you, baby."

I wiggle my eyebrows and grin.

"It helps when you've got the mafia boss wrapped around your little finger." I tap his cheek and try to walk away. I can't hide my giggle when he catches me by the wrist, lifts me in the air and throws me down on the bed.

"Hey, I love watching you be all ruthless and in charge. It makes me horny as hell. It's where you're happiest, isn't it?" I say, continuing to goad him.

"It's one of the places I'm happiest, yes."

"Hmm, what else then?"

"When I'm with you, Zara. That's where my true happiness

lies, with you."

"That's cute."

His fingers dig into my thighs and I try to wriggle away.

"Don't call me cute."

"Why? Have we got time for you to show me all the ways you aren't cute? I'd like the reminder that my fiancé isn't a big ball of mush. It's a bit of a turn off." I bite back a grin.

He looks at his Rolex and back to me, raising a brow.

"I've got four minutes to punish that little bratty mouth. Now on your knees, baby."

My eyes light up as his hands go to his belt.

This is exactly what we both need.

CHAPTER SIXTY-FOUR

Frankie

"Let's go, boss. Enzo's given us the green light," Jax shouts, throwing on his leather jacket.

As I guide us towards the patio, Zara's grip on my hand tightens. We make our way past the pool towards the steps leading to the beach, where Luca and Nikolai are diligently loading our explosives onto the boat.

Once Jax hops onto the board, my focus shifts to Zara.

"You ready for this?" I ask, searching her eyes.

"Damn right, handsome." She tugs on my tie, crashing her lips over mine.

"Are you kidding? We have shit to do!" Jax whines, hitting his ringed fingers against the side of the boat.

I don't look at him as I cup her cheek. "I suggest you shut up. At least I'm getting some."

He fakes a hurt face. "Trust me, I'm doing just fine. Girls love a biker with a massive dick and a tongue piercing."

After the few weeks Jax has had after losing Kai, I'm cutting him some slack. If anything, today will give him what he needs to move forward.

He clicks that bar against his teeth dramatically louder than usual, knowing it pisses me off. He winks, flipping me off as he does. Zara laughs next to me.

Carefully, I support Zara as she steps onto the boat, and then swiftly jump aboard.

"We're all set, Frankie," Luca says, rubbing his hands together.

"Let's go and end this once and for all."

The sooner Romano dies, the sooner my life can start. I wrap an arm around Zara's shoulder, pulling her close as the wind rustles through her long, dark locks, while we head towards the yacht anchored a few miles off the coast.

"Wow, now that's a boat." Jax lets out a low whistle as we approach.

"Not for much longer. It won't be."

By the time we're finished, there won't be a trace of Romano nor the Capri's.

Their reign will be over.

CHAPTER SIXTY-FIVE

Zara

The warm breeze brushes across my skin as I sit with Jax on the skiff waiting for Frankie to give us the all clear to climb up onto the yacht. I squeeze my eyes shut as another gunshot goes off. Jax fidgets next to me, clearly itching to get up there and join in. But, Frankie, Luca and Mikhail seem to have it covered.

I whip my head around as a splash comes from behind me. As I look up at the side of the ship, I can see Mikhail's black balaclava as he hurls a second body over the railings.

"How many people are on this damn boat, Jax?"

He gives a dismissive shrug, his tongue clicking in his mouth. "He's a mafia don. He was always going to have some protection."

I tap my fingers on my jeans. Another shot fires and I stand. Fuck this. I can reach the ladder, why should I sit here and do nothing?

Before I can even move, Jax abruptly steps in front of me, his gaze piercing and serious.

"Frankie gave me my instructions. You don't move until he says. Now sit down, Zara."

I raise my chin, waiting for a response, but he shows no sign of flinching.

"Sit. Frankie is doing just fine." His tattooed finger points at the hard bench behind me.

I slump back down, letting out an exasperated huff as I push my aviators up to perch on the top of my head.

Despite his constant teasing, he has Frankie's back. He wants Romano dead as much as we all do. My heart aches for him. Today could heal some of the pain he carries.

"Jax, we're all good," Frankie calls down. I blow out a breath and look up at him holding onto the metal railing. As the sun hits his tanned skin, it highlights the bloodied state of his hands.

He walks over and confidently scales down the steps onto our small boat, the sound of his footsteps blending with the lapping of the waves.

"Ladies first." He winks, tapping my ass as I squeeze past him to the stairs.

"Jesus, this is one hell of a yacht," I say. Its extravagance is almost overwhelming as I glance at the bar area in the dinner lounge.

"It will be a shame for something worth so many millions to go up in flames," Jax chuckles behind us before sliding open the glass doors and heading to the bar.

"No booze until we're done, Jax!" Frankie calls out.

"Yes, Dad." He holds up his hands and sits on the leather couch.

"You all good here?" Mikhail asks as he walks over. I expect him at some point to remove his mask, although I can imagine his face is as scary as the rest of him.

As he stands in front of us, I crane my neck to look up at him, and a shiver runs down my spine. I'm glad he's on our side.

"Yes, Miki." Frankie nods.

"I'll get in position with the rest of my brothers," Mikhail says, and disappears over the side.

"Anything yet from Enzo?" I ask, looking up at Frankie.

Tension radiates from his tightly clenched jaw.

"We have five minutes."

This will all be over in less than half an hour. Then, we can start our lives again.

"Let's go get ready, baby." He presses a tender kiss to my temple and guides us towards Jax. A sound shifts my gaze to the corner of the room where Luca appears, dragging the body of a waiter with blood pouring from his wounds that leaves a trail on the polished wooden floor.

"Zara, behind the bar for me," Frankie demands.

I don't argue with him. Even if I have a vest on, I know it isn't enough. As I attempt to leave, he seizes my wrist, yanking me back towards him, and crashes his lips onto mine.

"One more taste, just in case," he whispers against my lips.

"I won't let anything happen to you," I reply.

"I know, baby. I love you."

I feel my heart rate increase as I lock eyes with him.

As my hands travel down his back, I can't resist giving his ass a playful squeeze, only to be met with a stern look. One I know

I'm going to get punished for later. I give him a sly wink before swiftly darting behind the gleaming gold bar. Dropping onto my knees, I reach for my gun and pull the slide to make sure I have a bullet in the chamber. I position myself strategically, ensuring I have a clear view of the door through the narrow gap.

Jax and Frankie stand on either side of the main entrance, their guns raised and ready. Luca is waiting just behind them, hiding in the shadows.

"Copy that, Enzo," Frankie says.

I hear an engine outside and my palms start to sweat as my nerves kick in.

This feels as euphoric as I thought it would. I can't imagine how Frankie must feel.

I want this for him, for us both.

CHAPTER SIXTY-SIX

Frankie

Song- Final Judgement Day, Five Finger Death Punch.

The sound of several heavy sets footsteps grows closer.

"I haven't heard from George in days. Find him. I need to see if Mikhail's offer is legitimate. I need to form an alliance with the Russian before Frankie does." Romano's familiar voice is like music to my ears.

A subtle smile twitches on my lips.

"It gets me the cash I need to go after Frankie. He's going to be after blood. I don't have any other options."

The door slides open and I waste no time in pressing my gun against Romano's wrinkled forehead.

"Looks like I found you first," I say with a hint of amusement.

I glance back and see a man with a ponytail attempting to flee as Romano remains frozen in place, the phone slipping from his hand.

"Useless prick," Romano mutters.

"Shut the fuck up."

"Going somewhere?" Mikhail's hulking frame appears.

I glance over and find him holding up the scrawny ponytail by his neck with one hand. The frantic man claws at his black suit, his face reddening and his eyes bulging.

The sound of the gunshot echoes through the air as my bullet finds its target, tearing through Romano's hand as he reaches for his jacket.

"You fucking asshole," he screams out, holding his hand up with blood spilling down his arm.

With my gun pressed against his temple, I lean in and relieve him of his weapon.

"You're still using this old thing?" I say, holding his gun up between us that looks as ancient as he is.

"I was saving the last round just for you, Frank."

"I'll be sure to make sure it ends up lodged in your flesh then," I say and grab him by the scruff of the neck. He doesn't resist as I drag him towards the chair in the center of the room and toss him down onto it. Jax joins me, looping the rope around Romano's wrists behind the chair.

I hear the faint sound of Zara shuffling around behind the bar. I want him to witness the fury in her eyes as she exacts her revenge on him.

"Just kill me, Frankie. You fucking win," Romano shouts. He's red faced and tugging on his binds before Jax moves behind him and covers his mouth with a gag.

Mikhail has the ponytail sidekick slumped over his shoulder. He places him down on the chair next to Romano and Jax gets to work restraining him in the same way.

"Zara." I hold up my finger and motion for her to come to me. We have the Russians surrounding the boat until we're finished.

Zara steps around the counter, her sole focus on Romano. Her lips are tight, almost unreadable. When her eyes meet mine and that flash of darkness appears, I know my girl is okay.

Looking down at my Rolex, we have ten more minutes before we have to get off this boat.

"Jax, Luca, Mikhail, it's time."

They begin to douse the room in gasoline. I rip off Romano's gag and he sucks in a breath.

"Does it feel as good as you thought it would?" he taunts.

"Knowing that I took everything from you, including your life, means I can sleep soundly at night, Romano."

He turns to Zara and his face darkens. I take a shot at his kneecap with the bullet he had meant for me. He screams out in agony.

"You don't get to look at her. You shouldn't even be breathing the same air as her."

"You little shit," he spits out. "Just kill me, get it over with," he says breathlessly.

I tip his head up with my gun, looking into the hollow eyes of the man who altered my entire existence. There is only one thing I can ever thank him for, changing that path to allow Zara to be given to me.

"You're going out in the only fitting way possible. What better way to enter hell by turning up in flames?"

Images flash in my head of Leila, the house exploding and my life with it. As Jax douses the room, the pungent smell of gasoline burns my nostrils.

"You'll never be happy, Frankie. What are you going to do without your hunt for my blood?"

I tilt my head to the side, a smile spreading across my face. "I get to live."

Zara's smile lights up her face, and I can feel my heart racing in response. Revenge isn't the center of my universe, not anymore. She is. I step back from him to where I belong, by Zara's side.

"I'll see you in hell, Mr. Falcone," Romano grits through his teeth.

I know I'm no saint, I've never claimed to be. I have no doubts I will meet him again and I will continue to hunt him there, too. "I look forward to it."

I turn to face Zara, pulling her gaze away from the man who tried to destroy her, too.

"What do you say, dolcezza, shall we go and watch it burn?"

Our eyes lock, and in that moment, the world around us fades away.

"Hell yeah."

Lacing my fingers through hers, I lead us towards the exit without a glance back. Our past. It's over.

"Fuck you, Frankie!" Romano yells as we descend the steps where Mikhail's men are waiting for us on the speedboat. I pull out the zippo from my pocket and hesitate before throwing it onto the yacht. This truly is the end.

"What are you waiting for, throw it." Zara nudges me and I look at her. She should be the one to end his life. Her revenge.

I hand her the lighter and she furrows her brow in confusion.

"You do it for us, baby."

"Are you sure?" She hesitantly takes it from me.

"Positive." My hand finds the small of her back as she throws.

In a matter of seconds, the flames ignite. Nikolai starts up the boat. The flames grew taller in the distance as we moved further away.

"Stop," I shout. It won't be long before it goes bang with the number of explosives the Russians put on the boat.

I take a seat and pull Zara onto my lap. The deafening silence fills the air as the flames consume the yacht. She settles against me, her head resting in the crook of my neck. I inhale a deep breath of her vanilla scent and calm washes over me.

The moment I've waited for, for what feels like my whole life. I squeeze her tight. This wasn't just about me. This was for us, for our baby, for everything we've lost.

I know nothing can ever bring them back, but this is enough for me to move forward. To focus on what is truly important, our new family and our legacy. We will rule over New York together and there isn't a single person who can stop us.

Together, we are unstoppable. Just like I knew we would be.

I rest my head against hers. The moment when the yacht explodes a weight is lifted from my shoulders and I can't hide my smile. Sitting here, with the love of my life nestled against me, our enemies going up in flames.

Ending a war that has consumed my entire existence for a long time.

"I told you we'd set the world on fire together, dolcezza."

As she spins around in my lap, her hair brushes against my face. I don't give a fuck who is around us. All I see is her. The flames blaze in the background as I get lost in her sparkling green eyes.

"You did. Now you have to make good on your second promise."

"And what would that be?"

Her embrace tightens.

I instinctively bite down on my lip, trying to contain the rush of emotions.

"Marry me."

"That's first up on my agenda, angel. There is never any going back now, mine forever," I utter against her lips.

"That sounds perfect to me, Mr. Falcone."

CHAPTER SIXTY-SEVEN

Frankie

There's a somber feeling in the air. Kings gym is lined with our men, full to the brim. In hindsight, we didn't lose many, but any is too much.

Jax, Grayson, and Luca join me and Zara up in the ring. I need to do what any good leader does; show them their worth, and keep them loyal to me.

I tighten my grip on the red ropes. Just because Romano is gone, doesn't mean we start slacking. There is always another enemy waiting to swoop in for power. We're now working with the Russians who have enemies in the country.

It's always going to be a dangerous life.

"Romano is dead, the Capris are no longer an organization, nor a threat to us." I start my speech off with, which earns me a cheer from the crowd.

"Each and everyone of you have earned your place here, and will be compensated well for your work."

What they don't know yet is each of them will be receiving a hefty financial bonus.

"Now, business will return to usual. We have more shipments

coming in and deals with the Russians to take into consideration. Jax will lead the front with them and Grayson will continue with your training, both combat and boxing."

I glance at my two main men, both sporting grins.

"Zara and I are exploring expansion opportunities. Mainly with clubs and properties, potentially into the takeover in Sicily. The End Zone will be coming back. Some of you will work on that until Keller is ready to help."

I let out a breath. He's awake, he's in recovery. Despite having some touch and go moments, he pulled through with his wife by his side. I know he will be back in action in some form as soon as he can.

"He'll be back, but sticking to training this time."

"And I'm sure you've all noticed the reappearance of the other Russo brother." I turn and gesture for Luca to join me.

"Now, this asshole, he's not going anywhere. He might not be the boss anymore, but he will be my right-hand man, working closely alongside Enzo." My hand claps him on his shoulder.

Luca nods and waves like he's on a Sunday float. With a baby on the way, he's moving back to New York. He made it clear he had no intentions of leading alongside me.

Zara takes her spot beside me and holds my hand.

"And we will celebrate this victory at our wedding in a couple of months. I expect you to all be on your best behavior. Now, get back to work. We don't stop, we don't slow down, we expand. New York is ours. This time we fucking keep it that way. Who is with me?"

The men roar, and I squeeze Zara as Grayson and Jax join us to look out at the army we've built.

We may be the most fucked up family to walk this earth, but I wouldn't have it any other way. Family are the ones you choose. Zara and these men beside me, they are my family, the ones I will kill for, or give up my fucking life for.

The ones I will have by my side as we rule over the city.

There is just one last piece to put into place... making Zara my wife.

My forever.

CHAPTER SIXTY-EIGHT

Frankie

Two months later...

I jog down the stairs. I need some air. After seeing Zara in her wedding dress and her begging me to make her ass red, I had to drag myself out of that room. I follow the smell of cigarettes that wafts through the window and head out into the yard. Grayson, Jax and Luca sit around the table with a bottle of scotch.

"Starting without me?" I ask as I stride toward them.

"We didn't realize you would be so damn long," Grayson says, pouring me a glass and sliding it across the table.

"Sorry, Zara needed me."

Jax rolls his eyes. "Needed a dicking more like."

I slap him in the back of the head. "Watch your mouth."

Luca and Grayson hold back their laughter. He's not wrong though.

"You never know, Jax, you might find a woman one day who can show you a thing or two."

"Quality over quantity," Grayson adds, and holds up his

glass.

"Yeah, easy for you guys to say that. I'll stick to my plan, thank you." Jax knocks back his scotch and lights his cigarette.

"And what plan is that?" Luca asks. Rosa comes through the door and sits on his lap. I smile as I watch him cuddle her against him, pressing a kiss to the side of her head, his hand protectively stroking her little belly bump.

"What plan?" she asks, looking around the men with a questioning stare.

"Oh, my plan to stay single forever and fuck my way around New York," Jax replies with a smug grin.

"And how's that going for you?" she asks, making us all laugh.

Jax rests his arm up on the chair next to him, tugging at his tie. "I'm pretty happy."

There is no disguising the lie in his tone. He's still young. He has plenty of time to work it out. Even if we all have to give him a bit of a push in the right direction.

Keller and Sienna walk out hand in hand, with Max and Darcy in front of them. Keller cradles their newborn son, Nico, in his arm.

"Looking good, Mr. Russo." I greet him.

"Getting there." He smiles back, running a tattooed hand across his stubble.

"Darcy, wait for Daddy!" he calls out as his dark-haired daughter runs off into the yard.

"I'll go get her, Dad," Max replies and runs after her.

After pouring him a scotch, I hold it out to him.

"Are you ready to get back to work?" I ask.

"No. He's not." Sienna replies while side-eying him.

Keller chuckles and pulls her snug into his side before placing a kiss on the side of her head.

"Not that kind of work, princess. Helping out with the End Zone renovations is what he means."

"It better be."

I hold my hand up and chuckle. "I swear."

The revamp of the End Zone is in full swing, and in typical Keller style, he wants to be involved. Seeing as that will be primarily his base from now on. The hottest club will be back, even bigger this time.

The doors slide open and a red faced Maddie comes storming out, pointing her finger at me as she stomps closer in her black dress and heels.

"You, Frankie, ruined Zara's hair and make-up," she says, jabbing her nail into my chest.

"I'm not apologizing, Maddison." I hide my smirk.

She huffs, looking at her husband.

Grayson shrugs. "I'm not getting involved."

"You men, you need to get going. You need to be at the venue." She grabs my arm and looks at my watch. "Ten minutes ago!"

"Calm down, I've paid enough for them to not care." I ruffle her blonde hair, making her glare at me.

"Grayson, get him out of here before I kill him."

The men all stand up while she gives me a scowl.

"I'm going, I'm going." I hold my hands up in surrender.

"Sorry Frankie, I'm just a bit stressed," she pouts.

"It's okay. I appreciate all your help organizing this for us."

"You're going to love it, it's spectacular. Very 'you'." She grins.

"As long as my girl is happy, I'm happy. Is her bag all packed?" She nods.

I have a little surprise up my sleeve for my wife tonight.

CHAPTER SIXTY-NINE

Zara

Song- Rain, Sleeptoken

As Rosa helps me out of the limo, I spot my mom standing outside the grand hall. Without thinking, and gripping my bouquet of black roses in my hand, I sprint towards her and hug her tightly.

"Mom!" It comes out more of a sob as I squeeze her tight, closing my eyes.

"Zara, sweetie. I've missed you so much."

"I missed you, too." I cling to her neck and kiss her cheek.

We've spoken on the phone and I've been out to visit her a few times with Frankie. With her being in this new treatment facility, she wanted to get as well as she could for our wedding.

She also needed time to grieve, away from New York.

"Well, we won't ever be spending that much time apart again," she says.

I pull back to look at her. "What do you mean? Have you finished your treatment?"

"I have, for the most part. I'm moving back, well, in, with you and Frankie, if you'll have me."

I tilt my head. "Have you spoken to him already?"

She gives me a smile. "It was his idea."

My heart flutters; I love my man. "Well, we'd love to have you."

Maddie's heels click against the pavement behind us. "Everything is ready for you. Are you ready, Zara?"

Rosa stops by Maddie's side with her camera in one hand, resting her other on her protruding belly.

"I'm ready." I lace my arm through my mom's.

Sucking in a deep breath, I hold my bouquet in front of me, standing in front of the gold doors that will lead to our ceremony room.

The doors slowly open, revealing the white pillared room, surrounded by arrangements of black and white flowers.

Our friends, our allies, our family, all in one room.

My eyes lock on the man standing at the end of the altar. His hands clasped in front of his legs. His eyes rake up my body as he bites down on his lip.

He takes my breath away.

With each step I take towards him, the rest of the room fades out. It's only Frankie.

I can feel him as my dress brushes against the welts on my ass that he left me with earlier.

I wanted this.

To be his in every sense of the word.

As I reach him, I stop and turn to Mom.

She sniffles and kisses me on the cheek.

"I'm so proud of you, Zara. You've got yourself a keeper there." She winks and looks to Frankie, who smiles at her.

Handing her my bouquet, I step in front of the man who owns me with a grin on my lips.

He leans forward and my breath hitches as his neat beard brushes against my jaw.

"Beautiful," he whispers and I blush as he pulls back, lacing his hand through mine.

The officiant clears his throat as I stand beside Frankie and I squeeze his hand. I look up at him and lick my lips, causing Frankie to raise an eyebrow.

He leans down, still facing the officiant.

"What's up, angel?"

"Does this go on for long? My ass is stinging, and now I'm all horny."

Frankie chokes on a cough, and I hold back a laugh.

"Careful, baby." The warning in his tone has me clenching my thighs.

I spent the entire wedding ceremony squeezing my thighs together to try to relieve some of the pressure. No thanks to my new husband. Who not only looked damn fine in that black suit, he kept eye fucking me the entire time.

He knew what he was doing.

It was perfect. And now, I am officially who I was always meant to be.

Mrs. Falcone.

Now, the party is in full swing. I look over to Mom, who is sitting with Sienna and Maddie. She smiles and gives me a wave.

My heart swells as she makes her way over to us, resting her hands on mine and Frankie's shoulders. She leans down, whispering something in Frankie's ear and he laughs. I shoot her a questioning look, and she simply grins at me.

"A beautiful couple." I close my eyes and she kisses my cheek.

I stroke her frail hand.

"I love you, Mom." I whisper.

"I love you more than life. I'm happy I got to see this day." I look up and smile at her.

Frankie rubs his fingers along my wedding ring, just a simple touch has me almost sweating.

"Now, I'm going to get some more cake," Mom says, tapping Frankie on the shoulder.

"Not long, baby." He leans in and whispers.

I groan, just those words are setting off fires.

I look across the crowd, all of them together with their kids. They're all in love, and dare I say, happy. Even after everything they've been through, they fought and came out the other side stronger than ever. Just like Frankie.

I spot Jax sitting at the Russian's table, deep in conversation. I think this is the first time I've seen him with a serious expression on his normally teasing face.

"What's that about?" I nudge Frankie to look at their table.

"Their proposal for Jax. Him working alongside Nikolai. It's a big step up if he takes it." Frankie sips on his champagne.

Jax is one of his best. He seems to work well with the Russians on the shipments. He's been struggling with Kai's death. We've all seen it. Even if he tries to mask it with his humor.

"Jax doesn't look too happy about it."

He shrugs. "I'll talk to him soon."

Luca and Grayson appear in front of us, and I take the opportunity to slip away.

"I'll be right back." I drop a kiss to his cheek, my lips grazing his ear as I whisper, "if you find me, you fuck me."

I don't give him a chance to reply before hitching up my dress and running out the door. The fresh air hits me as I kick off my heels and run across the acres of grass lit up with festival lights.

My heart rate picks up. I know he's behind me. I need to get him alone. I dart behind the nearest tree and press my back against the bark. Excitement sparks through my veins as his footsteps get closer.

"What did I tell you about running from me, wife?"

I can't help but bite my lip when I hear his deep voice.

The first thing that hits me is his intoxicating, masculine scent as he towers over me. The sparkling from the lights reflecting in his icy gray eyes.

"What am I going to do with you, dolcezza?" He tilts his head, tracing his index finger along my arm in a soft motion all the way up towards my neck. "I found you. Have you been a good girl for me, hmm?"

I nod, feeling a surge of anxiety coursing through my body. I can't keep the secret any longer. It's killing me. I thought I could keep it to myself for a little longer, but the worry is taking over. I need him to keep me sane.

Would it be better if he never knew? Do I want to put him through that again? I quickly decide he deserves to know, to share this moment of joy together.

It's a blessing. A second chance. Together, we can get through anything. We've proven that already. With him by my side, nothing can bring me down.

"What's the matter, baby? Something is eating at you." He tips my chin up, searching my eyes.

"I'm pregnant," I almost whisper; I've been scared to even say it out loud.

Seeing the smile on his face in this moment is something I will never forget.

He pulls me into an embrace and his face presses into my neck.

A tear slips from my eye in happiness.

I have everything I could ever want, a husband who would burn down the world with me and I'm carrying his baby.

"Thank you," he whispers, squeezing me tight.

"It was half you. You've been pretty relentless with the trying part."

As he pulls back, his hand cups my cheeks. The cool metal of his wedding ring contrasts against my warm skin. It's my mark on him.

"I fucking love you, Zara Falcone. Today, tomorrow and every single moment until I take my last breath. You are the best thing to ever happen to me, and I will cherish you and all of our babies forever."

My tears erupt into full-blown sobs. I rest my forehead against his chest, feeling the steady rhythm of his heartbeat.

"Don't cry, baby." His palms rub soothing strokes up and down my back.

"What if it happens again?"

"We can't live with what 'if's'. We take the punches as they're thrown and we fight back harder. Together, we are unstoppable, baby. Never forget that. I've got you."

He pulls my face back up and presses his lips against mine.

"I love you, Frankie. I just want to give you everything, like you have for me."

"You already have, angel." He places my palm on his cheek. "We've got this," he whispers.

I believe him.

We have strength in each other, in our new family.

"Now, mama, I have to get you out of here. I've got a surprise for you and I can't wait a second longer for it," he says with a mischievous grin.

I sniffle, and he kisses my forehead. We stand there in each other's arms, soaking up this moment of perfection.

"Let's say our goodbyes, and then you are mine for the night,

Mr. Falcone."

"I am all yours, always have been, let's face it." He winks.

I slide my hand into his and squeal as he bends and scoops me up into his arms, cradling me into his chest as he walks us back towards the party.

He places me back on my feet before bending to retrieve my heels. He drops onto one knee so I can hold on to his back as he puts my shoes on for me.

"Fuck, you look so hot," I say as he stands and dusts off his suit.

"Not as gorgeous as you, wife." He holds out his hand with a smile and leads us back into our reception.

Jax is up on the table, swinging his jacket around and pouring champagne straight from the bottle into his mouth.

"Someone cheered up," I joke.

Frankie watches him with amusement, as do Grayson, Keller and Luca as they stride towards us.

"They're going to have fun with him in Vegas," Grayson says as he reaches us.

"He needs to blow off steam. He'll do just fine."

Jax catches us watching and gives us one of his cocky smiles.

"Make sure he keeps his clothes on," Frankie says to Grayson.

"I'm just going to say goodbye to the girls, okay?" I look up at Frankie.

"Be quick." He taps my ass as I head over to my new girl-friends, the first ones I've had since I was sixteen.

I'll be as fast as I can. I can't wait much longer for him.

I need to know how he fucks as a husband.

Chapter Seventy

Frankie

Song- Ex Habit- love me.

Zara gazes out of the helicopter window, captivated by the twinkling lights of nighttime New York as we make our way to our suite. The penthouse's magnificent views of the city left me with no choice but to purchase it for us.

It will be our escape from the world where we will always be just us.

A place where we can remind ourselves of our power, and where pleasure is the only thing we feel there.

"This is beautiful, Frankie."

My heart races just looking at her in all her radiance.

As we approach the skyscraper and begin to land, she squeezes my hand. I look down, seeing the wedding ring on her finger. Never in my life did I think I would find love again. Let alone, a love more fierce than anything I'd ever experienced. A part of me will always miss Leila and grieve the life we lost. Yet at the same time, I'm leaving that in my past to enable me to embrace my future.

I'm confident everything in my life has led me to Zara. She is who I have always belonged to. I know my true meaning, to love this woman with everything I have.

Zara was never meant to be broken to fit any mold for the world. She was created to lead, to be a force. She might break for me, but that was only ever for one reason. To show her the true potential she has. To set her free.

The door opens and I help her out of the helicopter onto the roof. The wind blows her hair in her face as she laughs. And fuck, I love that smile of hers.

I unlock the door with my keycard and take her down the flight of steps to our penthouse. As she steps in, I hold her hand tighter to stop her.

"I want you naked and down on your knees facing the window."

"Yes, sir."

I head past the living room and into our bedroom, which has everything set up that I need for tonight. But first, I'm taking us back to where this all began. Unzipping my bag, I pull out that damn ghost face mask, her handcuffs and the new addition to the collection- one of the rarest pink diamonds in the world that I've had put on a butt plug as a wedding present.

My wife is about to have a multi-million-dollar diamond in her ass tonight, and it will be worth every single cent.

Stripping out of my suit and boxers, I put on the mask with the handcuffs and plug in my hand. I stop by the entrance to the main living room, surrounded by black roses, to find my wife on her knees facing away from me.

Beyond her is the twinkling New York skyline.

Our city.

She keeps her head bowed as I stalk forward. I know she's itching to move; I can sense it as her fingers tap her bare thigh.

Raising her chin, I rub my thumb across her full lips. That perfect, deep red blush spreads across her chest as her eyes work their way up my bare body.

Her mouth parts in surprise as she reaches the mask.

"Remember this?"

She nods, the rise and fall of her breathing picking up.

"I still think about that night, you know. The first time I tasted your sweetness. I knew then that you would be it for me." I lean down, taking one of her nipple piercings between my fingers.

"Let's see if you've been a good girl for me. Spread your legs," I command.

She shuffles them apart, allowing me access to her.

"Hmm, just as drenched as you were that night," I grunt.

She pants as I stroke her pussy before sliding two fingers in.

"Your body is begging for me, wife."

That unmistakable sound of her desire fills the room, only making it harder for me to concentrate on anything other than the blood rushing to my dick. Taking the diamond plug in my hand, I slide it inside her, letting her coat the metal in her succulent juices.

"Oh, fuck." Her head tips back, arching her neck in a delectable invitation.

If I wasn't wearing this damn mask, I would have bitten her there, marking her for the world to see.

"On all fours." I pull it out of her and she drops onto her hands, her eyes fixating on the gem in my hands.

"Shut up. Is that real?" She frowns as it sparkles against the lights.

"Only the best for an ass as perfect as yours, baby. Now, watch me in the window."

I drop onto my knees behind her and spread her ass apart, revealing her puckered hole. As I slowly guide it in, she tries to lean forward, so I squeeze my free hand on her hip to hold her in place.

"Just breathe, gorgeous."

When it's all the way in, I take a moment to admire her sparkling ass. Wrapping my arms around her waist, her body presses against mine as I lift her up, placing her on her feet.

Her head rests against my shoulder, and my cock pulsates against the small of her back. Sliding my hand down her stomach, I slip between her legs to circle her clit, and with my other hand, I play with her nipple.

"Look at our reflection in the window, baby. Look how beautiful you are. Everyone outside that glass, you own them. All of it is yours. You're the most powerful woman in the city."

"Hmmm," she moans. "I don't care about them. Just you."

I thrust into her making her screams fill the room. Her hands shoot forward and she braces herself up against the window.

"I love you, husband," she pants out between thrusts.

"Oh, fuck," I hiss, her words fueling me and almost sending me over the edge. "I love you, Mrs. Falcone," I grit out.

Trailing my hand up to her neck, I squeeze my fingers around her throat. Her walls tighten around my cock.

"Such a perfect slut."

"Yes."

As soon as I'm close to exploding, I tighten my grip.

"Come for me." I just about make the words out before I erupt inside her.

Her body trembles around me as she screams out my name.

Without removing myself, I hold her waist and sit us down on the floor.

"Spin around, baby," I whisper against her shoulder, brushing my fingers along her skin.

She does as I say. Her flushed face meets mine as she settles her legs on either side of me.

Her hands delicately lift the disguise off of my head, allowing my skin to feel the cool air.

"I want to see you," she says.

With a flick of her wrist, she tosses it across the room.

"That's better. I love your handsome face."

Her lips land on mine and her hips grind against me.

I am consumed by a renewed craving.

"Without the costume now, please," she pouts.

Everyone hides under a mask of some description. It's who we are as mankind. There will always be parts of we want to conceal. The trick is to find someone who sees every part of you, no matter how ugly. They won't try to change you, they embrace the darkness.

This is the only one I'll ever be wearing with Zara. Because it has her absolutely soaking for me.

"That was just the warmup, dolcezza," I whisper against her jaw.

"Bring it on, sir. Show me who I belong to."

Oh, I will.

Every damn day. There isn't a thing I'd change about her. Not even that bratty mouth of hers.

And I vow to show her that she owns me completely, no matter what life may throw at us.

There is not a single doubt that our love will give us the power we need to take on the world.

And, if all else fails, we will have one hell of a time burning it to the fucking ground together.

Now that is true love.

EPILOGUE

Zara

8 months later

Blinking my eyes as I wake up, I find Frankie standing at the end of my hospital bed, cradling our son. His mop of black hair rests on Frankie's tattooed arm. He is whispering something in Italian to him, and in this moment, my heart is full.

Even if giving birth was excruciating. The second I did my final push and his cries filled the room, with Frankie holding my hand the entire time, I was complete.

Frankie looks up and his gray eyes meet mine, full of admiration.

"Did you have a good nap, mama?" he whispers.

"I did, although I could do with some more painkillers."

I can't even pinpoint where the pain is coming from. I might as well have jumped in front of a truck. I don't care. I'll take this agony any day to have my boys standing in front of me.

"I'll take care of it, angel." Frankie pads over to the side of the bed. "You want a cuddle?"

I look up at him and his eyes glisten.

"Gimme."

I hold my arms out, and he carefully leans over, placing our baby into the crook of my elbow. Closing my eyes, I take a deep inhale of that perfect newborn scent and press a kiss to the top of his head. Tears start to well in my eyes.

Frankie gently strokes my hair away from my face, pressing a soft kiss to my temple.

"I love you, Zara," he whispers.

"I love you, too, both of you. My boys."

"We did it, Frankie. We really did it." I sniffle, and he continues to stroke my hair. A sob catches in my throat as Frankie leans down and kisses the baby's head.

"This is just the start, dolcezza."

"He looks like a Leo, don't you think?"

He raises a brow. "Leonardo."

"Yes, *Leonardo.*" I roll my eyes and he pins me with a stare.

"After what I just witnessed, you can name him whatever you like, baby."

"Was it that bad?"

"I've seen some things in my time, but that may be one of the most brutal."

Freeing my arm, I lace my fingers through his.

"Don't you wimp out on me. We want to do this two more times, remember?"

He chuckles, squeezing my hand back, his lips hovering over mine.

"I can handle it. I was worried about you, that was all."

I look down as Leo starts to stir, his tiny mouth opening.

"Hey little man," Frankie coos beside me, stroking Leo's face with the back of his index finger.

I lean back and rest my head against his pec.

We have everything. An empire, a family and all the love I could possibly need to last me ten lifetimes. I got lucky. I can't wait to see what the future holds for us.

"What are you thinking about, dolcezza?"

"Just how much fun we're going to have."

His fingers grip my chin and push my head back to meet his gaze.

"That we will, baby," he says, before pressing his lips over mine.

EPILOGUE

Frankie

With a box of blue decorations firmly in my grasp, I stride into the dining room. My eyes find Zara at the table cradling our baby, Leonardo, with a smile on her face that makes my heart flutter.

Setting the box down on the table as instructed by Maddie, I make my way over and slide in next to Zara.

"So, how are you finding being a dad?" Grayson asks with a grin.

"Perfect," I reply without hesitation.

Because it's true. Every day I wake up with the two loves of my life, I'm a happy man.

My arm snakes around Zara's shoulder, and I pull her flush against my side. She looks up at me with a grin. I cast my eyes round the room, filled with blue balloons and a play area in the corner where the rest of the kids are already causing havoc.

"Sorry we're late!" Rosa calls from the door. Luca follows behind her, holding their new baby boy, Elio. He was born just two weeks before Leo.

Maddie jumps out of the booth and rushes over to them.

"Looks like you'll be adding to the crew again soon." I gesture my drink at the shuffling blonde before knocking back my scotch.

Grayson grins and looks over at his wife.

I shake my head with a chuckle. "Fucking hell, I told you we should have just made this into a daycare," I mutter and they all laugh.

Not that it's a bad thing. We have a new bloodline, a legacy here. Sienna has Nico, their newest son, in her hold. Max is busy on his computer game in the office while Darcy and Hope play in the kiddie zone.

Luca and Rosa slide into the adjoining booth.

Maddie cuddles Elio while beaming at Grayson.

"Anything to tell us, Maddison?" I ask, biting back my grin as I watch her cheeks flush a bright red.

She shoots a scowl at her husband. "Grayson! I told you not to say anything for another two weeks!"

"I said nothing," he laughs and blows her a kiss.

"Congratulations," I say, holding up my glass. "Now, pass me my nephew." I hold out my arms and reluctantly Maddie carefully places the little one in my arms. Rosa's watching with a smile on her face as she sits herself down next to me.

I lean over. "I'm proud of you, little thorn," I whisper.

"And I'm proud of you, Uncle Frankie." She nudges me back.

"Where the hell is Jax? He's supposed to be here," Keller asks.

He was back in New York for his brother's wedding yesterday, so he should be here.

"Probably still wasted," Grayson chuckles.

"Hold on, let me call him." I slide out my phone from my pocket with one hand and dial his number before putting it on speaker.

After a few rings, Jax's croaky voice comes through the speaker.

"Where are you?"

"Frankie, I fucked up. Big time." There's a panic in his voice that has me straightening my spine.

"What do you need? Where are you?" I look up to Grayson with a warning look. I'll need him to be ready if we have to leave.

"I'm good, boss. I just gotta get out of the city before I end up killing my brother."

I blow out a breath. Since Kai's death, he hasn't been himself. More reckless than usual. I'm keeping tabs on him with Mikhail. They're happy with his work, but they don't know him like we do.

"Why, what'd he do?"

Jax's laughter makes me relax slightly.

"He isn't the one who did anything. I am. But I'll have to kill him if he starts anything. I can't stand the asshole."

"I get it." Blood doesn't make a family.

"Jax, what did you do?" Grayson shouts.

There's a pause as Jax clicks his tongue bar. "I fucked his wife."

I burst out into laughter. It's typical Jax style. The King of Chaos living up to his name.

Zara's hands fly over her mouth as she tries to hold in her hysterical giggles.

"It's not funny!" Jax whines over the speaker.

Once I get a hold of myself, I ask the important question. "Well, was it any good?"

Zara nudges my side, still snickering next to me.

"Oh, fuck yeah, totally worth it." He didn't hesitate in his response.

"Well, get your ass over here, Jax. You're family. We want to see you before you head back. Okay?"

"Yes, *Dad*. I'll be there soon."

I hang up just as Elio starts to wriggle in my hold.

Luca is whispering into Rosa's ear as she smiles. We made it through the other side. Life has never been better. Leo's cries distract me from my thoughts.

I hand Elio over to Rosa and pick up Leo from Zara.

"Come on, son. Let's go for a walk," I say, resting his head on my shoulder.

Zara's hand lands on my thigh and electricity shoots through me.

"I'll come with you."

THE END.

THE MEN OF THE BENEATH THE MASK SERIES BONUS EPILOGUE

Keller, Grayson, Luca, and Frankie

*F**ive years later...*

Keller

Letting Max connect a jab into my stomach, I barely feel it.

"Try harder. If you want to slack off in school, that's one thing, but I'm not tolerating it here. Gloves up. Again," I order.

He sighs and I glare at him. I found him on my way to King's Gym, screwing off with his new girlfriend. So, I did what any father would—drag him into the back of my black Range Rover and shoved him in the ring.

"Look, I said I'm sorry, Dad."

He's a damn good kid. Well, teenager. He's seventeen. To me and Sienna, he will always be our first.

"Yeah, you tell your mom that."

She was furious when I called her. She worries that she isn't good enough. After her childhood, I get it. I make sure I spend every day reminding her how perfect she is.

Our kids have the best mom. We do everything we can to give all three of them the childhood we both wished we could have had.

Pulling back his glove, Max's glove connects to the pad with force, giving me the perfect combination.

"Better."

A grin lights up on his face. It quickly morphs into fear as the doors to the gym open and Sienna's heels click along the floor.

"Oh shit," Max whispers. "How pissed is Mom?" he asks nervously.

"Very. Apologize to her, and she will be fine." I nod to him as Sienna storms up into the ring. I toss my pads on the floor to help her.

"Hey, gorgeous," I murmur into her ear and press a kiss to her jaw.

Her bright blue eyes meet mine and my breath catches in my throat.

"I'll deal with you in a minute, Mr. Russo." She taps my chest.

I chuckle, wiggling my brows at her.

A blush spreads up her neck and she quickly puts her stern

face back on, stomping over to Max.

When she points her finger at him, he looks to me for support.

Won't be happening. My alliance is with my wife, always.

"Again? Really, Max! You're grounded. And I'm taking away your car until you learn to listen. School first, boxing after. Girlfriends, even lower down that list."

"But Mom," he whines, pushing his blonde curls away from his sweaty forehead.

"I don't want to hear it, Max." Her knuckles rest on her hips in a perfect motherly pose.

I step next to her to show her my support. "Apologize to your mom, Max."

"I am sorry, Mom. I didn't mean to upset you. I promise I won't do it again." There is a sincerity in his voice. He's a good kid. If skipping some classes is the worst we have to deal with, I'll take it. At his age, I was fighting in the street and getting my ass arrested.

Sienna moves forward, wrapping her arms around him.

"I love you, Max. I just want what's best for you."

He nuzzles into her embrace, and they release.

Max looks up to me. "I'm sorry, Dad."

I reach out and ruffle his hair.

"You're good, Maxy boy. Now go over there, grab a rope and get skipping." I lace my fingers through Sienna's.

Her bright eyes look up to me, raising her eyebrow.

Max ducks under the ropes.

As he gets further away, I blow out a breath, turning to my wife. Leaning down, I brush her dark curls away from her shoulder.

"Hi, princess. I believe it's my turn," I say with a hint of amusement.

Turning in my arms, her dainty hands wrap around my tattooed neck.

"You could have just taken him back," she whispers back.

"He's seventeen, baby. He's a good fighter, one of our best. He's doing something productive, have some faith in him."

"I do. You really think he can make it?" Her eyes light up.

"With me and G training him, he's got this. Now..." I brush my finger along her cheek and her eyes flutter closed. "How long have you got before you have to go back to work?" I raise a brow.

Her bright blue eyes light up as she bites down on her lip while tapping her chin. "For you, however long I want."

After taking over the Hideout from Paula, Sienna is busy running the charity. It's her passion, and I love her even more for it.

Tugging her by her hand, she squeals with excitement as I race us into the office and slam the door closed behind us. I lift her into my arms, her legs wrapping tightly around my waist before I crash my lips over hers.

"What does my gorgeous girl need from me?" I grunt out as she rolls her hips, sending blood straight to my cock.

"Surprise me." She pants out, dragging her fingers through my hair and yanking me down to kiss me.

As I lay her down on my desk, my phone lights up. She turns her head and groans in annoyance.

"It's Nico's school."

Unbuttoning her jeans, I snatch the phone up and answer.

"Hello, Keller speaking," I say, resting the phone on my shoulder as I peel off her jeans and panties.

"We need you to come and collect Nico, sir."

I stop what I'm doing. For a five-year-old, I've lost count of the number of times we've been pulled in for him.

He's mischievous. He's a mini me.

"Why?"

"We will explain to all the parents when you arrive."

"Give me ten minutes. Is he okay?"

Sienna sits up with worry etched across her features.

"He's fine."

I cut the call.

"What's happened?" Her eyes are wide and fearful.

"Nico is in trouble again."

I step forward, cupping her face in my hands and dropping a hot kiss to her lips.

"I'll finish this tonight, princess."

Grayson

"There are two more crates in the back," I order our guys, pointing over to the last of our drugs. Enzo reported police interest in two of our warehouses. So while Luca is securing deals for new, more discrete locations, I'm in charge of moving our supplies for the time being.

Rubbing my hands together, I pick up the gasoline from against the wall.

Time to burn it down.

The familiar rumble of my new Audi RS7 catches my attention outside. I slide my phone out of my pocket and see a missed call from Maddie. Dropping the canister to the ground, I rush to meet her as she parks.

Walking over, I open the door and she slips out, pulling on the hem of her yellow sundress. My favorite one. Pushing her oversized sunglasses to the top of her head, her bright blonde hair cascades over her shoulders. A smile creeps up on her lips.

"Maddie, what are you doing here?"

She tugs on my sweater, pulling me towards her. Resting my hands on the roof of the car on either side of her head as she looks up and bites down on her plump lip.

"My app just notified me. I'm at my most fertile. Right. This. Second."

I choke on a cough before a low growl rumbles through my chest and my cock twitches. Damn, this woman.

"I'm working, sunshine," I whisper, before stealing a kiss.

"Grayson Ward. I'm not taking 'no' for an answer. Please."

I pull back, making her pout at me. I look into her lust-filled green eyes. She's deadly serious. Her fingers trail down my sweater and underneath. I suck in a harsh breath as she strokes my six-pack.

"God, I fucking love you, sunshine."

"I love you too, big boy. Now, knock me up."

Chatter comes from the guys behind me. I whip my head round to them.

"You can go, I'll finish up here," I call out, then tense as her hands reach the top of my jeans.

The men stop and give me a questioning look.

"I said, fuck off," I growl. That kicks them into gear as they rush over to their trucks. Grabbing her by the hand, I drag her into the warehouse and set her down on the last remaining crate.

As soon as I hear the engines fade into the distance, I twist her hair around my fist and yank her head back, sinking my teeth into the base of her neck.

"Fucking gorgeous."

She spreads her legs and gets to work on my pants.

My own hands grab the fabric next to her thighs and push up her little dress.

"Jesus Christ, Maddie. No panties?"

She shakes her head, licking her bottom lip. "I don't need them. You'd only steal them anyway,"

I shrug, crashing my lips over hers.

We have our daughter, Hope, who is now seven and has the attitude of a fifteen-year-old. And then a son, Kai. He's five and obsessed with learning to box to be like his daddy. And now, she wants another to add to our crew.

My fingers lace around her throat making her suck in a

breath.

"Be a good girl. Put my dick inside you."

She shuffles her hips towards me, and I push her back so she's laying down. Her legs wrap tighter around my waist and she tugs me towards her.

My cock lines up, teasing her soaking entrance. "So perfect, sunshine."

I toss my head back as I thrust inside of her, with her name escaping my lips.

"More, Grayson."

As I bend forward, my phone rings in my jeans on the floor around my ankles.

"For fuck's sake."

I only have a ringtone for important calls. Reluctantly, I slide out of her and retrieve it.

"Are you serious?" Maddie hisses.

I hold up my finger when I see Kai's school flashing on the screen.

"It's Kai's school. Now, can you be quiet?" I ask, raising a brow.

She pretends to zip her mouth closed and lays back down. Returning to between her legs, I rub my hand up her smooth thigh.

This is the third call in two months. Each time, worse than the last. I didn't realize a damn five-year-old could cause so much trouble.

But do we want more? Absolutely.

Luca

"There you go, tesoro. Your favorite." I place down the plate of pancakes in front of her, smothered in strawberries and whipped cream.

"Ugh, what did I do to deserve you, Mr. Russo?" She looks up and smiles at me. I can't help but steal a kiss from her.

Every day, I love her more. I didn't know it was possible. She's given me everything I could ever ask for in life. Two beautiful children. Elio, who's five and a complete handful. And our daughter, Evangelina, who is asleep in her crib upstairs.

"Just by being you, my perfect girl," I whisper against her lips.

I take my seat next to her, placing the can on the table.

"Are you going to feed me, then?" I ask, biting the inside of my mouth.

Her brown eyes light up.

"Tip your head back and close your eyes."

I raise a brow but follow her instructions. With my mouth wide open, she stands and runs her fingers along my cheek, squirting the cream straight onto my tongue.

I swallow the disgustingly sweet fluff and lick the remnants from my lip.

"My turn." I say, picking her up by the waist and she squeals.

I prop her on the dining table, lacing my tattooed hand around her throat, and she tips her head back.

"Open up, my dirty girl."

I squeeze enough to fill her mouth and bring her face back to me. Her throat bobs as she swallows. Inching forward, I lick the cream from her lips, my tongue swirling around with the remainder of the cream.

"So fucking sweet," I groan, my dick painfully straining in my pants.

She nudges herself forward, wrapping her arms around my neck.

"How long are you at work for today?" she asks with a seductive smile.

"I just have to secure a deal on a warehouse with Enzo. So not long." I pause, looking at my Rolex. "I have an hour. You're off today?" I nuzzle beneath her ear, inhaling her sweet scent.

She shakes her head.

"No weddings booked in until next week. I'm all yours, Luca."

"Mine always," I growl against her skin. "Now, go and run us a bath. I have something to try."

She shivers at my touch.

I slap her ass as she saunters off.

My phone vibrates in my jacket.

"What now?" I mutter to myself, pulling it out and seeing Elio's school on the screen.

This kid is aging me.

I don't know what I expected–he's half me. He's rebellious and mischievous. I love him for it. The school, however, is not as amused by his disruptive behavior.

I answer the call, making my way up the stairs to Rosa.

"Hello, Mr. Russo?"

My mouth gapes open when I walk into the bathroom and find Rosa completely naked in front of the bath. I clear my throat,

"Yes, I'm here." Is all I can manage to croak out.

Frankie

I step back as Zara plunges the knife into the guy's thigh.

He screams out in agony.

She laughs, turning to look at me.

Fuck, she's beautiful.

"I wasn't joking when I told you my wife would do that if you didn't answer my question."

I yank the blade from his flesh and watch the tears roll down his cheeks.

"It's simple. Why were you snooping around my warehouse? Who sent you?"

He shakes his head, squeezing his eyes shut.

I press the tip of the bloodied knife just under his jaw. My eyes flick to Zara as she pulls her phone from her back pocket.

"It's Leo's school." She frowns at the screen and walks up the stairs.

Leonardo, our genius five-year-old. A perfect blend of both me and Zara. He will be our future in this empire.

"Well?" I return my attention back to this street rat.

"They'll kill me!"

"You think I won't?"

"You've got to go pick him up," Zara announces as she re-enters the room.

"Oh really? You get to stay here and have all the fun?" I ask with a smirk as she approaches me.

She nods, taking my tie between her fingers and pulling me towards her.

"I went last time. It's your turn, Mr. Falcone." She pulls me down, her hot breath beats against my ear. "If you do it, I'll do anything you want later."

I let out an exhale, tightening my grip on the knife. My cock twitches in my pants.

She knows how to get me.

"Damn. Fine, dolcezza."

She releases my tie and steps back, retrieving the knife from my hand.

"Don't worry, I won't make a mess. I'll pick the twins up from daycare." She winks, turning her attention back to our latest victim.

"Make all the mess you want, baby." I blow her a kiss and double take the stairs up from our basement.

Swiping my keys up from the table next to our family picture. The twins, Isabella and Rocco, were only a few days old here. Now, they're two-year-olds running around, shouting dada at me every two seconds.

Isabella, much like her mother, has me wrapped around her little finger.

My princess and my Queen.

My heavy footsteps echo along the hallway until I stand in front of Keller, Grayson, and Luca, leaning against the wall outside the office.

"What the hell have they done this time?" I ask.

They all shrug.

"They won't tell us anything, boss," Grayson replies.

"Why the hell are we waiting out here?" I shake my head, and stride to the principal's door and open it.

"I'm here. What can I do for you?"

Her eyes flick up from the screen and land on me. Enough to make her sit up straight in her chair.

"Come on." I gesture to my guys and they follow behind me.

My eyes zone in on my eldest son, Leonardo. A spitting image of his mother with bright green eyes and black hair, but my tanned skin.

For a five-year-old, he's a genius with a smart mouth like his mom.

Leo shifts uncomfortably in his seat as I approach him. The other kids look horrified at their father's appearance.

"Well, what did they do?" I straighten my jacket.

The woman pushes her glasses up her nose. "We found out that Leo—"

"Leonardo," I correct her.

She nervously shuffles some papers on her desk. "Yes. Sorry. He has been arranging fights on the playground. It appears he has set up a gambling ring, betting on the winners."

I have to bite the inside of my mouth to stop the laughter.

Grayson didn't quite get the memo, as I hear him chuckle behind me.

I look over at Keller and Luca's sons. Elio's hair is scruffy and Nico has a tiny graze on his eyebrow.

I give Leo a disapproving look, yet deep down, I'm impressed. Five years old and running a gambling ring.

I glance to the guys, all red faced trying to hold back their laughter. Luca fidgets with his watch. He can't even look at me. The longer I watch them, the harder it is for me to keep a straight face.

"And the punishment?" I ask, turning back to her.

"They will all be suspended for a week."

I tilt my head and take a step forward, resting my hands on the edge of her desk. "If you do that, I'll pull my funding for an entire year. Was anyone hurt? Any of the kids in the hospital?"

She shakes her head, her hands starting to tremble.

"We will deal with this matter in our own way, in the privacy of our homes."

The color drains from her face.

I'm not going to stop these kids from building their own

empires. Nor am I letting a school punish my child for showing fantastic business skills.

I tap my finger on the oak, waiting for her to respond.

"Sir, we can't have them fighting at school."

Keller steps next to me.

"They won't. Will you, boys? You know we only fight at Kings Gym. Nowhere else, unless absolutely necessary," he says sternly.

"We won't," they all mutter.

"See, lesson learned." I smile at her, but it's a warning.

"How about we take the boys home for the afternoon? They'll be back tomorrow." I face the boys. "And no more fighting."

They nod quickly. Leonardo holds my stare and I give him a wink.

"Okay," she whispers.

"Glad that's settled." I clap my hands together and walk over to my son, resting my hand on his shoulder.

"Time to go."

The boys all run out the door. Keller, Grayson and Luca follow behind. Without looking back, I lead Leonardo towards the car. As soon as we're away from the office, I lean down to him.

"How much money did you make, son?"

He stops and faces me, a grin spreading across his face.

"Two-hundred dollars, Dad!"

I ruffle his hair and pull him into my side.

"Good job."

ARE YOU READY FOR CHAOS?

The Beneath the Mask Series might have ended, but this doesn't mean the end of the 'Beneath' universe.

Do you want to visit the guys five years in the future? If so, sign-up to my newsletter and you'll receive a bonus epilogue with a chapter from each of the MMC's of the series:

https://BookHip.com/XGSGZSL

Jax 'The King of Chaos' Carter will be spinning us off into a new series, **Beneath The Secrets**. His book, CHAOS, will be the first, releasing on **April 12th 2024.**

You can pre-order it here:

https://mybook.to/PMlBU

Blurb:

Everything is falling into place.

A new life in a new state, living up to my name 'The King of Chaos'.

This is our new bratva empire where we take what we want.

And what a perfect way to leave behind my old life, *by sleeping with my brother's new wife... on the night of their wedding.*

The only problem is, I may have left my heart with her.

The one woman I could never have, that didn't stop me getting a taste.

When fate puts her on my lap for a second time, I'm determined to make her mine.

But my sweet Sofia is keeping a secret, one big enough to turn my world upside down.

Will our love survive the truth that is waiting to explode?

If you haven't had a chance to read the first three books in the Beneath The Mask Series, they are all now live on **Kindle Unlimited.**

Distance, book one, Keller and Sienna

Detonate, book two, Grayson and Maddie

Devoted, book three, Luca and Rosa

ABOUT THE AUTHOR

L una Mason is an Amazon top #20 and international best-selling author. She lives in the UK and if she isn't writing her filthy men, you'll find her with her head in a spicy book.

To be the first to find out her upcoming titles, you can subscribe to her newsletter here:

You can join the author's reader group (Luna Mason's Mafia Queens) to get exclusive teasers and be the first to know about current projects and release dates.

https://facebook.com/groups/614207510510756/

SOCIAL MEDIA LINKS:

http://www.instagram.com/authorlunamason

https://facebook.com/groups/614207510510756/

https://www.tiktok.com/@authorlunamason?_t=8j38Hlk CYmP&_r=1

Acknowledgments

The list of people I am grateful to for their help on not just this book, but my entire series, is almost endless.

The team I have created around me is nothing short of special. I love each and every single one of you guys. Without you, I am not sure where I would be right now.

To my author friends I've made along the way. I couldn't do this without your support, your guidance and love. I'm so incredibly lucky to have met such amazing people and get to call you my friends.

To my family- thank you for always believing in me. For helping me out at the drop of a hat. For listening to me go on and on about this crazy stuff that goes through my head on a daily basis and still being proud of me. I love you all, very very much.

This series has undoubtedly changed my life so there is one particular group I'd like to thank.

MY LOYAL READERS, MY NEW READERS, MY ARC TEAM, MY FILTHY BOOK CLUB, TO THE ONES WHO WITHOUT FAIL SHARE AND GET EXCITED OVER MY ENDLESS TEASERS.

Your love for my filthy men is everything. I see every post, comment and DM. You keep me inspired to write. You keep me excited for what's to come. You have helped me build respectful and open communities where we are free to discuss our love of smut.

So, this one is for you. From the bottom of my heart, THANK YOU.

Printed in Great Britain
by Amazon